ELITE OF ELMWOOD ACADEMY

RIVAL

USA TODAY BESTSELLING AUTHOR

J.L. WEIL

Published by J. L. Weil
Copyright 2022 by J. L. Weil
www.jlweil.com/
All rights reserved.

Edited by Hot Tree Editing
Cover Design by Wicked by Designs
Photo by Lindee Robinson

ALSO BY J. L. WEIL

ELITE OF ELMWOOD ACADEMY
(New Adult Dark High School Romance)
Turmoil
Disorder
Revenge
Rival

DIVISA HUNTRESS
(New Adult Paranormal Romance)
Crown of Darkness
Inferno of Darkness
Eternity of Darkness

DRAGON DESCENDANTS SERIES
(Upper Teen Reverse Harem Fantasy)
Stealing Tranquility

Absorbing Poison

Taming Fire

Thawing Frost

THE DIVISA SERIES

(Full series completed – Teen Paranormal Romance)

Losing Emma: A Divisa novella

Saving Angel

Hunting Angel

Breaking Emma: A Divisa novella

Chasing Angel

Loving Angel

Redeeming Angel

LUMINESCENCE TRILOGY

(Full series completed – Teen Paranormal Romance)

Luminescence

Amethyst Tears

Moondust

Darkmist – A Luminescence novella

RAVEN SERIES

(Full series completed – Teen Paranormal Romance)

White Raven

Black Crow

Soul Symmetry

BEAUTY NEVER DIES CHRONICLES

(Teen Dystopian Romance)

Slumber

Entangled

Forsaken

NINE TAILS SERIES

(Teen Paranormal Romance)

First Shift

Storm Shift

Flame Shift

Time Shift

Void Shift

Spirit Shift

Tide Shift

Wind Shift

Celestial Shift

HAVENWOOD FALLS HIGH

(Teen Paranormal Romance)

Falling Deep

Ascending Darkness

SINGLE NOVELS

Starbound

(Teen Paranormal Romance)

Casting Dreams

(New Adult Paranormal Romance)

Ancient Tides

(New Adult Paranormal Romance)

For an updated list of my books, please visit my website: www.jlweil.com

Join my VIP email list and I'll personally send you an email reminder as soon as my next book is out! Click here to sign up: www.jlweil.com

For everyone who asked for more. I listened!

PROLOGUE

MADS
Junior Year - High School

The rumors were true. Micah Bradford's dick was goddamn heavenly. Not that I was the most skilled lover at sixteen, but holy fuck. Sex with Micah had been better than ecstasy. I also wasn't an expert at drugs, so the comparison didn't hold a lot of weight. Yet still, Micah's dick and ecstasy? I couldn't even let my mind consider the pleasure. Nope. It was too much.

Tonight was the first night I'd see him since our hookup. Butterflies of excitement zipped and buzzed inside my stomach as I climbed the stairs of Brock Taylor's house to the second floor. Brock was the elite of the Elite, and his parties were legendary in Elmwood, probably in the entire state. They were constantly being crashed, especially by our rival school, Elmwood Public. I didn't give two shits about other schools. I barely gave a shit about my own school. I should, of course, because it had been pounded into my head that education was the key to my future success. It was like the academy motto.

I hooked around the corner, scoping out the kitchen, seeing Micah nowhere in sight. Neither Fynn, Brock, nor my cousin Grayson were anywhere to be seen either. *Just where the hell is everyone?*

I turned and spotted Porter Beck, one of the football jocks who played with the guys. "Have you seen Micah?" I asked him.

"What?" Porter hollered back, putting his hand to his mouth as if that would make a difference in me being able to hear him better. The music competing with the chatter was too much. Porter wavered toward me, a little too close.

I scowled, lifting my chin. "Have you seen Micah?" I shouted, making sure my voice projected much louder, and I emphasized each word for him. I was pretty sure he was drunk, a typical Friday night after a game win.

"Bradford?" Porter blinked with hazy, droopy eyes and a leering smile. The beer in his red cup sloshed over the side as he bumped into me. "Upstairs, I think."

I jumped back but not fast enough. My new fucking Converses got splattered with beer. *Fucking great. Asshole.* Rolling my eyes, I shoved his chest and took off toward the stairs, eagerness fluttering my heart.

Why was I so damn giddy? This was just Micah Bradford. I'd known him my entire life.

We slept together.

Don't make a huge deal out of this, Mads, I scolded, even as I raced up the stairs. I hadn't been able to see him after the game, but he was easy to find. There was only one place Micah went after a victorious game—the nearest party.

I didn't want to admit how long I'd had a crush on Micah. It was too damn embarrassing and made me feel like those girls at school who hung on the guys, just waiting to jump on their dicks. I refused to be one of those needy, attention-seeking whores. I was not a standby girl.

That was what the guys called them. They were basically booty calls.

Micah knew how I felt about those girls, knew I wasn't like them. I was the cousin of his best friend. The one thing the Elite didn't do was mess around with family. Unlike those girls, I had integrity and self-worth. And popularity meant dick to me, despite my best friend, who also happened to be my cousin, being one of the most popular girls in school. Perhaps I never cared about it because I'd always been associated with the Elite in a way.

No, I had no intention of ever being a standby girl. Something I intended to make very clear to Micah tonight. I didn't want him to get the wrong impression about the other night.

It had meant something... right? This wasn't all in my head?

It better had, or Micah Bradford would lose a limb—a vital one.

I wasn't naive enough to think we were dating, but I hoped

we were headed there. Never in a million years would I have believed I'd be dating an *Elite*. We might have done things a bit out of the normal order, but it was hardly like he was a stranger. Micah and I had been dancing around each other for years. Flirting and bickering were our thing.

Micah Bradford was part of the Elite, the four most popular guys at the academy. They all came from influential families. Some with old money and others new fortunes carved out by their parents, but for as long as I could remember, they had been known as the Elite. I couldn't recall if they'd given themselves that title or if it had just been something our peers started referring to them as. Regardless, it stuck. And now the four of them did whatever the fuck they wanted, when they wanted, and no one said a damn thing.

It was a power I didn't quite understand, but the shit they did and got away with, not just at school but everywhere, should have gotten them arrested on more than one occasion.

Weaving my way around a couple making out on the staircase, I headed to the second floor. Brock's house was filled with drunk teenagers, many of whom I'd never seen before. Typical. The Elite were famous, not just in the football scene, but they knew how to throw renowned parties. The booze was endless. The girls were desperate. And drugs were readily available. Everyone within a fifty-mile radius flocked to Elmwood for the free stream of drinks, sex, and a fun time. The Elite provided it all.

Downstairs, music pumped throughout the house, slowly drifting away as I reached the top of the stairs. There were a few closed doors, but I was familiar with the layout and what rooms were off-limits—like Brock's bedroom. No one was allowed to step a toe in that space.

Not that I blamed Brock. I wouldn't want random hookups happening in my bed every other weekend. Luckily, his house had many rooms for people to find a private spot. The indoor pool tended to be popular, one I stayed far away from.

Taking a left down the hallway, I decided to check the first door as thoughts of the text Micah sent me earlier tonight replayed in my head.

You're coming tonight, right?

Maybe, I'd replied. Football wasn't my thing, and I only went to games at Kenna's insistence. She was the typical popular, rich girl on the cheerleading team, and I sometimes wondered how we were best friends when we were so different, but then I remembered she was family. I overlooked her flaws and forgave her shallowness.

Come to the game. I need to see you, he'd sent back.

This could go one of two ways. He wanted to tell me this thing between us had been a mistake, that he shouldn't have slept with me, and we needed to end it before things got tangled. Too late. I'd been tangled with Micah far longer than a few weeks. This was the very worst thing he could say to me. The *mistake* excuse was nearly as bad as being a standby girl. Mads Clarke would never be someone's regret either. This was all my head messing with me. It never failed—when something good was going on in my life, my brain immediately went to worst-case scenario. Every time. It was annoying.

The other outcome: he wanted to hook up.

I was going with the latter.

I'll think about it, I responded.

The only thing you're thinking about is me.

He hadn't been wrong about that. Micah invaded my thoughts more than he should.

My fingers carefully turned the knob, and I pushed the door open slightly. A stream of light from the hallway hit the floor as I peeked inside, but it was the soft moan of pleasure that had me halting before going any farther into the obviously occupied room. I winced, having every intention to back out of the room before anyone noticed I had intruded. But my eyes had other plans. They lifted, a jab of curiosity forcing them to glance at the bed.

Only I wished I hadn't.

I blinked, certain that bleached-blond head of hair nuzzling on some girl's neck couldn't possibly be...

My entire body leaned forward to get a better view, the door squeaking with my movements, no longer caring what I was interrupting or that the guy on top of the girl was shirtless.

I knew that ass, was damn familiar with the tattoo covering his right shoulder, the dragon curling around to cover his front pec. Just days ago, I had been tracing that scaled tail with my fingertips.

My head shook, my lips mouthing, "No."

I must have done more than just mouth the word, because the guy fondling the girl's tits turned his head toward the door.

I gasped, not certain how I even found the air to do so.

The room spun.

My earlier excitement dropped into horror, dread, and gut-twisting pain.

Motherfucker.

Micah Bradford stared wide-eyed at me with those killer light blues, beads of sweat gathering on his brow, where his messy hairline began. Not that long ago, my fingers had been twisted into his hair.

Fuck. I wanted to kill him. My bewilderment and confusion swiftly turned into outrage and red-hot anger.

I flung the door wide open, not giving a rat's ass who saw the   well-on-their-way-to-being-completely-naked   couple.   I didn't care a single bit for the girl's privacy or her reputation. She was insignificant. Just another one of Micah's conquests.

Was that what I'd been to him?

Another fucking notch on his belt?

Screw him.

"You fucking prick," I gritted out between clenched teeth. My knuckles went white as I gripped the door.

"Mads?" Micah murmured, the haze of desire clearing from his eyes, replaced with confusion.

I could tell by looking at him that he'd been drinking, but that was no excuse in my book. "How the hell could you? I let you fuck me," I shrilled. "God, I think I'm going to be sick." My hand moved to clutch my stomach.

"It's not what you think," he defended, not even bothering to cover himself, too comfortable in his own skin.

"Really," I snapped sarcastically. "Let me guess. Your clothes just accidentally fell off, and your dick landed inside her. Spare me the excuses."

The girl under him squirmed uncomfortably, pushing at his chest for him to let her up. He ignored her, not sparing her a flicker of a glance. However, he shoved himself off her, sitting up on the edge of the bed.

Did the corner of his lips actually move into a smirk? Did he find this situation funny? What I said hadn't been a joke.

Unable to look at him for another second, I spun, shoving down the hot tears that threatened to spill. I refused, absolutely *refused* to cry in front of him. He didn't deserve them.

"Maddy, wait," he protested. I heard the rustling of sheets and assumed he stood up. Footsteps padded toward the open door.

I whirled back around, my honey-colored hair flying through the air, and Micah paused, buck-ass naked. He hadn't even had the decency to put some damn clothes on. His fingers forked through his hair.

Fiery anger licked through my veins, making my skin flush, some of it embarrassment. "You know I hate it when you call me Maddy." I held out a hand when he went to move closer. "And if you come anywhere near me, I'll cut your dick off. Are we clear?"

I didn't bother waiting for a response, didn't care to hear one, if I was being honest. My heart hammered in my ears as I stormed off into the hall, leaving Micah in the doorway. A group of guys hanging out in the hallway snickered, and I flipped them off as I walked by. "Get fucked," I mumbled, recognizing one of them as Warren Foster.

"Looks like someone already did," the smartass replied to his friends.

I halted, turning back around and getting in the douchebag's face. My knee came up, and a moment later, the only things coming out of his mouth were groans of pain and the hissing of a foul name. "If you want to keep being a man, get out of my way. Otherwise, I'll make good on my threat and cut yours off instead."

His other friends gladly stepped aside, and I bolted past.

"Crazy bitch," I heard them mumble, but honestly, I didn't give a shit what they thought about me. Warren and his buddies were a bunch of posers.

The image of Micah Bradford kissing and fondling some random chick on the bed burned in my mind with each step I took down the stairs. *Bastard.* Why had I thought for a second he might be different, that he'd changed? That I had been different... someone special?

God, I'd been so stupid.

He'd made me look like a fool. No one made Mads Clarke into a fool. I didn't give a shit who they were, how much money they had, or the amount of influence they wielded.

Never fucking again.

Micah Bradford could crawl on his knees, beg in front of the entire world, and I still wouldn't give him a second of my time.

I was canceling him.

From my phone.

From my social media.

From my life.

I wanted to live in a world where he didn't exist, because from this day forward, Micah didn't exist.

Not to me.

I grabbed a cup out of someone's hands as I hurried through the house, needing to escape the crowd. The girl protested, but I kept walking, not giving a shit about anyone or anything. Pressure clamped down on my chest, the beer-infused air stale and suffocating as I drew in short breaths. Slamming back the contents, I shoved open the front door and stepped out on the porch, dragging in the cool autumn air greedily. It did little to ease the pain digging its nails into my chest. I tossed the empty cup to the ground, immediately looking for another to replace it.

"Having a bad night?" asked a deep, husky voice.

I whirled, spotting a guy sitting on the banister of the porch, back pressed against a column, his face partially shrouded in shadows. From what I could see of him, he looked older, possibly in college. His hair was black, blending too much with the shadows that I couldn't tell if it was long or short, straight or curly. Not that it really mattered what he looked like. All I cared about was how full his cup was and how quickly I could snatch it and down the liquor.

I let out a short, bitter laugh, wandering closer to him, my eyes darting to the cup in his hand. The other brought something to his lips—a cigarette. "Bad doesn't begin to describe my night," I muttered.

The cherry end of his cigarette flared as he inhaled a long drag, eyes raking over me leisurely, his lips hooking in a lopsided smirk.

Maybe I should hook up with him for revenge, or to get Micah out of my system. Something. Anything to dull this stabbing pain, this feeling of being used and betrayed. He seemed interested enough and was easy on the eyes. It was hard to be on the same hot scale as Micah, but—

No! I am not going to do that, compare every guy to him.

And I wouldn't use someone the way Micah used me just to numb my mind. Alcohol was better suited for my needs.

"You look like you could use this." He took the cigarette from his lips and held it out for me.

I eyed the slim white smoke. "Fuck it. Why not?" I'd rather die of cancer than ever let Micah Bradford touch me again.

So it was, in fact, Micah's fault that I picked up the bad habit. He was to blame for a lot of shit, including my vow to never trust a flirt like him.

As I put the cigarette between my lips, the front door burst open. "Maddy." Micah's voice echoed over the porch into the long driveway.

The back of my neck tingled, which then pissed me off on top of him still not getting my goddamn name right. I hated that my body betrayed me. *Traitor.*

I didn't turn around, didn't look at him, but instead kept my eyes on the stranger as a stream of smoke expelled from my lips. I hadn't truly inhaled, just let the smoke swirl around. The mysterious guy lifted a brow, his dark blue eyes twinkling as if he could read my mind. *"I'm fair game if you are,"* he seemed to say with a cocky grin.

The cigarette wedged between my fingers, I moved in, pressing my lips to his. He didn't pull away or hesitate, just kissed me back, letting me decide how far or how deep I wanted to take it.

It was stupid, considering a few seconds ago I decided not to use someone the way Micah used me, and yet faced with the opportunity to make him jealous, to let him know he hadn't hurt me, that he meant nothing to me, I jumped at the chance. All lies.

But I didn't regret it. Not like my choice to sleep with Micah Asshole Bradford. I wasn't a pawn in a game I never agreed to play—the Elite's game.

I don't play games.

CHAPTER ONE

MADS

Present day

Squinting against the sun, I stared at the map on my phone, trying to figure out where the fuck I was. Kingsley University campus was like navigating through a foreign city, and right now, as I stood on the sideway, spinning in a circle, I looked every bit like a lost tourist. It was obvious I was a freshman.

Kenna, Josie, Ainsley, and I had moved into our dorm a few days ago, and after getting settled, we had spent the days leading up to orientation wandering the expansive campus and attempting to acquaint ourselves with the layout. On the map, it made sense, but out in the wild, I couldn't tell the science hall from the library, and I'd been too damn busy giggling and talking as the four of us strolled through campus instead of paying attention to where we'd been going.

Now I was paying the price. Lost on my first day of class. If I didn't figure this shit out soon, I would be late as well.

Fucking great.

Way to make an impression.

Not that I cared what anyone thought of me. I'd gotten over that insecurity in high school.

Right?

A group of girls passed by, giving me a once-over and then not-so-inconspicuously laughing. I rolled my eyes and mentally flipped them off. Girls were pretty much the same no matter where you went, and it seemed college would be no different. It didn't help that most of them came from money. KU wasn't an easy school to get into if you didn't have wealthy parents or influential connections. I had both, not that any of it mattered to me. I knew my lifestyle was posh and pampered, that not everyone had the same opportunities, and because of that, I tried not to take it for granted. I never splashed my money around. I didn't care about designer clothes like Kenna. That didn't mean I didn't appreciate them; I just bought what I liked, regardless of the name sewn on the tag.

Returning to my map, I chewed on my lip and lifted my head, staring at the white brick building in front of me. If this was the A4 building, then I needed to... Twisting my body so the phone lined up right where the building was, I needed to take a right at the end of the pathway.

I was pretty sure.

Why did I think this would be easy?

I started walking again, readjusting the bag on my shoulder. Why did I have to be so damn stubborn?

Fuck. It was pathetic that I had to use Google Maps to get around school, but if I ever wanted to get to class, I would have to rely on an app to get me there, because my map reading skills were obviously shit.

The sun was warm for ten in the morning, but I didn't mind. I liked the heat and preferred summer over winter. Snow and ice could kindly fuck off. It was so bright that I regretted not grabbing my sunglasses this morning. Normally they were in my bag, but I'd been in a rush to get out the door this morning thanks to Kenna and Ainsley, who were arguing over whose shirt Ainsley had been wearing. I didn't know how I got dragged into it, but after less than a week of living together, this was just a prelude to things to come.

Four girls plus one dorm room equaled recipe for disaster.

We were two sets of best friends who last year, under unusual circumstances, were thrown together, which created a bond not many people understood. Ainsley and Kenna didn't know each other well, but it wasn't off to a good start. Their personalities clashed like Titans, leaving Josie and me stuck in the middle.

Story of my life.

"Turn left here," the voice on my phone instructed as I walked past the roman fountain, a landmark of the university. Water trickled into the round pool from the raised stone bowl held up by a circle of four carved gods. The turnabout path tended to be a popular place for students to gather or meet up. Checking the instructions Google was spewing, I glanced at my phone, blowing up the map with my thumb and index finger. I only looked down for a second or two, literally, but that was all it took, a moment of distraction for me to ram into a wall.

Son of a b—

I stumbled back a step, my eyes quickly darting up. *Who the fuck put a wall by a fountain?* It made no sense, but it all came together when my gaze landed on not a wall but a body. A hard, muscular form wearing a loose T-shirt that looked comfortable as fuck. Almost as toned as my boyfriend but not quite. It was hard to compete with a wide receiver who spent hours at the gym and on the field. My boyfriend was lean and fit in all the right places.

Still, it hadn't felt good and startled me, which in turn pissed me off. My brows bunched together as I searched for the face attached to the body standing in my way.

The sun glared at his back, mostly blocked by his form, but as my eyes moved, I had to angle my head to avoid the bright beam. A bit of dark scruff adorned his jawline and chin, making me think he'd been in a rush as well this morning and hadn't had time to shave. His lips were full and curved; chiseled cheekbones carved the side of his face. Warm amber eyes sparkled as I stared into them, a wisp of dark hair falling over the side of his face. His features made me think he might have a bit of Asian descent in his family tree. Most girls would find him attractive, and he was, but he wasn't my type. Too pretty. Too smug. And something naughty.

No fucking way.

It couldn't possibly be him.

He took the few moments I glanced him over to do the same

to me. The smirk hooking on his lips spiked a flare of irritation, and I swore that, despite my taking a step back, he was closer than he should have been, invading my personal space. I could smell the traces of cologne that clung to his black T-shirt.

"Hey. I know you. Where have I seen you before?" he pondered in a rugged voice, rubbing a hand over his stubbly chin.

I backed up a step and then another, my calves bumping into something hard and damp. Then I was falling, arms flailing out in front of me.

He reached for me, amusing eyes going wide with surprise. My fingertips just touched his as a shriek escaped, but I slipped past before he could latch his hand to mine.

Splash.

My ass landed on something hard, legs up in the air as my hands caught me from going flat on my back. Water soaked my clothes, a splatter of droplets spraying over my face.

I didn't move. Not immediately. Just sat in the fucking fountain, unable to believe what happened.

I squeezed my eyes closed and groaned.

Fuck. My. Life.

Like why? I knew I should get out of the fountain, that the longer I sat here, the more of a spectacle I made, but I wanted nothing more than to sink into the water, crawl into a cave, anything but open my eyes and see *him* staring at *me*.

I'd only seen him once—the night I chose to erase from my memory—but seeing him brought it all back. I worked hard to forget and forgive, for both Micah's and my sake. Micah had always been important to me—always would.

But this guy... he'd been a fleeting moment's mistake. A blip that meant nothing other than the intent to hurt someone else. I had used him, and that wasn't something I was proud of. Even if he knew what I had been about that night, I still couldn't wipe away that he was also the start of my vice. I couldn't really blame him for the addiction that was still a part of my life, despite that I kept telling myself I'd quit. It had given me something to do other than dwell, something to ease the turmoil that had spun within me.

I never did get his name, then or now.

"Are you okay?" he asked, his tone gentle, perhaps even with traces of humor. I couldn't fault him for finding the situation amusing. In a few hours, I would definitely be laughing about it with Kenna, Josie, and Ainsley. I hoped.

Forcing my eyes to open, I shoved down the embarrassment, trying to gain some semblance of dignity. Kind of difficult when I looked like a drowned cat. I shoved strands of my wet honey-colored hair off my face.

He extended a hand, concern warming those amber eyes.

Whispers and a few giggles fluttered from the dozen or so people passing by. Most of them kept casting glances at the guy offering to help me. He had a look that people took notice of. He was that kind of guy.

And me, apparently, I was the type of girl who made a fool of herself. What a way to make a spectacular first impression. I had a feeling this would haunt me the entire four years of college. I would be known as fountain girl or some other more genius nickname since I couldn't seem to come up with anything catchy.

Why me?

I took his hand, and he pulled me to my feet, helping me step out of the fountain. In the process, my foot got twisted at my poor attempt to gather my bearings. I fell into him, my palms flattening on his chest. He chuckled, despite his shirt getting wet.

My cheeks burned.

Wow. You would have thought I didn't know how to walk. "I swear I'm not drunk or this clumsy," I assured, backing up, my eyes on the front of his shirt.

"If you say so," he said as if he didn't believe me.

I glanced up then, detecting a trace of humor that had my hackles rising. If there was one thing I detested in this world more than liars, it was being laughed at. "This is your fault, by the way," I replied, my voice sharpening a bit. I shook out my arms. "Fuck, my phone," I muttered, realizing it was no longer in my hand.

The guy and I both glanced at the fountain.

"Do you want me to fish it out for you?" he offered, regardless that I had hurled the blame of my shitty situation on him. It really hadn't been his fault, after all. *I* hadn't been paying attention and had been in a hurry.

"What? No," I retorted, shaking my head. "Don't bother. There's no reason for us both to take a dip in the fountain today. I'll get it." Shoulders sagging, I resigned myself to today being the shittiest first day possible. I mean, every day after today had to be better.

Right?

Lying on my belly over the ledge, I leaned forward, arms

stretched out toward the glinting screen reflecting in the water. I sensed his presence beside me, ready to catch my legs if I toppled forward. A sigh of relief breezed through my lips as my fingers clasped around my phone and I pulled it out.

"You might be able to revive it. Try soaking it in rice," he suggested, seeing me stare at my phone hopelessly. "I heard that works sometimes."

Where the fuck would I get rice? I didn't have a bag lying around in my dorm. I'd have to go to the store and buy some, which I didn't have time to do right now. And I still didn't know where the hell my class was. Not that it mattered. I couldn't go to class like this.

He angled his head to the side, an expression of intrigue and thoughtfulness on his features. "I feel like I've seen you before. Are you sure we haven't met? Hooked up perhaps?"

I choked, and it wasn't on fountain water.

This guy had a knack for being too close. He moved in without me being aware of him doing so. I got the feeling he rather liked making people uncomfortable with his presence, the direct stare of his eyes.

It worked.

"Mads?" someone called from behind me.

Holy fuck.

That voice. It couldn't be. What were the fucking odds that my boyfriend would happen upon me at this moment?

Are you kidding me?

Sadly, it was no joke.

Groaning internally, I turned around, wishing once again that I could duck under a tree and hide. Micah Bradford stood gaping at me, his light blue eyes brimming with disbelief and confusion. His blond hair had grown darker over the summer and fell haphazardly down his forehead, ruffled just the way I liked it. He had the kind of face girls sighed over, including me. I had fallen for his charm not once but twice.

He glanced over me, taking in the wet clothes plastered to my body, and then his eyes promptly turned shrewd as they landed on the hand attached to my hip before raising up to the owner of that hand.

Why is the guy's hand on my hip?

I couldn't remember how it got there.

"Micah," I breathed, the back of my neck getting hot. I jumped back, rubbing a hand over the nape of my neck. My hair hung in damp strands, tangling with my fingers. This was definitely not how it looked. Then again, I wondered what the fuck it looked like with me soaking wet. God only knew what kind of conclusion Micah drew.

Would he recognize the guy who I bumped into? Would he remember what we had done on the porch that night two years ago? He couldn't possibly know what happened after, could he?

Things had been going so smoothly between Micah and me. The last thing we needed was a ripple in our semi-new relationship. We'd only been together five months.

And neither of us wanted a reminder of *that night*. It had been a boulder-sized hurdle between us for two years before things took a turn last year. It was amazing what a life-threatening situation could do to one's perspective on life.

Brock Taylor, my roommate and best friend's boyfriend, was beside Micah. I'd known Brock for as long as I had Micah. They were childhood friends with my cousin Grayson, and along with Fynn Dupree, the four of them made up the Elite. Our group was interlaced in complicated knots.

Their longstanding friendship allowed them to assume unspoken roles. It only took a look, a nod, or often no gesture at all. They had each other's back, no questions asked, which was exactly why Brock stared hard at the guy I had hoped to never see again while Micah focused on me.

Micah lifted a brow. "What happened? Did you go for a morning swim? Don't tell me someone dared you to jump in the fountain. You know, rush week isn't until the end of the month."

Everything with Micah was a joke, but he had another side, one he only showed to those he was close to and could trust. I was one of those people. Not to mention, he knew I had no interest in sororities.

"Not intentional. I didn't think you had class until later today," I replied, not wanting to relive the awkward moment. He'd hear the details from someone by the end of the day. I wouldn't be surprised if a gawker had captured it on video and it was already circulating around campus. That was how these things worked. The power of social media. It could not just drive you to popularity but also ruin you within seconds.

"I don't. I'm on my way to the gym," he informed me. Explained why Brock was with him, and why they were in school T-shirts and basketball shorts. Micah and Brock were both on KU's football team. "I'm still waiting for you to tell me what happened."

"Is everything okay?" Brock added, his voice deepening as

he slid suspicious eyes to the other guy, who remained quiet, observing our interaction.

He didn't shrink or fidget under Brock's scrutiny. Most people did, and I couldn't decide if that made him stupid, brave, or foolish. Perhaps all three.

"Yeah," I assured. "I'm fine, but I don't think I'll make it to my first class." I pulled my bag around in front of me, unzipped the pocket, and pulled out a soggy pack of cigarettes.

Damn it.

"Here." The guy I'd rather forget offered me a smoke, which I gladly took with a sheepish smile and a mumbled "Thanks."

Micah's eyes flared. He folded his arms and faced the reason behind my bad habit with an inferior scowl. "Hey, I'm Micah, her *boyfriend*. Who the hell are you?"

"Micah," I gritted through my teeth, sending him a look that warned him to be nice.

"Boyfriend?" my past echoed, then flicked the lighter he pulled out of his pocket. "Interesting."

I leaned forward, letting the end of the cigarette hover over the flame as I dragged in my first puff. How the fuck was the fact that I had a boyfriend interesting? Did that mean he'd hoped I didn't have one?

Micah didn't particularly like that I smoked, but I didn't particularly like that he slept with countless girls whose names he never bothered to ask. It didn't matter that we hadn't been together. I never agreed with the Elite's carelessness and disregard for girls. Josie had been the only exception until me.

Micah's lip curved up, but there was nothing friendly about

the smile. Tension suddenly sparked in the air. "You still haven't told me who you are."

I had been around the Elite long enough to almost be desensitized from their ploys, their mistrust, and their fierce protectiveness. Almost, but not quite. They were notorious for not letting new people into their lives. This guy never really had a chance at receiving a warm welcome from either Brock or Micah.

Taking a long drag on my cigarette, I let the smoke trickle into my lungs, eased by the familiar feeling and taste of nicotine.

"Sterling Weston," he stated, his lips twisting at the corners, a tinge of arrogance in his amber eyes.

"Why do I know that name?" Micah muttered, the wheels in his head turning as he searched his brain.

Even Brock looked like he was trying to figure out the same thing.

And I didn't really give a shit. I just wanted to get away from here and out of my wet clothes. It was such an uncomfortable feeling, the damp and heaviness of them against my skin.

"Yo, Sterling." A group of guys was passing by, and one of them clasped Sterling on the back. "You still having the first party of the year tonight?"

"When don't I?" Sterling replied aloofly, pulling a cigarette out of the pack before shoving it in his back pocket.

"You never disappoint, man." The whole conversation happened as the guys continued to walk by, never missing a beat. Excitement buzzed between them but not on Sterling's face. A speck of boredom dulled his eyes at the idea of throwing a party, like it was a duty rather than a pleasure.

Micah's eyes brightened under the sun as the answer came to him. "That's it. Frat house. You're the president of Chi Sigma."

I blinked at Micah, taking another inhale. How the hell did he know that? I hadn't thought he was interested in fraternities, which, now that I considered it, was ridiculous. Why wouldn't Micah be interested in the part of college that majored in parties? He was literally the quintessence of a party boy. If Micah wasn't at one of the parties in Elmwood, then it hadn't been a party at all.

"Of course you're in a frat. You look like the epitome of a rich, pompous, selfish, frat asshat." The thought came tumbling out of my mouth, and I cringed inside.

"Wow, grudges much?" Sterling commented, grinning. "You guys should come tonight," he offered. His gaze slid to me in a way that suggested the invitation was for me, but he included Micah and Brock out of politeness.

Warning bells went off in my head. Had I not made it clear that I had a boyfriend? That I was unavailable? Or did he want to take a stroll down memory lane, reminiscing about the girl who had kissed him at a party, dragged him to his car, and then dashed off, never to be seen again?

Uh, no, thank you.

Sterling hooked a thumb to his right. "I need to get to class. It's been... interesting." He pivoted to leave but then snapped his fingers and faced me. "Oh, now I remember. I never did get your name that night. Mads, is it?"

Mads was a nickname. My birth name was Madeline

Clarke, and if a person really wanted to get under my skin, they called me Maddy.

My pulse skipped, and I couldn't shake the feeling that Sterling was playing with me. He hadn't just remembered where he saw me but chose this moment to pretend that he had. Why? What was this guy's deal?

Of all the college campuses, he would have to go to this school.

Micah lifted his hand to tuck a damp piece of hair behind my ear, but his hand halted midair at Sterling's jogged memory. "What is he talking about? You've met before? When?" His tone sharpened with each question, but I knew it wasn't me he was irked with. Sterling had ruffled Micah's boxers; jealousy and something else flared in those light blue eyes.

My fingers rolled over the cigarette. "It's not important." He wasn't important. That was basically what I was trying to tell Micah. "And neither is my name," I snapped to Sterling, shoving my waterlogged phone into my bag. Dropping the cigarette on the ground, I smashed it under my foot, smothering the cherry.

The playful smirk on Sterling's lips widened. My purpose hadn't been to amuse him, and yet that was precisely what I did. "See you around, *Splash*."

Splash! Not funny. Or cute, for that matter.

Micah didn't think so either. He stiffened beside me, and for a second, I thought he might do something like hit him.

"The next time you fall in the fountain, I'll try to be around to catch you," Sterling added with a wink before strutting off.

My mouth dropped open. The audacity.

This was turning out to be the weirdest day I'd had in a really long time, probably since I found out that Josie, my best friend, turned out to be my not-so-dead cousin who had been kidnapped as a baby.

Yeah, my life was complicated, but not as complicated as Josie's. Some days, I didn't know how she handled it all. Her mom—well, kidnapper mom. A new family. Suddenly having a brother and a sister the same age as you. They were triplets.

Although my problems weren't on the same scale as Josie's, that didn't mean my life wasn't without its bumps and bruises. And I concluded that Sterling liked drama. He also had a death wish.

This might only be the first day of class, but I'd bet my left tit that most students had already heard about the Elite. Whether he knew it or not, Sterling had just put himself on their radar, not a place you wanted to be.

The last guy on their radar was in jail. But he deserved to be there.

Micah's hand came around me to rest on the small of my back. His touch, as light as it was, sent a tingle dancing up my spine. There had always been something about Micah that my body immediately responded to. "Stay away from him," he warned, his eyes trailing after Sterling.

Brock also glared at Sterling's retreating back. "I have to agree."

I shook my head, sighing. "Do you trust anyone?" I didn't expect an answer. It had been more of a rhetorical question, and neither of them responded anyway. "It's too early for this. I need to go change. I'll see you later tonight?"

I left Brock and Micah scowling.

* * *

Rushing back to the dorms, I hit the elevator call button and waited, tapping my foot on the floor as the numbers counted down. In a dorm this size, it often took a few minutes to retrieve an elevator, and I was too damn antsy to sit still, not to mention the odd looks I received from my fellow dormmates.

I contemplated hiking up four floors of stairs when the elevator finally dinged, the doors opening. Waiting for a few people inside to shuffle out, I ignored their weird glances and brushed past them, hitting my floor number. Water dripped from my clothes, leaving behind a tiny puddle on the elevator floor.

Annoyed. Anger. Confused. Frustrated. Disappointed. Those were only some of the emotions spinning within me. I had this picture of what college life would be like, and so far, nothing was going as planned.

Ding.

The elevator door opened, and I shoved off the wall, dragging my soggy ass to my dorm six doors down. I wiggled my key into the lock and opened the door to my shared room. Four beds butted up into each corner, a nightstand beside them, and a small desk on the wall parallel to the beds. More than half the room was divided down the middle by a bathroom and closets. A small entryway connected the two spaces. We had one of the nicer rooms, which had everything to do with how much money our parents had, minus Ainsley. She lived on the other side of

Elmwood and didn't have her parents' wealth to rely on. Since she didn't have classes today, she was out looking for a part-time job.

We had each decorated our little corners of the room to fit our personal style. I found that it helped to have familiar things around me. Regardless of how excited I was to be spending the next four years here with Micah and my friends, I did miss home and my parents.

My older brother, Jason, was in his last year at the University of Dalton, the same school Fynn and Grayson attended, before heading to medical school. He wanted to be a doctor. It was still hard for me to imagine Jason having the discipline to finish four more years of medical school and then go on to his residency. With my brother and me gone, my parents were empty nesters, but instead of moping around the house missing me as I thought they would be, they had taken off on vacation to Tahiti.

God, some sun, the beach, and a rum barrel sounded divine right now

I dropped my bag in the entryway as the door swung closed behind me, then stripped out of my wet clothes, letting them fall to the floor. Kenna had left a minute or two before me for her Intro to Business class, which just left Josie.

A candle burned on top of her desk, scenting the room with oranges and smoked vanilla. She and Ainsley shared the right side of the space, while Kenna and I had the other half. Josie's bed was closest to the door, as was mine, but I didn't see her.

In nothing but my lace bra and underwear, I padded over to the small dresser and rummaged through the clothes I carelessly shoved inside. My side of the room might look like a bomb went off, but it was an organized mess. At least, that was what I liked to say. Unlike Josie or Kenna, who were two of the neatest people I knew, I hated order and thrived in clutter.

But I was beginning to think my life was too much of a mess. Especially if today was an indicator.

"What happened to you?" a soft voice behind me asked.

I glanced over my shoulder at Josie, my hands still digging through the disorder. "Don't even ask."

Josie still rocked her vibrant pink locks, freshly colored before school started. She had similar features to her sister, Kenna. The same chocolate eyes, high cheekbones naturally dusted pink, and golden skin. The shape of Josie's face was a bit more like Grayson's, rounder than Kenna's, but there was no mistaking when the three of them were together that they came from the same gene pool.

But Josie had a hardness to her, a toughness she had earned from growing up on the other side of the tracks like Ainsley. Kenna, on the other hand, had been sheltered and spoiled her entire life, but that didn't mean she hadn't suffered or felt pain. Kenna hid her damage and trauma with expensive clothes, makeup, and pretty smiles, whereas Josie used a cloak of sarcasm. They were two sides of a coin, and together they could be fucking troublesome and troublemakers.

One minute they were teaming up, taking down a common enemy, and in the next breath, they were at each other's throats, cursing and pulling each other's hair. In a way, despite their unusual circumstance, they loved and fought like real sisters.

The difficult part for me was not getting caught in the middle. I loved them both and refused to take sides.

A year ago, they had been strangers, and here we were, all living together. To their credit, Josie and Kenna had come a long way in that year. Virtual strangers who didn't even know the other existed.

I wasn't sure if the dorm could handle having both Edwards sisters under the same roof.

"Ooookay," Josie drawled, plopping down on my unmade bed. She crossed her long legs into a pretzel. "Aren't you supposed to be in class right now?"

I pressed a hand to my temple, where the dull ache of a headache throbbed. "Yes." I sighed, grabbing a random T-shirt before slamming the drawer shut.

"Is everything all right?" she asked, concern etched into her features.

I snatched a pair of jeans off the floor, not caring that they had been worn, and paused at the front of my bed. "I need a new phone. It fell in the fountain. Do you have any rice by chance?"

"Rice?" she echoed, brows bunching in confusion. "I don't think so. Is that why you're wet? You had to fish your phone out of the fountain?"

It was a good assumption, just not the whole story. "Not exactly. I was already in the fountain when I dropped my phone."

Josie's lips twitched, fighting back a smile. "Makes total sense."

I dropped down onto the bed. "No it doesn't. None of this does. I completely embarrassed myself."

"And how is that different than any other day?"

I tossed my bundled-up shirt into her face. Nothing like my best friend to put shit into perspective.

Laughing, she flung it back at me. "Whatever happened, I'm sure it's not that bad. And we'll get the rice... or a new phone. I don't have class until after lunch. We can go once you put some clothes on and dry your hair. You might want to check your makeup too," she added, her gaze bouncing from one of my eyes to the other.

"Mascara?" I guessed.

She nodded.

Wiggling on the jeans, I left them unbuttoned as I went into the bathroom to check out the damage. My eyes were sporting the raccoon style, as expected. I glanced at the tube I had left on the sink this morning. *Waterproof, my ass.* Grabbing a makeup wipe, I cleaned up the dark smudges under my eyes, salvaging what I could.

"The day wasn't a total loss. I did get an invite to a fraternity party tonight," I said, raising my voice so it carried out into the bedroom as I tossed my damp hair up into a messy bun. It had started to curl, and since I didn't want to deal with that and the humidity outside, it was best to just secure it up.

"You didn't," she proclaimed, but at the same time, I could hear in her voice that she really wasn't all that surprised. When it came to those of us who were raised in the upper side of Elmwood, parties were as common as brunch on Sunday.

Discarding the towel on the floor, I made a mental note to it pick up later before Kenna could scold me yet again and walked back into the bedroom. "I did, at Chi Sigma. Have you heard of them?" I asked, remembering that Micah and Brock both knew Sterling. Apparently he had a reputation here. I shouldn't have been, but I couldn't help but be curious about what kind of reputation that was.

I could hardly believe *he* was the same guy. Seeing him had dredged up too many memories and feelings, almost all of them ones I wanted to forget.

Josie lifted a brow in intrigue as she pressed her palms into the mattress behind her, leaning back slightly. "So, are we going?"

Reaching for the old T-shirt I left on the bed, I slipped it over my head, tucking a corner into my jeans. "Probably not a good idea. Micah and Brock both warned me to stay away."

"When has that ever stopped you?"

True. I wasn't the kind of girlfriend who let her boyfriend make decisions for me. There was open communication, and then there was control. No one controlled me. In Micah's case, he was legitimately looking out for my safety. As a female, we had to be more aware of our surroundings. There were so many guidelines that came with being a girl. Don't walk alone at night. Go to bars, parties, concerts, and such in pairs or groups. Always watch your drink, because God forbid someone slipped something into it.

Kenna and Josie both had firsthand experience with just how dangerous a drugged drink could be. I'd never forgive the bastard who hurt them, and Kenna and Josie made sure he got what he deserved... and then some.

"Look at you being a bad influence," I replied, a smile breaking over my lips.

"Hanging around the Elite, it was bound to happen. We can't miss the first party of the year. We promised that we would make the best out of the four years we have together."

"Did someone say there was a party tonight?" Ainsley leaned in the doorway, her once rainbow hair now a deep chestnut, honey highlights framing her face. It looked good on her, natural, but that didn't mean she had lost her fun factor. Hell no. If anything, I swore she was wilder than when her hair was ten different shades. Someone only had to utter anything that remotely sounded like a party and her ears perked up.

"No. No party here," I lied. The truth was it wasn't the party I was avoiding but the person throwing it.

Like, who the hell has a party on a Wednesday?

The Elite does, a little voice in my head chimed.

Suppressing an eye roll, I ignored that stupid voice of reason.

"That's not what I heard," Ainsley said, grinning so big she damn well nearly beamed. "Chi Sigma is hosting their annual back-to-school event."

I snorted at her choice of words. This was not an event but a frat party. I had to give her props for trying to make it more sophisticated than it was. Only Ainsley.

She moved to join Josie and me on the bed. I scooted over to make more room. It wasn't like there was much space to begin with; anything bigger than the twin beds we had and our entire dorm would have been one massive bed. "I also heard that some girl got shoved into the fountain. Can you believe that?"

My mouth flattened into a disapproving line that bordered on a pout. "I didn't get shoved. I fell," I corrected. Were people actually already talking about it? Instinct told me this was all Sterling's doing. He might not be going around directly telling everyone, but if he was as well known around campus as I was beginning to believe, then just being seen with him brought attention to me.

Ainsley blinked at me, taking in my appearance—the wet hair, the lack of clothes—for the first time. "It was you?"

I didn't confirm or deny but stood at the foot of the bed giving her a pointed look. I didn't want to talk about this anymore.

"Oh my God," she exclaimed, mossy green eyes widening. "I would give up my vibrator for a month to have seen that."

My nose wrinkled. "Ew. TMI. Keep that shit to yourself."

Josie just laughed, used to Ainsley spewing any and every-thing that came to her mind. She had no filter, and most days, I liked that about her.

A wicked smile curled on her dark cherry lips. Ainsley loved makeup. A lot of makeup. "As if you didn't bring yours."

"Have you seen my boyfriend?" I countered. "Vibrator completely unnecessary."

"So, you and Micah have..." She made a crude gesture with her fingers.

"None of your business," I smacked in return.

"That means no. What are you waiting for? It's not like you guys haven't slept together before."

What was I waiting for? The truth—I was afraid of being hurt again, of being vulnerable. Sex for me wasn't a basic need like it was for Ainsley. It was an emotional connection, and it wasn't easy controlling my body when I was alone with Micah, because wanting him was never the problem. How *much* I wanted him scared me.

And we did have sex. Just not every night.

"Who said I was waiting?"

She didn't look convinced. "Not all of us came to college with hot-as-fuck boyfriends, and the only way I'm going to get the real deal is by meeting people. And to do that..." Ainsley glanced at me expectantly, giving me her pleading eyes and pouty lips.

My shoulders sagged, and I could feel myself caving. "I get it."

"Come on, let's make memories. For tonight, it doesn't have to be about guys. It can just be the four of us. A girls' night to celebrate our first week on campus." Ainsley had about a thousand excuses for why a party was a good idea. She always had a reason to celebrate. The moon was out. Party. A new season of the Kardashians came out. Pour the champagne. And so forth.

My first day at college had been memorable all right, just not the kind of memories I'd been looking to make. Did I really want my stumble into the fountain to be the only memory I had of today? The only way to change that would be to make new ones.

"Fine, but I'm not dancing on the tables... tonight," I said, certain I would regret the decision later. "I have class tomorrow. We can pop in for a little bit, check out the scene, and then be back in the dorms at a decent hour without a hangover. That's the deal."

Ainsley squealed, launching herself at me as she threw an arm around my neck and then moved in to include Josie, causing the three of us to fall onto the bed.

A bead of apprehension curled in my belly. Why did I have such a bad feeling about this party? Was it Sterling? Or something else entirely?

CHAPTER TWO

MICAH

"Fuck off, Micah."

I smirked. I'd heard that phrase so often in my life, it was more of a nickname than an insult at this point, particularly from Brock motherfucking Taylor's mouth.

Only a handful of people could get away with speaking to me that way and not end up with a split lip. Worse if they deserved it. Brock was my best friend. Had been since the first grade when Tommy Ricci shoved him on the playground, and I gave Tommy his first black eye. No deeper friendship could be formed over standing up to a bully. Although, when I thought about it, we became the bullies—Brock, Fynn, Grayson, and me. Not for sport or shits and giggles. We did it to stop anyone from thinking they could mess with us. The four of us hadn't set out to be these icons in school, but it hadn't taken long for us to make a name. And that name stuck with us, even now.

We were the Elite.

Chuckling, I shut the door to the rowhouse Brock and I rented for the year. It was supposed to be for the girls and us, but they had insisted on staying in the dorms their first year, which was one of the campus rules. Brock didn't have much regard for rules, and it only took a donation from his father to make an exception for us. "You can see Josie after. It won't take too long," I assured, bounding down the front steps.

Brock sent off a text, assumingly to his girlfriend, and shoved his phone into his back pocket. "Why don't I believe you?"

A gust of warm air blew over the side of my face, a bit of moonlight streaming through the red oaks scattered over campus. "I just want to check it out. Who knows? Maybe I'll rush."

The sidelong glance he gave me called out my bullshit. Grayson or Fynn was more likely to join a fraternity than I was. "Are you sure about this?" he asked as we walked down the pathway lit up by round street lanterns.

"When am I ever sure about anything?" I didn't even know my major. It was best to just take shit as it came, not overthink crap.

Brock ducked under a low branch hanging over the sidewalk as we approached Greek Row. Just a few more blocks. "What do you hope to find out tonight?"

Over the years, we'd gone through so much shit together, and Brock had always had my back, which was why I knew he would have mine tonight. "I'm not sure exactly, but I've heard rumors about this fraternity, about its president."

"What kind of rumors?" he muttered, brows drawing together.

"Like there's a reason they only accept pledges from wealthy families with connections that could be useful. Political. Financial. Legally. You get my drift."

"Unfortunately, I do."

We were all too familiar with how this world worked. It could be both a blessing and a curse.

As we hooked a right onto Greek Row, more people were about, hanging out on the porches or in the yards, others crossing the street or walking along the sidewalk. KU's campus had a way of making you feel safe as you strolled down the streets at night, but I was glad to see many of the students still went out in groups. If they didn't already know about a party, they were looking for one, and this was the place to be. "I think Chi Sigma is more than just a fraternity," I said.

Brock looked at me. "Why do you care?"

My shoulder lifted in an offhanded shrug. "I don't really." What went on behind or inside Sterling's fraternity didn't concern me, not unless he made it my concern. There was only one way that happened—you messed with someone I cared about. That list just happened to be getting longer lately. "Well, I hadn't until today," I amended.

"Mads," he guessed as his gaze darted to the house on the corner.

I nodded, following his gaze. "Yeah. There's something about him I can't shake off."

Two guys were shoving each other on the front lawn, and it looked about three seconds away from escalating to fists. Brock kept a watchful eye on them, but neither of us would intervene. Most likely. "And this has nothing to do with you seeing her talk to another guy?"

"I'm not that jealous. Usually," I added at his smirk. The level of jealousy I had felt earlier seeing Sterling's hands on Mads irked me. Insanely so. My blood pressure hadn't spiked that high in years.

Was it because Sterling was better boyfriend material on paper? Someone Mads deserved?

I was sure her parents weren't thrilled that she was dating me. They had never said anything or treated me disrespectfully, but my reputation for changing girls as frequently as I changed my shirt went beyond the halls of Elmwood Academy. Sex had been a tool, a means to dull the anger inside me, to forget the pain or the agony I often felt. A short-lived remedy that, after a while, I realized wasn't the answer.

I tried therapy once. It led to sex with my therapist but not much else. I didn't have anything against seeking professional help. It just hadn't worked for me.

But truthfully, sex never filled that void, need, or whatever it was I was missing.

I could tell Brock thought I should leave the thing with Mads and Sterling alone, but my gut was urging me to keep a close eye on Sterling Weston, that he was more than just a resident frat guy. I didn't like the way he looked at my girl.

Was my decision to go to this party tonight crafted from jealousy?

Probably.

But my instincts were telling me to check him out. More

like demanding it. I learned to trust that intuition inside me. Even when it got me in trouble, it had been for a reason.

Most people don't take me seriously. Came with the territory of being the jokester and the town flirt, but that was precisely what I wanted people to think. If they didn't believe I was a threat, then they didn't see me coming when shit got real. It made me dangerous in my book and was a whole lot more fun than having a stick stuck up my ass.

The Elite had two rules.

Protecting each other. No questions asked.

And never screwing with the same girl. Standby girls excluded—girls we could fuck around with but never date. This was a fairly new rule that came about when Brock decided to fall off the deep end for Josie James.

Our fearless leader in love. Who would have thought, and with his best friend's sister too? How cliche. Talk about crossing all the lines, but Josie wasn't any girl. Even I could admit she was different.

She was one of us.

The first girl we ever adopted into the Elite.

Josie had changed us.

Brock, Fynn, Grayson, and I had protected a girl before her, and it had ended badly. Left scars not just on us but the girl as well, who happened to be Grayson's sister, Kenna. None of us ever forgot how we had failed her—never forgave ourselves either.

Perhaps that was why Josie was different—why she became so important to the four of us.

We hadn't wanted to fail a second time.

It helped that she was cute as fuck, and so damn spunky. She was also damaged, something I related to on so many levels.

Truth be told, if Brock hadn't claimed her first, I might have done more than flirt with her. But that was all. Josie and I were better at being friends who edged the line into something more but never crossed it.

That was all before Mads gave me a second chance, of course. I wasn't sure I deserved another opportunity to make her happy, considering how I had colossally fucked it up before. I had my reasons for what I had done, but they didn't excuse the hurt I caused.

I never wanted to inflict that pain on her again, but the reality was my world was brimming with shit that could do more than hurt her.

For me, it had always been Madeline Clarke, the girl who had constantly been there. I had many regrets in my life, things I'd done and choices I'd made that I had to live with every day, but none of which I regretted more than seeing the pain in Mads's eyes. She deserved someone better than me, and I tried to stay away, tried to keep her at a safe distance. But I couldn't. It took one moment of weakness for all the walls we'd both built to come crashing down. I wasn't about to make the same mistake again. This playboy had retired.

I would do everything in my power to make sure Mads never hurt again.

And that meant protecting her from guys like Sterling. Or protecting her from me.

Just how the fuck did Mads know him? He'd made a point to make sure I knew.

Brock and I had arrived at the Chi Sigma house, easily the largest on campus, and I didn't just mean the size of the house, which was expansive. Perhaps that was why there were so many people inside and outside the two-story colonial. I stared at the Greek letters on the front of a stunning brick house with black shutters and white columns. The front porch had a balcony above it that circled over the section where the entrance was.

"Isn't your dad an alumnus of this fraternity?" Brock asked, adjusting his ball cap as we lingered outside, eyeing the house.

I was surprised he made the connection or remembered. Alexander Bradford still kept a photo of his fraternity brothers in his home office. Nothing big or flashy, just a frame that sat on the bookshelf. The corners of my mouth hardened as I replied, "It is."

"And he wanted you to pledge," he concluded, putting more pieces together and knowing just how my father thought, what was expected of me. Brock understood my feelings about my father. We didn't always see eye to eye. In fact, my father and I hardly did. He wasn't an easy man. Not in business, and not on his family. I learned at a young age how to deflect his sternness and disapproval from my mom to me. She didn't deserve it, and if he was going to dish it out, why should we both suffer? Alexander Bradford was a man who didn't take no for an answer and knew how to push people past their limits.

For me, it had been school and football, and now college. Going to KU hadn't been an option. It was expected. Part of my growing up as a Bradford meant attending KU and getting into Chi Sigma just as my father, grandfather, and generations before had.

I despised having to live up to someone's expectations or dreams. And I had no intention of following the Bradford legacy.

"He did." It was why I knew who Sterling was, but after seeing him, I hadn't liked what I saw. Not the way Sterling looked at Mads or the interest I saw on his face. Mads was a beautiful girl, and I didn't fault other guys for looking, but when things went beyond an appreciative glance, that was when it got my attention.

"Then what the fuck are we doing in front of his house? I just want to make sure you know what you're getting into."

I appreciated Brock looking out for me. "We're just scoping him out." I wasn't here for my father. This had nothing to do with him. "If there's nothing to be worried about, then we leave. That simple." I needed to make sure this guy didn't get Mads mixed up with his fraternity shit. Although I didn't know the details from my father, I knew him and his less-than-honorable business discussions. He had hinted at the importance of this fraternity for too long, and it had made me both curious and suspicious then. Now, I was on full alert.

Brock's scowl deepened. "It's never that simple."

A handful of guys and two girls hung out on the front porch. This was a drill I knew well. The beefy linebacker dude was security, and the scrawny guy wearing sunglasses at night was in charge of finances—cover charges. That wouldn't go over well with Brock. The Elite never paid to party. "Do you think I'm overreacting?"

"Honestly, if it had been Josie, we'd both still be here. So no, I trust you and your gut feeling." Brock was the best kind of wingman. He always had my back, and that was exactly why he was with me tonight, despite him wanting to see Josie.

My lips curled. "Besides, it doesn't hurt to check out the competition. The only parties anyone will be talking about on campus are ours. I need to see what we're up against."

We started for the porch, walking up the stone pathway. "Since when did we agree our house would be party central?"

I playful whacked him on the back. "That was a given."

"Why the fuck did I agree to room with you?" he muttered, shaking his head.

"Because no one else can tolerate your ass, excluding Josie," I added. "I don't know how she puts up with you." Brock made it far too easy to harass him.

"Christ, Micah. It's only the first week and you're already gung ho to make enemies."

The bulky security guy with pythons for muscles tipped his gaze up as we approached the porch.

"You can take the guy out of Elmwood, but you can't take the Elite out of him."

Letting out a sigh, Brock said, "I'm not getting a busted lip tonight."

"Fine," I relented, cracking my knuckles more for fun than intimidation. "No blood. Just a few bruises," I conceded.

Brock rolled his eyes as we climbed the three stairs leading to the porch.

We were greeted by the scrawny douche. He had one of those sleazy smiles that bookies wore, sly and devious. Definitely, someone you didn't trust with money, and yet the Chi Sigma did. Dressed in pressed khaki shorts and a polo, he looked like every rich kid who just got off the golf course. My first instinct was to hit him, right smack in his smirking mouth. I clenched and unclenched my fingers.

"Hundred each or find somewhere else to drink," he said, placing the bottle in his hand on the porch ledge.

"Hundred?" I repeated, my brows lifted. "A little steep for such a small gathering, don't you think?"

His nothing-special hazel eyes twinkled with arrogance and humor. "Hundred or get lost." He held out his hand, waiting for Brock or me to slap on some bills.

Brock folded his arms, the biceps from a discipline of daily hours at the gym stretching against the material of his shirt. "Such a warm greeting. If I hadn't been invited personally by your president, I might be offended." Brock had this presence about him that I had always admired. It was more than the commanding tone of his voice or the confidence of his posture. He just had it. Whatever *it* was.

"You know Sterling?" the door-douche asked, his cocky smirk faltering ever so slightly.

"That's not important. You should be more concerned with who the fuck *I* am." My friend just glared at him.

"Uh, should I know you?" He glanced over Brock's face, confused.

Brock took a step forward. "If you don't, learn the name. Brock Taylor." His gaze slid down to the doorman's waiting hand and lifted a brow.

Panic sliced into the dude's eyes at the recognition of Brock's name, his hand lowering. "You're like a football legend, man."

"So I'm told."

"Here, let me get you a beer." The guy looked left and right, eyes darting in search of a full bottle. He ended up grabbing the one he had set on the ledge and offering it to Brock.

My friend took the bottle, not because he planned to drink a half-drunk beer but because he *could* take it. I snickered as we passed by, respecting the magic of Brock Taylor.

I didn't know what I expected when I walked into the house, but unimpressed was my first thought. My gaze did a quick sweep of the lower floor, and nothing exciting or unique struck me. Music pumped from speakers set throughout the main rooms, someone with an iPhone controlling the songs. A small group of drunk girls danced. There were a few rounds of beer pong and other drinking games going on, but the whole thing seemed so... tame.

Chi Sigma was supposed to be so exclusive, yet their party failed to be anything beyond what a fucking five-year-old could have thrown. It was just so fucking... average.

The disappointment was real.

Despite Brock using his name to get us inside, neither of us looked to draw attention. That wasn't the point of this little social experiment. We were to blend in and go unnoticed so we could observe the fraternity and its members. Beer and parties tended to have people let their guards down. I hoped that was the case tonight, as I wanted to do a little snooping while I was here. It couldn't hurt.

No one took much notice of us as we weaved through the crowd, making our way into another part of the first floor, a game room equipped with pool, Ping-Pong, and Foosball tables, as well as a wood-burning fireplace. Trophies lined the deep walnut mantel. The walls were a rich forest green with pictures of past alumni hanging in frames. It wasn't a bad place to hang out, but why did the room feel so stiff to me?

"Someone needs to show these guys how to party," I mumbled, picking up a beer from the small bar in the corner and handing a fresh one to Brock, who discarded the other one in the garage bin sitting beside the bar. The glass clinked as he dropped it, but the sound was muffled by all the voices and music.

"Do you see him?" Brock asked.

Taking a swig of my beer, pleased to find it was cold, I shook my head. "No, not yet."

"Is there anyone else we should take note of? Friends? Fraternity brothers? A girl?" He casually assessed the room. Casually to everyone else but me, that was. A shrewd light glinted in the center of his aqua eyes.

"Everyone."

Brock snorted. "I thought you said this would be quick."

I gave him a sharklike grin. "How hard can it be to spot a bunch of preppy douchebags?"

"At a place like this?" His eyes panned the room of guys who could have all been carbon copies of each other.

"Point made. Come on, let's check the rest of the house."

"This is your gig. Lead the way." He waved the beer out in front of him.

Tossing a grin over my shoulder, I maneuvered around a cluster of girls. I felt their eyes on Brock and me, but I didn't give them a second glance. "I like you taking orders from me."

"Funny," he said flatly. "Enjoy it while it lasts."

We sauntered through the first floor, going into room after room, even checking the patio out back, but Sterling was nowhere to be seen. Just where was this asshole? Hidden away in one of the bedrooms?

I couldn't decide which was more annoying, dodging the advances of girl after girl or hunting down this asshole. Stopping at the bottom of the staircase, I glanced upward, surveying the second floor. A hallway stemmed from either side of the top landing. This place had to have a least a dozen rooms or more to house a fraternity of this size. When one of the Elite threw a party, we closed off sections of our houses. Our bedrooms were always off-limits, but it didn't seem as if Chi Sigma had any regulations or restrictions. To me, that was a fucking invitation.

Waiting until the couple coming down the stairs reached the bottom, I hooked around the banister and started up, Brock on my heels. As we reached the top, a door down the hall opened, and a female laugh fluttered into the hallway.

We weren't the only ones upstairs. A handful of people lined up against the wall to use the bathroom. From the corner of my eye, I watched Sterling come out of a bedroom with a girl behind him. She tugged at the end of her skirt before smoothing her tousled strawberry blonde hair. It was pretty fucking obvious what they had been doing behind the closed door. Not only were her hair and clothes disheveled, but her lips were puffy, her lipstick smeared.

I couldn't judge him for doing something I had done time and time again, but I wanted to, mainly because I had changed. It had taken me some time to work through my shit, but living an empty life with different girls every night was so unappealing compared to waking up next to Mads.

"Do you see him?" Brock asked, noticing the change in my expression and the sudden stiffening of my shoulders. His back was to Sterling.

I nodded. "Yeah, he's approaching the stairs."

Brock continued to lean against the banister, his baseball hat pulled low to shield his eyes. "How convenient for us."

Clutching the beer bottle in my hand, I tipped my head down as Sterling and the girl passed by and trotted down the stairs. They rounded the bottom landing and disappeared into the crowd. The asshole walked right by the two of us without a glance. Perfect. It meant we didn't stand out for once, which I admitted was an odd feeling.

Brock clasped my shoulder. "Let's move."

I grinned, loving that he knew what was on my mind without me having to say a word. This shit was a typical night for us.

We headed down the hall, and Brock leaned against the wall, blocking me with his body as my fingers wrapped around the doorknob of the room Sterling and the girl had just exited. It turned freely. "These guys should learn to lock their doors during parties. Amateurs."

"Make it quick," he advised, his eyes canvassing the hallway and staircase.

I handed over my beer for him to hold while I did a little search and seizure. "I know the drill, boss." And as quiet as a shadow, I slipped inside the bedroom, keeping the door cracked just enough for Brock to alert me of any potential problems. He would stand guard in case Sterling decided to wander back.

A small table lamp had been left on, bathing the room in a soft yellow glow. He had a single room to himself, which made my job easier. I didn't have to sort through whose shit was whose. However, the amount of black plaid in the room made me queasy and dizzy.

Dude seriously needed some style. There was such a thing as excessive.

Hints of smoke and tobacco lingered in the air, faintly reminding me of Mads, and it instantly angered me. I wanted no part of another guy to make me think of my girl.

I wasn't a fan of cigarettes in general or what they did to the body, and as much as I would like her to quit, I also oddly loved the way her perfume and shampoo mixed with the aroma of cigarette smoke. It was her scent. Sexy, just like she was.

Shaking my head, I refocused on why I was inside his room. It was pretty basically furnished with a bed, desk, and lounging chair in the corner that had a shirt thrown over it. All the furnishings were black. Big surprise.

Rushing for the desk first, I rummaged through the drawers, searching for what, I didn't know. He had his laptop on top of the desk, along with a picture of him and another girl. They bore a similar resemblance that made me think she might be a relative rather than a girlfriend. A sister, perhaps?

The old Micah would have used her for information any way I could have gotten it out of her. I wasn't proud of the things I'd done in my past, but I also didn't regret them—not all of them, anyway. I had a few things I would love to do over—one in particular.

As I flipped through a stack of papers and notebooks, my elbow hit a book on the side of the desk, sending it thumping to the carpet. I bent down to pick it up and noticed something had slipped out between the pages. It looked like a photo. How fucking unoriginal hiding shit in a book.

I plucked the book off the floor and tugged at the end of the photo, pulling it out completely. I sucked in a sharp breath. Surprise quickly turned to boiling fury as I stared down at a face I knew well.

"What the fuck is this?" My fingers pressed hard into the corner of the photo.

Why does this asshole have a picture of my girlfriend?

I took a moment to study Mads's face and the background, trying to place when and where this had been taken. It was an older picture; I could tell by her hair color and style that it was at least two or three years ago. She smiled, but her face was angled away from the camera, and it made me wonder if she knew someone had taken her picture. It had been snapped in front of her house.

Had Sterling captured this moment? Was this the night he'd been talking about? How did he know *my* Mads? And why the fuck did he have this picture stashed away like a secret piece of treasure?

It was time for Mads and me to have a little talk.

Many scenarios had played through my head when I decided to come here tonight, but this... this had not been one of them.

I still didn't know what it meant, if anything, but my gut told me not to take this lightly or ignore Sterling.

It took all my self-control to not crumble the picture in my fist or take it with me. I ground my teeth to the point of pain as I tucked it back in between the pages of the book, wanting to leave no trace of someone having ransacked his room.

My jaw locked as I replaced the book on the corner of the desk and moved back toward the door. I'd seen enough for one night. And I honestly didn't care what else the fraternity might be up to unless it had anything to do with Mads.

Then it was game on, bitches.

Brock kept his eyes down the hallway as he asked, "Did you find anything?"

I clicked the door softly shut behind me. "The bastard has a picture of Mads."

That drew his attention, and his gaze swung to me, brows pinched together. "What kind of picture?"

"Not a nude or he'd be fucking dead already, but it's from a few years ago. Maybe junior year."

He handed me back my beer bottle. "Why would he have an old picture of Mads?"

"Exactly. I intend to find out." I tossed back the bottle, draining it, but the alcohol did little to ease the burning inside me. I'd been itching for a fight before, but now I fucking craved it. I had to hit something or someone.

"Fucking hell," Brock cursed under his breath, sensing the fury pounding inside me. If it had been a photo of Josie, he would have felt the same. He forked a hand through his dark hair. "So much for thinking college was going to be chill."

"Tell me about it." I wasn't thrilled with the turn of events either. I had not been expecting this. My emotions were reeling.

He clasped a hand on my shoulder. "We need to get you out of here before you do real damage."

"Probably a good idea." I dropped my empty bottle on the floor in front of Sterling's room. It was too much to hope he would step on it when he took his drunk ass to bed. God, I was in a fucking foul mood. Only two things could cure the turmoil within me—a fight or Mads. "You think the girls are still up?" I asked, shoving my way past the bathroom line, which had grown longer while I'd been inside Sterling's room. It extended beyond the stairway now.

"Only one way to find out."

"I like the way you think." Jogging down the stairs, I thought Mads and some fresh air were the better options, and I was kind of damn proud of myself for controlling my impulses. The urge to do physical harm still radiated inside me, but the thought of Mads's lips sparked a different fire in my gut.

Eagerness spurred me forward down the hallway. We passed the game room again, and I glanced in, dying to run into Sterling. I told myself if I made it through the house without seeing his mug, I'd save the fight for another day, despite my fists begging for confrontation. But if I saw his smug face right now, I'd beat the bloody shit out of him.

"I know what you're thinking," Brock said, raising his voice so it carried over the music and drunk nonsense, "and you need to keep your cool. We need answers. Then we kick his ass."

Brock was right. Of course he was right. He was good at thinking ahead, plotting and planning. I didn't have as much discipline, not when my blood pounded in my ears, and especially when it came to Mads. My judgment became clouded. For as long as I could remember, she was the one person who could turn me inside out and not even try.

In typical drunk girl fashion, four girls were shaking what God gave them on top of the pool table. One of them laughed, or maybe they all did—it was difficult to distinguish—but only one of their laughs hit me in the chest.

I did a double take, coming to a sudden halt, my head whipping back inside the game room to the pool table.

What the fuck?

"Mads?" I whispered, blinking, positive I was seeing shit, but I hadn't drunk that much, and unless someone dosed my beer, then...

She wouldn't have come to the party, right?

Then I remembered who her roommates were.

Son of a bitch.

Brock's head whirled beside me, his gaze zeroing in on Josie. Like me, his expression went through a series of emotions, and I waited to see him realize that it was indeed his girlfriend dancing on top of a pool table and not an illusion.

The scowl on his lips deepened, and I swore I heard him growl her name. Normally this would amuse me. Not tonight. Josie and Mads, along with Ainsley and Kenna, had their hands in the air, swaying back and forth barefoot as the room watched.

This wasn't the first time Mads danced on a table, nor did I think it would be the last. I had hauled her ass off them time and time again throughout high school, protecting her even when she didn't want it or remembered the next day. Her love for tables and dancing extended beyond parties. I had this vivid memory of the first time I'd seen little Mads at six years old, with pigtails and ribbons. She'd come over to Grayson and Kenna's house for their birthday party. When I walked into the backyard, there she was, on one of the white banquet tables, dancing with Kenna, a blue balloon clutched in her hand.

I think I developed my first crush that day.

But nothing stayed innocent or pure for long. After the whole thing with Kenna and that bastard Carter Patterson, she'd become more cautious and distant. For a while, she avoided everyone, including the Elite. It had bothered me, but as long as she was safe, I had told myself it was for the best.

I tore my eyes from Mads and browsed the room. My gaze landed on the corner, where Sterling sat on a barstool near the bar watching. Not all the girls. No. His eyes were solely fixed on Mads.

Blood rushed through my veins, hot and fiery.

This bastard is dead.

I took a step forward, eyes set on Sterling. Brock clamped a hand down on my shoulder, stopping me. "Not here. Not now. Let's just get the girls and go. We don't know what he wants. Not yet. But we will. I promise."

It took more than a few breaths to steady the rage pumping through me. I gave him a nod, assuring him that I wouldn't sink my fists in Sterling at this moment. He released my shoulder and strolled into the game room, heading straight for the pool table. I strutted right behind him.

A bold, desperate girl walked into my path, smiling coyly at me. She twirled her hair, and before she could open her mouth, I said, "Not going to happen."

Her jaw dropped, and I walked around her, irritated at the interruption.

I sought out Mads, hating that I'd been distracted even for a second. Her light brown hair fell down the center of her back in loose waves that swung with her hips. Drunk or not, she knew how to move, and I appreciated the way her body rolled and dipped with the beat of the music. Her lips moved with the words to the song. No matter how many girls were in a room, my eyes only saw Mads.

Stopping at the edge of the pool table, I glanced up at her, thankful she hadn't worn a skirt tonight but also a little disappointed. "What did I say about dancing on tables?"

Mid-giggle, she swung her eyes toward the sound of my voice. "Micah!" she squealed as those beautiful gray eyes landed on me. The glass bottle in her hand dangled in the air.

Lifting my hands, I slid my fingers up to her waist, plucking her off the table. She leaned into me, twining her arms around my neck. "You're here. I was thinking about you."

Even drunk, Mads was cute. Too damn cute. "Really? Would you like to tell me what you're doing here?" I intended for the words to come out sharp, but she wrinkled her freckled nose at me, smiling.

She started to sway. "Dance with me."

My dick hardened in my jeans as her body rubbed me in just the right place. *God, she fucking drives me crazy.* Hands still at her hips, I leaned down, murmuring in her ear, "How about you and I have a private dance back in my room?" Regardless of what was happening in my pants, my goal was to get her out of here.

"Mads told us about the party tonight," I heard Josie say to Brock. He must have asked the same question I had. Josie sat on the edge of the pool table, her legs dangling off as she clutched the front of his shirt.

Brock lifted an amused brow. Where Josie was concerned, his cold heart melted. "She did, did she?"

"You don't actually think we're going to sit and study in our dorm every night, do you?" Kenna, the walking, talking tornado of drama and trouble, plopped down beside her sister. It still bewildered me, seeing the two of them together. Kenna and Josie were pretty freaking close to being carbon copies of each other until one or the other opened their mouth. Then it became clear who was who.

Kenna, Josie, and Grayson were triplets—the Edwards threesome. Not as dirty as it sounded.

I blinked at Kenna, and my eyes portrayed my answer. Fuck yes, I thought the four of them were tucked away safely in their dorm every night. To see otherwise didn't make me feel good.

Mads rolled her eyes at me, reading my expression.

Taking the bottle from her hand, I downed the remaining beer. "Party's over, *Maddy*." She hated to be called that. I emphasized the nickname because I wanted to annoy her—an angry Mads would get out of this house faster than a drunk one.

CHAPTER THREE

MADS

A frown tugged at my lips. He knew how much I hated that nickname. "I know what you're doing. And it's not going to work," I said. Never in a million years would I have believed I'd end up here... with Micah. I was either growing soft as I matured or dumber. The jury was still out. I'd never been a believer in second chances, yet Micah had a way of getting a person to do the impossible, the unexpected.

A lot had happened over the last two years. So much, and because of it, I learned not to take life for granted, or those I cared about, and the truth was, regardless of our past, I had always loved Micah. He had the power to make me ridiculously happy or crush my soul. It had been difficult allowing him back into my heart, and so fucking scary. Opening up meant I could be hurt again. I would rather feel physical pain than the grueling agony of a broken heart.

Micah's eyes darted over my head, and despite being

slightly inebriated, the hardening of his jaw didn't escape my notice. When his eyes meet mine again, he tried to cover his irritation with a lopsided grin. "I have no idea what you're talking about."

"Why are *you* here?" I countered, vaguely aware of Kenna and Ainsley hopping off the pool table. How the hell had I let those two talk me up there to begin with? I strictly remembered mumbling something about no dancing on tables, and yet...

I had no excuse.

Booze, tables, and dancing went hand in hand for me. It was like pizza and pop. Or milk and Oreos.

Micah reached out, twirling a strand of my hair around his finger and lightly tugging on it. "Do I need a reason?" He was doing that thing again, trying to distract me, but my brain couldn't figure out why.

Our relationship was fairly new and far from perfect, but I had known Micah forever. I knew him. Although I didn't want to jinx what we had going, we had a lot to work on. Trust was our biggest obstacle. No surprise considering our history. Micah and I both tended to be rash, acting before we thought, a trait that could get us both in trouble.

It had been a long time since I thought about the night Micah destroyed any hope I had of having a healthy, trusting relationship. I had become jaded and cynical since that night, and despite all that, I had done exactly what I told myself I would never do: I gave the jerk a second chance.

Except Micah really wasn't a jerk. He was a lot of things, including a flirt, reckless, and facetious, but he was also incredibly generous, attentive, funny, and always there when I needed him.

Clean slate, I kept having to remind myself, but still, the memory of him sleeping with another girl would always haunt me. She hadn't been his last. We had both been with other people since then, and yet we found our way back to each other.

Not easily either.

Suspicion shoved aside the warm fuzzy feeling of the few beers I'd had. I wasn't ashamed to admit that, regardless of all the parties I attended, I was a lightweight. No matter how much I drank, my tolerance never grew. "Normally I'd say no, but this is a party, after all. Since when do you ever voluntarily leave a party early?" I pressed my lips together as I stared at him, the buzz I had going fading a tad. "Why do I feel like you have ulterior motives for being here?"

His hand slid to the small of my back as he leaned closer to my ear. "Turns out I'd rather spend the night with you. And this party is so dull, it could hardly be considered a party."

Smooth. But that was Micah.

Curse him and his damn light blue eyes and cocky dimples. Ugh. I was such a sucker for dimples. And tattoos. Micah had both. It was like a double whammy straight to my ovaries. "I bet."

Kenna stumbled into Micah's side, latching on to his arm to catch herself. "Why are you being such a douche? It's our first party."

"Thanks for the invite, by the way," he retorted, giving her a butt-sore glare.

My cousin rolled her eyes. "The Elite don't need an invitation."

This was true. Micah grinned in response. "Damn right we don't." But this was college, not Elmwood Academy. He might not admit it, but I knew he and Brock were a bit uneasy. They were at a new school and down two Elite.

"Okay, then." Kenna exhaled like that matter was settled.

It wasn't.

Brock shook his head. "Not okay. We're going," he stated firmly, not an ounce of wiggle room in his tone or in the pointed look he challenged Kenna with.

She crossed her arms and glared back. "What the hell is happening? You're killing my buzz. I'm not ready to be sober. You used to be the fun Elite." She pouted at Micah.

He flashed her a grin. "Manipulation won't work on me."

Josie studied Brock's face; I could see she sensed something weird was happening. He tended to be overprotective of her, but with good reason. According to Brock, there was always at least one guy at a party with nefarious intentions and looking to take advantage of a vulnerable girl. "Did something happen?" she asked, no longer dancing or smiling.

"I can't talk about it here." An understanding passed between them, and judging by the downturn of her lips, Josie wasn't happy about having to wait but would.

Irritation flashed over Kenna's eyes. "Wow. That didn't take long. We've been on campus for like a week and you're already starting in on your secrets."

Brock shifted his body to face her, shooting her a warning

glare. "I promised Grayson that we'd look out for you. Now stop being a pain in my ass and go the fuck back to the dorms."

Kenna huffed, and her butt dropped against the pool table, a speck of defeat darkening her chocolate eyes.

"I will haul your ass out of here," Brock threatened.

Unlike my threats, Micah's and Brock's were very real. "Don't bother. I'm going," Kenna conceded, but not happily.

"That goes for the both of you as well," he ordered Ainsley.

She blinked. I felt a little bad for her. She was also figuring out where she belonged, not just at KU but within our group. We had all hung out over the summer, but I could tell she still didn't think of herself as one of us.

Then again, I wasn't sure Josie did either. She balanced this thin line between two worlds, unable to leave her past fully behind.

It looked like we both had loose ends that needed to be tied.

Kenna grabbed a beer off the edge of the pool table and stormed out of the pool room, but not before flipping up her middle finger as she left.

My lips twitched. Josie must have been rubbing off on her sister, and I liked it. It was past time that Kenna stopped being the girl she thought everyone wanted her to be and started just being herself. Whoever that was.

"I'll go after her," Ainsley offered, most likely to avoid being a third wheel, something that bothered Josie. And me. I wanted Ainsley to be comfortable with us. All of us.

Brock nodded, and she raced after Kenna, despite them not getting along. Ainsley was a decent person. I respected her for putting aside her differences to watch over Kenna.

Josie tugged on the front of Brock's shirt, drawing his gaze to her. "We should make sure they get back to the dorm."

Brock slid a hand to the small of her back. "I'll see you at home later," he said to Micah.

"Yeah, we're right behind you. Mads and I need to have a chat," Micah replied.

Josie sent me an empathetic look.

Winking, I lifted the corners of my mouth, telling her not to worry about me, but the grin didn't reach my eyes, not when my stomach had knotted.

Micah laced his fingers through mine, leading me toward the door. My foot had just touched the threshold when a voice stopped Micah dead in his tracks. "Leaving so soon?"

I groaned, wanting to keep moving, but Micah's hand in mine tightened, and he slowly turned around.

Sterling Weston stood behind us clad in black jeans that hugged his toned legs, a fitted shirt the same color, and combat boots. Always black. Always smug. Always a hint of danger. And yet, despite the outward appearance, he smelled of money, a wealth he tried to hide behind a bad boy exterior. His dark hair fell to one side, revealing the shaved sides. He had no tattoos but looked as if he should under those clothes. At least there hadn't been any over two years ago. He could have gotten one since then, but I somehow doubted that. His vice wasn't tattoos. It was cigarettes.

Inching closer to Micah, I stared into Sterling's face. His eyes twinkled mischievously, and he wore a smug grin. I could tell he enjoyed torturing me. Realizing that, I made the decision right there to tell Micah tonight what happened between Sterling and me. Another one of those life mistakes I longed to erase. I refused to let another guy hold any kind of power over me. Besides, Sterling couldn't possibly know that I hadn't told Micah. He was guessing, and based on my reaction earlier, he had guessed right.

Prick.

I was done. What was the point in hiding from my past or pretending it didn't exist? At some point, the truth always came out, and it was better if it came from me.

I didn't know what I was so scared of. It wasn't like Micah hadn't done the same thing or hadn't been with other people. For two years, we had a history of throwing people in each other's faces. Healthy reactions? No. But when did teenagers ever make healthy choices? My decisions had been spurred by hurt, anger, and often jealousy I refused to admit burned within me.

Seeing him with other girls had sucked. Communication had definitely been something both of us lacked. We were working on that, among other things, because the bottom line was I loved Micah.

God, what the hell was I thinking coming here tonight?

In my defense, I figured it was likely that I would run into Sterling. This was his house. Hence the three beers in less than an hour. Not the brightest idea, but the first beer had been to take the edge off so I could work up the courage to talk to him. I didn't want or need any unexpected bumps in the road or skeletons to come out of the closet. The second and third had been to calm my nerves since the first didn't do shit. And now that warm, loose feeling I had worked to obtain was quickly draining.

And I never did get the chance to speak with Sterling.

Now was not the time. Micah first, then Sterling. I refused to spend the next year or two until Sterling graduated waiting for the bomb to drop. This was my mess, and I would clean it up.

I firmed my chin and replied to Sterling. "I have an early class in the morning, and considering I had to skip my first lecture today, I can't afford to miss another."

He toyed with the rim of his beer bottle, running his thumb over the opening. "That was unfortunate, but how crazy that we ran into each other. We'll have to get coffee and catch up."

My cheeks warmed, ribbons of embarrassment weaving inside me. Could he make me any more uncomfortable? I frowned. Why did I let Ainsley talk me into coming? I should have stayed home.

Micah's muscles tensed at the invitation. "She hates coffee," he blurted, an utterly false statement.

Sterling lifted a mocking brow. "Really?" he retorted as if didn't believe Micah and knew for a fact that I did like coffee, which I did. "Tea, then," he amended.

Sterling had fucking balls, I'd give him that. He wasn't asking me out on a date, but it felt that way, and in front of my boyfriend, no less.

"Sure. Next time," I said, grabbing Micah's arm. I desperately wanted to leave, quickly before Micah acted on the impulse to plant his fist in Sterling's face.

"Next time," he agreed. "Thanks for coming, *Splash*."

Micah's muscles flexed under my fingers, and he cocked his head to the side, a telling sign he was about to throw a punch. Hostility burned from him, nearly setting my skin on fire. It emitted off him in waves.

Spinning so I stood in front of Micah, I flattened a hand on his chest, giving it a firm push. "He's not worth it," I muttered.

Micah's eyes remained fastened over my head on Sterling, and I worried for a second that he might indeed cause a scene. What was it about Sterling that had him so worked up? Had he found out about...?

No. He couldn't have.

Or had Micah recognized him? Was that why he and Brock came to his party? That night, he hadn't paid much attention to Sterling. He had been focused on me, and it had been dark. Perhaps he hadn't gotten a look at the guy I kissed in front of him out of revenge. When my lips had finally left Sterling's and I had glanced at where Micah had stood, he was gone.

A tight smile appeared on Micah's lips, a mask descending and concealing his true feelings. "Thanks for the beer." He tipped his head at Sterling. "I have a feeling we'll be seeing quite a lot of each other."

What did he mean by that? And why did that sound like a threat and not a thing of friendliness?

I inspected Micah's expression, attempting to figure out what the hell was going on with him.

He turned to leave once more, and as we entered the hallway, something brushed down the side of my arm. Not something. Someone. And because Micah had a hold of my other hand, I was all too afraid of just who that someone was.

I shivered, but not like the warm, stomach-flipping tingles Micah's touch created. No. This was a cold, hair-raising sensation that made my veins freeze.

Was it because Sterling was a secret I wanted to stay buried?

My gaze shot over my shoulder, unable to stop from looking. It was a knee-jerk reaction from being touched unexpectedly and unwantedly. I narrowed my eyes at Sterling, conveying a simple message.

Don't. Touch. Me.

He received the message loud and clear, but the asshole didn't give a shit. He smirked, and I didn't like the devilish glint sparkling in his amber eyes.

I wanted to do something foolish like flip him off or stick my tongue out of him, but I did nothing and kept walking straight out of the Chi Sigma house.

CHAPTER FOUR

MADS

"Are you okay?" Micah asked when we stepped outside.

I nodded, drawing in a deep breath of the night's air. "Yeah. Just a bit tired now," I admitted. Alcohol tended to have that effect on me.

"How much did you drink?" He was still angry. Not with me, but I could visibly see him slowly pushing aside his temper so he wouldn't direct it at me. Micah's ability to control his emotions like that and be aware of them was impressive. I respected that. My emotions tended to just fly, and it wasn't until after the damage was done that I realized I could have handled the situation better.

"Just a few beers," I admitted.

His fingers were still interlaced with mine, our arms swinging between us as we walked down the side of the street. Occasionally someone would hoot or laugh in the distance, people still milling about, excited over the prospect of a new semester. For a few minutes, we walked in silence, the crickets singing in the grass and the moon glowing brightly in the dark sky. I loved summer nights just like this. It was still hot, but traces of fall lingered in the breeze, the in-between stage of seasons.

My head heavy with thoughts and still a bit clouded with beer, I moved into Micah's side, laying the side of my head on his shoulder. I thought about how to begin what I needed to say, but the words were scrambled in my head. How did one start a conversation like this?

We'd both done a shitty thing, but over the last two years, we'd grown up a lot. Life had a way of forcing your hand sometimes, even when you weren't ready, but what sixteen-year-olds didn't make colossal mistakes? What Micah had done... was nearly unforgettable and would have been if we'd been in a relationship, but the truth was we hadn't been. Not officially. We'd hooked up, and I got ideas, those girlish dreams of romance and love. When it came to Micah Bradford, I had nothing but glittering stars in my eyes. How quickly an illusion can be shattered.

That had been the hardest year of my life, and only a fraction of it had anything to do with Micah. It had been all kinds of fucked-up, and I thought that was one of the reasons the memories of Micah and Sterling were so vividly implanted in my head.

Shortly after the incident with Micah, my best friend left. Kenna moved to another town, transferred schools, and because of the distance, our relationship suffered.

All my relationships suffered that year.

The world changed. *I* changed. Gone was the girl who believed nothing bad ever happened, that her life was full of cherries, roses, and cotton candy. My cousin became a victim, someone out of a true crime story we used to watch on TV, and I was the powerless witness who could do nothing to stop her from getting hurt.

When she escaped Elmwood, I became secluded, not giving a shit about friendships, school, or any of the things I used to love. My guilt crippled me, made me feel useless. I never wanted to go back there.

And during all that bullshit, it had been hard to go through it without my best friend, but I understood why she left, why my aunt and uncle sent her away. So much anger had festered inside me for what she'd been through and the reason she left.

It was difficult to put your past behind you and move forward. Some things followed you. Some haunted you. Some invaded your sleep when you were vulnerable and open. And others crept up when you least expected them to.

Sterling was the latter. A dark stain on my past that appeared out of nowhere.

I had just about worked up my courage to tell Micah as we turned on the street of his house with Brock. I hadn't noticed until then that we were heading there instead of the dorms. Seeing the rowhouses come into view, I realized how much I wanted to spend the night in his bed, sleeping in his arms.

After the day I had, I needed the comfort and security he gave me.

This was the first time I'd ever been away from home,

excluding vacations, and I missed my parents. Unlike Micah, Brock, and Josie even, I had a good relationship with my parents. They might not approve of all my decisions, but they also didn't make me feel like a shitty person. It was because of them that I'd been able to get through some of the darkest times in my life.

I was lucky.

Micah released my hand, running his fingers through his hair. He stopped under a streetlight, the yellow glow illuminating his face. "I thought I wanted to know how you know him," he said, not needing to explain who *he* was. "But now I don't. It doesn't matter. The only thing I care about is you, and I'm not saying this as a controlling, possessive boyfriend who's insecure and jealous as fuck."

My lips twitched. If anyone was jealous in this relationship, that title went to me. Insecurities were a motherfucker.

"But you need to stay away from Sterling," Micah warned with a trace of desperation that I'd never heard from him before.

Surprise fluttered into my chest and something else. An emotion I couldn't quite grasp. Sadness, perhaps? "Why? What is it?" I could tell something weighed on him. What did he know about Sterling that I didn't? But to be fair, I knew very little about him... now *and* then. I hadn't wanted to know anything. Not even his name.

His gaze held mine. "I don't have the answers yet, but he's bad news, Mads. I can feel it."

The new phone I picked up before dinner buzzed in the back pocket of my white jeans. I ignored the persistent rumble. It was most likely Kenna, wondering where I was or wanting to complain about having to leave early. She would have to wait. "Is that why you were there tonight?" I asked.

He nodded. "Yeah."

"Micah." I sighed, stirrings of worry fluttering in my gut. "I don't want you getting into any trouble." It was the first day of school, for heaven's sake. Was it too much to hope that the quiet we had over the summer would carry into college?

"Trouble seems to find me. Trust me, I didn't go looking for this."

No, he hadn't. I had brought Sterling into this. Whatever had Micah feeling uneasy, it had been enough to check Sterling out after only one short meeting.

That he'd gone to Sterling's house to satisfy a hunch didn't shock me. This was the Elite. It was what they did. They found out your secrets, even the ones you thought were buried deep, without a trace. And then they kept that information tucked away to hold over your head. I didn't have any idea the number of people they had collected information on over the years, but this was a new place, a new crowd, and plenty of scandals.

I had seriously hoped the four of them had put their little *hobby* behind them.

It didn't look that way. Some habits die hard.

Micah reached out and grabbed my hand, yanking me toward his chest. I tumbled into him, his hands already around my waist to steady me. He pressed his cheek against mine, his lips hovering close to my ear. Through his shirt, his heart beat rapidly with mine.

"Promise me you'll stay away from him," he whispered, his

breath warm and ticklish on my skin. "At least until I get some answers."

Rubbing my cheek against the just-scratchy surface of his face, I replied, "I promise."

The words rolled off my tongue before I even contemplated what I'd agreed to, or how hard it might be to avoid Sterling Weston.

Buzz. Buzz. Buzz.

My phone's alarm went off, rumbling on the nightstand. Without opening my eyes, I reached out, fumbling for my phone. It took a few tries, but eventually, my fingers landed on the vibrating device. I quickly silenced the alarm and dropped the phone onto the bed.

Five more minutes. That was what I told myself every day, and yet five often turned into ten and then twenty. I'd been late to school many times due to this *fail-safe* practice.

Yet something nagged at the back of my mind, an echo of the annoying ring from my alarm, telling me I had to get up. I groaned, rubbing my hand over my eyes. They slowly opened, and the dull ache behind them reminded me where I went and what I did last night.

I checked the clock, trying to remember what day it was. Thursday?

Fuck!

I blinked at the blurry time on my phone. There had to be a mistake. I had class in thirty minutes. And... I glanced at the rumpled bed, the tan, firm body tangled in the sheets with me. His dark blond head rested on the navy pillowcase.

This wasn't my dorm.

And that meant I didn't have any of my stuff. No clean clothes. No toothbrush. No deodorant.

Fuck!

Not only would I have to wear the clothes I'd worn to a party last night, but I also didn't even have time to at least shower. Smelling like a guy all day was the least of my worries. I needed my laptop. This trend of starting the school year off on the wrong foot every day had to stop. The universe couldn't possibly be against me that much. At some point, the odds had to swing in my favor.

Right?

One thing was certain—sitting around in Micah's room definitely wouldn't make time stop or turn back. If I planned on making it to any of my classes this week, I needed to move my ass now.

Tossing back the covers, I rolled out of bed, eyes scouring the floor for my clothes. I vaguely remembered Micah loaning me one of his T-shirts to sleep in. We hadn't slept together, just shared a bed. He was notorious for being the world's best cuddler.

Speaking of the big teddy bear... He groaned from the sudden movement of the mattress and the loss of my weight. I snatched my jeans off the floor and tugged them on as I peeked over at him. Big fucking mistake.

Micah first thing in the morning, all sleepy and nearly naked, was a sight to behold. My heart fluttered in my chest, and for a split second, I wanted to crawl back into the bed with him.

Half-lidded light blue eyes lifted to my face, lips curling just enough for the dimples to peek at his cheeks. "Where do you think you're going?"

God, no. Not the fucking dimples. I shook free the stirrings of desire. "To class." I dragged my gaze away from the bed, looking for my shirt.

"Too early," he mumbled. "Need more sleep and snuggles."

I rolled my eyes, quickly backing away from the bed to avoid the hand Micah stretched toward me. I knew his tricks. If I let him pull me back into his arms, I wouldn't leave this room for another hour or more.

Not today.

I was getting to that class even if it killed me—and leaving a shirtless Micah in bed was close to dying. Finding my shirt under the one he'd worn last night, I grabbed it and padded toward the bathroom. "I need to borrow your laptop and some toothpaste. You don't have class, right?"

"What time is it?" he mumbled, having rolled onto his back.

"Almost ten," I replied before shutting myself into the bathroom.

"Who the fuck schedules class so early? I swear, woman, you are not human." His complaint came through the closed door, and my lips twitched as I peed. Micah was not a morning person.

I didn't particularly like getting up early but hated wasting my day even more. Once I got out of bed and usually had a cup of coffee, I was good to go. Today would be one of those days I'd have to forgo the coffee, and in a few hours, my body would be regretting the lack of caffeine. I'd just stop and get something from a vendor after class.

Tossing on my shirt, I left Micah's on the bathroom counter and opened the door. "That means you're dating an alien."

"Sexy," he rasped, voice still heavy with sleep. I loved the gravelly texture of his voice when he first woke up.

Rolling my eyes, I tossed my hair up and smeared a dab of toothpaste onto my finger, using it as a makeshift toothbrush. Not very effective, but at least it chased away the morning breath.

"Laptop?" I asked, stepping back into the bedroom. It was days like today that I was grateful Micah and Brock didn't share a bathroom like we did back in the dorm.

His hand made some sort of swirling motion toward the desk, his head still snuggled up against the pillow. Envy struck me. I wanted to be back in that bed, not rushing to a lecture on the principles of marketing. As a marketing major, it was a requirement.

Picking up the laptop, I shoved my wallet and phone into my back pockets. Before heading out, I leaned down and kissed Micah's cheek. He was quick. Before my lips eased away, he grabbed my wrist and yanked, sending me tumbling forward. I landed sprawled on top of him, the laptop between our chests, no doubt exactly what he planned.

Blowing pieces of my hair out of my face, I glared down at him. "Keep your hands to yourself, and don't you dare think about kissing me. I've got to go."

"I know. Are you sure you can't spare one kiss?" he asked, intentionally dropping his tone.

My heart skipped. *Be brave. Be strong. Be resilient.* A breath later, I replied, "I already did."

Micah's fingers roamed over my jeans. "Cheeks don't count."

"Does a knee to your junk count?" I wiggled my knee up between his legs to get my point across. It would only take one quick jerk to bring my point home.

He laughed as he squirmed on the bed and pushed me off him. "Go. Get out of here before I change my mind and ravish you."

I scooted off the bed, clutching the laptop to my chest, and walked backward toward the door, grinning. "Tonight?"

A hand dove into his hair, causing some of the strands to stick out. "I don't think I'll be able to wait that long."

I reached behind me for the doorknob, my eyes still on him. It was like I couldn't look away. "You're ridiculous."

"And you like me. What does that say about you?"

My lips moved up, and I opened the door. "That I need to study harder," I said, walking out and leaving behind temptation.

I raced across campus to the business division, not far from Micah's house, thank God. I pounded the pavement, zigzagging around students, and came to a fast walk once I was in front of the building. Rushing into the hallway, I found the stairs, taking them two at a time to the second floor. The room was easy to find, the second door on my left.

My breath came out ragged from my haste, but my efforts paid off—I got to class with a minute to spare, just enough time to find a seat. I quickly scanned the rows of theater-style seats. This was one of the larger classes, seeing as it was a requirement for most of the business degrees and plenty of others. I entered an empty row and plopped down, my racing heart slowly returning to normal. Before the professor entered, I opened Micah's laptop and was greeted with a password screen.

Shit! What the hell is his password?

It would be something stupid, nothing practical or sentimental like his birthday or my name. I didn't bother to try and crack it; that was Fynn's department. Instead, I dug out my phone and sent him a text, praying to God he was still awake and hadn't already fallen back to sleep.

This cannot be my luck. What are the chances that I finally make it to class but am so damn unprepared? I didn't even have a notebook or pen. These days, those were practically archaic.

A body dropped down in the seat to my right as I waited impatiently for Micah to text me back. I stared at the screen, begging those three little typing dots to appear.

The person next to me shifted, settling into their seat. My knee bounced under the laptop, and I nibbled on the end of my nail.

Come on, Micah.

A throat cleared, drawing my gaze to my right. I didn't pay him much attention, my mind on other matters, until I saw a flash of his amber eyes. Then I fully looked at the person next to me, hoping I was wrong. It couldn't be him.

It was.

Sterling.

Of all the classes, did he have to be in this one?

He slouched deep into the worn fabric of the chair, his knees pressing into the back of the one in front of him. He slipped a pencil behind his ear and grinned at me. "Hey, Splash. It's nice to see you finally made it to a class... and not soaking wet."

I stopped fidgeting as a curse flew through my head. Not all the events of last night were crystal clear, but one part was stamped into my memory—my promise to Micah. Keeping that promise might be more difficult to uphold if Sterling kept showing up everywhere. "Sorry, that seat is taken," I said the first thing that came to me in a pathetic attempt to get him to move.

Not a single muscle moved, except for the one controlling his eyebrow. That muscle lifted. "There's an empty seat on the other side of you."

I opened my mouth.

"Don't tell me. That one's taken too," he cut in before I could say precisely that.

Gnawing at my lower lip, I contemplated the best approach to handle him. "Yeah, by my invisible friends Get Lost and Can't Take a Hint."

Sterling chuckled. "How did I know you would be funny."

Despite he and I being acquainted, we knew next to nothing about each other and yet had shared some intimate moments.

Fuck me.

This wasn't going to work.

"Fine, I'll move," I huffed, snapping the laptop closed and preparing to stand up.

The professor chose that moment to stride into class, her classic black heels clapping over the floors.

How many times would the f-bomb run through my head today?

Sinking back into my chair, I glared at Sterling. The bastard smirked at me, looking like a very pleased cat after a meal. I half expected him to start licking his paws.

The professor's briefcase dropped to the floor with a clatter, jolting my attention to the front. Silence fell over the classroom auditorium. She wore a very practical black pencil skirt that came past her knees with a matching blazer and a white button-up underneath. No jewelry. Auburn hair swept away from her face into a neat but not tight low bun, a few loose pieces framing her face. She wore natural makeup, nothing bold or distracting —simple and professional, like her attire. A pair of sleek glasses sat on the bridge of her nose.

Shoulders back and spine straight, the professor faced the class. She had impeccable posture, reminding me of a New York businesswoman. Tough. All business. Classy. Ambitious. And wealthy.

"Good morning. This is Introduction to Marketing. I assume if you're sitting in this room, you're supposed to be here. If you're not, you know where the door is." Her voice carried beautifully, even to the back of the room where I sat. It was as if her voice had been made to give speeches. She waited for a few beats to see if anyone needed to leave.

A chair squeaked a few rows in front of me, followed by a shuffling of feet. The guy was clearly rattled and fumbled with his stuff as he rushed out of his seat into the aisle, walking briskly toward the exit.

"Never fails," the professor commented once he left. "There's always one every semester." She smiled, clasping her hands in front of her. "Now that that's settled, I am Professor Davis."

Settling into my chair, I did my best to forget Sterling beside me and focus on the professor as she went over the syllabus. Since I couldn't log on to my KU portal and follow along, I just listened, but I did notice that Sterling came to class about as prepared as I had—less so, even.

Why did I care?

I didn't.

It wasn't my problem if he failed the class. Sterling could handle his own shit. I needed to worry about myself. And that was all.

Then explain why the fuck my eyes shifted to my right even after I told them not to.

I snuck another peek at him, curious if he listened as the professor moved on to providing a little detail about herself. Relaxed and utterly still, I wondered if he had fallen asleep.

Elbow propped on the armrest, the side of his cheek rested on the knuckles of his curled hand, head bent at an angle toward me. He wasn't asleep, but he also wasn't paying attention to the professor. No, his eyes were watching me.

I shifted in my seat. "Stop it," I hissed lowly, my lips barely moving.

He remained reclined. "Stop what, Splash?"

He knew damn well what. I faced forward, keeping my voice low. "Don't pretend to not be a dick." Although I wasn't looking at him, I sensed the twisting of his lips.

Despite being aware of Sterling, I still managed to get sucked into the lecture. Professor Davis had a presence that demanded everyone in the room focus on her. I found her interesting and wanted to know more about her.

An hour or so went by when my phone buzzed in my hand. I'd been so engrossed in the lecture that I had completely forgotten about my frantic text to Micah.

The quiet hum drew Sterling's gaze, and he glanced at my phone before those amber eyes lifted to my face. Switching armrests, he leaned close to my ear, his arm brushing against mine, and whispered, "Boyfriend?"

I jerked away from him, tilting my phone so he couldn't see the text—that was if his spying eyes hadn't already. "None of your business."

We drew a few eyes from in front of us and across the aisle.

"I noticed you're in the same clothes as last night." He pinched the fabric on my shoulder, eyes running over me before letting the material fall back to my skin. "A little walk of shame on a Thursday. Who would have thought? So scandalous, Splash."

"Stop calling me that," I hissed under my breath, my eyes darting to the front of the class to make sure the professor wasn't frowning at me. I wanted her to like me, not see me as a nuisance Sterling so clearly wanted to make me out to be.

His face was too close to mine, yet I had nowhere to go, not without letting him see how uncomfortable he made me. "What should I call you?" he countered.

I stared him down, my fingers clutching the closed laptop resting on my lap. "Nothing. Now please be quiet. Some of us are here to learn." I snapped my gaze back to the professor.

The tension didn't leave me, and it didn't help when he did little things like bump my leg with his or lay his hand close to mine. Those were done to make me uneasy. Well, mission complete.

It wasn't until class ended and Professor Davis dismissed us that I released a hunk of the stress stiffening my muscles. Bolting out of my seat, I walked around Sterling and merged with the sea of students shuffling into the hallway.

I couldn't get away from him fast enough. All I wanted was to drag in a breath of fresh air and clear the scent of him from my nostrils.

An arm caught me before I reached the stairwell. I whirled, already knowing who it was. "What do you want?" I snapped, cradling Micah's laptop to my chest like it was a shield to protect me.

Sterling's eyes gleamed playfully at me, and I wondered if anything ever intimidated him. In a way, that trait reminded me of Micah, but unlike my boyfriend, Sterling wasn't a pretty boy. "You still owe me that tea, Splash."

My promise to Micah came back to me again. This whole thing had turned into a mess. Maybe if I just had a drink with

Sterling and explained everything, he would go away or back off. I somehow had to make the point very clear to him. Nothing would ever happen between us. Again. But if Micah found out I didn't keep my promise... The very last thing I wanted was to do anything that could jeopardize my relationship—the relationship we were working hard to build, and that started with trust.

Pressing my lips together, I replied, "I changed my mind. I want nothing to do with you."

He shifted, moving in closer to me. "Well, that's a shame, because I very much want to get in your way." He still had a hold of my arm, a fact I'd just realized when the pad of his thumb brushed over the inside of my wrist.

My gaze flicked to where his fingers were wrapped around me. I jerked my arm, surprised that his grip had been firmer than I judged. He didn't release me immediately, only after I tried to pull away a second time, as if he, too, hadn't been aware of the strength in his fingers. "Why are you doing this?" I demanded, my gaze imploring his.

The smirk permanently affixed to his lips faded as a speck of seriousness shadowed his eyes. "You know why."

My gaze lingered on his. "I don't. Really. You know I have a boyfriend."

"For now," he admitted, implying he had every intention of changing it.

I snorted, shaking my head. "I'm not the same girl I was back then. If you're looking for a quick fuck, I'm not your ticket." What Sterling insinuated left an icky feeling from his touch.

Mads Clarke was no slut—not that I thought having sex or a

one-night stand made you a slut, because by those definitions, half the girls I knew were, including me.

No, I had standards, but I wasn't a prude. I wanted to be respected and... loved. There it was. The real reason I was taking things slow with Micah and not giving in to all those raging hormones sparking and lurking around inside me.

I wanted Micah to fall in love with me. That hard, deep, passionate love. I wanted to hear the words, and for him, they were difficult to say. He wasn't the type of guy who tossed them around. As far as I knew, he had never said them. Of course, he playfully told the guys he loved them and shit like that, but he was extra careful about using those three little words with females. There might be a few exceptions, like Josie and Kenna, but that was sisterly love or playful banter.

Never the real thing.

Sterling shoved his hands into his pockets and rocked on his heels. "Then I'm looking forward to knowing who you are now."

He just didn't give up. Why me? What was so special about Madeline Clarke? I cringed internally at my full name. "Is that the point of this? To break Micah and me apart?"

He shrugged, his expression confirming he gave no real thought to my relationship. "It matters little to me that you have a boyfriend. I'm more concerned about what you can give me."

Oh. My. Fucking. God. This self-entitled prick. "The only thing I'm going to give you is a bloody nose."

"Why does *that* even sound fun coming from you?"

He made me want to thump my head against the nearest wall. "You're twisted."

"And if I remember correctly, you like it twisted." He hadn't even bothered to lower his voice.

A small gasp bubbled up my throat, and my cheeks grew warm. "If you think I'll sleep with you, I have news for you, Sterling Weston. You'll never touch me again." The last place I wanted to have this discussion was standing outside my classroom.

He held out his hand to me, and I gave him a weird look. "Should we bet on it?"

I ignored his outstretched hand, not wanting to touch him again. "Why bother? You'll lose."

He flicked the end of my nose, and I thought about biting him, but I didn't want the taste of his skin in my mouth. "I can't wait to prove you wrong, Splash."

CHAPTER FIVE

MICAH

After Mads left this morning, I didn't get much sleep, regardless of my efforts. I noticed that I tended to sleep deeper when she was in bed with me. Before college, there hadn't been a lot of opportunities to spend nights together. Unlike my parents, who rarely knew when I was home, Mads's were the opposite. They were very involved in their daughter's life and her whereabouts, but not enough so that she felt suffocated or wasn't able to spread her wings. They gave her freedom without losing touch. I envied that about Mads, having parents who were sincerely interested in you and your life.

I took a quick shower and threw on a pair of sweats and a shirt, intending to hit the gym before I had football practice at 3:00 p.m. and class tonight right after practice ended, which meant I wouldn't see Mads again.

That didn't work for me.

Checking my phone, I saw I had a text from her. My lips bent at the message, and I could picture her frantically typing it in class. She had about fifteen minutes left, just enough time for me to run over and greet her before heading to the gym.

I sent back the password for my laptop, adding a few explicit emojis that I knew wouldn't just make her smile but also put a bit of color on her cheeks. I fucking loved making that girl blush.

I headed into the main living area, finding the room and kitchen were both empty. The utter quietness of the house led me to believe Brock was already gone for the day. We had similar schedules with practices, working out, and classes. Perhaps he had gotten an early jump at the gym or was grabbing a protein shake with Josie. Either way, it worked out with my plans.

Stepping into the bright sun, I cursed for not thinking of grabbing my sunglasses. Despite it being close to the end of August, the heat of summer still clung to the air, which I both loved and detested. This kind of weather was fabulous for parties on the beach and going on long rides on my motorcycle but not so great for football practice. Sweating under a helmet and tights was not something I recommended, not to mention the dirt and grass stains.

I ran my fingers through my slightly damp hair and rounded the corner to the business division. With just a few minutes to spare, I plopped under a shady tree and screwed around on my phone while I waited for Mads.

Not big into social media, I rarely scrolled through my accounts, but I used the little time I had to do a bit of cyberstalking on Sterling. Not that I found much. He also didn't seem to be active in sharing his life online. Inconvenient but smart, especially for someone who had secrets to hide.

An increase in activity drew my gaze up. Students meandered out of the building one by one, headed to their next class or back to the dorms. Locking my phone, I stood, keeping my eyes on the door, and waited for Mads. After a minute or two, I shifted my weight, becoming a bit restless.

Where is she?

Had she stayed behind to speak with the professor?

No, that was a very un-Mads-like move.

Just when I was about to go inside and look for her myself, she rushed out of the building, her dark blonde hair flying out behind her. I only got a glimpse of her face before she was briskly walking away from me, but it was enough to catch the hard set of her features. She was pissed.

I started after her, convinced I had somehow unknowingly upset her, but the reason she'd been late and for her sudden aggravation made itself known a few moments later when the door opened again. I wasn't sure why I glanced over my shoulder as I jogged to the pathway, but I was glad I did.

Sterling fucking Weston.

Skidding to a halt, I swore under my breath and veered paths, heading straight for the son of a bitch. He hadn't seen me yet because he was too busy scanning the grounds as if he was looking for someone. I didn't have to follow the line of his gaze to know it was Mads he sought.

His lips curved, informing me that he'd located her not too far ahead up the sidewalk leading to the dorms. My brows furrowed together. I was about to do something stupid, but it couldn't be helped.

I stepped right into his line of sight, blocking his view of Mads. "See something interesting?" I asked, my lips pulled tight into a hard smile. It was forced but effective.

Sterling blinked, and I caught a flicker of annoyance before he quickly shifted to condescending, like he thought I was beneath him. As if. I made a note of how quickly he masked his emotions. It was good to know your enemy and what he was capable of, physically and mentally, and Sterling struck me as more of a mental fighter. Those were the ones you had to watch out for.

"Bradford, right?" He posed the question as if he wasn't quite sure who I was.

I wasn't buying it. My eyes narrowed. "Let's cut the bull-shit. What are you doing?"

Stoic, Sterling's lips quipped. "Right now? Grabbing lunch."

Smartass. That title was already taken. By me. "What do you want with Mads?" I demanded.

He started laughing. "Want with her? I'm not sure what you mean."

I kept seeing that photograph flash through my memory. Over and over again. Were there others? The thought made me see red. Anger zapped through my veins. I cursed myself for not taking another minute or two to continue searching his room. I had to know what else he might have of her, stashed away like little trophies for him to jack off to when the mood struck. Pervs like Sterling collected shit.

Okay, I didn't for a fact know he was a perv, but my mind had already shoved him into that category. I needed to get back there. I had to know what else he had. More importantly, what he planned to do.

"I think you do," I growled.

Sterling straightened his shoulders, rolling them in the process. "Does this have something to do with the fact that I know your girlfriend?"

The more ignorant he played, the more pissed off I became. It had everything to do with Mads and the picture he had of her. Was it possible that they'd known each other and he just happened to have a picture of her? Sure. I could rationalize that, probably. What I couldn't accept was, why bring that photo to college with him? Why hide it in a book that he probably thumbed through a dozen times a day? "So, you understand that she's *my* girlfriend. Just want to clarify."

"You seem a little on edge. Maybe too much sun, buddy," he suggested, clapping me on the shoulder as if we were friendly.

Casting a shadowed look at Sterling, I frowned. "I'm on to you."

He leaned forward, his voice just above a whisper as he retorted, "Then you better work hard to catch up, Bradford, because I'm way ahead of you."

Just what the fuck did that mean? I jerked back, glaring into his eyes. "Stay away from Mads."

His lips wrenched to the side in humor. "Unless she's a pet you keep in a cage, I think *Mads* is capable of figuring out who the good and bad guys are on her own."

The balls of this jackass. Did he really suggest I treat Mads like a dog? I should put my foot so far up his ass that he couldn't walk for a week. That sounded way more efficient than talking. I could run my mouth with the best of them, but eventually I got to a point where words were no longer doing the job. I wanted to bust his balls over the photo and demand he tell me why he was keeping it, but I also knew it was better if Sterling kept his guard down. The moment he learned I'd found the picture, he would be more careful, more cautious, and that was exactly what I didn't want. I needed him to make a mistake, to fuck up, so I could nail his ass.

I craned my head to the side. "You're not the only one with patience."

The asshole shrugged. "I guess we'll both have to just wait and see." He sidestepped me, our shoulders grazing as he passed by, and it took every single ounce of my control to not do more than bump shoulders.

My fingers balled into a fist, pressing deep into my palms. That urge to hit something pulsed down my arms. It was a good thing I was on my way to the gym. I needed to burn off some serious steam, but first I needed to find Mads and see for myself if she was okay.

A full minute went by as I stood in front of the business district building, doing my best to suppress my fury. Taking off in the direction of Mads's dorm, I kicked up to a jog, hoping to catch her before she went inside.

I almost dashed right by her, not thinking that she might not have headed straight to the dorm, but as I sprinted through the courtyard, a whiff of smoke tainted the air. I should have guessed she would need a cigarette to calm her nerves.

Mads leaned against a tree, a lit smoke pressed between her lips as she inhaled. *Why the fuck does that look so hot?* My eyes were drawn to her mouth, a dozen impure thoughts skipping through my male brain. They couldn't be helped. I was just wired to think of sex. It didn't matter what Mads was doing. She could be blow-drying her hair or chewing on her nails and my mind would somehow turn those simple, innocent acts into something sexual.

Slowing down to a lazy walk, I approached my girl, who looked lost in deep thought, frown lines creasing her brow, and all I could think of was that I needed to put a smile on her face. "I got something you could put between your lips."

Her gray eyes flew upward, relaxing once she realized it was me. An elbow flew into my gut, and I groaned with a smile on my lips.

"You are so damn cute when you try to be tough," I said, rubbing the spot on my abs.

"*Try?*" she echoed, clearly insulted, but she couldn't fully hide the smile that hinted at the corners of her mouth as she lifted her hand in the air to smack me.

I chuckled, catching her wrist before her hand could land on my chest. Spinning her around, I enclosed my arms over her stomach, pressing my chest to her back and resting my chin on her shoulder.

She turned her head to the side, careful to keep the cigarette away from me. "Nice move, Bradford," she murmured. Traces of smoke mingled with her breath, a combination that had no right turning me on but did.

I could spend hours bantering with and teasing Mads

Clarke. The only thing I enjoyed more was kissing her. "I have a few." And because I wanted to, I lifted a hand to her chin, tipping her face a bit more to the side so I could kiss her.

My lips lingered, drawing in the warmth from her mouth, needing to feel her safely against me. It also just felt so damn good. I wasn't one to deny myself things that made me feel. My intention had only been to offer her comfort, a quick distraction, but the taste of Mads's lips awakened other parts of me.

I twisted her in my arms, wanting to feel the length of her body against mine. Not giving a shit that we were in a public place with eyes everywhere, I pressed her into the tree, letting her feel just what she did to me with a single kiss.

Catching her quick inhale of surprise, I slipped my tongue into her mouth, rubbing, taunting, teasing it with hers. She was quick to respond. Mads had always been quick. I liked that about her.

Slim arms tangled around my neck, and fingers not quite gentle shoved into my hair. The little purr she made in the back of her throat had me longing to be back in my bed. Her dorm was closer. Maybe her roommates were gone. Highly unlikely when there were three of them. One good thing about living with Brock—not only did we have our own rooms with locks, but I only had to worry about *him* being home and walking in on something.

Fuck. I have to stop kissing her before I rip her shirt off in public. Embarrassing Mads was not on my agenda today. Despite knowing I should pull my lips off hers, my fingers slipped into the back pocket of her jeans, squeezing her ass.

This girl had the power to make me forget myself and so

much more. I didn't think she fully grasped the influence she possessed, not just with her lips and what was between her legs, because it was so much more than sex for me, something I never imagined I'd feel—didn't deserve to feel. There was nothing in this world I wouldn't do for her.

Her long lashes, coated with last night's mascara, fluttered open, and I adored the little dazed glimmer in her dove-gray eyes. "What was that for?"

My hands continued to rest on her hips. "No reason. I just wanted to." We both had needed it, a moment to forget Sterling. I refused to let that asshole come between us. Mads and I had worked hard to get to this point. I wouldn't let anything or anyone take her from me.

Not again.

I was damn close to being in love with this girl.

Or perhaps I already was but just wasn't ready to admit it.

"I'm glad." She let out a long sigh. The cigarette that had been between her fingers sat burning on the ground. Mads crushed it under her white sneaker before meeting my gaze again. "I needed that."

"Bad day?" I thought back to Sterling. What had he said to her? If he hurt her in any way, emotional or physical, I'd kill the bastard. If he kept messing with my girl, I would make him wish he'd never laid eyes on her.

"You could say that." A few moments of silence passed as I let her sort out the turmoil I sensed from her. "Sterling was in my class today," she explained what I'd already learned.

I brushed the side of her cheek with my knuckles. "Did he bother you?"

She dropped the back of her head against the tree. "It's nothing I can't handle. I'm more upset about not being able to keep my promise to you."

Right. My promise about her staying away from Sterling. The last thing I wanted was for her to feel guilty. "You didn't go out of your way to hang out with him. Coincidences happen." Except I fully didn't believe him being in that class with Mads was a happenstance. The prick was up to something. He had an agenda, and I planned to uncover what the fuck it was.

"Are you going to tell me what's going on?" she asked, studying my face.

"I will. Just not today." She had enough on her mind, and I didn't want to add to it. "How was class?" I asked, taking her hand and pulling her out from under the tree.

"Wait." She dug her heels in and turned around, grabbing something in the grass—her discarded cigarette to dispose of properly. After she gathered her stuff, we traipsed through the courtyard to the sidewalk. "Surprisingly it didn't suck completely. I like my professor."

The scent of steamed hot dogs drifted in the air as we walked by one of the street vendors on campus. "Is she hot?" I asked, failing to keep a straight face.

She pinched me in the side, but I only chuckled. "Oh, before I forget, here." Extending my laptop, she waited for me to take it. "Thanks for letting me borrow it."

I took the computer, tucking it against my side. "Are there any notes you need?" I inquired, making sure she had everything.

She shook her dark blonde head. "I ended up not needing it today."

"Did you at least take a few nudes for me?"

Her nose scrunched. "And when would I have had the time to do that?"

I slung my arm over her shoulder. "I don't think about the details, babe, just the outcome."

She shoved me away. "Don't call me babe." Mads loathed the use of cute couple nicknames. She thought they were cliché and gag-worthy. Her words, not mine.

"Sweetie. Cookie. Honey. Doll. Love. Are any of those better?"

Shooting me a deathly side-eye, she replied, "Not if you want to keep both your balls attached."

"Such violence." I grinned, moving in to nuzzle the space behind her ear. "No wonder I'm crazy about you."

She rolled her eyes.

We came to an intersection in the pathway. The right would take me to the gym, and the left would take her to the dorms. This was where we split off, yet I was reluctant to leave her. "I need to go shower and change. I've had enough of these clothes," she said. "I'll text you later?"

I nodded.

Waving, she flashed me a smile before turning and heading to the dorms. I stayed and watched her receding back for a few minutes until I lost her behind a building.

At least she was smiling, the shadows no longer clouding her gray eyes. I'd done my job.

* * *

Thirty minutes into my workout, Brock came sauntering in. I barely spared him a glance, but our gazes connected for just a moment in greeting. I pulled out my earbuds, shoving them into the pocket of my basketball shorts.

The machines only went so far to burn off the frustrations clawing inside me. I used the time not just to relieve the stewing need to hurt someone but also to think. I had come up with some of my best plans at the gym. Brock might disagree, but he sometimes lacked imagination. Although he made up for it in calculating strategy.

It was weird being here without Grayson and Fynn. The four of us had been together for so long. We practiced together, worked out together, partied together, and took down together. Now we were divided by whole two hours.

I made a mental note to text Grayson later, to get his take on this whole Sterling thing. Mads was his cousin, after all, and he would want to know if someone was messing with her.

Brock sat down on the ab bench beside me, his legs straddling either side as he prepped to use it. "Why do you look like you're trying to murder that machine?"

I extended my legs, inhaling. "I'm pretending to kick Sterling's face."

He lay flat on his back, ankles hooking under the footrest. "Okay, that explains a lot. Did something else happen that I'm unaware of?"

Releasing the weight pressing against the top part of my

feet, I wiped at the sweat beading over my brow. "We had words this morning."

He only got one curl in and was already lying on his back, head twisted toward me. "Already? Christ, Micah. It's barely noon."

Noon was early in our world. "I know. I caught him staring at Mads after her class today, a class he also just happens to be taking."

"I see." And he did. If it had been Josie, Brock would be right where I am, doing the same shit, taking out his anger and frustration at the gym. It helped, but it didn't fully take the edge off—not like smashing his face into the floor would.

Fuck yeah, I wanted to hit him. Almost as much as I wanted to keep Mads from getting hurt.

"And you just had words, nothing more?" he clarified as if he didn't believe my fists hadn't been involved.

"This time," I grunted through another rep.

He nodded, knowing my restraint only went so far. "Coming here was the best move for the time being."

My legs burned as I pushed the muscles in my legs, but it was a good kind of burning sensation. I enjoyed working out, the rush of dopamine, serotonin, and adrenaline. It was the one place where I didn't disappoint my father, where I could escape from the pressure of being Alexander Bradford's only son and heir to the multimillion-dollar empire he and my grandfather had built. I was expected to join the family biz, regardless that I had no interest in the finance world.

With each rep, I pushed through all the expectations and pressure bearing down on me. I had to be the best wide receiver, yet not pursue a career as an athlete. I was expected to marry a girl with family wealth and influence, a merger of families rather than love.

I wanted none of those things.

And if I thought the little bit of freedom college gave me would ease the pressure, I was dead wrong.

My phone buzzed. Normally I avoided my phone during workouts, but on the chance that it was Mads, I scooped it off the floor and checked the screen.

I swore. It was if as my father had an internal buzzer that went off every time I thought about him. The old man, doing his weekly check-in, reminded me who I was, how I was to behave, and what he demanded from me.

My fingers tightened against the phone as I read the message again. *Asshole.* I clicked the lock button on my phone. The screen went blank, and I set it back on the floor alongside the water bottle. The old man was used to me ignoring his messages. He would think nothing of my lack of response, but the texts—and calls, when necessary—would continue.

As if I needed this today on top of everything else. I couldn't deal with the old man or the path he'd carved out for my future. Not now. Not today.

A vein in my neck ticked.

"Everything okay?" Brock asked, seeing the way I chucked my phone to the ground.

I switched machines, moving to the seated arm curl on the opposite side of him. "Just the old man riding my ass again," I said dryly.

He understood all too well what it was like having a father

who only wanted perfection, a portrayal of a son rather than an actual son with flaws. "I'd tell you not to sweat it, but we both know neither of us has that luxury."

Wrapping my fingers around the bars, I curled my arms, the muscles tightening in my forearms. "I'm calling our guy."

His reaction didn't change, but Brock excelled at keeping a neutral face. It kept those who didn't know him from being able to see what really went on behind his often-cold eyes. "Normally I'd say you're overreacting... but I think having Sterling checked out wouldn't hurt. Has Mads said how she knows him? That might be helpful information."

I continued the reps, raising and lowering my arms. "No, not yet. We haven't had much time to talk."

"Didn't she spend the night?"

I grinned. "Do you and Josie talk all night when she's in your bed?"

His lips twitched. "Touché."

We got into a routine, working through our reps. Twenty minutes later, Brock dabbed the ends of the towel hooked around his neck over his face. I grabbed my water off the floor.

"You have something else planned. I can see it. What is it, Micah?" he pressed.

Sitting on the edge of a bench, I took a long drink of water before answering. "I'm going to rush for Chi Sigma next week." I had decided before Brock showed up. It was my way in, to get information that outsiders wouldn't have and the private investigator might not have access to. Drunk guys liked to talk. I needed to be there when the lips loosened.

Brock's brows bunched. "You're really going to join a fraternity?"

Thanks to my father, I pretty much hated everything about Chi Sigma, and the fact that I was breaking my personal vow to never have anything to do with the fraternity my father loved and held in high regard meant something. I hadn't been kidding when I claimed I would do anything to keep Mads safe, even at my own expense. "It's the only way I'm going to find out what the fuck he wants with my girlfriend."

"Just promise you'll be careful, and don't do anything stupid," he warned, being the serious leader he was.

Unable to suppress the one-sided grin, I said, "I can do one or the other. Not both."

Brock heaved a heavy sigh of acceptance. It was the best he would get from me, and he knew it.

Sterling would quickly learn he was messing with the wrong girl.

CHAPTER SIX

MADS

"That's my shirt," I heard Kenna snap as I opened the door to our dorm room.

The headache I'd been dodging pulsed at the sides of my head. Half tempted to walk out unnoticed and find a quiet corner in the library, I chewed on my lip. This might only be the first week of school, but that didn't mean our professors took any mercy on us. I had assignments due on Monday, and although I had the weekend ahead of me, I also knew I wouldn't get much studying done.

Grayson and Fynn were coming up tomorrow night to hang out Friday and Saturday. That meant parties, late nights, and general fun. I needed fun after the week I'd had, which meant homework now since I had two classes tomorrow.

Ainsley shoved her laptop and a few other belongings on her bed into an over-the-shoulder bag—black, of course, because that was literally Ainsley's signature color. "Right, because every black crop top in this place is yours," she hurled back at Kenna, giving her the scrunched-eye glare that looked like a cat with the way she applied her makeup—dramatic and stunning. Ainsley might not like to be the center of attention like Kenna, but she liked to draw attention with her appearance. Perhaps that was why the two of them didn't get along; when they were both in a room, they competed against each other for all eyes.

Kenna hovered at the foot of Ainsley's bed like a feisty hummingbird about to peck Ainsley's eyeballs out. "Not every one, just *that* one," she barked like it was a reasonable explanation.

I stood in the doorway, still gnawing on my lip and debating whether to get involved or just let them hash it out.

"Since when do you ever wear anything black? You're like a walking pink Barbie," Ainsley retorted, securing the snap on her bag in place.

And the saga between Ainsley and Kenna continued. It had been seriously stupid to think having these two live together in close quarters would somehow make them closer—friendlier.

Still not saying a word, I glanced at the top in question. *Top* was a loose word to describe what Ainsley wore. I was going more like a bra or bralette. Cropped was stretching it. Neither of them noticed that I stood in the doorway.

Kenna made a huffing noise of outrage. "I don't know if I should be insulted or flattered. Coming from you, probably the latter."

Ainsley rolled her mossy green eyes. "Take it however you please, but I'm not a thief." She tugged on a sheer black button-up top that hung over her green and dark gray plaid skirt. On

Ainsley, the ensemble was cute and edgy, just like she was. Maybe that was what had Kenna in a tizzy.

"What do you call borrowing without asking?" Kenna asked snootily. We might have been related, but that didn't mean I always condoned her behavior. Everyone familiar with Kenna knew how much of a brat she could be.

Facing Kenna so they were almost nose to nose thanks to the two-inch platform boots Ainsley wore, Ainsley snapped, "If you have a problem with me, take it up with our RA."

This was going well. Perhaps it was time I intervened and tried to diffuse the escalating situation.

Ainsley hiked the strap of her bag over her shoulder. "I don't have time for this. I have class." Stomping around a fuming Kenna, she finally noticed me. "Oh hey, Mads. See you later," she muttered, rushing out the door without a second glance.

Drama. Drama. Drama. Was there an inch of this school that wasn't dripping with it? Or did drama just follow me around like a gloomy cloud?

Kenna flopped onto Ainsley's bed, not giving a shit about personal space now. "Can you believe her?" she complained, immediately starting in.

Although it might seem as if Kenna had more flaws than virtues, that wasn't always true. She could be a good friend. Correction, an exceptional friend when she tried. Sometimes it just took her a few minutes to shift the focus off herself and onto the other person.

I didn't have time for this. Bypassing Kenna, I went straight into the bathroom for a bottle of aspirin. Fumbling through our drawer of meds, I pushed aside the cold medicine and Pamprin until I found the pain reliever. I unscrewed the cap, dropped two in my hand, and filled a glass of water. As I tossed the little white pills back, something black hanging from the hook near the shower caught my eye. It was partially hidden behind a white towel. Shoving aside the cotton material, I found a black bralette, bra, crop top, or whatever correct term, much like the one Ainsley had been wearing. I picked it up by one thin strap and walked out of the bathroom. "Is this what you were looking for?"

Kenna's gaze lifted at my voice. She frowned. "Are you guys screwing with me?"

Balling up the lacy top, I tossed it at her. "It was in the bathroom, Kenna. You should apologize."

"And the Toros should have beaten the Clovers at Nationals." As a cheerleader herself, Kenna's favorite movie of all time was *Bring It On.* The number of times she made me watch that movie, I could still recite the Toros' cheer in my sleep.

"Where's Josie?" I asked, needing to unload my problems on someone.

Kenna shot me a sour frown. "What, I'm not good enough to talk to? I can tell something is bothering you. You used to tell me everything."

It wasn't that Kenna and I weren't close anymore. We were, just not as much as we had been prior to her leaving for two years. During that time, it had only been natural that we drifted, but Josie and I had this bond. She understood me in ways that sometimes I felt Kenna couldn't. Of course, I couldn't tell Kenna that, not without hurting her feelings, which I wasn't about to do.

It wasn't just that Josie and I were both dating an Elite. We'd also shared experiences that changed a person, and we'd gone through those altering events together.

Kenna had her own shit.

We all did.

Sighing, I rubbed at my temples and sat down on Josie's bed across from Kenna still on Ainsley's. She twisted around to face me, waiting for me to say something. "That's not it," I assured. "You know this isn't a competition over who's the better friend, right? I love you both."

"Then what is it? What's wrong?" she pushed. "And don't give me that crap about nothing, because I'm all you got at the moment. Josie has class, and then she's stopping by to see her counselor afterward. So spill it, cuz."

Kicking off my shoes, I agonized over where to start. A part of me was embarrassed by my actions, despite knowing Kenna wouldn't judge me. We both had a past where we hadn't made the best decisions. I was my own worst critic. Not to mention it would take Kenna back as well to her tragedy. Did I want to do that?

I sighed. "Remember when I told you about that guy I hooked up with after…"

"After you caught Micah in bed with that girl," she supplied, nodding. "Oh, I remember."

I tried to be cautious as I relayed the events, trying to keep myself from saying something that might trigger her. Kenna had come a long way from the withdrawn, depressed girl she'd become a few years ago, but the road to recovery after what she suffered was more of a twisty path than a straight road.

"The mysterious hookup," she added, grinning as if it was a fond memory—and it kind of had been at the time. We'd laughed and joked afterward, giving him an outlandish story and making him into the mysterious hookup. For me, it had all been part of getting over Micah. Clearly that didn't work.

"Well, he isn't so mysterious anymore," I muttered, toying with my earring.

A hand flew to her mouth, her brown eyes going wide. "Don't tell me you saw him again? After all these years?"

Perhaps Kenna was the right person to talk to about this. She already knew many of the details. I loosened up, feeling a bit less tense. "He's a student at KU."

Kenna blinked, and then her lips curved wickedly. "Shut the fuck up. You've seen him."

"Yesterday. And today," I admitted.

"What! I can't believe this. Did you talk to him? Does Micah know? Did you get his name this time? Why am I only now hearing about him?" She rapid-fired everything that came to her mind.

The ache in my head intensified, and I wished the pills would hurry up and kick in. I dropped back onto the bed, my feet dangling over the edge. "I have no idea what I'm doing or why this is even a thing. It happened two years ago." Rolling to my side, I propped my head up on my hand, waiting for Kenna's reaction.

Concern clouded her eyes at the mention of that time in our life. "What exactly did happen?"

"You remember that party we went to last night, the one at Chi Sigma?"

She toyed with strands of her loose, dark hair that had fallen over her shoulder. "I remember most of it. I definitely remember Micah killing the party. What the hell was up with him?"

That I could answer. "Sterling Weston."

"Sterling Weston," she repeated, connecting the dots. Then her eyes grew wide. "Holy shit. You banged Sterling Weston? Do you have any idea who he is?"

Picking at a white thread on the bed that had come undone, I mumbled, "The president of Chi Sigma."

"No. I mean, yeah he is, but that isn't even the tip of the iceberg." A bit too much excitement laced her voice, and I began to worry. "He's one of the *Weston*s," she stated as if I should be impressed.

I stared at her blankly. "Is that supposed to mean something?"

She shook her head at me, looking disappointed. At what, I didn't know, but I was confident she would fill me in. "Mads, you need to pull your head out of that cloud of cigarette smoke. The Westons are one of the oldest and wealthiest families, not just in this state but in the country. They're like the Hiltons of the East Coast."

Unlike Kenna, I didn't keep up with who was who in the world of old money. Or even new money. I could barely keep the Kardashians straight, let alone an entire society of rich people. "And you're sure Sterling is one of *those* Westons?" He hadn't struck me as someone who dripped money. Then again, I hadn't even known his name. Did I have any right to assume anything about who Sterling was?

I didn't.

Just as he knew nothing about who I was.

Kenna rolled her eyes. "Is cotton candy pink?"

I gave her a flat, unamused stare.

Getting a little too enthusiastic about a guy who I wanted to avoid like last week's moldy pizza, Kenna said, "It's him. I'm sure of it. My grandfather knows Sterling's grandfather, who happens to love to brag about his perfect grandson."

This must have been her paternal grandfather, as we shared the same grandparents on her mother's side.

"It doesn't matter to me where he comes from. I just want him to forget we ever met."

"I get that considering what you have going on with Micah, but this is *Sterling Weston*."

"Are you actually encouraging me to go out with him?" Something dark and uneasy slithered over my mind, confusing the situation more.

She scooted closer to the edge of the bed. "Did he ask you out? If the answer is yes, then so is mine."

"Kenna!" I groused. "I am not going out with him, so get it out of your head. You are not helping."

"I'm still not understanding what the problem is."

I was two seconds away from burying my head into the pillow and screaming. "I'm not sure, but I think he seems to be under the impression that I'm into him or something."

"Again, how is that a problem? This sounds like a good thing. Sterling is, like, a big deal on campus."

Only Kenna would think another guy hitting on me was a good thing. "I have a boyfriend, who also happens to be your brother's best friend," I reminded her. Where was the loyalty?

She might think Micah wasn't good enough for me, but weren't my feelings what was important?

"Aren't you over him yet?" she asked dramatically. "You've been pining after Micah for so long, I can't remember you ever being into another guy."

That was because I hadn't. Even when I was angry, bitter, and basically boycotting all things Elite, I still thought about him. "No." I tried to make it clear and simple for her.

She snapped her fingers. "So that's why Micah was such a dick last night. The pieces are starting to fit. Okay, I have a plan to solve both our problems." Swinging her legs over the side of the bed, she settled again, a glint in her eyes that made me leery.

"I didn't realize you had a problem." Kenna had a frightening knack for turning everything back to her. Selfishness? Just one of her many personality traits, but to be fair, she was also loyal, protective, and sometimes crazy.

Excitement glimmered in her brown eyes. "I do. I'm boyfriendless, and I told myself college would be my year. I'm starting fresh. New school. Fresh faces. And he checks all the boyfriend boxes."

"Are you sure you're ready to start dating?" Kenna never had the chance to date like most high school girls, not seriously *or* casually, and I could understand her interest. She strived to be normal, regardless that her life experiences had been anything but. Being raped at almost sixteen put a screeching halt on her dating life. I took it as a good sign that she wanted to try, but with Sterling, a guy who I had a one-night stand with? Not what I would call a prime candidate. Although, I didn't think he would hurt her. He wasn't that kind of guy, not like Carter.

I hoped.

The truth of it was I didn't know. He could be a serial killer for all I knew, which would be pretty fucked-up, considering I'd slept with him. Not something I wanted on my résumé.

But the fact that I'd hooked up with Sterling made the idea of Kenna dating him weird, and it had nothing to do with me having any lingering feelings for him. To have lingering feelings, you needed to have them to begin with. There had been none. Not from me. He'd been nothing but someone to numb the pain.

Fun fact: that shit never worked.

Kenna gave a half shrug. "I won't know until I try."

Thinking about it for another moment, I said, "I fully support you dating, but I don't think Sterling should be your first target."

A tad of the excitement died in her eyes. "You make it sound like I'm going to the shooting range. But maybe your right. I need a few practice rounds to see how things go before moving on to the main event."

I groaned. How did my problem suddenly become bigger? Kenna interested in Sterling, romantically or otherwise, filled my chest with pressure. Why did I feel so uneasy about this all? Was it because of Micah's warning? What did he know that I didn't? If he hadn't found out about Sterling and me, then why did Micah seem so adamant about me staying away from him? Surely that same warning extended to Kenna and my other roommates.

I needed to ask Josie if Brock had said anything, and then I was going straight to the source. Micah needed to tell me what the hell was going on before one of us did something regrettable and stupid. Like let her cousin go out with a serial killer.

Stop! I hissed to my overactive mind. *So not helping. He is not a killer. I did not sleep with the next Ted Bundy, for God's sake.*

At least I was pretty sure I hadn't.

It had to be me, right? Just my wild imagination getting the best of me, because people weren't giving me odd glances. Yet I remained unconvinced and unable to shake the feeling that everyone I passed stared and whispered.

This had to be a dream. One of those nightmares where you found yourself naked in a crowd, like the opening scene in *Bring It On* when Torrence ended up shirtless in the middle of a cheerleading routine, only to wake up moments later in her bed. That was what this had to be—just a bad dream.

Except... I glanced down quickly. I wasn't naked. And... I pinched my underarm and jerked at the quick stab of pain.

Nope. Definitely awake.

Then what was the fucking deal? Had I become so paranoid that I believed everyone had nothing better to do than talk about me behind my back, including people I'd never seen or met in my life?

Apparently so.

I was not that important.

Seconds away from stopping in the middle of campus and screaming, *"What?"* I ducked my head, increasing my pace to a fast walk before I made a pariah of myself. I dashed into the café, hoping to escape the noise going on both inside and outside my head. Plus, I needed a tall flat white coffee pronto. Anything to calm my frazzled insides.

I had just put in my order at the counter when my phone buzzed in my back pocket. When I fished it out, my eyes roamed over the message.

Josie: Did you see this?

The text included a link to a KU school website.

A hard knot formed in my throat, making it next to impossible to swallow around it. Tapping on the link, I ambled down the counter to wait for my coffee and the website to pull up. The Internet in the café wasn't the greatest, so it took a few seconds. The crunching and hissing of the coffee grinder suddenly hummed, and the air brimmed with fresh coffee beans, a scent that filled me with happiness.

As the machine trailed off, someone giggled from behind the counter, distracting me again. Popping my hip against the half wall dividing the dining area from the ordering section, I scrolled through the link to the *Kingsley Informer*, the school's online newspaper.

Why did Josie send me this?

With the pad of my index finger, I swiped the screen, flipping through the articles until I came across... me.

Well, a fucking picture of me, which had no right being in the paper.

Legs sprawled up over my head, water sprayed down over

my shocked face, mouth open in a silent scream, and arms flailing like an inflatable tube guy on a windy day. Mortified at the image mocking me in full color for the world to see, a little shrill of horror escaped my lips.

Son of a bitch. Really? They couldn't have gotten a more flattering photo? Or at the very least one where you couldn't so clearly see my face.

The headline read **The year starts with a splash.**

My fingers went lax, and the phone began to slip right through them. I fumbled to keep it from crashing to the floor, bobbling it a few times before I secured it once again.

For the love of everything holy, could I get through a day of college without being humiliated? I didn't want this to be an omen of how my time here at KU would be remembered. Not for me or my peers.

All those stares and mutterings began to make sense but didn't make me feel better.

Who wrote this? Why? It couldn't possibly be the most newsworthy thing that happened this week.

And yet that was exactly what it was.

I skimmed back to the top of the article, and just under the title, a name in black ink popped out.

Sterling Weston.

Motherf—

The prick wrote an article about shoving me into the fountain.

Who does that?

Okay, fine. He hadn't actually shoved me, but still, the point was why write about the incident at all? Was this some cry for attention? If so, what a shitty way to gain a girl's interest. Was he trying to ask me out or destroy me?

What he did manage to accomplish by his cheeky antics had been to further embarrass me.

Fuming, I spun and burst through the café door with only one thought on my mind. *I'm going to murder Sterling Weston.*

That would be the headline tomorrow for the *Kingsley Informer*. Nothing like getting my name in the press two days in a row.

Striding through campus, my cheeks warmed not from the sun but anger, I headed to Greek Row with no idea if Sterling would be home. My feet moved of their own accord as my mind stewed over the photo.

I made it across campus in record time, storming up the porch of Chi Sigma. It had only been two nights since the fraternity hosted its first party of the year. Two days since I first laid eyes on Sterling that night. I didn't know exactly what I wanted from him, an apology perhaps, but I had to confront him.

Without hesitating, I rapped my fists on the door, growing louder and faster with each passing second, much like my outrage. It felt like a full minute of pounding before the front door swung open with an almost inaudible grumble from the person standing on the other side. It became clear I had woken them up. The person wore just a pair of gray sweatpants that hung low over their hips as if they had mindlessly tugged them on before coming to the door. Fingers forked through their dark, disheveled hair, further disrupting the strands as half-lidded amber eyes lifted to mine. When they registered who I was, his lips curved.

Just the man I'd been looking to see... except preferably with a shirt on.

I hoisted my gaze away from his chest, which I hated to admit wasn't bad to look at, just not as impressive as Micah's.

Who the fuck answers the door shirtless?

Sterling lazily crossed his arms, leaning against the door with a smirk that riled my composure. What was it about this guy that could make me feel so uncertain about... everything?

"Splash. Miss me already?"

Oooh. My hand, already sore from knocking so long, itched to connect with his guy's cheek, and I might have given in to the urge if his chest were covered. I did not want any flesh-to-flesh contact with him. "You wish, dickhead." I thrust my phone in front of his eyes. Too close. He had to back up a step to see what filled the screen. "Explain this."

Those sleepy eyes blinked twice before focusing on the phone. Was it just me or did that shit-eating grin grow wider? "What makes you think I had anything to do with it?" he countered.

"I don't know, your name on the article," I snapped, nearly baring my teeth.

"I wrote the article, but the pic isn't mine, doll," he responded flippantly.

"I'm not your doll. And I don't give a shit if the fucking boogeyman took the photo. You're the one who stuck it online."

"Guilty as charged. Do you want to handcuff me now?" He held out his wrists like this whole thing was nothing but a joke. And maybe it was to him. But to me... not so much.

"Take it down. Now," I demanded.

"Have a drink with me," he said instead, throwing me for a loop.

Had we not just been talking about the ridiculous article. How did we go from that to a drink?

"I haven't had any coffee yet," he explained, "seeing as someone rudely pulled me out of bed with the incessant knocking."

"Do you think I give a shit whether or not you've had coffee or that I woke you up?" *Fuck. My coffee.* In my haste and anger, I had completely forgotten about the flat white I had ordered and paid for, which was now undoubtedly cold.

He ran a hand through his hair and leaned against the doorframe. "Look, the article was nothing but fun, a little harmless humor to start the year off before the stress begins. If I remember correctly, you were a girl who wouldn't have given a shit about what other people think."

"I don't."

He lifted a brow. "Let me buy you a cup of tea as an apology." Holding up his hand, palm facing me in an upright salute, he said, "I promise to never publish another piece without your permission first. Deal?"

My eyes narrowed, not humored by his act. "Why would I agree to that?"

"For one, if you're so worried about other people talking, being seen with me will give them something else to attach your name to."

I choked. That was his solution. "No fucking thank you. I'm not interested in being involved in a campus scandal."

"It's just a drink, Splash," he said, making it sound like a dare.

I lifted my chin, lips pressing into a thin line. "You say that, but your tone suggests something more. And in case your pea-size brain has already forgotten, I have a boyfriend."

Sterling took a step forward, his frame just outside the door now. "And I don't care."

Whoa. Why did I suddenly feel like that girl in the movies who went into the scary house alone while running away from a serial killer, only for the serial killer to be waiting inside for her? Various degrees of warning bells chimed inside my head. I resisted the compulsion to take a retreating step, refusing to let him think he could intimidate me. "Back off," I warned, firming and deepening my voice. For one damn second, I wanted him to take me seriously.

He disappointed me. Again. "I'll wear you down. I always do."

"You might want to get out your phone and record this. I'm giving you a quote for your next piece on me. Never going to fucking happen. I would sooner kiss a dozen poisonous frogs than be seen anywhere with you." Feeling pretty fucking good about myself, I whirled and tramped down the stairs.

His laughter followed me to the pathway leading to the side-walk. I stalked off, giving him an image to remember as my middle finger went up in the air.

Put that in your paper.

CHAPTER SEVEN

MADS

Four o'clock rolled around, and I'd just finished my final class for the week. Sometime between storming away from Sterling's house and taking notes in my English lit class, I decided I had to talk with Micah.

If I hurried, I could catch him after practice. He had only three weeks until their first football game. Practices would be grueling until then, not that he complained. And once he finished running through their drills for the night, Grayson and Fynn would be here, not leaving me a lot of time to squeeze in the kind of conversation we needed to have.

I didn't want to ruin the mood or the weekend before it had a chance to begin, but a nagging voice in my head told me I shouldn't put this off any longer. I could continue to dodge Sterling's advances if he insisted on not taking no for an answer, but Micah deserved to know that I was in no way encouraging him.

Dropping my laptop off at my door, I made a quick bathroom run and touched up my makeup. I caught a glimpse of myself in the full-length mirror Kenna kept in the corner. The jeans were good but the top... could use an upgrade. Something a little less practical and a bit more flirtatious. There was nothing wrong with distracting him with the goods while I explained that a guy I once hooked up with went to school here. I was sure Micah had already guessed, but it would be better if he heard it from me.

Tucking a loose curl behind my ear, I locked our door and headed outside. The hot August air smacked into me, and I thought about ducking back inside for another few minutes of air conditioning. The weather had been yo-yoing between the idyllic temp of seventy-five and being able to fry an egg on the blacktop. Today the bottoms of my flip-flops were melting, and a dip in the fountain sounded like bliss right now.

I counted down the hours until the sun retired for the day, offering some relief from this sweltering heat. My heart went out to the guys who spent the hottest part of the day out on the field in uniform, running, tackling, and basically sweating their balls off.

When I got to the practice field, most of the players were gone, just a few staff stragglers gathering equipment and herding the lingerers into the locker room. I walked around the perimeter of the field to the athletic building, hoping to catch him before he left the locker room, if he hadn't already.

I paced up and down the treelined pathway, wringing and twisting my fingers together as I thought about how I would start this conversation. It wasn't something I could just blurt out. There needed to be a lead-up, and that was where I got stuck.

As I walked past the wooden bench for the twentieth time, I lifted my head at a group of guys piling out of the locker room. I scanned their faces, looking for Micah. Disappointment trickled into my belly, only asserting the restlessness within me.

The dozen or so guys paraded around me, chuckling and talking among themselves. It was only natural that I turned my head when someone called the name of a player. "Yo, Rivera."

I cringed before my eyes connected with the owner of the voice.

Are you shitting me?

Sterling held his hand up in the air farther down the walkway, coming straight toward the group.

"Sterling. Just the man we were looking for," Rivera greeted.

I immediately ducked and turn my back to the group that halted in the middle of the path to... I don't know what, bullshit about a party or some crap. My ears stopped listening and started buzzing.

I didn't want him to see me. Not now.

"Shit," I whispered under my breath and darted toward the athletic building's glass door, only thinking that I had to get away before he noticed me. One confrontation with Sterling a day was my limit, and the last thing I wanted was for any of the guys to recognize me from the photo. If they were friends of his, chances were they had seen the article swirling around campus.

Had Micah seen it?

Josie had, so the probability that Brock had as well was high, and he would have shared it with Micah.

Cool air immediately washed over my flushed body, offering much-needed relief from the heat. I snuck a glance outside to make sure no one noticed my less-than-stealthy escape. I exhaled, relief unfolding in my chest to see no one chasing after me. I should have known better than to drop my guard for even a moment. My nose was still pressed to the glass when a dark head turned toward the door, and I panicked, flattening myself against the wall.

My heart hammered in my chest, threatening to crack a rib. *Now what, smarty-pants?*

I didn't have time to properly think. The squeaking of sneakers on linoleum, the shuffling of feet, and the voices that followed from down the hallway drew my attention, presenting a new set of worries. They grew closer and spurred me into motion yet again.

My head flipped left and right, desperate for an escape. Going through the door I'd entered from was not an option, seeing as Sterling still stood with part of the football team.

Why me? I internally groaned, my mind blanking.

Scampering into the first door on my left, I let it softly click shut behind me, pretty sure no one had seen me.

I hoped.

Now all I had to do was wait until they exited the building, and I would creep my ass right back out of here. That was the plan. How could it go wrong?

My fingers were still gripping the handle when I felt it shake. I bit down on my lip hard to keep a shrill of surprise from tumbling off my lips and scrambled away from the door before it burst open. I hadn't paid attention to where I was in the athletic building until I darted behind a row of lockers.

The second time they tried the handle, it turned, and the door squeaked open as I pressed my back against the metal compartments, taking a deep breath and holding it.

What is even happening right now? How did meeting my boyfriend after football practice turn into me sneaking around the football locker room?

"Are you sure she went in here?" a deep voice asked.

My eyes popped. *Shiiiit!*

Tiptoeing as quietly as possible, I inched my way down the aisle, putting distance between myself and the door. If they were looking for someone, I was so fucking screwed.

"I could have sworn I saw..." They trailed off, and I went instantly still at the sound of Sterling's voice.

No fucking way had he followed me inside the locker room. I could only assume it was me they were looking for unless girls sneaking in here was a common occurrence.

Had I made a noise?

I hooked a right at the first corner. It was a goddamn maze of lockers in here. I didn't even know if I would be able to find my way out, but my immediate concern was just how long I'd be stuck hiding or possibly running into another football player. Most of the guys had already hustled out, but in the distance, I heard at least one shower running, which I planned to stay clear of. I did not need any unexpected peepshows. I cringed at the thought. My reputation couldn't handle any more hits.

"Who is this girl? Is she the one you wrote about? Because that would be classic, man."

Their voices were a tad farther away than before, giving me a fraction of space to work with. My behavior bordered on plain stupid. Why was I avoiding Sterling to such a degree? Because of a ridiculous article? Or was it because I feared he might ask me out again? Because he reminded me of a time I wanted to erase?

Yes, to all the above.

I wanted him to just go away.

"She's someone I shouldn't have let disappear on me," the bane of my existence replied.

What the fuck did that mean? Was that regret I heard in his voice?

Questions and confusion swirled in my head, but I didn't have time to dwell on Sterling's words as someone grabbed me from behind and spun me around. My furrowed brows quickly morphed into utter shock as a scream surged up my throat, but before I could let it wail, a hand clamped over my mouth.

Everything about my captor's movements was smooth. He managed to secure me without making any noise. The little beads of fear that had been trickling in the bottom of my stomach rose and became claws, raking down the inner walls. I'd felt true terror in my life, and this wasn't quite on that level, yet adrenaline burst through while my brain figured out what its response would be—fight or freeze.

I froze.

My gaze lifted, seeing a familiar pair of light blue eyes. I loved that shade of blue, and somehow the color shoved my trepidation away in a single swoop. Micah waited until he saw recognition in my startled expression and felt my tense muscles go lax. He pressed a finger to my lips, and the message came through loud and clear.

Don't make a sound.

He kept me pressed against the locker, trapping me with his toned body that I'd just noticed was only partially clothed. I didn't have time to fully appreciate his bare chest or the sweat-pants-material shorts, but it didn't stop me from taking a quick glimpse.

His damp sandy hair looked as if he'd just come from a quick shower and had shaken the water right out, the ends curling and falling into messy disarray that made my insides purr.

Sometimes, his looks caught me off guard and made me completely forget about the world. Everything around me ceased to exist, and if he smiled at me, those dimples winking on his cheeks... fuck, it was over. Instant lust. Hell, I was surprised my panties didn't drop of their own accord; that was the kind of power a true smile from Micah had over me. Not the cocky smirk —that did things to me as well, but that one I found the strength to resist, mostly because it could entice an array of emotions, from amusement to "I'm going to fucking kill him." That pretty much summed up our relationship. No one else drove me absolutely insane and also instilled an animalistic hunger like I'd never felt.

I should be glad he kept the dimples under wraps.

"Hey, Boyd" came a voice I knew well from the other side of the locker wall—Brock Taylor running interference. I should have known he wouldn't have been far away. Brock and Micah almost always worked together. "Sterling, right?" His tone hardened slightly. Anyone who didn't know him probably wouldn't notice, but I did.

Micah's gaze remained on mine, and although they were chips of ice, I also noticed a flicker of something else in his eyes. It captured me, holding me prisoner as much as his hard body did.

"This is the guy I was telling you about," Boyd jumped in. I assumed it was him. I didn't know a Boyd, but he had to have been on the football team with the guys. "This man is going to take us to the finals. I'll bet on it."

"We just might have to do that. Quietly, of course. The school frowns upon gambling," Sterling said with a slight sneering undertone.

Brock chuckled. "Let's see how the regular season goes."

Micah's fingers came to rest at my hips, warm through the thin material of my white shorts. A thrill ribboned within my belly at his touch, at the pressing of each finger, not hard but not gently either, just enough for me to be fully aware of how close they were to my skin.

What is wrong with me? Now was not the time to get all hot and bothered, and yet I couldn't seem to stop the flush that crept up my neck. I tried to focus my attention back on the conversation a few rows over.

"We might actually bring home a national trophy now that we have Brock and Micah on the team," Boyd gushed. "Our biggest competition will be Dalton."

Fynn and Grayson went to Dalton. How strange to think that the Elite would be playing against each other. They'd only ever been allies. I didn't know how I felt about them pitted against one another. Who the hell did I root for?

Bigger problems, Mads. You have bigger issues right now, like the mindless circles Micah's thumb is creating at your hips.

Sometimes I needed to slap my mind back on track when it wandered, as it often did.

No, what I needed was for Micah to stop touching me.

A shiver twirled over my heart as the hem of my shirt lifted with the rise of my chest and that thumb brushed over my skin. My sharp inhale followed, and Micah's head dipped to the side of my ear. "Shhh," he whispered so quietly it was almost inaudible, but I felt his breath, and that became an added distraction—*a* torture of its own.

"You should pledge for Chi Sigma," Sterling said. "I think you'd be a good fit. We're pretty selective, but something tells me you would be right at home."

I snuffed a snort at the suggestion of Brock Taylor in a fraternity. The only way that worked was if he became president. He needed to be in charge.

Micah bit the lobe of my ear, a punishment of sorts for making yet another sound, except the pressure of his teeth on that sensitive part of my body caused a whimper to bubble up.

"I haven't thought about a fraternity," Brock admitted, sounding genuinely curious at the idea.

It took everything in me not to cough at the absurdity. Did Sterling have no idea he was being played right now? I guess it was a good thing he didn't.

Micah's *punishment* was far from over. Every reaction I

made earned one from him. His lips had moved to my neck, and all I could think was *I'm in big trouble now.*

"We're having a get-together tonight. You should come," I was pretty sure I heard Sterling offer, but I was having a difficult time listening.

Micah's fingers at my waist trailed up along my sides, skimming my breasts. Little fires erupted all over my skin. My head fell back against the locker, eyes closing as my boyfriend's sweet torment continued. *He's trying to kill me.*

His lips only curled.

"Can't. I have friends coming in for the weekend." Brock's voice was a bit farther away, making me think they were walking as they talked. He was maneuvering them toward the door.

I hooked my fingers into the waistband of Micah's shorts, clasping the material. My nails skimmed the edge of his stomach, and the muscles there quivered. Lust and a heady sense of female power whirled inside me. He wasn't the only one who could play this game.

"Bring them," Sterling said.

Such a friendly guy, I thought sarcastically. His lack of morals and decency was why I'd been drawn to him in the first place. I hadn't wanted good and sincere; I'd wanted someone who wouldn't get attached or ask questions.

Sterling had done neither—at least I hadn't thought so at the time. Maybe I'd left a lasting impression? It didn't matter. I wanted nothing from Sterling, and the sooner he backed off, the better. The line had to be drawn in definite blank ink. We could be friends or friendly but nothing more.

The moment the door to the locker room swung closed, muffling their voices, Micah's hips ground into mine as he took possession of my lips. My body went on sensory overdrive, spinning me wildly out of control. I no longer cared where I was or how I got here in the first place. The conversation I'd overheard was forgotten. All that mattered was Micah.

His name became a chant in my head as rolled his hips into mine again. The hardness I felt through his shorts sent heat radiating between my legs, punching a soft moan through my lips, only to be captured in our kiss.

"God, I love when you do that," he breathed, his mouth hovering over mine.

My hands took a tour up his chest, starting low at his solid abs before slowly exploring the plane of muscle. His skin was hot, and he was so fucking hard.

The button on my white shorts popped up, Micah's fingers fumbling with the zipper. "Let me touch you," he implored, his voice husky as he kissed a path down my neck, leaving no spot unadorned.

His eyes were half lidded as they looked at me, need churning in them. "I'm not stopping you," I whispered.

I was lifted in the air and pushed against the lockers. My legs locked around him as he pressed into me, his lips covering mine for a brutal kiss that didn't last long enough. He lowered his mouth to my breast, taking my nipple between his teeth. I gasped, my head dropping to the back of the locker, and arched into him. His fingers came to the front of my shorts, fumbling with the zipper. "I need you naked," he panted. If I'd been wearing a skirt instead, he would have already been inside me.

His lips fused to mine again as his finger looped inside my shorts, but as long as we stayed in this position, they weren't coming off. I wiggled, unfolding my legs.

A locker slammed shut, echoing throughout the room as if a rifle had gone off. I jumped, pulling away from Micah like we'd just been caught making out in my bedroom at home.

We stared at each other for a few breathy moments, our chests rising and falling rapidly in sync. I could read his expression. It was the same that was reflected in mine. Did we say screw it and keep going or let our senses return?

He waited until the lingerer left, slowly returning my feet to the ground, and hooked his finger under my chin, drawing my face up to look at him. "Care to explain what you're doing here?"

I rested my hands on his bare chest, the scent of him screwing with my thoughts, scrambling them. "Here, like right this minute? Because I thought it was pretty obvious what we were doing."

"Maddy," he growled, not finding my avoidance cute.

It took me a moment to respond and form coherent words, my entire body still buzzing, little electric flutters pulsing between my legs. "I have a very good explanation. It's a long story, though, and I don't even know if you'll believe me." We kept our voices low, because despite the locker room being mostly empty now, the shower in the other room still ran, meaning we weren't completely alone. Not yet.

"Try me," he challenged. From the hard set of his jaw, I could tell we wouldn't be leaving until he got answers.

"I came to see you."

Micah lifted a quizzical brow that didn't look content with my response. "That's your long story?"

"No," I huffed, toying with the ends of his damp hair. Nerves made me want to pace, but he wasn't letting me budge. "Do we really have to do this—" My eyes flicked from corner to corner. "—in here?" I whispered. "What if someone else walks in?" I asked, clearly uncomfortable.

The water running in the shower turned off, bathing the locker room in eerie silence and driving my point of getting caught home. What were the odds that whoever emerged would come down this particular row of lockers, stumbling upon Micah and me? I didn't want to take that chance.

His eyes dipped to my lips, and some of the harshness in his features softened. "You're with me. It's fine."

I drew my bottom lip between my teeth, a gesture that drove him crazy. "Oh really? So, guys bring girls into the locker room all the time to seduce them?"

Wickedness flashed in the center of his eyes. "Under the bleachers, in the bathrooms, on the coach's desk, in the storage closets. There are a hundred different places we could be doing this." As if he needed to show me what he meant, his lips cruised over my cheek.

My heart drummed in my chest, quickening. "Your mind is seriously warped," I said with no real bite to my tone, zipping and buttoning my shorts.

"Maybe we should continue what we started..." He crowded me with that edible body, smelling of pine and hints of the sea, his hands flattening against the lockers on either side of my head. My hands on his chest automatically wove up around his neck or risked getting smooshed between our bodies.

He wasn't serious.

Oh, but the glint in his eyes said Micah was dead serious.

My blood soared as his lips skimmed along the column of my neck, to the space behind my ears. A hum rose in my throat. "Micah, don't start again. We should leave."

His mouth hovered dangerously close to mine but never claimed it as I craved. "Or you could put me out of my misery, Mads, and kiss me."

He knew I hated that nickname, and usually it infuriated me, but somehow hearing it said with such desperation had the opposite effect on me. My poor heart dipped as need filtered into every part of me. Micah and I had this uncanny ability to get sidetracked so easily. It was both maddening and intoxicating.

I felt myself being swayed by his eyes, by his lips, by the plea in his voice. He could shred my willpower with a glance, a smirk, and even simply my name. And sometimes it was the knowledge that he could do all of that effortlessly that infuriated me. How could it be so damn easy for him? And why was I so weak around him?

Lifting on my toes, I brought our lips closer, intending to tease him, but like usual, that plan always backfired on me. It was as if he could read my deviant mind and countered my maneuvers with his own.

His hands cupped my ass, hauling me against his chest, and just as his lips descended on mine, the lights went out, cutting off the kiss that could have shattered me.

"What the...?" Micah muttered, his hands steady on my waist, keeping me close to his side.

I took in a shaky breath. "Micah?" Blinded by darkness, I blinked, trying to get my eyes to adjust to the sudden deprivation of light. It wasn't working; the contrast from light to dark had happened too swiftly, essentially leaving me sightless. A shiver crawled up my back, trepidation forming a tight ball in my gut. I didn't suffer from nyctophobia, but I also knew that not only good things happened in the dark.

"It's okay," he whispered near my ear. "I got you."

Strong fingers laced with mine, carefully leading me through the darkness. I trusted that I wouldn't faceplant into a locker or trip over someone's forgotten cup.

Why did my brain have to go there? Of all the football equipment in this room, why a damn jock cup?

"Ouch," Micah hissed, coming to a halt, and despite only being able to see the shadow of his outline, I felt him bend over slightly, his free hand moving to his leg.

"What is it?" I asked, the question racing out.

"Nothing, I just rammed my shin into a bench." I didn't have to see his face to picture the deep scowl on his lips.

An unbalanced giggle worked its way up my throat at the image my mind created, born of part fear and part amusement at the tough football player being taken down by an inanimate wooden object.

Micah glanced over his shoulder as he straightened up. "Are you laughing right now?"

Since he stopped so suddenly, I was nearly plastered to his

back. "I can't help it. This situation is just so outrageous it's funny."

He resumed moving toward the exit, hobbling a step or two and taking me with him. "Is that so?"

I rolled my eyes at the back of his head.

Micah finally pulled open the door, a stream of light pouring into the locker room, chasing away the darkness behind me. Still shirtless, he tugged me outside, and I'd never been so happy to see the sun. I rubbed my eyes, the brightness stinging after coming out of a room with no windows. "What the hell was that?"

"Either someone messing with my game or just screwing around in general." He didn't seem all that worried, and that normally calmed me, but traces of uneasiness lingered inside my chest.

I panned the area outside the athletic building, making sure we were alone. Sterling was nowhere in sight, and I didn't see Brock either. "This is too much excitement for me in a week."

CHAPTER EIGHT

MADS

Micah sensed the tension in my body. He placed a comforting hand on the small of my back. "You don't need to worry, Mads. It was nothing but a stupid prank. Let's go. I'll walk you back to the dorm. I'm still waiting to hear how exactly you ended up in the locker room. Not that I'm complaining."

I relaxed against his side. "I bet," I mumbled, my feet moving automatically with his, matching his strides.

His shoulder lightly bumped into mine, and he winked. "We'll have to try that again without the disruption."

"I'd rather not if it's all the same."

Halfway to my dorm, that feeling of drawing attention returned and I remembered the article, but it wasn't me this time everyone stared at. I watched as a pair of girls passing by ogled Micah. And when it happened again and again with different girls each time, even a few guys, a glare formed on my face. "Should you be walking around campus half naked?" I was used to the attention he and the Elite drew, but for some reason today, it got to me, and a protective streak rose in me. Or jealousy. Whatever. It didn't matter which emotion, only that I didn't like it.

My lip curled into a snarl at the next pair of girls eyeing Micah appreciatively, but it was useless. It was as if I didn't exist next to the guy at my side, even though he still held my hand. They giggled all giddy-like.

He flashed me a dimpled grin that made me regret asking. "God, I love it when you get all possessive."

I rolled my eyes. "You have issues."

"Don't we all?"

We arrived at my dorm, and I shifted on my feet, standing in front of him. With all the unexpected drama over the last hour, the reason I'd gone to see Micah had been temporarily shoved aside, but now... I chewed on my lip.

His words from the other night came back to me as I glanced up into that boyishly handsome face. *Stay away from Sterling.*

Micah had a hunch, a boyfriend instinct that told him just how I knew Sterling, and I guessed that hearing me confirm his suspicions would hurt him.

The last thing I wanted to do was cause him pain. He had enough of it on his own without me adding to his suffering. I wanted to do just the opposite for him. I wanted to be a place where he could find happiness, love, and comfort. And yet it wasn't Micah's past coming to haunt us. No, it was mine.

My choices.

My mistakes.

My regrets.

Could I not handle Sterling on my own? Did I need to be shielded by my boyfriend?

No. I handled my own shit, and I would deal with Sterling.

I'd been independent for years, living without the Elite, shunning their existence, until Josie, but I was still that girl who could stand on her own two feet.

Micah noticed the shadow that spread into my eyes and brushed his thumb over the corner of my temple as if he wanted to banish the trouble brewing inside me. "Maybe we could finish what we started later tonight?" He leaned down, dropping a kiss onto the right side of my mouth.

Before I got the chance to sink in and enjoy the tingles dancing on my lips, we were interrupted by a voice that sounded an awful lot like my cousin Grayson's. "God, it's bad enough that my best friend is hooking up with my sister. And now you and my cousin... I just can't."

Grayson Edwards and Fynn Dupree sauntered toward us, both looking like they just stepped right off the runway onto campus. Neither had on anything fancy, just jeans and a T-shirt, but it was the way they wore them that made the clothes look expensive and more than casual.

Fynn stood an inch or two over my cousin, the tallest of the group. He came from a mixed-heritage family that gave him the most envy-worthy and stellar features, and the fact that he was actually a nice guy made him not just desirable by many but popular as well. Fynn had always been levelheaded and the quieter one of the group, but that didn't mean he wasn't still dangerous. It was the quiet ones you had to watch out for.

Then, of course, there was Josie and Kenna's brother, Grayson. The triplets shared more than winning the lottery in the gene pool. They could be quick-tempered, reckless, and irrational, but they were also loyal as fuck. Not just to each other but to their friends as well. Josie only found out last year that she was an Edward and a triplet from a very wealthy family, giving her a different outlook than Kenna and Grayson. As the only boy in the trio, Grayson had a better understanding of girls in general, and because of it, he rarely fell for the usual tricks girls used to gain a guy's attention.

I swore someone whistled as they came to greet Micah and me. My gaze landed on the culprit. A cheeky redhead with tits that threatened to spill out of her deep V-neck tank. One extra bounce in her step and it would be a free show for all to see. The three other girls with her giggled despite the guys completely ignoring them. Sometimes I wished I had their ability to be impervious to the heads that turned their way, or the suggestive whispers in their ears.

Micah broke out into a wide grin. "About time, fuckers." He clasped Fynn's extended forearm and did the same to Grayson in some kind of ritual bro greeting.

My cousin made a face, shoving his hands into the pockets of his shredded jeans. "Yeah, but I'm instantly regretting coming. I'm not spending my weekend watching my friends grope my family."

I scrunched my nose. "You have such a way of putting

things into perspective." Shifting, I moved in to give them both a hug.

Those brown eyes identical to his sisters pinned me with a narrowed gaze. "Where are the hellions?"

"Josie and Kenna are probably in our room," I replied. Now that the Elite were back together for the weekend, it didn't look like I'd be having that talk with Micah tonight. I didn't want to ruin his excitement.

"And Brock?" Fynn asked.

Micah and I shared an awkward moment, both remembering how Brock had run interference to keep Sterling from discovering me. "He's probably back at our house, showering or some shit," Micah said.

"Why the fuck are you running around without a shirt?" Grayson asked as if he just realized Micah's bare chest was on display for all to appreciate.

"Jealous?" Micah flexed his defined pectoral muscles.

Grayson snorted. "Get the fuck out of here. I was actually thinking it looks like you've been slacking in the gym, bro."

Barbs like that only bounced off Micah, making him grin deeper. "Not a chance."

Fynn chuckled, a deep and sexy sound.

This could go on for hours, and I suspected it to continue far into the night. "As much as I would love to stand here and listen to the three of you be utter assholes, I need to get ready."

"I'll see you later?" Micah asked, rubbing a hand over the back of his neck as he glanced down at me.

I nodded. "Of course. Don't cause trouble," I warned the

three of them, which I realized was an invitation to do exactly that. Shaking my head at the twinkle in Micah's eyes, I lifted on my toes and pressed a parting kiss to his lips.

"That's it," Grayson groused. "I'm banning any form of lip touching for the weekend."

"Does that include you too?" I implored, lifting a brow at my cousin.

"No, because my lips won't touch someone I'm related to," he retorted.

"Do I need to remind you of that night when we were thirteen and you—"

"Get out of here, Mads. You're eating into my guys' night," he snappily interrupted before I could finish bringing him down memory lane.

My lips twitched smugly. "Like I wanted to hang out with your dumb ass tonight."

They could have their boys' night. I had my girls.

Chaos greeted me as I walked into my dorm room. When you lived with three other girls, chaos became a default state. One half of the room looked like a hurricane had attacked Kenna's closet and deposited her clothes everywhere. And by everywhere, I meant the floor, the bed, the desk, and even the lamp had an article of clothing strung over it. But it wasn't just her side of the room that suffered destruction. I couldn't even see my bed.

On the other side of the room, Ainsley curled Josie's hair, a random slew of makeup and hair tools covering Josie's desk. BTS harmonized from someone's iPhone, filling the space with a mixture of English and Korean lyrics. Ainsley's newest obsession. I had to admit, despite not being into K-pop or anime, two things Ainsley loved, I didn't hate either. I found myself weirdly sucked in.

We had plans to go out tonight and hit a few college bars, which were supposed to be fairly easy to get into even though we were underage. It was all part of the college experience, but wrangling four girls who had to share one bathroom? Far more difficult than being served beer at a college bar.

Dropping my bag on top of Kenna's shit strewn on my bed, I stepped over a discarded bra and a pair of jeans, making my way to my closet. It wasn't easy. "Why did you bring so much crap with you?"

"Options. I need options," she insisted from somewhere buried in her closet. I had no idea how there were still clothes hanging in the small wardrobe.

Skimming over my selection for the night, I ran my fingers over one of my favorite tops, considering. "If I see you with a single shopping bag this semester, I'm purging your closet myself," I informed Kenna.

A dark head popped out from behind the slim white door. "Just wait until you need to borrow something."

"Like this?" I said, bending down and scooping up a black skirt that sat on the floor by my feet. After closer examination, I turned my lips upside. "Hey, this is mine," I told Kenna, holding it up. "And I'm wearing it tonight," I declared, taking it with me as I maneuvered my way to the bathroom.

"Leave the door unlocked," Kenna called after me.

Rolling my eyes, I shut the door and turned on the shower water to warm. The steady spray hitting the tub drowned out the music from the other side of the wall. I stripped and stepped under the stream of water, letting it soak my face. I stayed in that spot, allowing my problems, worries, and insecurities to wash down the drain.

A knock broke me out of my trance seconds before Kenna said, "I need to grab the curling spray." She was in and out without me having to say anything.

As I toweled off, feeling cleansed inside and out, I told myself that tonight was just about my friends.

No Sterling.

No boyfriends.

No drama.

Just booze, greasy foods, laughs, music, and unforgettable memories with my three best friends. This was college, and it was damn time it lived up to the hype. After this weekend, all that shit I needed to deal with and figure out would still be there.

Hair wrapped in an old T-shirt of Micah's, I strode into the bedroom, a cloud of steam behind me, in my black skirt and lace bra. After taking a shower in a bathroom that small, it was nearly impossible to use the mirror, so the desks we were supposed to do homework on became vanities. I had a white Ikea tower of drawers that just fit under the desk filled with my hair, skin, and makeup essentials, and a mirror with lights propped up against the wall on top of the desk.

I sat in the chair and pulled open the top drawer to apply my skincare. In the mirror, I caught a glimpse of Kenna behind me on the opposite side, applying layers of mascara on her lashes. The music still played on the other side of the room but had been turned down to a low hum of background noise.

Josie came dancing over to me, her long hair falling and bouncing in loose curls. Ainsley came in right behind her, singing the words to whatever song played on her phone. She was dressed in all black, the fishnet tights, combat boots, and decorative chains hanging from her belt making the rather plain skirt and cropped top edgy. She often altered her clothes, adding personal touches like the metal rings embedded in the bottom of her skirt.

"What's up with you? Are you still upset about the article?" Josie asked, immediately noticing something off with me. The two of them climbed onto my bed, feet hanging over the side.

I rubbed moisturizer into my face. "Yes. No." Sighing, I twisted in my seat, facing them instead of looking at their reflection. "It's not so much the embarrassing photo, because whatever, who doesn't have moments like that in life? It's that *he* put it there."

"He?" Ainsley repeated, her mossy green eyes confused.

"Sterling," I stated flatly, turning back to the mirror.

"Who is Sterling?" Ainsley whispered to Josie.

"The fraternity guy, I think," she explained, but not entirely confident in her response.

Ainsley's eyes widened. "Does she know him?"

So much had gone on this week that I hadn't had a chance to talk to either of them, but I could count on Kenna to fill them in.

"She banged him a couple years ago, right after Micah crushed her heart," my cousin divulged from the other side of the room, not missing a beat.

"It was a mistake," I declared, pulling out my tube of primer with a frown. As I applied my makeup, Kenna joined Ainsley and Josie on the bed, giving them a rundown of my history with Sterling, including the last few days. She got most of the facts right and didn't leave anything out, surprising me. I guess she had listened to me the other day.

When she finished, I informed them about my confrontation today and the locker room incident. "I'm not acting completely out of my mind, am I? Who does that? I can't shake this feeling that he wants something from me."

"Uh, he does. Your pussy," Ainsley so eloquently advised.

The eyeliner pencil I had pointed at my eyelid veered off to the side in the craziest cat eye ever. I scowled, glancing at the reflection of my roommates.

Two seconds went by, and they burst out laughing.

"I'm glad you guys can find humor in my misery." I grabbed a wipe to clean up the mess of eyeliner, but as I did, my lips curved at the corner.

Josie crossed her legs, leaning back on her hands. "I'll admit it does seem a bit much, but maybe he sincerely likes you and doesn't want you to run away like you did the first time," she suggested.

"Perhaps," I agreed, pressing my lips together. It was a reasonable explanation.

"But your instincts are telling you something else?" she guessed, seeing the unsettled look still on my face.

Giving up on my eyeliner, I moved to apply my blush, picking out a big, fluffy brush. "I honestly don't know. At first, I was afraid Micah would find out, which is crazy. We both have pasts. Why should I feel ashamed about mine? He sure as shit isn't about his." Micah had regrets like most people, but he didn't hide or shy away from his mistakes. I could take a page from his book. My irrational behavior and decisions the last few days didn't make any sense to me. How could they make sense to someone else?

"Did you tell him yet?" Kenna asked, twirling a piece of her hair.

A hot flush stole up the back of my neck as I remembered just why I'd been so preoccupied that my mind basically stopped functioning. "Not yet."

Josie frowned. "This isn't good. If he finds out that Sterling is flirting with you, or worse, making moves on you..."

I swiped the brush over the apple of my cheeks, my eyes darting away from hers in the mirror. "You don't have to tell me. And to think, I'd hoped we would be able to leave all the Elite drama back home."

Kenna snorted. "When it comes to the four of them, trouble is never far. They're like a package deal. When you date one of them, you don't just get the Elite, you get the baggage the four of them come with."

Truer words couldn't have been spoken.

* * *

Several bars edged the outer perimeter of campus, and the school offered golf cart shuttles that ran all night both Fridays and Saturdays to take people to and from the downtown area. It was part of the Allie Viscount Safety Movement that started a few years back after she'd been kidnapped and assaulted on her way back to the dorms. KU was normally a safe and peaceful school, and when Allie's body was found a week after she disappeared, it rocked not just the college but the whole state.

It didn't matter how safe you felt in a community. Evil lurked in some of the unlikeliest places.

Groups were key when going out clubbing or to bars. The four of us, we stuck together, we watched out for each other, and we had the Elite on speed dial. They were never really far away, and we would all be in the same area tonight if anything arose.

Ainsley and Kenna walked a few paces in front of Josie and me, the two of them bickering over who was hotter, Loki or Thor. I didn't even know how they got on the topic. Like all conversations with the four of us, shit derailed fast. Kenna's heels clicked on the pavement as Ainsley's boots clomped. Yin and yang.

I toyed with one of my dangling earrings, bright neon lights flashing over my face advertising beer brands, live shows, and quirky slogans. Music from country to classic rock and everything in between filtered into the street from the different venues. The downtown area pumped with life. It was Friday night, and everyone wanted to forget about the essays and upcoming homework assignments because despite it being only the first week, some teachers were merciless. We were all here to get hammered and have fun.

Why did that seem so hard for me?

I didn't have to get shit-faced, but a few drinks would help me loosen those tense muscles in my neck and other places. Food would be good, too, seeing as I hadn't eaten anything since late this morning.

"Are you sure you're up for this?" Josie asked, brown eyes brimming with regard.

Putting on a smile that I knew not just my friends needed but I did, too, I looped my arm through hers and dragged her into the bar behind Kenna and Ainsley. "I need this," I assured her.

For it being only eight o'clock, the bar was busy, most of the tables already occupied.

"I know that feeling all too well," Josie replied, raising her voice over the increased volume of chatter and music. A few guys fumbled with band equipment on the small stage in the corner, setting up for their performance later tonight.

"Bourbon, isn't it?" I asked, raising a brow. It was Josie's drink of choice. If there was a bottle nearby, she would reach for the bourbon over any other, but she'd cut back on the drinking since Angie's trial. Angie was the woman who'd kidnapped Josie as a baby and raised her as her own, and last year she'd finally been sentenced. Three years, the minimum amount of jail time, and thanks to her husband's money, she would be eligible for parole next year. She'd gotten off easy, as far as I was concerned.

Not only had Angie been a kidnapper, but she also had a

penchant for alcohol morning, noon, and night. Angie hadn't discriminated when it came to her booze, nor in her neglect of the daughter she'd wanted so desperately that she committed a felony to get her.

I didn't know how the woman managed to have a daughter as amazing as Josie. It had to have been Easton's influence, the man who thought he was Josie's dad for nearly eighteen years.

Josie groaned at the mention of her favorite liquor. "No matter what I say or do, keep the bourbon far away from me tonight."

Ainsley turned around and faced us, walking backward through the bar. "Where's the fun in that? I've had some of the best nights of my life with you and bourbon."

Josie rolled her eyes. "My point exactly."

Kenna joined in on badgering her sister. "Wasn't bourbon the reason you slept with Brock?"

Josie wrinkled her nose at them. "Not entirely," she snipped back.

"Regardless, I think you owe bourbon a celebratory shot." Before Josie could protest, Ainsley grabbed her hand, leading her to the bar.

"Exactly," Kenna agreed, looping an arm around my shoulders. I already anticipated her next words. "We need shots!" She tossed her head back, sending her long silky locks swinging. Kenna didn't need booze to look or act drunk. Sometimes it was her default behavior with or without the aid of alcohol.

The magic word caused a chant to break out within the bar. "Shots! Shots! Shots!"

"Fine," I relented, the only way to get Kenna to stop. "A shot, and then we dance," I said, offering a compromise.

She did a little bounce, smiling. "Finally you're saying something that makes sense."

I should have known that starting the night with a shot was a bad idea, but making bad choices was my thing. I had to live up to the reputation.

The first shot had been the bartender's choice. Fruity and smooth, it went down like a juice box. Then I switched over to cocktails, ordering my usual Long Island iced tea. IDs weren't a problem because no one checked, and I wasn't about to offer up my real age, so getting drinks wasn't an issue. The real issue was the consumption of said drinks.

Feeling my stress lighten with each sip, I sucked down my first Long Island effortlessly and made the stupid mistake of thinking another round of shots was wise. This one tasted like an oatmeal cookie. Yes, please. After that little delight, I obviously needed another, because what girl could say no to a liquid cookie?

Not this one.

I had no excuse for the Long Islands that followed other than they made me feel good, they numbed all those negative thoughts, and they made me forget everything but present moments with my roommates.

Dancing after shots was a definite requirement. With a freshly topped-off drink in hand, I swayed my hips right to the makeshift dance area, joining Ainsley and Josie with Kenna close behind me. Half the crowd in the bar already moved with the beat of the music.

Into the fourth or fifth song, I noticed Kenna's eyes browsing the bar as if she were looking for someone. My empty drink had been cast aside on a table, and I signaled for Kenna to come with me to the bar. She didn't need much enticing. As we waited for the bartender to take our order, she continued to scan the bar.

"What are you doing?" I asked, pressing my back into the counter.

She took the corner of her bottom lip between her teeth for a moment in consideration before replying, "Checking out the merchandise. There must be at least one guy here worthy of my attention." Her critical eyes moved from guy to guy, and I followed along with her gaze as she sized up her options.

The front door of the bar opened, drawing Kenna's attention and mine. I could practically hear her thoughts. *"Please be hot and available."*

Fynn Dupree's fine ass strolled through, and I grinned.

Kenna scowled as her eyes landed on Fynn, clearly stating that he was not who she had in mind for tonight.

His height made it easy for him to see over the crowd and find Kenna and me. His green eyes glittered under the mood lighting that outlined the ceiling. He smiled after spotting us at the bar.

Behind him, Brock, Grayson, and Micah sauntered in, and I swore the entire place paused for a second and then sighed. It could have also been all in my head, my heart stopping for a beat and the sigh escaping my lips.

Would that feeling always exist when I laid eyes on Micah? Or would it fade over time? Doubtful, seeing as for more than two years I tried to get my heart to stop tripping every time we crossed paths. Never once did my heart listen to me.

A flutter whirled in my chest when Micah's gaze collided with mine. It didn't matter that he was across the room. I was drawn to him. He made me feel too damn much, enhanced by my current blissfully happy, drunken state.

Kenna ordered us drinks as the Elite made their way to the bar. On some unconscious level, people tended to shift out of the way, carving a path for the four guys like they owned the damn place.

"Fynn!" I sang, throwing my arms in the air and then around him for a hug. "Kenna needs a dancing partner." I put my hands on his back, nudging him toward my cousin. "Your turn. My feet need a break."

Brock bypassed us and went straight to Josie, who was still dancing. The man had a one-track mind when it came to her, something I never thought I would ever see in my lifetime—Brock Taylor hopelessly in love. I had to admit I was a bit envious of their relationship.

Micah came up behind me, his fingers grazing my hand as he brushed a kiss on my shoulder. "You look hot, Mads."

"I do," I agreed, my lips curving as I twisted my head to the side. "You, on the other hand, look like trouble. What are you up to?"

He flashed me those fucking dimples. Nothing good happened when the dimples appeared. Just mischief.

"We're not staying," Grayson answered.

Kenna's lips formed a half pout. "You're not?"

Fynn's dark brows knitted. "No, we were just looking for someone."

I had an inkling of who that someone might be. Between the look in Micah's eyes and Grayson's shitty attitude, it wasn't hard to conclude that it was likely Sterling. What concerned me was what the four of them planned to do if they found him.

"Who could be more important than me?" Kenna asked, and the thing was, she was totally serious.

Grayson rolled his eyes. "Do you want me to make you a list?"

Kenna dipped her middle finger into the center of the glass, pulled it out, and turned it around, flipping her brother off. "Suck on this."

Scoffing, Grayson shook his head. "Could you be any more childish?"

I leaned my back against the bar counter, regarding Micah. "Should I be concerned?"

He closed the space between us, slipping his hand behind me. The maneuver had the front of his button-down shirt rubbing against the thin material of my top and through to the lacy bra. He knew what he was doing. Every move, every touch, no matter how light, mattered, and Micah did so consciously. I'd never met a guy who could seduce me so effortlessly with such simple gestures.

His hand came back with my drink, and he brought the straw to his lips and sucked down half. "About me? Never."

I couldn't stop staring at his mouth.

Grayson and Fynn both snorted but quickly covered with a

cough or cleared their throat like they were hiding something, purposefully failing to be discreet.

"Micah." I groaned. "I've had too much to fucking drink tonight to bail your asses out of jail."

"I'm too pretty for the joint," he remarked, half joking, half serious.

I narrowed my eyes. "As true as that might be, I doubt the officer making the arrest will agree."

"It's fine. I'll be out in the morning. Right, Dupree?" Micah lifted his sparkling light blue gaze to his friend and winked.

Taking my glass from Micah before he could drink the entire contents, I stirred the cocktail. "Not funny."

Fynn leaned an arm on an annoyed Kenna. "We'll make sure he stays out of jail tonight."

"Now leave. You're distracting my girls." Kenna shooed her brother and Fynn, waving them off with the back of her hand.

I shot her a pointed look. "Weren't you looking for a guy to hook up with just a few minutes ago?"

Yes, I just threw my cousin under the bus. And I didn't give a damn, or maybe it was the booze that didn't care.

Curiosity filled Grayson's eyes. His arms folded as he stared at his sister.

Was it my imagination, or did Fynn's gaze just darken? Weird. The lighting was dim, and my vision was altered by the alcohol, but...

I glanced again at Kenna and Fynn and saw... nothing. My imagination was getting the best of me.

"Don't give me that look," she scolded both Grayson and Fynn. "It's no different than what you do every weekend."

Micah chuckled at my side.

The Elite left, but not before Grayson and Ainsley exchanged the ritual glares and sarcastic mumbles under their breath of two people who could barely tolerate being in the same room together, even when that room was filled with a hundred other people.

All summer the two of them had been throwing barbs at each other. I still couldn't figure out if my cousin wanted to drown her or fuck her. Honestly, probably both. But the tension between them could easily kill my party mood. It was time for another fucking drink.

The band went through a few minutes of soundcheck and instrument tuning before starting their live show with a bang. Literally. Cymbals crashed together right before the guitar riff echoed through the bar and the crowd got rowdy.

An hour into the set, I leaned in toward Josie. "I'm stepping outside for a smoke," I yelled loud enough for her to hear.

She nodded.

I might be the only one in my group who partook in what Kenna coined as my "ratchet habit," but my friends cared enough about me to brace cold winters and hot-ass summers while I indulged.

Josie started to follow me through the cluster of bodies, but I shook her off. "Stay," I insisted. I could tell she didn't like the idea. "I'll just be a minute," I insisted.

Ainsley fell into Josie, which turned into a hug. I left them like that and began making my way toward the door. It was like playing a game of human Tetris. I moved my body this way and that, trying to fit through open space. By the time I made it to the entrance, I didn't just want a cigarette, I needed it like I needed a gulp of fresh air, which I did.

The bar had become stuffy, and I couldn't tell if just my ears were ringing or my entire fucking head.

I stepped outside into the night air, which was only slightly cooler than the temperature inside the bar, yet it still offered a reprieve to my flushed skin. Digging into the small wristlet hooked on my arm, I took out a smoke and slipped the thin stick between my lips. The familiar weight and taste of the tobacco instantly calmed me, and I closed my eyes for a moment to appreciate the paper hitting my tongue. Anticipation of the first drag shrank the ringing in my ears.

I loved smoking as much as I loathed it. Cigarettes and I had developed an unhealthy love/hate relationship. They did something that no counselor or pill had been able to: quiet the noise inside my head, allay the overwhelming feelings, and soothe those nasty bouts of anxiety.

The flame from my lighter jumped to life, warming my face as I brought it to the end of the cigarette until it caught. A handful of other people loitered along the building, either smoking or talking in a group with their friends. Knowing there were people around made me feel less likely to be snatched off the streets and murdered in a ditch. As a girl, night or day, thoughts of safety were always in the back of my mind, especially when alone. Sad facts about the world we lived in.

But no one paid any attention to me, and I took comfort in being invisible, just a no-name girl hanging in the corner by herself.

Yet it didn't take long for that safe feeling to morph into

something unnerving. It kind of crept up on me, like a spider dangling from the ceiling and landing on my shoulder. I glanced behind me, half expecting to see the shadow of a giant bug looming over me, but nothing scary or unusual lurked in the darkness. Not that I could see.

Shaking my head to clear the negativity that tiptoed in, I lifted my cigarette to my lips only to have it plucked from my fingers before it reached my mouth.

I whirled my head to the side. *What the hell—*

CHAPTER NINE

MADS

The last person I wanted to see tonight took a quick inhale of my cigarette, his lips curving at the corners. Sterling Weston. He wore a black V-neck tee and jeans tucked into a pair of combat boots. Nothing about the way he looked screamed president of a fraternity, and that threw me off. His look and attitude didn't align with the stereotypical frat brat.

To think, if the Elite had shown up at the bar an hour later, they might have crossed paths, and the night would have had a very different ending than it was about to.

My gaze narrowed on Sterling as I slumped against the building. "Do you seriously have nothing better to do than stalk me?"

"Is that what I'm doing?" Exhaling, he was close enough to me that the smoke reached my nostrils.

He seemed to be everywhere I went. I didn't know if it was

intentional or just because we went to the same school. Regardless, he was making me uneasy, more so as I thought about hiding out in the locker room just to avoid him. My gaze stayed on him warily. "To be honest, I don't know what it is you're doing."

He leaned a shoulder on the brick exterior, angling his body to the side so he faced me. "This feels awfully familiar, except it was you bumming a smoke off me."

A flashback to the night I'd met the nameless boy on the porch of an Elite party flipped through my mind. "I'd rather not take a stroll down memory lane with you. Not now. Not ever." My fingers twitched, missing the weight of a cigarette between them. I should just go back into the bar, but the urge for another smoke grew strong inside me. Damn addiction. It had become a crutch I couldn't kick.

He didn't move a single muscle other than his lips. "I don't recall you being so prickly."

Confiscating my cigarette from his fingers, I took a quick drag. "I don't recall you being so clingy," I snapped as the smoke coated my lungs.

"You want clingy, Splash?" He moved as quick as a hiccup, trapping me against the wall with his body so fast that, for a few breaths, I couldn't process what happened.

Music from the live band pumped from the other side of the brick wall, but I barely heard it over the pounding of my heart. "What are you doing?" I demanded, attempting to move out from the prison he created with his arms and body.

"We had fun together, didn't we, Mads?" he murmured, his breath stroking my cheek.

The way he used my name, it felt like a felt punch in the gut, and not in that take-your-breath-away feeling I got when Micah kissed me.

Twisting my head, despite the fact that the movement had the tips of our noses brushing, I blew a puff of smoke into his face. "I'm not having fun now." Most of my blissful buzz had fizzled out, leaving me weary and annoyed.

Sterling angled his head to the side, his golden gaze drifting to my tight lips. "I guess we'll have to change that."

Gah! How was I ever attracted to him? Let him touch me? Kiss me? Sleep with him? The thought only repulsed me now. "Get out of my way." I used my stern voice, praying he would take me seriously and realize how uncomfortable I was.

"Not until I get what I want."

Panic exploded inside me as I jumped to a conclusion about just what Sterling might be after. He had insinuated more than once that he would like to be more than friends, regardless that I had a boyfriend. My brain stopped thinking logically, forgetting that we were in public with other people around, not that they were paying any attention to me. I suspected that, to someone glancing our way, we might look like lovers, or drunk—drunk lovers.

Sterling rolled his eyes. "It's not that. At least not tonight, not here. But if the mood ever strikes, or your boyfriend isn't fulfilling your needs..." He ran his fingers down the back of my arm.

"Don't count on it," I spat, putting my shoulder into his chest, hoping to break free from him.

No such luck. The asshole didn't even flinch.

Disappointment and dread slithered inside me like a slimy snake.

He had this habit of always touching my hair when he was near me and did so now, brushing at a dark blonde strand. "I'm counting on a great deal from you," he whispered leaning closer.

Is he going to kiss me? My first instinct was to shrink away or turn my head, but there was nowhere to go. Rough bricks pressed into my back. "Sterling, don't—"

I heard the shutter of a camera. It was faint, nearly overrun by the music from inside, but I swore I heard it.

What the fuck? Who was taking a picture, and why?

Momentarily, Sterling's impending lips flew from my mind at the new possible dilemma. It could be anyone taking a photo, and it didn't have to be of me. After seeing that picture in the article, I was paranoid, and yet... that snap of a shutter had been close. Too close for me to disregard it. As if it had been...

My eyes went to Sterling's lips. The prick was grinning. Not just a normal grin but a wicked one, and it became obvious he was up to something.

I didn't think, just reacted. My hand holding the nearly burned-out cigarette lifted, pressing the end onto Sterling's arm. It was the easiest patch of exposed skin I could reach.

"Mads," he hissed, but it ended in a growl.

Shoving hard at his chest, I managed to put some distance between us, not much but enough to see the phone in his hand. I caught a glimpse of the screen lit up in the night.

He hadn't.

Had he?

Did the bastard take a picture of us?

Darkened eyes bored into mine. "That wasn't very nice."

Nice? We were way past pleasantries. "What the fuck, Sterling!" I lunged for his phone, my thoughts only on the photo that might or might not be on there. I couldn't care less about his little burn. But Sterling was quick and jerked the phone over his head.

He tsked like he was scolding a three-year-old who wanted something that wasn't hers. "I don't think so, Splash." The deepening of his grin infuriated me.

I gritted my teeth. "You took a picture of us." And I needed to see what it looked like.

"A keepsake, nothing more. No need to get worked up."

A new wave of anger rushed to my head. "Delete it."

A dry laugh came from him. "Not happening. I need something to remember you by."

"You don't need to remember me at all." I jumped at the phone again, but his damn long arms were out of my reach, and for a guy who didn't play any sports that I knew of, his reactions were freakishly quick. "The last time you got a pic of me, you put it in the blasted school paper!"

He shook a finger in front of my face, and I wanted to snap my teeth at him. "That was different."

"Forgive me if I don't believe you." Sarcasm dripped like poison from my words.

He slashed a hand through his midnight hair. "I figured you for a smart girl. For once, I'm glad I was right about you. It's just a little insurance," he proclaimed, backing up a step away from me, and I realized he was preparing to leave... with the photo. I couldn't let that happen. That shit was gone, even if I had to destroy his phone.

Taking a step forward, I regained the space he put between us, my eyes flashing from the phone to his face. I didn't want to let the thing out of my sight. "Why are you doing this?"

He gave a one-shoulder shrug as if this had little meaning at all, just something he liked to do on his weekends. Harass girls and take their pics as trophies. Weird. And fucking creepy. "I might need something from you in the future," he replied.

Add deviant and sadistic to the list.

Why did this sound so familiar?

Maybe because this was the kind of thing Micah and Elite would have done, gathering evidence on someone to store away. But why? What did Sterling want from me?

"I'm not giving you anything. Keep the fucking photo." The brave words tumbled from me despite the knot forming in my stomach.

His eyebrows furrowed together. "I wonder what your boyfriend would say if this ended up in his text messages, from an anonymous number, of course. He does know about our history, doesn't he, Splash?"

"Don't flatter yourself. Micah and I don't have secrets. He knows," I lied, not willing to give Sterling the satisfaction of guessing the truth.

"Maybe he would be more interested in these." He started to flip through photos on his phone, making sure to allow me a glimpse at each one. "Or how I got them."

My fury turned into something cold and fearful at each image that scrolled across the screen. They were all of me.

"How the fuck did you get those?" A shiver pricked down my spine, seeing my face, my body in various ways on a bed. Some with my clothes on and others not. Most of them were single shots of me, but in a few, I wasn't alone.

I was with Sterling. And I mean *with* Sterling.

There were even some of me sleeping in my dorm bed.

How the fuck...?

They weren't tastefully taken photos, and as much as I wanted to believe he had photoshopped my head on another girl's body, it didn't look that way. I had a small beauty mark on the inside of my right thigh, and that little dot was present in a few pictures. Was it possible he'd found someone who was a close match to me? Sure, but would he put in that much effort?

The last thing I fucking needed was a bunch of nudes floating around campus. These were bad enough; however, if he had these, then he most likely had photos that had me completely unveiled.

I suddenly couldn't feel my legs, and my insides went to ice. The year ahead of me flashed through my mind, a nightmare. That was what Sterling promised me.

"I took them when we were together."

I shook my head. "No, that's not right." My voice came out weak and confused. The timeline was wrong. So very fucking wrong, because the girl in most of those pictures wasn't a nearly sixteen-year-old Mads Clarke. They were. Now. At eighteen.

The only pics I was sure were from that night were the ones of us together. It was crystal clear they had all been taken without my knowledge or consent. Sterling was living up to the bad boy I pegged him for but so much worse. This went beyond bad boy. This was stalking!

And blackmail.

My nostrils flared. "You set me up."

If I expected a denial, I was sorely disappointed. Sterling owned his crazy. "So what if I did? You wouldn't have given me what I needed otherwise."

I honestly still didn't know what he wanted, my head too busy whirling with pictures and tequila, rum, and vodka. "You're not a nice guy."

"Oh, and you're a nice girl? Are you, Splash?"

One photo of me had been irritating. Multiple images spelled catastrophe. "Who the hell are you trying to hurt? Me?" I studied his face, trying to figure out his angle. He wasn't easy to read, but what I did see gave me pause. "No. Not me," I muttered more to myself as I continued to scrutinize his expression. Then who? Someone close to me, obviously. One of my friends? But they didn't give a shit about some images of me with a guy. There was only really one person who would be hurt the most.

Dread stretched tight inside me, and my mouth went dry.

Micah.

Alarm churned like sour milk in my stomach. "I won't let you hurt him."

He stared at me hard now, all traces of humor and smugness at having the upper hand gone. "You really do deserve a better boyfriend."

And he deserved a kick to the nuts, which I was seriously contemplating. After his phone met the bottom of my shoes, of course. My resolve to get those pictures strengthened, and so the awkward battle for the phone began. It became a game of cat and mouse, and to any onlooker, it probably appeared as if we were flirting. That couldn't have been further from the truth. He dodged and ducked my hands as I grabbed and jumped for his phone, chasing him around the sidewalk area and into the edge of the street.

Sterling chuckled at another one of my failed attempts at snagging his phone, and I swore he was enjoying this. The last thing I wanted was to cause him any type of enjoyment. I had to resort to a new tactic because this was not working. If I could catch him off guard...

The back of my heel hit the curb, causing my equilibrium to go off-balance, and I started to fall backward, my arms outstretched in search of something to grab, something to save myself from hitting the ground.

Sterling's hand clasped around mine and yanked me forward. The momentum sent me tumbling into his chest, my nose bumping into his hard form. A curse went off in my head as I gathered my bearings, but my heart never got the chance to calm down.

A heartbeat later, a deep voice that wasn't Sterling's said my name. "Mads?"

My blood went cold.

Micah had Sterling up against the wall a second later. "Stay the fuck away from her."

Sterling's shoulders lifted, his chest rose, and the veins in his neck pulsed, but his anger didn't hold a candle to Micah's quiet fury. "I think you got it all wrong, man."

I stepped forward, but a hand landed on my shoulder, keeping me from intervening. "You don't want to do that," Brock warned. "He needs to do this."

Do what exactly? Beat the living shit out of Sterling? Not that I didn't think he needed it, but it wouldn't solve anything. I could tell Micah that this form of intimidation wouldn't work with Sterling. It shone in his amber eyes. If anything, the slight hook of his lips told me Sterling craved the fight as much as— perhaps more than—Micah did.

Time slowed as I waited to see what would happen next. A girl came out of the bar and shrieked, but I barely noticed her, not with my attention fixed on Micah and Sterling.

A cold mask descended over Micah's features. "Do I?"

"She's drunk," Sterling started his defense, and I couldn't believe my ears. The jerk wasn't trying to pin this situation on me. Fuck no. Yes, I was drunk, but not drunk enough to believe his bullshit. Besides, the shit with the photo had more or less sobered my ass up really quick. But he continued spewing lies. "I was only trying to—"

Micah's fist slammed into Sterling, hitting him right on the corner of his mouth. "I don't want to hear your fucking excuses."

Sterling's face jerked slightly to the side from the impact. He kept his gaze downward, working the pain I was sure throbbed on his jaw. Blood beaded at his lip, bright against his creamy flawless skin.

If Micah hadn't hit him, I would have. My fingers were balled together at my sides, nails digging into my palms.

Sterling spit a pool of blood at Micah's feet, his back still pressed into the bricks. "You shouldn't have done that."

Undercurrents of violence and tension built between them like a volcano about to erupt. "That's where you're wrong. I should have done it sooner," Micah snarled, nostrils flaring.

Sterling brought up a hand to block Micah's next hit, a crosscut, and a flash of something silver reflected off the bar lights hanging over the building.

Sterling's phone. Panic stampeded over my chest.

As if he sensed the trepidation racing inside me, Sterling glanced over Micah's shoulder to me.

"Don't fucking look at her," my boyfriend growled. Micah had never shown this magnitude of protectiveness, not for me, not for any girl, and I couldn't figure out what it was about Sterling that made him lose his cool. He had to know that Sterling and I slept together. Nothing else made sense to entice this lightning rage that zapped through his features.

He dodged Sterling's fist, and as it whizzed over his head, Micah delivered a blow to Sterling's ribs. Sterling grabbed the back of Micah's shirt, hurling him to the side and into the wall. He got one punch in before Micah planted his fist into Sterling's gut. And another. Sterling went low, bulldozing into Micah as he grabbed his waist, sending them both to the ground.

If Micah got hurt...

He couldn't. Football was important to him. Perhaps not as much as it meant to Fynn, who had the same goal for as long as I could remember to make the NFL, but still, for Micah it was a release, a way for him to unleash any aggravation or stress.

I rushed forward, not thinking.

"Grab her!" Brock's voice boomed, and seconds later, a pair of strong arms looped around my waist.

"I can't let you get hurt, Mads," Fynn said into my ear. "He'll have my ass if you get in the middle." The brute lifted me off the ground, and resistance became useless, like an uphill battle. I went still, letting him hold me, my eyes glued to the fight.

"Aren't you going to do anything?" I pleaded.

"When he's had enough," Grayson said. He stood to the left of Fynn, arms crossed over his chest, watching his friend pummel Sterling in rapid succession. While Fynn had detained me, Micah had pinned Sterling to the ground.

The area around the bar remained fairly quiet, onlookers gawking at the fight until three guys shoved through the crowd. I didn't know their names, but I could guess who they were. Sterling's frat bros. Word must have gotten out, and they came to defend their president, but they would have to get through the Elite first. The guys from Chi Sigma didn't stand a chance.

Before they could interfere, they rammed into a human wall. Fynn kept me tucked against his side.

Are they really going to have a brawl right here in the street?

One of the bar's bouncers came barreling out, assessing the situation. The crowd parted, but Micah and Sterling were oblivious to the security. "Break it up or I'm calling the cops!" the bouncer's voice exploded through the scene.

Sterling's boys continued to glare at the Elite. Brock cocked a brow, daring them. The Elite didn't give a shit about police being involved, but I imagined there were fraternity rules about fighting. Well, only if you got caught, and I doubted any of them were eager to have that strike on their record, but they also couldn't leave their president hanging.

The guy in the middle stared Brock down. "You're next," he promised.

Brock blew him a kiss before giving Grayson the signal, a slight tilt of his head.

Grayson pulled Micah off Sterling as one of the frat douchebags went to secure Sterling, who took a cheap shot at Micah, throwing a punch at his face the second Grayson tugged him away.

My cousin scowled, annoyance blazing in his eyes. While keeping a firm grip on Micah, Grayson kicked his foot to the side, striking Sterling in the back of the knee. The jerk's leg buckled, and he would have fallen back to the ground if his buddy hadn't been there to keep him upright.

Micah hurled a wad of spit at Sterling's face. "Stay away from her or you'll get more than a black eye and split lip. Do you hear me?"

Despite Sterling's swollen eye and bleeding lip, the bastard grinned. "It's not my fault my dick is better than yours." He yanked his friend off him, shoving his way through the crowd.

My mouth gaped open. *As if.* "Your dick isn't even the same playing field," I hurled after him, my chest moving rapidly. "It's tiny and weird," I added, as if that made it any better.

Did that actually leave my mouth? Color warmed my cheeks, realizing everyone in the vicinity had heard my proclamation. Nothing like drawing more attention to myself.

Not only would I be known as the girl who christened the fountain, a pillar monument for KU, but now I was also the girl who proclaimed Sterling, one of the most popular guys on campus, had a small dick.

The words really hadn't been about the size of his manhood, because truthfully, that shit mattered too little to me when it came to sex. I only sought to hurt Sterling. My words were more powerful than any punch I could have thrown, not that I didn't want the chance to hit him, because I did. And might the next time I saw him.

The bouncer shook his head, mumbling under his breath, "Fucking college kids." Then he proceeded to take his beefy self back into the bar.

Grayson released Micah now that Sterling left, his frat fucks right behind him. My boyfriend's eyes immediately found mine as he rubbed a finger across his lower lip, smearing a streak of blood. Fynn didn't try to stop me this time as I surged forward.

"Are you okay?" Micah asked, eyes like chips of ice boring into mine.

I nodded, a shiver tap-dancing up my spine.

A speck of relief surfaced in those cold blue eyes. He was still fuming, and for once, I couldn't tell if he was angry at me. This wasn't my fault... entirely. Did I play a part in it? Yes, a tiny, minuscule piece, but that was a mistake I made two years ago. Could I really be faulted for that now? The rest was all on the frat prick.

Micah was the one bleeding, yet his concern was for me. For those who didn't see this side of him, they wouldn't have thought it possible for the Elite playboy to be worried about anyone other than himself and his three best friends. Micah was damn good at projecting his image to the world. He knew his part, and he played it to perfection, often at the expense of others.

But I got to see who he truly was without the labels, the facades, and the expectations of others. He was the type of boyfriend who opened doors for me. He saw to my needs before his. He made sure I ordered first at a restaurant and that the servers set my food down before his. The list of little things he did without thinking scrolled endlessly.

And it would be one of those little gestures that cracked the last bit of shield protecting my heart from Micah Bradford. He had chipped it away, little by little, over the past few months.

Lifting my hand to get a close look at the cut, he jerked his head away from my fingers. Pain flared in his features, stabbing me in the chest. I had done nothing to feel guilty over, yet I was riddled with that horrid emotion.

This was such a mess, and I wanted to fix it. I had to tell Micah about the photos. It was the only way to prevent Sterling from using them to hurt him, but that meant *I* would hurt him. And knowing Micah, he would likely do more than beat the shit out of Sterling for threatening to use them, and for having taken them without my knowledge.

He held my gaze for another moment before brushing past me.

I whirled around, staring at his retreating back. "Micah, wait," I called after him, not wanting us to part like this. My heart couldn't take it.

He kept walking, taking a part of my splintered heart with him.

This wasn't happening.

Not to me.

Not when I had literally done nothing wrong, excluding

that enormous mistake of sleeping with Sterling two years ago. Never in a million years would I have thought an error in judgment would come back and bite me in the ass so fucking hard.

I started to go after him, needing to explain everything, but Grayson stopped me. "Give him some time to cool off."

"I didn't do anything. I swear," I said, desperately wanting, needing someone on my side.

"You don't have to tell me. I know you, Mads. And although it might not seem like it at the moment, Micah knows it too. He just has some shit to sort through."

"What shit?" I shrilled, my eyes imploring. If he had information, I wanted to know.

My cousin made an exasperated sound in his throat. "Just trust me, you need to stay away from him."

"I'm trying." A moment of silence stretched between us. I glanced down at my shoes, scuffing the toe over a pebble. "He has pictures of me, Grayson." I peeked up when he didn't say anything immediately.

Grayson's face had gone from concerned to scary. "What kind of pictures?"

A sense of foreboding built inside me. "The ones you don't want your boyfriend or your family to see."

He swore, forking a hand through his dark brown hair. "Seriously, Mads?" he reprimanded. "That's something I would expect from Kenna or Josie, but not you."

And why not? I wanted to argue—which was stupid, considering—but didn't get the chance.

"What would you expect from me?" Josie asked, appearing at Brock's side with Ainsley and Kenna.

Ainsley's gaze took in the disbanding crowd. "What the fuck did we miss?"

Kenna didn't even wait for me to respond. "We can't leave you alone for two minutes. Where the hell is Micah?" Her eyes bounced from Elite to Elite.

Grayson shook his head.

I wrapped my arms around myself, feeling small in this big world. "This is not my fault."

Josie stumbled slightly, struggling to keep her balance. "What isn't your fault?"

My hands went up into the air, full of animation, frustration, and sadness. "Everything."

"Will someone please tell me what I missed?" Kenna demanded, looking less drunk than Josie or Ainsley, though I wasn't sure how.

Fynn hooked an arm around Kenna's neck, bringing her in for a side hug that she resisted, only causing him to smile. And when Fynn Dupree genuinely smiled, it lit up the world. Not even the darkest of corners were safe from him. "Micah got into it with one of Mads's exes."

"She doesn't have any exes. I would know. You need to have a boyfriend first to have an ex," Kenna so dutifully explained, making me look even more pathetic than I felt.

"Kenna!" I snapped, glowering at her. "Could you just not?"

She lifted her hands in the air, taking a step back. "Whoa, someone is strung tighter than a girdle on a virgin."

I reached in my wristlet for another cigarette. It was either that or slap my best friend. "Good thing I'm not a virgin."

Josie giggled, falling into Brock, who secured her against his chest.

"Obviously," Grayson coughed under his breath.

I shot him a death glare, shoving the smoke between my lips. "Do you want to die tonight?"

He plucked the tobacco stick from my lips and snapped it in half. "I've seen enough violence for the night, thank you."

I dropped my head back and growled in frustration at the moon.

"Is Micah okay?" Josie inquired, looking up at Brock with sleepy eyes.

"Yeah, he'll be fine," Brock assured her, running his hands soothingly through her hair. "Nothing that won't heal."

"What about the other guy?" Ainsley slowly asked.

"Who gives a shit?" Grayson grumbled. "He was lucky it was only Micah he had to deal with and not the rest of us."

Four against one didn't seem like fair odds, and Ainsley thought so too. "You wouldn't," she appealed, narrowing mossy green eyes on Grayson.

"They would," Kenna replied.

She was right. They would have. And might still.

My head was starting to ache. I touched the throbbing spot at my temple. "I'm not letting you get kicked out of college or worse because of me. It's not happening. I'll handle this," I told him, but it was meant for the entire Elite.

Grayson tilted his head, considering my words. "Because you're doing such a bang-up job."

Gah! My cousin could drive me fucking crazy by just existing. Another sound of frustration left my lips. "God, don't be an ass."

The bastard grinned. "Too late."

I released a groan, doing my best to maintain my aggravation. "Fucker."

"That's right, girl. Let it out."

I turned my glower on Kenna.

"Look, I had my doubts before about this guy, but after tonight, I'm with Micah," Brock stated, drawing our eyes with his authoritative tone. "He's up to something, and until we figure out what his fucking endgame is here, we all need to be on the same page. I don't trust him, which means the four of you ladies need to be cautious. He's made it very clear that Micah is his target, and he means to use Mads to get to him. We just have to run a bit of interference until we figure out what it is he wants."

"To hurt Micah," I said.

Brock nodded. "Agreed. The question is why?"

"We mean to find out," Fynn stated, determination shining in his green eyes.

"And then he'll pay for messing with ours," Brock added grimly, that statement—no, the promise hanging between us.

CHAPTER TEN

MICAH

My clenched fingers slammed down on the counter, pain radiating up my arm, but my mind had gone numb to it. Anger still pulsed through my veins, taking over everything else. I couldn't see or feel anything past the fury. It rushed back in a sea of red, hearing Grayson tell me that Sterling has pictures on his phone and that he was using them against my girl.

Not fucking happening.

Perhaps using my fists hadn't been the most effective way to get answers from him, but it sure as shit felt fucking fantastic to lay into him. Now hearing this, I was ready for round two, and this time, I wouldn't go easy on him. He was about to get the full brunt of just how far a reach the Elite had.

His life was about to become miserable.

I blinked at Grayson, attempting to clear the film of red that had descended over my gaze. "He has what?" I stated, the lowness of my tone making the words a deadly whisper.

Grayson huffed, slouching in the chair. "I said he has photos of Mads on his phone."

"What kind of photos?" I demanded, thinking about the one he had hidden between the pages of a book in his room.

Brock sat across from me at the island counter in our kitchen where we ate most of our meals. "We didn't see them, but think *Playboy*."

"Are you—" I couldn't even finish the statement. A storm of fire raced through me, and I wanted to hit something again, but the counter wasn't going to cut it. I opened and closed my fingers to release the tension that had mounted from keeping them clenched for so long. It didn't help. "Why didn't she tell me?"

"You never gave her the chance," Fynn muttered.

True. I had walked off before I said regretful shit, not wanting her to be on the receiving end of the violence that continued to stir in me. I had pretty good control of my temper, but when I lost it, it was like a beast being freed from a cage. Wild. Untamed. Destructive. Unchained.

"He's so fucking dead," I rasped, brushing the pad of my thumb over the cut at the corner of my lip.

Grayson's head turned sharply in my direction. "I get you're upset, but none of this makes sense. It doesn't add up. My cousin wouldn't do that, not with a guy she barely knew, and she seemed genuinely confused about how he had them."

Brock drummed his fingertips over the wooden counter, a

frown pulling at his mouth. "I agree. Something is up. That girl has liked you far too long, which I'll never understand."

"Don't tell me we have another Carter on our hands. We just put that bastard behind bars," Grayson retorted.

The idea of Sterling being anything like Carter and doing what the prick had done to Kenna and Josie froze my heart for a split second.

Fynn scratched the underside of his chin. "I'm not sure. This feels like a personal attack on Micah. Mads is just a means to get to him."

"I'm thinking the same thing," Brock agreed.

I wrapped my fingers around the cold neck of a beer and brought the opening to my lips, downing half of it. "And that's what has me so fucking angry. Not at Mads. This asshole has me worked up, and it's the not knowing that's driving me crazy."

Brock's brows locked together, an expression he wore often. "We'll figure out his game."

Grayson glanced around the counter at each of us. "We always do."

Fynn held up his drink. "It's what we're good at."

The other three of us followed, clinking the tops of our beers together.

I didn't know what I would have done without these guys in my life. They'd saved me more times than I could count, had always been there when I needed them, even when I thought I didn't. Unlike Grayson or Fynn, I didn't grow up with a loving family, at least not the same kind of love they got from their parents. My father gave hard-ass a new name.

Tonight was supposed to be about getting drunk with the

guys and letting go after our first official week of college classes. Some days I doubted I would ever end up here. It had been drilled into my head from the time I was born that everything I'd been working for was to get me into Kingsley University. All Bradford men attended KU, and if it hadn't been for Mads and Brock, I would have flipped family tradition off in the face. I wanted to stick it to the old man. Instead, I shifted my fuck-you priorities, but even those weren't panning out. Like refusing to be a part of Chi Sigma, yet I was considering rushing.

Not that I stood much of a chance after tonight. Perhaps I never did. That would burn the old man's ass.

I didn't regret choosing KU. Mads could get me to do things I promised I'd never do.

It was as if the universe wanted me to walk in the old man's shoes, step by step. The harder I fought against it, the more parallel my life became with his.

Fuck no.

I refused to be like him. Not as a father. And certainly not as a husband. Those were two vows I'd made to myself that weren't negotiable. I would never budge on them. The other stuff like football, college, and a stupid fraternity mattered little in comparison to family.

"Has our guy come back with any information?" Brock asked.

I shook my head, taking another swig. "No, not yet." It had only been a few days, and as much as I would love to rush him, good dirt took time to unearth, and I wanted something to use against this bastard, something dirty enough to keep him far away from Mads. Sucking in a deep breath, I released it with a heavy sigh. "We need to get rid of those pictures."

"We will," Grayson said quietly, his eyes hard.

My fingers tightened around the beer bottle. "If he hurts her..." God only knew what the hell he planned to do with those photos.

"We know," Fynn assured me, holding my gaze.

And they did. I glanced around. They understood. They were in this with me. And we wouldn't stop until Sterling was no longer a problem.

Saturday was low-key. We didn't have much planned other than to recuperate from a night of drinking and hanging out. It was damn difficult to keep my mind from straying to the photos Sterling had of Mads. I wanted to see them, and at the same time, I didn't. What I should do was march into Chi Sigma and smash his phone repeatedly into the wall. It was either his phone or his face. The phone was less likely to get me expelled from school.

It was difficult to keep my thoughts from being dominated by Sterling and the anger that had yet to die down. I had to find other things to occupy my mind or go mad.

Maybe I should do something special for Mads, plan a date.

Having a group of friends that regularly hung out and then prepping for college, there hadn't been much time for us to be alone, something I figured we both currently needed.

A sort of reset from the rocky beginning of our college relationship. I wanted to give Mads the best possible four years.

These were memories we could reminisce over when we were fifty, sitting in front of the fireplace and preparing to send our first kid to college, because that was what I saw when I looked at her.

A future.

Our future.

Did it scare the shit out of me?

Fuck yes.

Everyone knew I wasn't husband material. It didn't matter that I was only eighteen. No one would have believed that I could ever be a one-woman guy. Those were the people who didn't really know me.

I built my playboy reputation to piss off my father, and it had served me well.

Until the day Mads decided to give me a second chance. That was the day I no longer gave a shit about the persona I'd crafted. Let them believe whatever the fuck they wanted about me, because I didn't want another girl. I only wanted Mads Clarke, and I would do whatever it took to make her Mads Bradford—to make her mine in every way possible.

The four of us decided to have breakfast with the girls, which would end up being brunch by the time we all managed to get up and ready. Rallying eight people was not an easy task, even when living together. In fact, I think that made it harder. Definitely true for the girls. Sharing one bathroom? No joke.

And that was how Mads ended up in my shower. Her text vibrated my phone on the counter as I towel-dried my hair, steam fogging the mirror. I glanced at the message.

Tell me you have hot water, she said.

Despite the shitty day yesterday had been, my lips twitched as I read the message, practically hearing the vexation of having three roommates come through. I could picture her sitting on her twin bed in the corner, fingers flying over the touchscreen on her phone.

Hot water, two bathrooms, and me. Take your pick, I sent back. I hadn't slept at all last night, only a few patches here and there as my mind whirled.

Her response came through almost immediately, short and sweet, kind of like the girl herself: **I'll be over in five.**

It turned out to be fifteen. I counted each minute, unsure if things would be weird between us after last night. We needed to talk. I needed to apologize for leaving like that, but I hadn't trusted myself, not when I'd been so enraged.

Memories of my father's fists and the fear in my mother's eyes during one of his rants had made me leave. I never wanted to be the cause of that brand of fear, not with her. I kept telling myself that I would never hurt Mads, that I had spent years being the exact opposite of my father, but in the back of my mind, doubts lingered.

And I fucking hated that my father put them there, that he made me feel like I could be anything less than a good man.

I'd never once brought Mads to my house, and I had no plans to bring her around that part of my life. No matter how much it might break my mother's heart, I couldn't let my father's abuse bleed into the only good thing in my life.

One of the other guys must have let her in, as I heard voices a moment before soft steps padded down the hall to my room.

From my bed, I glanced at the doorway, waiting for her to poke her head in.

A feeling of completeness filled my chest when I saw her face, every feature down to the freckle just below the corner of her right eye etched in my memory. I'd denied my feelings for her for so long that it was harder to embrace them than it was to shove them aside.

I was working on changing that, among other things.

In a way, every hurtful thing we'd hurled at each other over the last two years had really been little declarations of love in a fucked-up way—*our* fucked-up way, and I freaking loved that about us. She drove me crazy as much as she made me crazy.

Her smile reached her eyes, despite my sensing an uncertainty from her as she hovered in the doorway instead of bounding inside like usual. "Hey." Her soft voice felt like a breeze of spring air over my skin.

I showed her a dimple, knowing how much she "hated" them because they made her knees weak. "Hey."

The awkwardness only lasted a few more moments. She started to relax, leaning her shoulder against the doorframe as she dropped an oversized bag on my floor. It landed with a thump. She took in my damp hair, the dewiness that lingered in the air from the bathroom. "You better not be lying."

I raised a brow. "About?"

"The hot water," she stated.

A silent chuckle shook my chest. She had a way of humoring me without trying. Folding my hands behind my head, I stayed stretched out on the bed. "Did you decide?"

An adorable look of confusion descended over her features. "Decide what?"

"Which one you want?"

Her eyes glinted as she recalled our text messages. "Doesn't the hot water come with the bathroom?"

It took everything in me not to climb out of bed and go to her. Or better yet, tug her into the bed with me. I needed to feel her against me. "Then the only reasonable answer is all three."

"Funny," she said, averting her gaze from mine. She picked up her bag and slipped into the joined bathroom. "I only need like fifteen minutes," she said, closing the door behind her.

I lay on the bed, staring at the door, listening as the water turned on a few moments after she disappeared. It took no time at all for my mind to start thinking of inappropriate shit. Like the fact that she'd undressed in the next room, only a thin slab of wood separating us. For the next sixty seconds, I pictured Mads standing in my shower, rubbing soap all over her body, and I became instantly hard.

"Fuck me," I muttered, tapping my fingers against the mattress. I should stay right here and wait for her. I had no business interrupting her shower, except... My mind was already coming up with excuses, like how there was unresolved business between us. Somehow my warped brain convinced itself that now would be a good time to squash any unsettling feelings either of us might have when, really, I just wanted to see her naked.

I was a guy.

When didn't I want to see my girl naked?

The door was unlocked when I turned the knob, the patter

of the shower masking any noise it might have made as I carefully pushed it open. Her clothes were scattered on the floor, including a white lacy bra.

Dear God. She knew I had a weakness for white lingerie. Angelic and hot. How could you go wrong?

The shadow of her form, outlined against the frosted blocks, only added to the illusion of sexiness. She faced the showerhead, her chin raised as water rained over her body. For a few breathless seconds, I stared, watching as she lifted her hands, running her fingers through her hair.

My dick throbbed.

I moved soundlessly to the opening at the corner of the shower and stepped in. I didn't bother to undress and didn't give a damn that I had just showered myself. A body could never be too clean.

Mads turned around as I planted my bare feet on the wet tile floor. Her eyes were closed, still unaware of my presence. A smile curved at my lips, deflected drops of water spattering onto me. I gazed upon her face, taking in the high cheekbones flushed from the heat, the perfect cupid's bow on the top of her pink lips, and the slim arch of her nose. I couldn't help but wonder how the fuck I'd gotten so lucky.

Why did she pick me of all the guys in the world?

I'd never know what she saw in me. I could joke all day about my charm, wit, and good looks, but when you peeled away all the charisma and allure, what was left? A broken and tortured guy who had a long way to go to get his shit together.

Those long lashes, beaded with drops of water, finally batted open. Her eyes widened in surprise, and she let out a little squeal, splashing a spray of water in my face. "Christ, Micah," she swore a second before she slapped me on the chest. "You scared the shit out of me. I could have fallen and broken my neck."

I trapped her hand against my chest, partly to steady her but mostly because I needed to touch her. "I would have caught you."

She rolled her eyes. "What are you doing in here? And you're fully dressed," she said, gaze raking over me.

I gave her a lopsided grin. "I could remedy that."

"You being in the shower or being fully dressed?" she asked.

Mads and I always fell into this playful banter. Even when she couldn't stand me, we couldn't help but drop into old patterns. "I'll let you take your pick."

She shook her head, soaked strands of hair falling over her breasts and partially concealing them from view. "You're going to make us late."

I reached out, parting the hair to expose her nipples. We were always fashionably late. Why change our ability to never arrive on time? It was expected at this point.

"We should talk," I stated, my smile slipping a notch.

"Okay," she agreed, looking up at me with those big gray eyes that did me in every time.

Don't look down. Keep your eyes locked on her face. Nothing below the neck. Don't do it. Don't you think about—

My eyes took a stroll down the length of Mads's glorious body, ignoring the warnings in my head. How could I not look at the most beautiful female I'd ever laid eyes on? I'd seen her naked dozens of times, the first being when we had sex two years ago, and then I promptly screwed it up.

She constantly took my breath away.

I had every intention of just talking, but then Mads went and licked her lips, a smokiness I recognized in her eyes. A groan of desire started to work its way up my throat, and I only had one thought in my head.

Kiss her.

I had to. *Just one taste*, my inner devil reasoned, shoving the angel who had warned me before out of my mind. The devil had always been louder within me. That bastard always won.

Now was no different.

"I have to get this out of the way first," I said huskily.

She blinked. "What?"

"This." My hands swooped in to cradle her face as my mouth collided against hers. A gasp of surprise parted her lips, and my tongue swooped in, wild for a taste of her. When her tongue brushed against mine, I groaned, stepping closer to her and deeper under the shower.

I had been so fucking hard before I stepped into the shower. Now I pulsed with need.

The kiss wasn't gentle or tame. Our kisses rarely were. The first touch ignited a fire that consumed us both. Passion had never been our problem. I wasn't sure we would ever get enough of each other.

Craving all of her, I shifted us to the side, pressing her back into the tiles. I put my hand behind her head to keep it from thumping against the hard surface. Our lips never parted. I angled my head to deepen the kiss as impatient fingers went under my shirt. She ran her nails over my stomach, shoving at the material and hiking it farther up my chest.

"This has to go," she murmured, breaking the kiss.

I groaned at the loss of her lips, helping her tug the heavy, drenched shirt over my head. "And the pants."

Her eyes had darkened, turning them to more of a charcoal gray than the usual starlight color. "Those too. It all has to go. Now." But she didn't wait for me to strip, her lips attaching to my lobe before cruising down behind my ear, then down my neck. Teeth and tongue. Kisses and licks. She cupped me through my soaked sweatpants, squeezing the hard length of my desire.

"Are you trying to kill me?" I groaned.

"You know how much I love to make your life torturous." Her fingers edged into the waistband of my sweatpants and paused.

"Don't stop," I growled.

With a wily grin, she jerked them down over my hips. "I thought we were talking." She looked up like a damn temptress.

I kicked the sweatpants the rest of the way off. "We will. After," I said, shoving my hand into her hair and bringing her mouth to mine again. But kissing alone soon became not enough for either of us.

I moved my lips down to nuzzle her throat. She tilted her head back, the column of her throat pressing into my mouth as I sucked, nipped, and savored every exposed inch. When I grazed the rim of her ear with my teeth, she arched her back into me, taut nipples rubbing into my chest.

Fuck, I want them in my mouth.

What's stopping you? the devil in my head purred.

What indeed?

Taking my time, I moved to her shoulder and then to her chest. I licked a drop of water from her nipple, and her entire body shuddered, nails digging firmer into my back. I swirled my tongue over the nub, teasing and grazing it with my teeth, a fine line between bliss and pain.

She moaned, her hips rubbing against my leg nestled between hers.

I clamped my teeth against her nipple, sucking and still stroking with my tongue. Moving my mouth from one breast to the other, I lavished the nipple just as lovingly.

After I had my fill, I shifted to the flat of her stomach, going lower and lower still. Her fingers fisted in my wet hair, and as the water drizzled down her body, I ran my tongue over the center of her womanhood.

She swayed. "Fuck." The word came out as a whisper that could have been a curse or a prayer.

I brought my hands to her hips, a steady anchor because we were just getting started. My tongue moved faster, deeper, flicking over her clit. She was close to the edge, her muscles tightening.

Eyes screwed shut, her head fell back against the wet tile wall. "Micah," she panted.

My heart skipped, every cell in my body wide awake and pulsing. "Say it again."

"Micah, I can't," she whimpered.

I was almost blind with need, my mind full and scrambled with Mads. "Don't ask me to stop."

The fingers in my hair gripped harder. "I was most definitely not asking you to stop. I might kill you if you did."

"Just hold on to me." Her knees quivered, along with another part of her. "I want to feel you come on my mouth," I moaned against her.

She came undone seconds later, the center of her body trembling as she rode the orgasm until the last flutter.

The water drizzling over my back had cooled yet remained warm. I stood, shaking my wet hair off my face as I smoothed it back with my fingers, but before I could catch my breath, Mads's fingers wrapped around me.

"My turn," she purred, moving her hand up and down.

I opened my mouth to tell her she owed me nothing. This wasn't a give-and-take relationship. Sometimes I just wanted to give and give and give. But the moment her soft, tentative fingers firmed on the length of my cock, the only thing that came out of me was a moan.

I rested my forehead on hers. "Christ, Mads."

It only took a few strokes of her fingers to send me over the edge, my seed spilling into her hand and washing quickly away in the shower. I'd been that turned on, making me feel like a fifteen-year-old virgin.

I took a step back, gazing at her face. Euphoria stuffed into every pore in my body. "We should probably get you clean," I said, smirking.

The smile that started on her lips faded as her eyes roamed over me. I knew what she saw. I'd seen it in the mirror this morning after waking up. Her finger grazed over my lip before moving to my cheek, where another small cut marred my skin thanks to the ring Sterling wore on his middle finger. "Do they hurt?"

"I'm fine," I insisted, not wanting her to worry about me. I really was okay. As someone who fought like it was a hobby, the dull throbs on different parts of my body were familiar. I'd cracked more than a few ribs and broke a bone or two. It really wasn't that far off from being hit on the football field play after play.

She gave me her don't-bullshit-me frown.

"He only got a few jabs in. They'll heal. I promise. Besides..." I ran my hands down her smooth arms, flushing her ample body to mine. "I thought we agreed to talk after we showered."

She looped her arms around my neck. "Is that what we're doing? Showering?"

Grabbing my shampoo bottle from behind her on the shower rack, I squeezed a glob into my hand. "We are now."

She stayed still as I scrubbed the shampoo into a sudsy lather on her long hair. "I don't like seeing the cuts on your face or the bruises on your body."

"Are you sure?" My brows rose and my mouth curved. "Because I was under the impression that girls are into guys who are rough and rugged. You know, the street fighter type."

She took over, digging her nails deeper into her scalp. "I don't know about other girls, but this one likes it when you're not bleeding everywhere."

Fully scrubbed, I squeegeed the bulk of the bubbles down the ends of her hair. "But the tattoos you like?"

She bit down on her lip to keep the smile from blooming.

"This isn't a joke, but yes, I like the tattoos a hell of a lot more." She tilted her head back under the water, rinsing out the shampoo.

My mood sobered, the reminder of last night snuffing out the lingering orgasm high.

She dropped her head down, staring into my eyes, and noticed the sudden shift in my expression, an unspoken question forming in her gaze.

"I'm sorry," I whispered, casting my eyes down to her nose. I didn't want to see her reaction. "I shouldn't have left you like that." I felt her finger trace the edge of my lips, drawing my focus up. "I won't do it again."

She angled her head to the side. "You were right. It turns out I needed you more than the hot water or the bathroom." A soft smile played on her mouth. We always did this, deflecting, and it was her way of telling me that she understood.

Reaching for the hand hanging at her side, I interwove our fingers. "I could have told you that."

CHAPTER ELEVEN

MADS

The shower didn't take much time after that. Not with two sets of hands doing the work. Micah soaped up my body, which he might have enjoyed too much, while I conditioned my hair. I sat on his bed, fully dressed while I dried my hair with one of his old T-shirts.

"You know about the photos," I said, starting the overdue conversation.

He nodded, tugging on a light blue shirt that matched his eyes. "The ones on his phone. Yeah, the guys filled me in last night." The tone of his voice roughened a fraction, enough that I noticed, but someone who didn't know Micah wouldn't have. Sterling rubbed him the wrong way, that became very clear.

Bunching the shirt against the ends of my hair, I dropped the damp material into my lap. "I didn't know he had them. And honestly, I'm convinced he photoshopped them." The more I thought about it throughout the night, the surer I became, because frankly, the alternative scared the living fuck out of me. Imagining him sneaking into my room and snapping pictures of me while I slept just creeped me the hell out. He wouldn't have done that. Right? Who in their right mind would?

I needed another look. I'd been so distraught by the images that I hadn't paid attention to details like the room, the bed, the background. Those could easily prove they'd been altered.

But if they were of *my room*, the idea of him being there without my knowledge, watching me, invading my privacy, and taking advantage of me, felt almost like a form of assault. Definitely stalking.

Suggesting that I needed to see the photos again on Sterling's phone to Micah would not go over well. He would tell me it was bad. Dangerous. And maybe he had a point, but still, even if they weren't real, I had to get rid of them. It was the only way I could stop Sterling from exposing them. Once something got uploaded to the Internet, it never went away. The idea of my parents accidentally seeing or being sent those photos of me?

I would die.

"He wants something from you, but he wouldn't tell me what," I admitted. "I got the impression that he means to hurt you, Micah." I'd replayed the conversations I'd had with Sterling a thousand times in my head, looking for details I might have missed. How the fuck did a one-night stand turn into blackmail? Two years later?

It didn't make sense.

Micah flashed me a roguish grin. "Are you worried for me, Mads?"

Tossing the shirt onto the ground, I frowned at him. "I'm serious. I get that you think you're like fucking Superman. Invincible, bulletproof, and all that shit with your friends at your side, but newsflash, no matter how tough you are or who your friends are, you're still human."

He came to sit on the edge of the bed beside me, kicking the damp towel out of the way. "It was one fight. That I provoked."

"But it won't be the last. I can see it in your eyes. You're not done with him yet."

He didn't bat an eyelid. "No. Not by a long shot."

I narrowed my eyes. "What are you hiding?"

"I will always protect you." Determination and cockiness coated more than just his voice. His body was lined with it, the muscles in his shoulders firming.

I plucked at a string from my distressed jean shorts. "So what do we do now?"

His lips pressed into a flat line. "*We* do nothing. *I'll* take care of him. The photos too."

Suspicion knotted in my stomach. "What do you mean by 'take care of'?" Regardless that I had known the Elite nearly my entire life, I still didn't know about half the crap they pulled. Probably didn't want to.

"It's better you don't know," he retorted, mimicking my thoughts.

"Micah." I grimaced. "You're not talking about..." I made a slicing motion across my throat.

I could tell he didn't mean to smile because he tried to cover it up and failed. Then he gave up entirely and chuckled, shaking his head. "Is that what you think we do? Off people? We're not the mafia."

Shaking out my damp hair, I cursed myself for not remembering a hairdryer. "Close enough in my world," I muttered.

Leaning back on his hands, he eyed me. "Doesn't Grayson tell you anything?"

"No more than you do, and it's frustrating as shit."

Micah flicked the end of my nose with his index finger. "Good."

Sighing, I asked, "What should *I* do, then?" I couldn't just sit around and pretend like life on campus was normal, waiting for Sterling to make his next move. I'd go nuts.

The muscle along his jaw tightened. "Nothing. Just avoid him as much as possible. And don't get worked up," he added as if I could flip it off like a switch.

I snorted. "You realize what you're asking from me is unreasonable. I'm already worked up."

His lazy smile washed over me, my heart fluttering at the dimples. "You're cute when you're flustered."

He would regret those words. Lunging at him, I hooked an arm around his neck and used my body weight to tumble us backward onto the bed. Resting half on top of him, I glowered down at him. "Cute isn't going to make Sterling leave me alone."

Gentle fingers brushed at the strands of hair curtaining around my face, all traces of humor gone from his eyes. "No. You need to be the exact opposite of cute around him."

* * *

Monday morning, Josie and I had Econ together, a class neither of us was looking forward to. I get we had to take general education courses, but economics? Who in their right mind actually liked this stuff?

I was sure there were a few weirdos out there who did. That was what made us unique as individuals, but if Josie and I had it our way, we'd be sitting in Pottery or Film 101, a class with more color and less drabness.

We stopped and grabbed an afternoon coffee before heading to the business building. The iced Americano cooled my hands, beads of water dampening the cup from the afternoon sun that beat down over our heads.

Josie sipped her drink. "You feeling better?"

The rest of our weekend had gone by without a Sterling sighting, and I should have been relieved instead of stressed out. What surprised me the most was how much I didn't want Grayson and Fynn to leave. Having the four of them here made me feel safer, and now that the Elite had split in half again, I felt weaker somehow.

I swirled the ice in my cup. "Truthfully, I don't know how I feel. I'm all jumbled up inside."

"Confused about Sterling or Micah?" she asked, the wind picking up pieces of her pink hair.

I chewed at the end of my paper straw—the college had implemented a no-plastic movement a few years ago. "Both. But mostly Sterling. I can't make sense of it. And Micah always makes my head spin."

Josie frowned as she toyed with her straw, stirring around the ice that floated on top of her coffee. "It's creepy enough that he has nudes of you on his phone, but to also have pictures of you stashed secretly in his room is next-level disturbing."

My gut clenched, and the clear cup slipped an inch in my hand. I barely managed to keep from dropping it. "He has what?"

Her gaze flew to mine, and the change in her expression said it all. *Oh shit.* "I thought you knew."

The pit in my stomach hardened. "Knew what, Josie?"

Her dark brows bunched together. "This is why we can't have secrets. Brock told me that the night of Chi Sigma's first party of the year, they went snooping around in Sterling's room."

I shook my head. "Of course they did."

She huddled in closer to me as we walked, our shoulders brushing, and kept her voice lowered as she revealed, "Micah found a picture of you hidden in a book."

I grabbed Josie's arm, which happened to be the one she held her drink in, and the melting ice sloshed in the cup. "I'm trying to stay calm, but this crap is starting to make me paranoid."

Her eyes found mine, a cloud of disbelief darkening her chocolate eyes. "At first I thought he might have a crush on you or that the picture was some weird souvenir or something, like guys who steal girls' panties."

It was clear my friend needed to lay off the true crime shows, something I always found strange considering she'd actually lived one of those episodes. "And now?" I prompted, my brain still processing how unusual her thought process was.

She took a sip of her drink, the corners of her lips turning up as she sucked. "I think the bastard needs to go down."

My eyes widened, amusement tickling my mouth. "Whoa, Josie. Dial back the badass. That's supposed to be my title."

Rolling her eyes, she ducked under a branch hanging in our path as we cut through the courtyard. "I swear you and Micah are made for each other."

"Thank you, I think," I replied as we approached building D3, not far from the common hall library. Josie, knowing my need to get a nicotine fix before class, sat down at an empty bench under a large dogwood tree no longer in bloom. I took a seat as well, leaving enough space between us that she wouldn't be clouded with cigarette smoke, and set my coffee on the grass. "I can't believe I slept with him." Pulling a pack from my bag, I took a slim stick out and stuck it between my lips before reaching for my lighter.

"I had the same feeling about Brock, and look how that turned out."

I flicked my lighter and lit the end. "If you're suggesting that Sterling is my endgame, I'll take you out right here in front of the business building," I threatened.

She laughed. Josie had one of those laughs that was naturally sexy and girly at the same time. It only made her cuter. "God, no. I was only saying that you're not the only girl to have those kinds of feelings about a guy she's slept with."

I exhaled smoke from my lungs, watching it drift into the air. "What does that say about us as females?"

Josie crossed her legs and leaned into the wooden planks at

our back. "That we're human and we make mistakes, and those mistakes make the best learning lessons."

Smoking usually calmed me to some degree. Not today. "So you're saying we're also attending the school of hard knocks. Good times."

"This probably isn't any consolation, but Micah only wanted to protect you. I'm sure he didn't want to worry you if the picture he found turned out to be nothing."

Letting out a long sigh, I took another drag. "But it isn't nothing, is it?" When she didn't reply, I continued to speak my thoughts out loud. "I just wish Sterling would tell me what it is he wants from me. Other than to torment me, that is." It felt good to unload.

She eyed me, a corner of her mouth sinking. "Micah will figure it out."

"That's what I'm afraid of." I checked the time on my phone. We had about five minutes until class started.

"It's not easy dating an Elite."

This I already knew. Had told her the same thing last year when I warned her about the Elite, and yet despite knowing the difficulties that followed the four of them around, I still chose to start a relationship with Micah. One thing was for certain... "There are too many fucking secrets floating around in this group. We need to get together and... I don't know... share notes. Brainstorm. Have a bitch session."

A glimmer of intrigue sparked in the center of Josie's eyes. "The guys will never go for that," she said, shooting me down.

"You're right, but that doesn't mean *we* can't. The Elite have their inner circle. Who says we can't have ours? You never know, maybe we'll uncover shit the guys missed."

As a girl who should have majored in criminal law instead of child and adolescent psychology—which, considering her background, made total sense—I would have thought the idea of a little detective work would pique her interest. "You're not talking about using yourself as bait, are you?" she asked, disapproval lacing her tone.

"Maybe," I admitted, staring at the bright, burning end of my cigarette. "The only thing I am certain of is I'm not willing to just wait around until Sterling decides to hurt Micah. And after what Micah did on Friday night, Sterling might be interested in a little revenge."

"From personal experience, that's usually how this shit pans out." She thought over it for another few moments. "Let's do it. We'll get Kenna and Ainsley on board. Those two are always down for trouble and formulating some ideas."

My expression filled with gratitude. "I don't know what I would do without you."

"You'll never have to find out. We're family, and you're kind of stuck with me." Her shoulder lightly bumped mine. "I would hug you, but you smell like an ashtray."

"You're the worst." I laughed. "We should probably go in." I took one last inhale of my smoke before putting it out in the dirt and tossing it into the trash when we walked into class.

"If we do this, that means you'll have to see Sterling," she said as we rounded the doorway into the classroom already half full of our peers—a bunch of eager beavers. There was punctual, which I loved being, and then there was exuberant. I preferred to show up in that window of not too early but not too late.

"I know." A tiny shudder rolled through me. How the fuck had I ever been attracted to him? Even for a split second? I suppressed another shudder that threatened to make its way down my spine.

"And Micah?" she asked with an undertone that I didn't want to unravel.

"I'll handle him," I replied softly, taking a seat in the back of the room. "Besides, he's also keeping shit from me."

"When aren't they?" Josie muttered, unearthing her laptop as the instructor walked in.

When aren't they indeed?

CHAPTER TWELVE

MICAH

"This just keeps getting fucking more interesting," Brock said as if I already didn't know the Sterling situation was quickly tumbling out of control. That only meant it was my turn to take the reins.

So far Sterling had been calling all the shots while I played catch-up, trying to uncover his intentions. I still might not know what the fucker's agenda was, but that didn't mean I couldn't dominate the game.

I stared at the matte black envelope Brock had handed me. *What the fuck is he up to?* This felt like bait, and I didn't care that my name was Bradford. Despite my forefathers all being a part of Chi Sigma, I didn't believe with Sterling as current president that my name would have given me a free pass.

However, perhaps I could use this little ticket to my advantage. That had been my play from the beginning, but I assumed after I rearranged his face last weekend that rushing for Chi Sigma had been removed from the table.

Apparently not.

Weren't fraternities just concealed secret societies? Or a guise for asshole bullies who were one dead animal away from being serial killers in the making? There was something about the whole eternal brotherhood that I found disturbing. Not like what I had with Brock, Fynn, and Grayson. Our bond went deeper than parties, drunk nights, and being jackasses.

No one was more surprised when I got the invitation to rush Chi Sigma than me. Not even Brock appeared stunned by the letter, nor the identical one with his name scribbled on it.

"No shit," I groused, the letter in my fingers crinkling.

Brock tapped the envelope against his palm. "You have to admit, this guy has balls."

A growl rumbled in the back of my throat. "Which is exactly why I don't want him tangled up with Mads. He's made this personal." I tore open the envelope and slipped out the printed card. Only a date, time, place, and password were typed on the invitation.

August 29^(th)
Midnight
Ash Woods
PASSWORD: *Manwhore*

I read over the text again, fighting the urge to ball the shit up and burn it over our stove.

Brock glanced over my shoulder. "Manwhore, huh?" He

chuckled, shaking his head. "Fuckers. Why do I get the feeling that the passwords are actually frat-given nicknames?"

Reaching behind me, I plucked the letter from Brock's fingers. "What the hell does yours say?" My eyes went straight to the bottom of the card. *Midas*. "Midas," I repeated aloud after saying it in my head and glancing up. "You're shitting me. As in you have the Midas touch?"

Brock grinned. "Maybe they aren't as bad as we think?"

I socked him in the shoulder, my lips twitching despite trying to keep a straight face. "Get the fuck out of here. It's obvious they don't know jack about football."

He threw his head back and laughed. "Relax. They just want something from me. I'm intrigued to find out what that is." He clapped me on the back.

"It's either your dick or your money," I muttered, tossing the stupid invitation on the kitchen counter.

"I think based on our passwords, it's *your* dick they want." He couldn't pass up the opportunity to razz me as the smirk on his lips lingered.

Sauntering into the living area, I sank into the couch, kicking my feet up on the coffee table. "Mads might have something to say about that."

Brock snorted a sarcastic snicker. "All jokes aside, I'd feel better if we had someone tailing the girls." The other side of the couch groaned as he folded himself into the cushions.

"Mads and Kenna would spot them so quickly, and I'm pretty sure Josie's caught on to your tricks. They'll find a way to dodge him. They always do," I shot down the suggestion.

"And they always end up in trouble," he pointed out.

"So true," I grunted in agreement.

"Fine," Brock huffed, crossing his arms. "At the very least, one of us should keep an eye on them."

"This was easier when there were four of us, or when there weren't girls involved. Damn, they make life more complicated."

Brock chuckled. "No shit. But the sex is worth it."

I rolled my eyes. Sex was not the reason Brock was with Josie. He could get ass any time he wanted with a push of a button on his phone. The difference was having sex with someone you loved. I was just starting to realize that myself. I had plenty of opportunities, but none of them interested me. Not the way Mads did.

It took me two years to figure that out and endless meaning-less lays.

He twisted the watch on his wrist, checking the time. "Should we call in Gray and Fynn?"

I shook my head, glaring out the big picture window that overlooked the field. Patters of evening rain hit the glass and watered the dry grass. "Not yet." With this just being the start of the semester, they had plenty on their plates between classes and football practice. The first game of the year was coming up in two weeks.

His arms dropped down to the couch as he glanced sidelong over at me. "What do you want to do?" he asked, tossing the ball into my court.

He was letting me call the shots, something he normally took on himself. My mouth tightened as I thought about the numerous ways I wanted to destroy Sterling Weston. It wasn't just that he had intimate pictures of my girlfriend but how he was using them to manipulate her. "Did you call Fynn?"

Brock nodded. "He's working on it. I'll call him tonight, see if he can rush it along," he said, fishing his phone from his back pocket. "See if he can get access tonight and wipe it by tomorrow."

It was a start. "Good. I want those photos gone." My voice was dry and harsh, not bothering to conceal my resentment. If we took away his leverage, then perhaps he would stop using my girl and come straight for me.

Brock typed out a message as he replied, "He'll take care of Sterling's phone and computer. I also asked him to check into the other guys as well. I figured it couldn't hurt just in case this is a frat thing and not just a personal vendetta."

"Good thinking."

"It'll take him a few days to get through those." Brock had gotten a list of every member currently living at Chi Sigma. His gaze lifted from his phone. "What about any hard copies he has stashed?"

"I'll take care of those myself," I said with a tight smile. "I want another poke around the place."

His gaze flattened. "You thinking August 29 at midnight?"

I gave him a lopsided grin, appreciating that Brock knew how my mind worked. "I mean, it's fitting. He did give us an invite to rush."

"What if he finds it suspicious when we don't show?" he countered. It was what he did best, pulling apart ideas, looking for plot holes and unexpected errors. One small mistake or oversight could get us caught.

"That's why you're going."

I anticipated Brock's scowl, as well as the rebuttal I knew was coming. "I don't like it. You going into that house alone."

"I need you to keep Sterling and his cult buddies busy," I said. "Keep an eye on them. With just the two of us, it's the best idea we have."

He couldn't argue with that. "Grayson and Fynn are only two hours away. We might need to bring them down for this."

"It's too close to the first game. Fynn needs to keep his head on football, not what's happening here," I argued, serious for once in my fucking life. I didn't want anything getting in the way of Fynn's chance at the pros.

Brock dropped his head back onto the couch. "God, I hate it when you're reasonable."

My lips twitched. "I know. It feels wrong, doesn't it?"

The week flew by without a single sighting of Sterling. His silence made me edgy, and for good reason. Although he didn't show his face, which I had been looking forward to admiring my handiwork on, the prick had no problem tormenting me. The first photo arrived Thursday night right before I was about to drop off to sleep. It came from an anonymous number. Most weekdays Mads stayed in her dorm, but on the weekends, she was mine.

Had he deliberately sent these knowing she wouldn't be here? That I would wonder if she was safe in her room? If Sterling was creeping outside her dorm, staring at the light in her window? If he was lurking outside her door?

In the utter dark, I hurled my phone across the room, hearing it smash against the wall and shatter to the floor.

"Fuck," I whispered, realizing moments later that if Mads needed me tonight, she had no way to get a hold of me.

Sleep was pointless. No way would I be able to relax my mind enough to drift off, not without all these crazy scenarios running wild in my head.

Well past one in the morning, I tossed the covers aside and rolled out of bed. My intuition urged me to take a late-night jog to clear my head and perhaps cruise by the girls' dorm. It couldn't hurt and might just let me get a few hours of sleep that were left in this night.

Throwing on a pair of jogger shorts and a white T-shirt, I turned back toward the bed to grab my phone. "Shit," I cursed, remembering it was fucking toast. I made a mental note to buy a new phone as well as an Apple watch in the morning—I needed a secondary mode of communication, and I had a feeling midnight runs could be a nightly ritual in my future. At least on the days Mads didn't stay with me.

As quietly as my size thirteen shoes allowed, I slipped out of the house. A nearly full moon shone in the dark sky littered with millions of stars. They were perfectly visible in the cloud-less sky. Air still as a statue cooled the campus, a welcomed contrast to the warm days of summer that clung on. By the end of September, we would start to feel the shift into fall, my favorite season.

With the porch light glowing at my back, I kicked off down

the pathway, following the trees that lined the streets, and headed toward the dorms. An owl hooted above my head, hidden in one of the oversized maple trees as I trotted by, the only other sound beside my shoes hitting the pavement.

No matter how fast or how far I seemed to run, the image of Mads lying tangled in the sheets while some other guy snapped pictures burned behind my eyes. The fact that I had a face and name to put to that guy only made the flames licking my veins grow hotter. The jog was supposed to cool the fire, but the rage only built.

The campus was a graveyard, not a single soul about as I weaved through the buildings to the other side of the grounds. Damp blades of grass clung to the edges of my shoes, and the scent of something sweet like maple syrup perfumed the trees as I ran past.

By the time I got to the dorms, my sprints had turned into an all-out run. Panting, I slowed down as I approached the building, scanning the shadows for movement. Maybe I was looking for another chance to kick Sterling's ass, but it didn't appear I would get the opportunity tonight.

Doing a lap around the building, I stopped under a tree and glanced up to the fourth-story window—Mads's window. No lights were on, but I continued to stare, looking for shadows that weren't there. I should have been relieved. The pressure in my chest should have lightened. Neither happened.

Sterling's goal had been to rattle me.

And I let the asshole win. He had succeeded in doing just that, unnerving me to the point that I felt as if I were going to lose it.

The idea of sinking down the side of the tree trunk and camping out in front of her dorm occurred to me, but I quickly shut it down in the next thought. There was protective and then there was crazy.

Turning to leave, I took one last glance over my shoulder when something from the cluster of trees across the courtyard caught the edge of my eyes. I flattened against the trunk and watched as the shadow moved. A flash of moonlight cut through the leaves, hitting the figure for a split second. It was enough to confirm I wasn't alone.

The black hoodie they wore cloaked their face, but judging by the stature of the figure, they were small, like female small, ruling out Sterling.

Who the fuck else could be snooping around at this hour?

Only one way to find out.

They looked left and right before coming out from the flock of trees, and once I saw their back, that was when I made my move, coming up swiftly behind them. The grass cushioned my steps as I moved, and when I was close enough, I reached out, grabbing a hold of their forearm.

I spun them around. My eyes went wide as recognition swept through me, not expecting to see this face hidden underneath the hood. Brows bunched together, I scowled at the startled expression that turned to annoyance faster than I could chug a beer. "What the fuck are you doing out here at this time of night?" I demanded, still holding them by the arm.

She tilted her head back, and Kenna's lips unfurled into a tight smile. "I could ask you the same thing."

I grimaced. "I'm running. Now answer me before I call your

brother." She didn't need to know that I had no way of actually doing that. I could always steal her phone to make the call. Regardless, the threat did the deed.

"I snuck out," she snapped, jerking her arm out of my grasp.

Of all the people I imagined could be slinking around campus in the middle of the night, Kenna never crossed my mind. "Why?" I pressed, glaring down at her with hard eyes. For once, I had no flippant comments, my voice still sharp.

Shrugging, she replied, "Old habits die hard."

I knew all about old habits. And I knew Kenna. My eyes went to the bag slung over her shoulder and then shifted to her fingers, drawing conclusions. It was impossible to see if she had paint on and around her nails. "Are you tagging again?" Before she could respond, I snatched the bag, hearing a familiar jingle and clang of metal. "Kenna," I growled.

Long lashes fluttered at me. "The dad vibe doesn't suit you."

I didn't need to open her bag to know there were paint cans stashed inside. When things got tough or out of her control, Kenna's outlet was to spray-paint shit. "Who are you pissed off at now?"

Her small hands reached to take her shit back. "For your information, I'm actually doing you a solid."

"Is that so?" I asked, lifting a brow as she grabbed her belongings. The pea-size metal balls rolled around in the cans, jostled by her movements.

She held my eyes. "I'll take your thank-you now."

I huffed, crossing my arms. "I'm still waiting for you to tell me what kind of trouble you created tonight, and if it's something Brock and I are going to have to cover up."

The cockiness in her features made me nervous. Basically any time the girls got an idea, it fucking made me nervous. "Please, this isn't my first rodeo. I know what I'm doing," she said smugly, sounding a bit too much like me.

"The suspense is killing me," I retorted dryly.

She rolled her mischievous eyes that looked so much like Josie's and Grayson's it was eerie. There was something weird about seeing your best friend in girl form. Some days the three of them couldn't be more different, and then other days, it was like I was seeing triple. "Chi Sigma house," she said proudly.

My heart dropped. "You didn't."

Her dark ponytail bounced as she nodded.

"Fucking hell, Kenna. Do you know how reckless it was for you to go there by yourself?" In my current mood, I was close to shaking some sense into her. She was like a fucking sister to me.

Fury flickered in the centers of her eyes. "He needs to know that he fucked with the wrong girl."

"And you don't think my fist smashing into his face was a clear message?" I commended her for wanting to protect her cousin, but she shouldn't sacrifice her own safety to do so. "I get that you're pissed off. I am, too, but if anything had happened to you... Maddy would never forgive herself."

Her lips quirked at the mention of the nickname everyone knew Mads hated, but residual anger continued to cling to her eyes. "As you can see, I'm fine."

"That's because you got lucky. What if you had been caught by one of those fraternity assholes?" I snarled. "You of all people should know just how dangerous it could have been."

She flinched. Hurting her had not been my goal, yet I

somehow succeeded in doing just that. "Not every guy is like Carter," she snapped. "They aren't all going to rape me at the first given opportunity." Defiance shone in her dainty features. Kenna had always been so frail to me until she'd come back after a two-year hiatus. It had done her good because the girl had grit now, and a fierce determination that scared *me* at times.

A small frown touched my lips. "You don't know that," I said softly. "True, they might not all be as fucked in the head as Carter, but what if one of them had been drinking and stumbled upon you lurking about? He might not have forced himself on you, but he could have very well reported it to Sterling. The campus doesn't take defacing school property lightly. You could have gotten kicked out of school."

Her chin lifted, eyes sparkling with fierceness. "I'm not afraid of him."

Tugging on the ends of my waistband strings, I scoffed. "Okay, now I get why Grayson is constantly in a mood. I'll make you a deal," I rushed to say, seeing Kenna open her mouth to argue. "The next time you get an itch to vandalize shit, you fucking call me. No matter what time of night."

She didn't respond immediately but stared at me, chewing on her lip. "Fine," Kenna reluctantly agreed.

I flashed her my teeth. "I want to hear you say it."

Shoving back the hood, she shook her long dark hair out of its tie. "God, when did you become a nag? You're supposed to be the cool one."

"Exactly, which is why I'm not going to tell Grayson or Brock and I'll have your back in the future."

"Thanks," she replied with a grim smile. "It might not make

sense to you or the others, but I had to do something, even if it has no impact. I just wanted to take him down a notch, even if for a few minutes as he's wondering who dared to call him out."

I understood the frustration. "You really need a new hobby."

"Shut up." She eyed me, and I didn't like the glint in them or the way they narrowed on me. "Why are you pacing in front of your girlfriend's dorm like a lovesick puppy?"

Did I plan to tell Kenna that Sterling was tormenting me? No. Instead, I just skipped right over her question as if she'd never asked. Sometimes ignoring her was the only way to get her to stop probing. "Is she asleep?"

Kenna tugged at the cuffs on her sweatshirt so they nearly covered all of her fingers. "She was when I left."

"I need to see her." The statement burst from me. I didn't even know that was what I wanted until the words were out.

She held my gaze for longer than necessary, and I could practically see the wheels in her mind churning. "Why?"

"Does it matter?"

"Yeah, it does. It's not like you to be so... I'm not even sure what this is. Serious, perhaps, but it's more than that." She angled her head to the side. "Are you afraid?"

Only one thing in the world scared me: Mads getting hurt because of me. I forced a leisurely smile. "Of Sterling? Not a chance. But I don't trust him. I need to see that she's safe, and before you tell me she is, *I* need to see it."

"Okay, I get it." She pulled out her school ID card from the small zippered pocket in her bag. "Did something happen?"

Before she could sling the bag over her shoulder, I took it from her, tossing it over mine. "Nothing new. Where are we going?" I asked when she headed in the opposite direction of the main door.

"The side entrance. It's closer to our room, and we can avoid the main lobby," she explained like it was something she did regularly, and maybe she did, but Mads always took the main entry.

KU didn't have any student curfews, nor were there any rules or regulations about having visitors in the dorms. It wasn't weird or unusual for students to be coming and going at all hours of the night, but guests were supposed to check in by scanning their ID. "Aren't you worried the staff will think it's odd that you go out in the middle of the night so often?"

"Not when I have this." She flicked up the little white card in her hand. Her student ID. I didn't see anything unusual about it. We all had one.

I matched my strides to hers. "I don't understand."

Halting in front of the door, she turned to me, holding the card under the lantern above the door. "Look closely."

Squinting, I moved in, reading the text. "You got a fake ID? Kenna," I scolded. "I don't know whether to be impressed or disappointed."

She rolled her eyes and scanned the card in front of the reader to unlock the door. "You just graduated from dad to grandpa."

I couldn't help but laugh.

I followed Kenna into the elevator up to the fourth floor. She used the smart key in her ID to unlock the dorm room. Turning the handle and cracking the door, she glanced over her shoulder, putting a finger to her lips. "Take a good long look at your girlfriend and then go home Micah," she whispered. "I'm getting ready for bed. When I get out of the bathroom, you better be gone."

Nodding, I stepped inside behind her, cautiously closing the door behind me. I dropped Kenna's bag on the entry rug, careful not to let the cans rattle and wake up the others. Josie required white noise to sleep, so duel small fans ran from either side of the room, filling the space with a gentle lull that was relaxing but not good for detecting burglars. I had no clue if Ainsley had any sleeping quirks, but from the utter quietness of the room, I was guessing she didn't mind the steady humming of the fan blades.

Kenna tiptoed to the left side of the dorm toward the bathroom. It was dark, but my eyes adjusted after a few moments, and I went to the side of Mads's bed. Seeing her tucked soundly under the covers, the pressure clamping down on not just my heart but my lungs evaporated. I drew in my first easy breath of the night.

Strands of her silky honey hair spilled over the pillow where her cheek pressed against the white cover. The serene expression on her face made Mads angelic. Unable to stop, I trailed the backs of my fingers along the side of her jaw to her chin. Watching her sleep, it was hard to believe the things her mouth could say and do.

She tipped her head slightly into my touch, a soft purr-like sound that made my heart patter escaped her parted lips. My intent had only been to see her and leave, but now that I was here, I couldn't make my feet move. They remained rooted to the ground.

Kenna was still in the bathroom doing whatever the fuck girls did before bed. I nudged off the back heels of my shoes, slipping my feet out of them, and went back to check the door, making sure it was locked. Shedding my shirt, I pulled a corner of the sheet down and climbed into bed beside Mads. The twin-size mattress hardly fit me, let alone the two of us. I carefully gathered her in my arms, positioning her so she was more or less lying on top of me. She never fully woke up but snuggled against me, her face resting in the crook of my neck.

Soft whispers of her breath brushed against my throat, and although it was a simple action, desire curled inside me. Not the instant lust I often felt with Mads that drove me absolutely insane. This was a quiet need that settled inside me—comforting, even. I never thought need could be a source of contentment.

Inhaling her scent, I closed my eyes, my nostrils filled with sweet orange blossoms. My muscles, my limbs, my mind, and my entire body relaxed. Within minutes, I finally dropped off into a sleep I desperately needed.

Her side of the room was what Mads coined clean-chaotic, meaning it was clean for her standards. Clothes were scattered over her desk, a few underneath it, and more tossed over a chair. I didn't mind the messy side of Mads. She wasn't always put together and polished as so many of the rich girls at Elmwood Academy had been. She didn't mind that I saw her without makeup or care that her hair was out of place. Mads was real.

She also didn't bat an eye at finding me in her bed. Still half asleep, I felt Mads's arms tighten around me, and her face nuzzled against mine as she rained kisses on my neck and cheek. It was her morning ritual whenever she stayed the night with me.

It wasn't a bad way to wake up. No, it was fucking glorious to have her warm body pressed into me, to feel her nipples grow hard under the thin T-shirt and brush against my chest. Our legs were interwoven, and despite my eyes being closed, I felt her gaze on me and sensed the smile on her lips.

I wanted to be woken from sleep every day of my life just like this, which scared the shit out of me. For years, I'd loved Mads, but I never let myself fall in love with her. I couldn't. Once I admitted it not to just her but myself, then it became real, and I would never be able to let her go.

"Morning," her raspy-from-sleep voice greeted me, a whisper in my ear.

I grunted groggily, battling between more sleep and convincing Mads we needed to have morning sex. I wanted both. If only I could do both, like have sex while sleeping. God, yes. That was what I wanted.

Her laugh tickled the side of my face. "I am not having sex with you while you're asleep."

Had I mumbled something out loud? Probably. I did have a tendency to talk in my sleep, so I was told. I didn't believe it. There were secrets in this brain that I had to take to the grave. "But if I wake up, then we can—"

She pressed her lips to my mouth, silencing me. The kiss

didn't last long enough, my mouth clinging to the very last second as she pulled away. "When did you get here?" she asked.

I finally forced my eyes open. Mads's rumpled hair framed her heart-shaped face in a sexy disarray that made my fingers itch to dive into it and mess it up further. "Late," I responded, my eyes roaming over her face. "Why do you look so damn good in the morning?"

Her nose scrunched. "Did you lose your contacts?"

I didn't wear contacts or glasses, a fact she was aware of. My vision was fucking perfect. "I wish you could see yourself the way I do."

Flattery wasn't working this morning. "I'll pass." She snorted.

I imagined all she thought I saw were her tits and ass, and she wouldn't be entirely wrong. I enjoyed her body, all parts of it from her head to her toes, but she had this aura about her that seeped into me, and I absorbed it like a sponge, soaking up all her goodness.

A song started to play—Imagine Dragons, I thought. It was too early to be recalling song names off the top of my head. "What is that noise?" I groaned.

"My alarm," she said, a bit too chipper.

I shifted on the mattress, my fingers diving under the sheet to cup her tight ass. "Why? It's Friday," I replied, stifling a groan. She wasn't wearing shorts, just lacy panties.

Fucking hell. She's torturing me.

"And some of us have class on Friday," she said, the tip of her finger drawing mindlessly over the tattoo covering my chest.

My muscles responded to her touch, jumping under the

skin as her nails passed by. "What the fuck for? Isn't Monday through Thursday enough?"

"Josie and Ainsley are gone." Her hand stopped moving, and she tapped her fingers over my heart like a thought just occurred to her. "You haven't answered my question."

I blinked. "There was a question?"

A bit of the light in her eyes dimmed. "What happened last night?"

My chest rose as I inhaled, holding it before letting it out in a long release. "I couldn't sleep."

Understanding softened her gray eyes. I had so many demons that could keep me up at night, but she guessed which one it had been last night. "Still doesn't explain how you got inside my dorm. Not that I'm complaining."

She was too fucking quick in the morning. "Kenna let me in."

She tilted her head to the side. "Why didn't you just call me?"

Fuck. I couldn't rat out Kenna. "I had a little incident with my phone last night," I explained.

Her eyes narrowed as she sat up between my legs in the center of the bed. "What kind of incident?"

"It ran into my wall."

A small frown appeared. "Micah."

Sitting up, I scrubbed a hand through my hair. "I might have helped it run into the wall. That's not the point. I'm getting a new one today, so don't worry."

A muffled voice came from the other side of the room. "I

swear, you better not have your hand on his dick," Kenna warned, sounding like she had her head under the blanket.

My lips twitched.

"Kenna!" Mads shrieked and then laughed, color staining her cheeks.

"What? Are you saying it isn't a possibility?" Kenna proclaimed, her head popping out from the covers. Mads remained silent, neither confirming nor denying, and Kenna added, "My point exactly. And eww. I'm taking a shower. Finish whatever you started before I get out."

"Oh my God, Kenna! Nothing is happening," Mads insisted, dropping her head onto my chest.

Kenna rolled out of bed, grabbed some clothes, and padded to the bathroom. "Yet," she replied as she shut the door.

Mads waited until the shower turned on. "You're not going to tell me what got you so pissed off that you tossed your phone across the room, are you?"

That would be a big fat no. She didn't need to know that Sterling was sending me her nude pics. Perhaps I should send him some back of my own. A few dick pics? The idea made a smirk pull at the corner of my mouth, which I promptly tried to hide because Mads was suddenly looking at me weird. I cleared my throat. "In fact, I should probably get ready and go pick up that phone," I said, wiggling my way out from under her and to the edge of the bed.

She stayed under the sheets, watching me as I scoured the floor for my shirt. *Where the fuck did I toss it?*

"Don't touch anything. If you move it, I won't find it again," she explained in a way that only made sense to her.

I shot her an exasperated look. "Can you find my shirt, then?"

A playful gleam entered her expression. "Do you really need one?"

My fingers encircled her ankle, tugging her toward the edge of the bed. I dropped my hands to either side of her head on the mattress, leaning over her. "How much time do we have?" I asked, staring at her mouth.

She giggled, and I realized how much I missed hearing her laugh. The last two weeks had been hard for her, and Sterling would pay for the stress he caused her. I planned to end this... for Mads.

CHAPTER THIRTEEN

MICAH

Some people started their mornings off with a bowl of Wheaties. My favorite way to start the day was a dose of Mads. Morning sex was literally like my cup of caffeine. I felt energized and ready to show Sterling just how much he royally fucked-up messing with my girl.

Ideas bounced around in my head—too many. I needed a few moments to sort through all the crazy ones and flesh out those that had grit to them.

I drummed my fingers on the glass case as I waited for the employee to ring up my phone replacement. I smirked, recalling Kenna's foolish yet amusing antics last night.

She secretly had my stamp of approval.

If Grayson found out…

I swallowed a laugh, picturing him losing his shit as he often did.

Even if Chi Sigma didn't report the graffiti to the school board, the prank would spread through KU like a fucking STD, and that was exactly what Kenna wanted. It wasn't just the act itself, the danger, the sneaking around that drew her to her late-night hobby. It was the aftermath that gave her the thrill she sought, seeing how the people around her reacted and her watching in plain sight.

With my phone in hand, I hopped into my Hummer and booted the device up, going through screen after screen of prompts. I had a feeling this would be only one of many new phones in my future.

A breeze fluttered through my open window, ruffling my hair and carrying traces of the light rain that had fallen in the early hours of morning. It smelled fresh, like the world had taken a cleansing shower, washing away the sticky heat of the last few days. Even the birds were energetic, like the little fucker repeatedly tapping his beak against the tree trunk beside my car.

The phone went through the transfer of all my data, and as soon as the home screen appeared, a slew of text message notifications popped up. I didn't have to be a psychic to know some of them would be from Sterling.

I told myself I was prepared, that I could handle it, but fuck if my heart didn't speed up a little, adrenaline spiking in my blood as I tapped the messaging app. The unknown number stuck out. After having just left the warmth of Mads's body, a sense of wrongness or dirtiness ribboned inside me, as if Sterling somehow stained what Mads and I had, lessening the relationship we both worked to make happen. I couldn't let him come between us. Sterling had been nothing but noise, interrupting the steady frequency of our budding feelings.

I touched the anonymous number. No text, just another two pictures of Mads. Different poses and one of her sleeping, much like how she looked last night. Her face was perhaps a tad more mature now than in the photo. Despite hating that Sterling had these in his possession, I couldn't help but notice Mads's beauty. I glanced closely at the details, searching to see if something odd stuck out to me.

I recognized the room. I'd snuck inside enough over the years to know the different phases of Mads's style, and this had been taken during high school. A new layer of anger stacked on top of what I already felt, and my just-out-of-the-box phone was almost chucked into the street. I restrained the profound impulse, my knuckles going white as I squeezed the shit out of the mobile device.

Tossing my phone onto the passenger seat, I started the Hummer and rammed my foot on the gas. The engine roared, jerking off down the road.

When I stormed into my house fifteen minutes later, Brock sat in front of his laptop at the kitchen dinette. He glanced up as I went to the fridge and pulled out a chilled beer. I popped the cap off on the edge of the counter and pressed the bottle to my lips, tipping my head back.

"A little early, even for you. Did something happen last night?" Brock asked, watching me. "You didn't sleep here."

"I was at Mads's." My response came out clipped.

He took in the rigidness of my body and waited until I drained the beer, seeing I was in a fucking mood. "Is she okay?"

It wasn't Mads who needed me last night. It had been the other way around. "Yeah, she's good." I crushed the can in my hand. "He's sending me little gifts."

Brock twisted in his chair, the screen on his computer going black into sleep mode. "Gifts? You mean pictures?"

I nodded. He excelled at manipulation and torment tactics, so it didn't surprise me one bit that he'd guessed Sterling's next ploy.

Brock's lips pulled into an evil grin. "Then you're going to love this. Apparently your boy is claiming that you put him in the hospital that night."

I tossed the empty can into the sink. "What? Bullshit," I hissed. "He walked away. Same as me."

"We know that. But the school board..."

"Fuck. What a dick move." Had he actually gone and filed a report? Of course he had. It was just another ruse that pointed Sterling's target as me, not Mads. "Can you make this go away?" I had plenty of black marks on my record, and Fynn had always been our personal eraser.

"It's already done," he stated. "You don't have to worry about the school board. My parents and yours both made substantial donations. They won't risk losing any future funds."

I despised this side of politics, but money talked. Or, in most cases, shut the right people up. "Fucking pussy."

Perhaps sporting a black eye, a few cuts, and some bruises didn't live up to his frat boy reputation, but for someone who liked to pretend he was a bad guy, it didn't add up. Was that why he'd skipped classes this week? Hid away in his frat house, too ashamed to show his beaten-up pretty boy face? Licking his wounds and playing the fucking victim?

Lifting my gaze to Brock, I said, "I need to know who or what he cares about the most in the world." I would find a way to break Sterling before he did something to Mads that would destroy me. Everything in my bones told me the bastard was toying with me before he unveiled the main event, and my biggest fear was that Mads would be the star of the show.

"According to the info from Marlow, he has a sister."

Marlow was our private investigator. He did work for our parents, but the man loved a side hustle. He also loved money and knew we were good for it. He was the kind of guy who never asked questions, just delivered the goods. "You think she might be his weak link?"

His smile grew. "Only one way to find out."

My smirk mirrored his. "I love that devious mind of yours."

"I'll get Marlow to do a little legwork, and we can hash out the details tonight."

My phone buzzed in my pocket. I pulled it out and checked the caller ID. *SpermSac,* aka my father. I declined the call, dropping my phone on the counter. I didn't have the energy to deal with him.

"Fynn wiped Sterling's phone last night. The photos are gone," Brock informed me, though we both knew that even though we had his leverage deleted, Sterling would find another way. He was the kind of asshat who had a backup plan for his backup plan.

I hated assholes like that. Methodical to a fault.

Reaching in the fridge for another beer, I pulled out two. "I'll let Mads know. Thanks, man."

Brock took the beer I offered, removing the cap. "It won't end here."

The need to shelter Mads was fierce inside me. I wanted to tuck her away from all the assholes like Sterling and Carter, because there were too many of them lurking in the world, blending in with the general population, watching, waiting, stalking, like a hunter in the woods, far too patient and quiet. Those qualities made them dangerous as hell, whereas I came in loud with punches swinging. That was the difference between Sterling and me.

I tapped my finger over the bottle's cap. "I know."

"There's something else I think you need to see." The grim tone of his voice told me I should down this beer before he told me. Whatever Brock had found, it wasn't good.

"Fynn went through the others' phones. He isn't finished yet, but he sent me these." He dropped his phone on the table. "You might want to take a look."

I picked up his phone, staring at the image on the screen. It was a girl standing in one of the dorm rooms in nothing but her bra. She was bent over, picking something off the floor. The pose wasn't sexual, at least it didn't appear as if it was meant to be. In fact, due to the novice quality and pose, I suspected she didn't know the photo had been taken. There were more. So many more. I flipped through them, one by one. All girls, taken in the dorms. Ice trickled down my spine as I swallowed the bile that coated my throat. "Fuck," I hissed, forking my fingers through my hair.

Anger, like an old friend, came back into my life. "What the hell are they doing with all these photos?" Was the fraternity into some sort of amateur porn shit?

Quiet violence simmered in Brock's eyes as I handed him back his phone. "A part of me isn't sure I want to know. But then I thought about how I would feel if I came across a pic of Josie. I'd kill them all."

The bottle hissed as I twisted off the cap. "A killing spree probably isn't the answer, regardless that the planet would be a better place without them."

"You're not supposed to be the levelheaded one."

My phone buzzed, and when I saw my father's number again, I knew he wouldn't be ignored. I swore under my breath. "I need to take this. It's the old man."

He nodded. "Enough said."

Alexander Bradford didn't tolerate trouble of any kind. In short, he didn't tolerate me because I was literally made up of all kinds of trouble. He had a short fuse on his temper, which tended to make him trigger-happy. The one trait I inherited from the old man.

"Sir," I answered flatly, walking out of the kitchen and toward the stairs to the privacy of my room.

"Heard you've been making a name for yourself at KU." Nothing in his greeting hinted at pride. His voice was cold and sharp with heavy doses of disappointment. "You've only been on campus for two weeks and you already managed to provoke a fight. With the president of Chi Sigma, no less." He got right to the point. No pleasantries. He didn't have time for small talk or nonsense.

I wasn't surprised that word had reached my father. He had friends on the school board, and regardless that Brock had convinced them to discreetly turn a blind eye to the incident, someone would have passed the information along. If the board couldn't deal with my indiscretions, then my father would.

Somehow being away at college felt like I'd finally put some distance between the old man and me, but the second I heard the deep timbre of his voice and the criticism that went with it, all those miles were just gone. It was as if I'd been transported back to my bedroom in our house, the old man standing tall in the doorway as he scolded me on what I'd done wrong at his latest dinner party. They'd always been centered around his work and therefore, in his mind, were deemed important. Only perfection was allowed. Perfect home. Perfect wife. Perfect son to follow in his footsteps and take over the empire.

"It was nothing but a misunderstanding," I said, squeezing the phone. It wasn't like I could tell him what a creep Sterling was. He didn't hate Mads. He didn't have feelings toward her at all beyond that a girlfriend was a distraction I didn't need. College wasn't a time to be tied down in a teenage crush according to him.

He bulldozed his way through what was on his mind like I hadn't spoken at all. "Does this have anything to do with the Clarkes' girl?"

She had everything to do with why I'd hit the bastard and would gladly do so again. I was looking forward to getting my hands on him, but I knew I couldn't explain what was happening. Regardless of the truth, my father wouldn't care about what he would deem juvenile pranks. My focus was to be class, foot-ball, and getting into Chi Sigma, yet I'd managed to fuck up his plan in the first week. It had to be a record.

I closed the door to my room, pressing my back against it. "No, it had nothing to do with Mads, sir." I kept my tone neutral, the lie easily rolling off my tongue. *Deny, deny, deny.*

"Then why did Sterling end up in the hospital with a few broken ribs?" he snapped.

"Because he's an attention-seeking douchebag." The response slipped out of me before I realized what I was saying.

A harsh laugh came through the other end of the phone. "That douchebag holds the keys to your Chi Sigma alumni."

"I don't give a shit about some fucking fraternity."

"I've told you before. Chi Sigma isn't just a school organiza-tion. The connections you'll make are imperative to not just your future but this family. Perhaps if Madeline Clarke trans-ferred to another university, you would take it more seriously."

He didn't come right out and say it, but that had been a threat. He would use his influence and friendship with the Clarkes to do just that—remove her. If my father had his way, he would remove Mads from my life completely. After I graduated and came to work at the family business, he would, a few years down the road, find me a suitable wife, one who would fit the part of a prominent member of the elite society. Love had nothing to do with it, nor what I wanted. It mattered very little to the man who made every decision in his life methodically.

"You can mess with my life, but I swear to God, if you even think about meddling in Mads's, you'll regret it." The words came out low and bitter. I meant every one of them. I would stand in his way if he tried to impose on her life.

"Then stop thinking with your dick. There are plenty of girls."

He would know all about that. I don't think there had ever been a day in his life when he'd been faithful and honest with my mother. *Fuck that. Fuck him.* "As I said, she has nothing to do with this," I reiterated between clenched teeth.

Thick-ass tension oozed through the phone, wrapping around my neck and choking me. I had made a mistake, showing my father how important Mads was to me. He had my weakness now, and he would use it any time I strayed off the path he laid out for me.

Fuck. Fuck. Fuckity fuck.

"Don't screw this up," he stated. "Find a way to make it right. I don't give a shit how much you hate Sterling. In business, making friends isn't a priority. Sealing the deal. That's what matters."

"I get it. Message received, *Pops.*"

"Micah, I don't have to tell you what will happen if I receive another call."

I rubbed my temples, a dull ache pulsing behind my eyes. My room was dark, the blinds drawn closed and the lights off. I was grateful for the darkness. "No, sir, you don't, but if you involve her at all in this, you won't have an heir to inherit your kingdom."

"Remember that when you don't have a dime to your name." The phone went silent on the other end before the line clicked dead.

I smashed my fist into the door behind me, but it could have easily been my phone going across the room. I definitely wanted to throw shit, and before I destroyed my phone for the second time in less than twelve hours, I flung it onto my bed. Opening the side drawer of my nightstand, I took out a bottle of pills, dumped a few in my mouth, and tossed them back.

The headache that had been edging just above my temples was moving quickly into a migraine. As I sat down on the side of the bed, two things became painfully clear. Not only was Sterling using Mads but now so would my father.

I refused to let that happen.

No matter what the cost, I would stop him. Damn my soul to whatever Hell awaited so long as she remained protected.

She was in more danger than before, caught in the crossfires between this ongoing war with my father and now this budding feud with Sterling.

And secondly, I couldn't help but think that maybe the only way to keep Mads safe was for her to stay far away from me. I knew what I should do, but knowing wasn't the same as going through the motions. I so desperately wanted to cling to what we'd been building over the last few months, but this was precisely why I hadn't let myself say what my heart already knew, because speaking such strong emotions out loud gave them power.

It would hurt her, break her, something I vowed never to do.

She wouldn't be the only one broken.

Stepping away from Mads would be the hardest thing I'd ever do. I didn't know if I had the strength to totally push her out of my life. I was positive I couldn't do that. Selfish? Probably.

I refused to leave her unprotected.

But for a little while, just until I took care of Sterling and got my father to believe it was over. I had to undo the damage I'd created.

Fuck!

The curse screamed inside my head, and I longed to release it into the world, to belt it from the top of my lungs, rattling the walls of this room. Fury and pain, my two old friends.

Jogging down Stadium Drive toward the football field and the athletic building, I slowed my pace to walk. I had fifteen minutes to get my ass dressed and on the field for practice. Each minute I was late would result in an extra run around the field on top of my warm-up. It meant I would miss out on the first few drills. I didn't often run late. Today was an exception, my mind distracted from the phone call with my father and the photos from Sterling.

I had just reached the back of the bleachers when I heard my name. Stifling a groan, I turned toward the voice of a girl who'd just walked past me. I'd spared her nothing more than a glimpse, but now that I got the full picture, I wanted nothing more than to keep walking. In fact, I started to turn around and do just that. *Fuck this.* She was the last person I wanted to deal with. A part of me wished I was seeing shit.

She made a throaty noise of indignation. "Classy. Perhaps I

should see if Brock is around or what's her name? The newest standby girl you're all obsessed with? Josie, is it? I heard you pass her around from week to week."

Freezing, I waited for a heartbeat before I whirled. "Fuck off, Kate," I growled, my shitty-day scowl deepening. She knew precisely what buttons to hit. Today was not the day to screw with me. If it had been Mads and not Josie she'd chosen to insult, I might have broken my cardinal rule to never hit a girl.

Though in my book, Kate McGuire wasn't a girl. She wasn't even fucking human; therefore, did the rule really apply?

The Elite's biggest mistake. We didn't make them often, but when we did, they tended to be what I referred to as the three Cs: crazy, cunning, and clingy. Girls who didn't know how to move on. Kind of like Ava.

But Kate was way worse.

When she moved our junior year, I'd hoped to never see her vile face again. It didn't surprise me one bit that the obsessed princess kept tabs on us, particularly Brock. He'd been the brunt of her fixation, along with Grayson.

I'd never fallen for her bullshit, which had only infuriated the devious bitch.

She might look like a sweet peach with creamy skin, rosy cheeks, and sun-kissed blonde hair, and I could see why a guy might find himself captivated by her, but I knew what evil festered underneath the beauty.

I wanted her nowhere near me, Mads, or Josie for that matter. I wanted her off campus. Now.

Like the witch she was, Kate batted her fake eyelashes at me. "Micah," she purred and proceeded to wrap herself around me like a cat in heat with a suggestive smile that I'd seen plenty of times before... just normally not aimed at me. Kate usually reserved her seductive charm for Brock or Grayson, and I wondered if either of them knew what shady mayhem had blown into town. "It's been too long. Is that any way to greet an old friend?"

"What are you doing here?" I snapped, removing her spider-monkey arms from me and taking a step back. I needed the space before her perfume choked me to death.

She slipped her sunglasses down the bridge of her nose, peering at me from over them with coppery eyes that reminded me of a lioness on the prowl. "I'm just as surprised as you are."

"My ass. Don't play dumb. You forget that your pussy never enticed me," I stated like I was bored out of my mind.

Her laugh was as fake as the rest of her. She flipped her hair. "As crude as ever."

The sound of her voice, her laugh, basically everything about her grated on my nerves. "And you're still a fraud. How many friends did your parents buy you this time?"

She scrunched her face at me. "I'd like to say it's been a pleasure, but it hasn't."

"Wow, something we can agree on. If you're here for Brock, he isn't interested."

"Believe it or not, I didn't know that either of you was attending Kingsley."

"Bullshit," I coughed. "You expect me to believe that? If you know about Josie, then it only makes sense that you're still stalking my boys."

Her lips curved into a viper smirk, cruel and poisonous. "The world doesn't revolve around the Elite."

A harsh laugh bubbled out of me. "You should try listening to your own advice."

Fire flashed in her eyes. "Go fly a kite."

She and Ava were two peas in a pod. We should have been grateful that they'd never joined forces and couldn't stand each other. Kate and Ava considered one another a threat—competition. "Gladly, if it meant I never had to see your face again."

She touched my arm, her long white-painted nails trailing over my muscles. "You, Brock, and I should get together for a drink, catch up."

"Kate," I said, matching her fake sweetness, "I'm going to kindly ask that you remove your hand before I snap it in two."

Her giggle was forced. "You always were funny."

From the other side of the bleachers, my teammates began to hustle onto the field. I would for sure be doing some extra laps because of this unwanted pit stop. "Want to hear something funny? Stay the fuck away from Brock and Josie."

Everything I said seemed to bounce right off her like she was made from rubber ball materials. She cocked her head to the side with a befitting cruel smile. "Your father might be disappointed to hear how you're treating an old family friend."

Anger cracked like a whip inside me. "What does my father have to do with this?" I snapped.

Before she could respond, a soft voice said my name from behind Kate. "Micah?"

I lifted my gaze, clashing with a set of perturbed gray eyes. Her timing sucked. So much for keeping Mads off Kate's radar.

My girlfriend did not need the added drama Kate was bound to bring. "Mads, what are you doing here?" I didn't mean for the question to come out as unwelcoming as it had. Fucking Kate.

"I could ask you the same." Mads's focus slid to Kate, her eyes narrowing to daggers of disdain. Kate and Kenna had been on the cheerleading squad together, yet there had never been any camaraderie between them. High and mighty Kate had treated Kenna like she was the maid who cleaned shit off her slippers. That rotten bully-like attitude was what made Mads loathe Kate with every fiber of her being.

"Kate was just leaving," I said forcefully between clenched teeth.

Kate angled her body to the side so she could see both Mads and me. Her gaze volleyed between us, assessing before landing on my girl. "Mads, it's been a long time."

"Not long enough," Mads gritted, her voice flat and strained.

"I can't believe you're still hanging around. But you always were panting after the Elite's playboy."

"Retired," I warned. "And careful. She's my girlfriend."

Kate pressed her injection-puffed lips together. "Hmm. I guess desperate looks good on some of us."

"Get the fuck out of here, Kate," I hissed. "And don't hold your breath on that drink. Better yet, do." I didn't wait for her response. Didn't deem it worthy of my time, seeing as I was late and had places to be. Grabbing Mads's hand, I headed toward the athletic building. Her fingers were stiff. "You can retract the claws," I muttered when we were far enough away.

Mads's chest heaved as she let out a breath. "That bitch. I can't believe she had the balls to show up here."

"She's apparently a KU resident." I kept walking, determined to put distance between Kate and Mads. Although, nothing was stopping Kate from coming back and harassing Mads during my practice. It was something She would do.

"Are you shitting me?" Mads bit out. "Kenna is going to flip when she finds out."

Brock too. I wasn't looking forward to telling him. "Is everything okay?"

She nodded, giving me a small smile as she tried to shake off her sour mood. "I came to watch you practice."

"You did?" I couldn't stop the stupid grin from appearing.

Her eyes rolled. "I do sometimes come to support you." She leaned against my arm, moving into me, her fingers still interwoven with and clinging to mine. "Plus, I missed you."

It had been a busy week, the hustle of classes picking up, which hadn't left much time for us to hang out. "Didn't I see you this morning?"

We came to the athletic building, and she eyed it cautiously. Mads had an expressive face, revealing her emotions. I could see without asking that she was remembering hiding out in the locker room. Pulling her gaze from the door, she glanced up at me and smiled softly. "That was hours ago."

I bent down and kissed her lips, wanting to make her forget Sterling completely. She sank into me and sighed as I pulled away.

Her eyes grew somber. "Is she going to be a problem?"

I wanted to assure her that she didn't need to worry about

Kate, but when it came to those she loved, particularly family, she couldn't help herself. If Kate started harassing Kenna or Josie, Mads would take it personally.

I flicked the end of her nose, keeping my voice light as I said, "Looks like we both have ghosts of the past rising up out of the graveyard."

CHAPTER FOURTEEN

MADS

I didn't know what it was about Micah on the field, all sweaty and his uniform covered in dirt and grass stains. Maybe it was the way his ass looked in those tight pants. Or the way he shook his hair when taking his helmet off between drills. But dear God, it did shit to me that I had no right feeling in the middle of a football stadium.

Brock tossed another pass down the field, straight into Micah's hands, and then the man took off like he was born to run, shoes kicking up dirt. Only a small section of the stands was sectioned off for onlookers, the rest of the seats empty. For the size of the stadium, seeing all the bare rows made it feel like a deserted ghost town. Weird and kind of eerie. I was used to the deafening cheer, the crowded rows of fans, and proud parents. Elmwood had always been a big football town. Kingsley University was no different. This was only their practice field. It would be a different atmosphere game day.

I sat in the middle of the bleachers, close to the opposing team's tunnel. Doing a sweep of the stadium, I searched for Josie. She was supposed to meet me here but had texted earlier saying she was running late. With practice nearly half over, I wondered if she would make it at all. In light of the recent shit with Sterling, my motherly nature kicked in, and I couldn't but wonder if she was okay.

Was something or someone preventing her from showing up?

Kate immediately popped into my mind, and I groaned.

Fucking Kate McGuire.

God, had it been too much to hope that I'd never have to see her horrible face again? The girl was a damn walking scandal waiting to happen. As if I didn't have enough shit on my plate. I dug my phone out to text Kenna and send her a warning message that Kate was back.

Had Josie run into Kate? Josie might know her, but I wasn't stupid enough to think Kate didn't know Brock's girlfriend. She would most definitely take notice of the first girl Brock had ever been serious with, and I shuddered to imagine the trouble Kate would stir up.

She would do anything and everything to get in between Micah and me. Her nastiness wasn't just about having Brock, or Grayson, for that matter, remembering how hard she'd tried to gain my cousin's attention. Kate thrived on the chaos her actions and her tongue created.

Vile monster that she was.

After sending Kenna a quick text, I checked the time again,

beginning to worry. It wasn't like Josie was a huge football fanatic. Neither of us enjoyed the sport, but we surely enjoyed the men who played it.

Turning over my phone, I was about to send her a text when I felt a wisp of hot air on the back of my neck, causing my skin to prickle. Before he even spoke, I knew Sterling was behind me.

"I have to say, I might have underestimated your boyfriend. He moves quickly. If I remember, you like to draw out the anticipation."

I blanched at the insinuation. "What do you want, Sterling?" Exasperation covered the spike of fear. I was proud I managed to cover it up.

"I have a gift," he said, tugging a strand of my hair.

I'd bet twenty thousand dollars that his fucking gift would be more of a torture than it would bring me joy.

No fucking thank you.

"Funny. I have a gift for you too." Keeping my gaze centered on the field without really seeing the plays, I lifted my hand and flipped Sterling the bird. The players were in the middle of a drill, not paying attention to the stands.

His chuckle made the hairs on my arm stand up. "This is a gift you can't refuse, Splash."

Turning my head to the side, I caught a flash of the dark ball cap pulled low over his eyes. "I don't give a shit about your fuck-tangular problems. Take all the photos you want."

"Who said I just had photos?" His lips quirked.

Swallowing, I smeared my cold, sweaty palms over my jean-clad thighs. "You need help, counseling or some shit. I'm sure there's a hotline just waiting for your call." I started to fully turn around, but Sterling's voice stopped me.

"Keep looking forward," he ordered. "We wouldn't want your boyfriend to end up with a suspension so early in the term."

It was true. If Micah caught a glimpse of Sterling, he wouldn't hesitate to hurdle the steps and beat the shit out of him a second time in front of the coaches and his team. "Don't pretend like you wouldn't love that," I sneered.

Applause came from the sporadically filled seats around me, dragging my attention back to the field. I searched for Micah, but before my eyes could pick him out from the other players huddled together, a tiny prick pierced the back of my neck. I jumped at the sudden and sharp sting.

"What the hell?" I squeaked, my hand flying to the sore spot on my nape. It felt like I'd just been stung by a bee, which, being that it was the end of summer, was completely possible, but given the devil who sat behind, the probability seemed higher that Sterling was at fault. Forgoing his warming, I whirled and glared at him. "Did you just jab me?" I spat.

Shrugging, Sterling shoved something inside his pocket. A needle, perhaps? Alarm zapped like lightning through me, causing my pulse to race. "Don't worry. It won't kill you. I just gave you a little something to help you relax and kick-start the party a bit early."

"You drugged me." Fear made my voice higher and sharper. Everything in my head went haywire as I fought against the panic surging in my veins, along with the drugs. I couldn't believe he had the gumption to inject me with a substance in broad daylight surrounded by people! Who, I realized, weren't paying any attention to me. I needed a level head if I had any hope of getting out of this situation.

A finger traced down the inside of my arm as I clutched the edge of the bleachers, my head spinning with confusion. "It's more fun if you use your imagination, Splash."

Fucking fun? Nothing about this was *fun*. "I'd rather drown you in a lake." I shook my head, wondering how long I had until the effects showed. I'd never involuntarily been forced to consume something I didn't want. The feeling was pretty much as one would conceive. It. Fucking. Sucked. *Keep calm. You need to stay calm.* "You shouldn't have come alone," I told him, wanting to sound threatening. I doubted I succeeded on that front.

"I'm not stupid." He shifted his gaze from corner to corner before reverting to mine. "I brought a decoy. A little distraction to keep your boyfriend busy."

I glanced to the left and right, picking out faces in the bleachers that were semi-familiar, yet I could only pull out one or two names. It was enough to understand. Sterling had brought his fraternity brothers to the field, scattered among the stands. An intimidation tactic? If so, he needed to start taking lessons from the Elite instead of trying to best them. "I hate to be the one to break it to you, but this won't work. I know Brock and Micah. They already have something in motion to handle this."

An evil smirk curved on his lips. "We'll see. Would they

dare do anything with you in the middle? You might get hurt, and we wouldn't want that."

Son of a bitch.

I hated that he was right. Micah would see to my safety first, but my gut told me that Sterling's plan was to take me during the chaos. That was why he drugged me, right? To make me more compliant and cover up my cries for help. The liquid form of the drug would hit my system faster. I figured I had only a few more moments before the effects started to make themselves known.

Everything in me screamed at me to run, to get up now while I still had my wits about me. I squirmed on the hard surface. *Fuck it.* All I had to do was bolt down about a dozen rows of bleachers. No big deal. I could do this.

I moved, but before I could even lift my ass, a hand clamped down my arm, keeping me seated.

Sterling tsked. "Not so fast, Splash."

My butt fell back onto the bleachers. "I hate you." I didn't know how many ways I could say it, but I doubted the truth of my words would penetrate Sterling's thick skull.

"Hmm." He pursed his lips. "I'm a firm believer in there being a thin line between love and hate."

On the field, I watched as the offense switched players, sending Micah to the sidelines for a few plays. Brock stayed in as quarterback. From under his helmet, his sharp aqua eyes scanned the stands, looking for Josie. One of the coaches blew a whistle, and Brock's gaze passed right over me, returning to his teammates. Anguish pitted in my stomach.

"If you're trying to justify me having actual feelings for you that don't stem from contempt, I have news for you—you're way off base."

"It matters little to me." The fingers on my arm remained firm, tightening even. "That was a nice little touch, having your friend leave me a message. Colorful and bold. Makes a statement when you slap it on the front of the house. Although, I don't think the school board will agree once I send them the video."

"What the fuck are you talking about? What message?"

Everything about him was so damn cocksure. His demeanor. His tone. His attitude. He seriously thought he'd bested the Elite. "Oh, this is better. You don't know. Here, take a look."

My phone buzzed in my hand, and dread ribboned around my ribs. I didn't want to look. At the same time, I had to. I had my suspicions even before I played the video Sterling had sent me. It had Kenna written all over it, metaphorically speaking. In bright pink letters, she spray-painted the Chi Sigma house, just not with her name.

House of stalkers and horrors. S is for stalker, not Sterling. Say cheese for the camera.

Sterling's video wasn't all that incriminating. It was fucking weak. Not once did the camera pick up Kenna's face because my girl knew what the hell she was doing. It captured her back, the black clothes and hood concealing and blending her into the night. The slim figure and height gave away her gender, but that was all.

I turned my head to the side. "This could be anyone. And I can tell you for certain, it was not any of my friends. Perhaps you have a stalker of your own. How ironic. Smells like justice."

"The lies just roll off your tongue. You might have forgotten about me for two years, but I know a lot about you and your friends. Including what they did last year to... what was his name?"

I was not going to allow myself to panic at the thought of Sterling watching me all this time. Or that he learned about Carter. I clamped my teeth together. *Think, Mads. Think.* I had to get myself away from him.

"You can leave peacefully with me, or we can wait until the fireworks begin. The choice is yours."

And then what? I didn't want to think about what would happen next. My brain couldn't handle it. All I did know was that I couldn't be alone with him. An absolutely terrifying thought. A deep shudder of revulsion rippled through me. "How far do think you'll get? Micah won't let you take me out of this stadium."

His fingers pressed firmly into my arm, as if he was afraid I might bolt at any second. His worries weren't unwarranted. "God, I hope not. I would hate for him to disappoint me."

Was that what he planned? To get Micah alone? And for what? To beat the ever-loving crap out of him? "Tell me what you have against Micah," I demanded, the drug in my system finally making its presence known.

Silence lingered from behind me until he finally spoke. "He hurt my family."

I blinked, shocked that he actually answered, even vaguely.

The Elite had hurt a lot of people. What had they done to Sterling's?

Micah's eyes collided with mine as he jogged back onto the field after sitting out for a few plays. Twirling the football in his hands, the hotshot grin faded when he noticed the panic on my face. I hadn't been able to keep up the facade, not after our eyes connected. I let Micah see my mouth moving. He might not be able to make out the words, but he could catch on that I wasn't alone up in the stands. "So, this was always about him? Even then, when we first met?"

The rim of his ball cap grazed the back of my head as he leaned in close. Too fucking close. "It was no coincidence that you found me that night outside. I was waiting for you, Splash. But I'll admit, you took me by surprise. I figured it would take weeks for me to gain your trust and seduce you, but you were ready to go. How could I say no to such a sweet opportunity when it all but fell into my lap?"

"You bastard," I hissed as a glow started to form in the center of my gut, spreading out like a vine and infecting my arms and legs until it felt like I was lit up like a damn field of fireflies at night.

Micah's jaw had gone taut, and the muscles in his body coiled as he ignored his team, slowly walking toward my side of the field. His eyes were hard and remained locked on mine.

Sterling touched the brim of his hat and tipped his head. A signal, I soon realized, as one by one the Chi Sigma members stood up. To everyone around, it didn't seem that weird, not until they each cracked a slim, small tube. Some used their knees to break the seal, others just their hands, but each one led to the same reaction—smoke. It hissed and curled from the tubes, engulfing the stands.

"It's showtime, Splash," he whispered in my ear, gliding a hand under my elbow to assist me to my feet.

I resisted at first, but Sterling dragged his lips across the back of my neck, enticing sensations I'd never felt before. Warm. Loose. Light like I was floating on my own personal cloud. My reality softened. A part of me was still conscious that I loathed Sterling with every molecule in my body, but the sensory section of my brain was having the best time of her life.

Nothing I felt was real; it was the drug making me feel these things. A sober Mads would have nothing but contempt and disgust in her heart for Sterling Weston, would never let him touch her again.

"No," I combatted, despite getting to my feet.

He patted my ass like I'd just scored a touchdown. "Good girl."

Hardly. If he claimed to know me so well, then he should have guessed that I would never go anywhere with him meekly. Fuck no. He could pump me full of every drug he could get his hands on, and I would still fight him tooth and nail.

Commotion stretched through the stands, making its way down to the field. The mumbles quickly turned to people getting up from their seats, trying to make it off the bleachers and out of the colored smoke.

But I was too damn busy trying to keep my balance. I felt so off.

Instead of going down with the crowd, he took me up, confusing me, but it didn't stop my heels from digging in, a bit of lucidness creeping through the high. Not that it did much good. Sterling lacked Micah's physique, but he still outmuscled me. A swift yank and I staggered up the steps. It was either that or end up on the ground. Perhaps falling would have been better.

I gave myself a second or two to regain my composure, and then I screamed, "Micah!" A mouthful of smoke went into my lungs, and I coughed. It had been a weak cry for help, especially over the upheaval. I doubted Micah heard me, much less anyone else.

Sterling jerked me against him, slapping a hand over my mouth. "That wasn't very smart, Splash," he growled in my ear.

Yeah, well, neither is this. I clamped my teeth down on a finger.

"Bitch," he hissed, ripping his hand away from my mouth, but a moment later, that same hand was flying toward my face.

The asshole backhanded me.

I stumbled against him, my eyes rolling back, the tang of something metallic on my tongue. My blood. Pain throbbed on the left side of my cheek as I froze, my whole body and mind stunned. I'd been in a fight or two in my life, but nothing serious, just some hair pulling and shoving. Never had I been hit. Even when my older brother Jason and I were younger, he never hurt me. Sure, he would put me in a headlock or pin my arms behind my back, but I'd only really been protected by the men in my life. In my world, men didn't hit women. How quickly my world shifted.

"You shouldn't have done that," Sterling said as if it was my fault the asshole slapped me. "I never meant to hurt you. All you had to do was come with me for an hour."

A bitter laugh choked out of me. "Next time don't drug and force me."

"Mads!" a voice howled. *Micah.*

Thick smoke impaired my vision in a rainbow of colors. It looked more like a birthday party than a kidnapping. I couldn't tell how far away he was, but once Micah got a hold of Sterling, the asshole was dead.

Sterling's head whipped over his shoulder right before he bent and hauled me over his shoulder, the quick movement taking my breath away. Then we were moving as he rushed down the row toward the end. Squirming, kicking, and hitting, I did everything I could to get him to release me, but the bastard came to a halt before I could really fight. I didn't have time to grasp what he planned as he pulled me forward, grabbing the end of my wrists and pushing me over the edge.

A silent scream lodged in my throat, my mouth and throat so damn dry. *Oh my God? Does he plan to drop me?* I'd break an ankle for sure and God knew what else depending on the landing. Regardless, it would hurt like hell. I panicked, my feet kicking through air as I dangled.

"You ready?" Sterling hollered, and I wasn't sure if he was talking to me or not, but I was most definitely not fucking ready.

"Yeah. Drop her," a voice came from below. His accomplice.

No sooner did the words register in my head than I was falling. Another scream ripped from my throat, this one created from instinctual fear of plummeting to my death. My arms flapped like I was a bird with a broken wing trying to take flight.

Two large hands grabbed my waist, breaking what would have been a disastrous fall. It still didn't feel great. Sterling's partner in crime's fingers dug into my flesh, hard enough that I knew I would have another bruise on my body. At least this one I wouldn't have to cover up with makeup, not like the one I was sure to have on my face.

Once my feet were planted on the ground, the one who caught me pinned my arms behind my back as Sterling jumped, landing with a thud beside us.

"We need to move before they realize she's no longer in the stands," Sterling ordered his co-conspirator.

My cheek and lip still ached, pain pulsing, but the discomfort was the least of my worries. Sterling had hit me once. Nothing was stopping him from doing so again, and now there were two of them, but my survival instincts had kicked in. This was a fucking public place, for shit's sake. Surely someone would be able to hear my cry for help.

I opened my mouth and screamed. "Help—"

As expected, a hand slapped against my mouth. "Keep her fucking quiet," Sterling hissed, teeth gritted together.

The only way they were going to be able to do that was by knocking me out, which was always a possibility. I wrestled against the binds imprisoning my hands, attempting to break free, but there were some positions the arms were just not meant to bend. Switching tactics, I slammed the heel of my foot down on my captor's foot. "Go phhuck yourshelff," I snarled, my words muffled behind the hand.

Sterling laughed as he thrust his fingers into my hair, grabbing a hold of my head and shoving me forward toward the tunnel. "Watch it with this one. She likes it rough."

My feet were having trouble, getting tangled together and

lacking normal coordination. If he would just stop manhandling me for a fucking moment, I could get my bearings. I knew without certainty that I did not want to go inside the tunnel with the two of them. The farther they took me from the field, the more dangerous the situation became. I tried to free Sterling's fingers from my hair, as he used it like a leash to guide me, but to no avail.

All the lights in the tunnel had either been switched off or broken. Darkness yawned before us. Intimidating. Daunting. And desolate.

Only a few steps in, both Sterling and his partner came to a jarring halt. Before my eyes could find the reason why, I heard a familiar voice.

"Funny. I heard the same thing about you," the voice said sarcastically in response to Sterling's lewd comment about how I liked it rough. Knuckles cracked in the dark.

My world stopped, tilting sideways on its axis. Or maybe that was me being close to passing out. Or the drug. Probably all the above. I braced a hand on the cold, damp concrete wall.

Josie stood a few feet in front of us. Her pink hair caught on a beam of waning light shining from behind me. Her brown eyes were huge, and she gasped, the sound bouncing through the tunnel. But the menacing voice hadn't been hers. It had been Grayson's. I would guarantee it.

And then my cousin stepped out of the shadows, the sunlight just bright enough to give a face to the figure that came to stand beside Josie. Fynn appeared on the other side, the two Elite flanking my best friend. Their arms were crossed, and murder gleamed in their eyes.

Relief hit me like a tsunami. I hadn't intended to sway against Sterling. He just happened to be an available body to keep me from crumpling to the ground. Not that he offered much support.

"Oh, you're so fucked now." I giggled, a bit manic, and his fingers slid out of my hair. I tumbled backward, my back hitting his chest.

Grayson stared at me strangely as if a third eye had magically appeared between my other two.

Sterling gripped my shoulders, positioning me in front of him like a shield. As if I would protect him from a mosquito bite, let alone from the Elite. His idiot accomplice shifted warily on his feet, eyes darting between Grayson and Fynn.

"Let her go," Grayson said.

"Mads and I are old friends." Sterling patted my shoulder, not holding me captive but letting me know if I took one step forward, he would grab me, but really, he wouldn't have to try hard. I wasn't going anywhere. The drug made every part of my body feel heavier yet more lax than it was.

Fynn arched a mocking brow. "Do you usually hit your friends?"

I grimaced, staying still. My whole life I pretended to be the tough girl, and I thought I had done a pretty good job at it. But somehow, seeing the slightest bit of sympathy in Fynn's eyes broke something inside me. I didn't want to be weak, and that was how Sterling made me feel. It wasn't just that he'd hit me. I felt as if I hadn't fought back hard enough.

And that wasn't me.

The frown on Josie's face deepened. She might not have seen the tiny cut on my lip, but Fynn had.

"You assume I hit her. Did you ever stop to think that maybe I was the one who saved her?" Sterling countered.

My sarcastic snort echoed through the tunnel, slightly suppressed by the disorder still happening outside on the field. The team might not use this tunnel during practices, but that didn't mean someone couldn't wander in at any moment. I couldn't decide if that would aid or hamper the situation. Did it matter? "Add woman beater to his impressively growing douchebag résumé," I said.

Grayson pinned me with his turbulent dark eyes. "Seeing as you can find it in yourself to crack a joke, I don't have to ask if you're okay."

"I'm okay," I assured, but my body and actions were contradicting my assurance.

Grayson shifted his focus off me. "You have no idea what you've started," he said darkly. "You've been lucky up until now. That's all about to change. Once Micah sees her—"

"You've got the wrong idea," Sterling said shortly. "This is part of Micah's initiation."

"He drugged me," I blurted before he could spew more lies.

Grayson closed the space in a heartbeat, slamming Sterling against the wall, the side of his arm pressed into the fucker's throat. The restraint on Grayson's temper snapped. "Tell me why I shouldn't break your nose right now."

Sterling's waste-of-space friend moved to wrestle Grayson off him, but Fynn stopped him with a firm command. "Don't think about it." Fynn pinched the bridge of his nose, remaining at Josie's side. "You crossed the line. She's family."

Grayson shoved his arm deeper into Sterling's throat. "You don't fuck with family. If there's one thing we can't stand, it's the use of drugs to get a girl. It's weak and pathetic."

"I'm. Not. Weak," Sterling gasped, struggling for air between words.

"This wasn't our fight before, not when we thought you had a thing for Micah's girl. But now? All bets are off." Grayson's features were hard and savage. "You've made it personal."

"Me!" Sterling growled. "I'm not the one who started this—"

Grayson's arm dug in harder, cutting him off before he could dig his grave deeper. "He is going to kill you for this. I'd watch your back."

Fool. Sterling was a fool.

His friend was smart enough to reconsider his position. "Sterling, man, I think we should go." He glanced over his shoulder, hearing the voices outside the tunnel getting closer. A fight had definitely broken out on the field. Sterling's frat boys distracting Micah and Brock.

Her lips pursed, Josie asked the question that burned in all our minds. "Why don't you tell us what it is you think Micah did?"

Sterling made a grunt of disgust in the back of his throat, glaring at Grayson. He didn't struggle against my cousin's restraint. In fact, I swore he enjoyed the pain. His lip curled in derision. This was a different side of Sterling, a side that elicited cold fear and made me want to run from him.

"What's going on in here?" someone called from the opening of the tunnel.

It was one of the coaches. Heads whipped in the direction of the voice, but other than that, no one moved a muscle. Not even Grayson, who still had Sterling pinned to the wall.

"You shouldn't be in here," the coach informed us, scowling. "We're clearing the stadium. It's time to go."

"We were just heading out," Fynn assured him, shooting Grayson a silent message.

Grayson released Sterling, but not without one last shove.

The coach cleared his throat, sensing the tension that suffocated the tunnel. "Did any of you have something to do with the stunt that was pulled in the stands?" His focus went right to the president of Chi Sigma. "Sterling, this better not be one of your fraternity pranks."

Sterling adjusted his shirt, smoothing out invisible wrinkles. "Coach, I can assure you that my house wasn't involved. You know what big supporters my family is of the football team."

I wanted to laugh at the absurdity of his statement, but I also wanted to cry in frustration, because the coach looked as if he bought Sterling's bullshit. *Has everyone in KU drunk the Kool-Aid? What the fuck?*

"Let's go, Mads," Josie said softly, draping her arm around me and lending me her steadiness as we left the tunnel of horror. Or it could have been. I didn't want to think about what Sterling and his buddy would have done to me if Josie, Fynn, and Grayson hadn't shown up.

"Micah?" I rasped, needing to see him. Through all the

madness, he became the one thing I needed, the one thing my brain fixated on, and he was all I could think about.

My cousin steered me through the field. The air had lingering traces of smoke in it, reminding me of the bonfires my parents had back home. "I sent him a text and let him know we found you. We're meeting back at the guys' place," she told me.

Grayson and Fynn flanked either side of Josie and me. Both had their jaws clamped, nothing friendly in their expressions.

"I need him."

"I bet you do, honey." She brushed strands of hair out of my face, and it felt good. Too good, like when Micah played with my hair. I didn't want her to stop touching me and yet that felt wrong.

A whimper breezed through my lips. "There's something wrong with me."

Josie shared a look with Grayson, who gave her just the slightest shake of his head. "Micah will take care of you. Just hang on a little longer," she said, trying to placate me.

"Why did I wear a bra?" I mumbled, my undergarments causing friction I had no right feeling in front of them, but a part of me also didn't give a shit. "I'm so uncomfortable."

"One of you needs to carry her. It'll make this go a lot quicker," Josie ordered.

Fynn checked his phone. "Micah isn't going to like one of us touching her right now."

"I don't give a shit what he likes or doesn't like. Mads needs us. The Elite protect what's theirs. Is that not what you guys are always preaching?" Josie argued.

My feet did their best to keep up with her, but the extreme

sensitivity of my body distracted me. The way the wind blew my hair, tickling my neck and back. The way my jean shorts rubbed as I walked. Every movement, no matter how small, became heightened and had taken over my thoughts.

"Fynn, you got this," Grayson said, clapping him on the back.

Fynn cocked a brow at his friend.

"It'll be weird if I do it," Grayson defended. "We're fucking related, and she's too horny for me to deal with."

"He's going to kill me for this." Fynn sighed as he scooped me up, cradling me in his strong arms.

I didn't have to worry about stumbling or falling because Fynn would never let me do either. Clinging to him, I bit my lip to get keep from saying or making any embarrassing noises while being jostled in his arms, but Micah's name tumbled out anyway.

"Just a little bit farther," Fynn soothed.

"I'm sorry," I murmured, feeling tears sting my eyes.

"You have nothing to apologize for," he whispered. "This is not your fault, Mads."

I nuzzled my cheek against his, the bristles of his facial hair scratching over my skin. "I won't let him get mad at you."

Fynn chuckled, his warm breath created a string of tingles that nearly made me moan. I'd always thought Fynn was an attractive guy. I mean, I wasn't blind. What wasn't to like about him? But he'd only been a friend. So why was my body buzzing and so damn turned on?

My fingers itched to run through his dark hair. It had gotten longer, and I wondered if it would be as soft as it looked.

Specks of humor danced in his green eyes. "Thanks. I appreciate it."

"You have pretty eyes. I always thought so." At this point, I was just spewing random shit. True, though.

Another chuckle rumbled underneath me, and I felt him shake his head.

Micah sat on the front porch, still in his football practice gear, when we finally turned the corner onto his street. He was up on his feet and crossing the lawn the moment he laid on eyes on us. His eyes were hard while inspecting me. "What did he do to her?" he thundered, his voice so low, I swore the ground shook.

I squirmed in Fynn's arms, silently demanding to be put down. There was only one place I wanted to be. As soon as my feet touched the ground, I threw myself against Micah, his arms immediately surrounding me.

"She's rolling. Sterling injected her with Molly," Grayson replied, his tone dripping with loathing.

Micah's body jerked against mine, turning rigid. "He's fucking dead."

Grayson folded his arms. "Yeah, I told him that much already."

Somehow, I'd forgotten that someone did this to me. I nipped at Micah's ear, biting down harder the second time. He turned his head, looking down at me with watchful eyes, and I couldn't tell if he wanted to scold me or beg me to do it again. I knew which one I wanted.

Fynn's eyes were darker than usual. "You've got a problem

on your hands, Micah," he declared. "We got a glimpse of the real Sterling, and it was disturbing."

Grayson agreed, nodding. "I got the impression he wanted me to hurt him tonight. Like he craved it."

Micah's arm firmed against me, keeping tight to his side. "In that case, I'm happy to oblige. I'm more than willing to give him pain that will last for months."

"Not tonight," Josie stated, her hands on her hips as she put herself in front of Micah. "She needs you." Her sharp gaze slid to me.

Micah looked at me again, understanding shadowing those sky-blue eyes. "Fuck."

Grayson tried to contain the grin that pulled at his lips. "Just think of it as another way to burn through your anger."

Fynn smirked. "If you're not up for it, I could always step up—"

"Get fucking lost before I decide to break your neck instead of Sterling's." His implication was harsh, but it lacked substantial heat.

A husky laugh rumbled from Fynn's chest. "Get her inside. We'll make sure neither Sterling nor his boys come anywhere near this house tonight. Brock has us on rotation."

Micah raked his fingers through his hair. "I owe you."

"You know that's not how we work," Grayson said. "Nothing is ever owed."

Micah nodded.

Beads of sweat rolled down my shirt between my breasts. My neck was damp with perspiration, pieces of hair sticking to my skin. God, it was fucking hot. I had to cool off before I liter-

RIVAL   267

ally burst into flames. The sun was setting, yet it felt as if it had zeroed me out in the world, sending its sweltering rays just to me. I couldn't take it anymore.

"Maddy, what are you doing?" Micah demanded sharply.

"I need to get these clothes off," I confessed, lifting the hem of my tank up. The friction was bothering me, and in my current state, the only way to rectify the problem was to get rid of them. And I'd waited long enough.

"Shit," he muttered under his breath before hauling me over his shoulder, his long strides carrying us toward the house.

CHAPTER FIFTEEN

MICAH

I'd done my fair share of drugs. My life from a young age had been nothing but a stream of endless parties. What started out as business functions and high-class soirees turned into beach bashes and high school bingers. One thing they all had in common: booze and a cocktail of drugs, from street to prescription.

Those pretentious high rollers were no different from thugs in the streets. Dressing it up with glass tables, expensive tools, or hidden platinum gold jewelry didn't make the contents any less potent.

Mads, despite growing up in the same uppity world I had, rarely partook in the drug side of parties. The girl could down a bottle of champagne without taking a breath, but she never touched the *party favors*.

The fact that Sterling had given my girl a drug without her consent nearly put me over the top. The only thing stopping me from storming the Chi Sigma house was Mads. Tonight, Sterling got a pass, but tomorrow, all fucking bets were off.

I would be gunning for him, fully loaded and ready to hunt.

As I carried her upstairs to my room, I tried not to let my mind wander to what might have happened if Brock hadn't called Grayson and Fynn for the weekend. It only made me respect him more for the role he took in our crew. What if he hadn't called them? What if they had been five minutes later? What if Sterling's sadistic plan had gone off without a hitch?

I fucking hated the what-if game.

I don't know what made him change his mind, but I would be forever grateful.

The smoke. The crowd. The chaos on the field. All of it contributed to the panic I had felt when I lost sight of Mads. My gut immediately understood what was happening. I'd been the foreman for too many pranks in my day not to recognize what was going down.

And now she was suffering. I only knew one way to relieve the agony she felt. The idea that Sterling might have been the one to touch her, to ease her distress, sent blistering fury blazing through my blood.

"Micah, the world is upside down," she whined, and the little quiver in her voice broke something in my chest.

Anger wasn't what Mads needed. I had to bank the flames and find a way to remain calm. "We're almost there," I reassured her, kicking the door wider with my foot.

I set her down in the middle of my bed. She shoved tangles of hair out of her face, glancing up at me with those teary starlight eyes. "What did he do to me?"

My jaw clenched, and I fought the urge to punch a wall. "The bastard shot you up with Molly."

Her bottom lip trembled. "Why?"

I trailed a finger over her jawline. My desire to take away her confusion and make her forget the heightened emotions coursing through her slowly overrode my anger. "It would do neither of us any good to theorize about his motives."

She reached up, her hands slipping under my shirt, pulling me between her legs. "You're right. Let's not talk."

"Mads." I put a bit of sternness behind her name. "I want you to stay here. I need five minutes to shower. Can you do that?"

"Micah," she pleaded, her lips forming the most adorable pout. In a different situation, I would have been amused.

"Stay put," I ordered, pointing to the bed.

Her fingers went to the elastic waistband of my shorts, brushing over my lower belly. "Don't leave. I don't want to be alone."

I sucked in a breath. "I'm not going anywhere. Why don't you lie down?"

She scuttled back on the bed, tugging at my waistband as she went. "I like touching you. It feels good."

"Uh-huh," I agreed, removing her hand gently from my shorts before I jumped on her, stinky and sweaty as I was. Backing up to my bedroom door, I shut it, flipped the lock, and glanced one more time over at Mads to make sure she hadn't moved before strutting into the bathroom. I left the door open.

Taking a two-minute shower to rinse off, I didn't bother to shampoo. The water was cold, but damn if it didn't alleviate the churning of both desire and fury pumping inside me. It seemed like a dangerous concoction that I needed to gain control of fast.

Lucky for me, the moment I stepped back into my bedroom with just a towel draped around my waist, one emotion became predominantly brighter, snuffing the anger out completely.

Mads lay on my bed without a stitch of clothing, her shorts, tank, and undergarments tossed into different sections of my room. I hovered in the doorway. "Jesus," I whispered to myself.

She groaned my name groaned as she squirmed on the bed. She ran a hand down the side of her hips, her glazed eyes finding me. "Micah, you left."

I moved to the bed—to her. "I'm here now, and I'm not going anywhere. I'll be by your side the entire night."

She sat up, reaching for me, and this time I didn't step away. I sank into the bed beside her. "I need you to touch me. I need you to—"

I brushed my fingers over her lower belly, moving up between her breasts. "Like this?" I murmured.

"Yes. More. I need more." She arched her back, tilting her body slightly to the side so my hand grazed her nipple.

I rolled the bud between my thumb and index finger, applying a bit more pressure with each turning pass. She wrapped her arms around my neck, drawing me closer. I kissed her gently, slanting my lips over hers, but the featherlight teasing of our mouths lasted only seconds. Mads wasn't having it. She swept her tongue in between my lips, deepening the kiss. Nothing about her suggested she wanted tenderness or a slow pace.

What Mads wanted, I would give her.

"You make me dizzy," she said.

"Then you better hold on," I instructed, wrapping my fingers in her hair and pulling her back to my lips.

She took my bottom lip between her teeth and bit me. The smile that curled on her lips was devilish. "You taste good." As if she needed another taste, her tongue swept over my mouth.

With clever, impatient fingers, she pulled at the towel around my waist, the loose knot unraveling. She shoved aside the terry cloth material as her lips fused to mine. Our tongues tangled, and I gasped into her mouth at the feel of her hand wrapping around my dick. I barely caught my breath before her fingers were moving, teasing me into a frenzy of need. Sparks of desire pulsed.

Her hand pumped over the hard length of me, and I nearly came as the pad of her thumb grazed over my tip. This wasn't supposed to be about me, but damn if she didn't make this situation fucking hot.

"Wait," I moaned pathetically. Not even I believed I wanted her to stop.

"I'm done waiting. I want to watch you come." She climbed on top of me, legs straddling either side of me, and I groaned. My fingers went to her hips, steadying her, but she began to rock against me. "Stop talking. More kissing." Her mouth fused to mine, and we fell onto the mattress, a tangle of tongues, limbs, and hungry kisses. She needed this. Needed me.

And I was selfish enough to take it.

She positioned herself over me, guiding my pulsing cock inside. I slipped in effortlessly. She was already so damn fucking wet.

A sigh of pleasure escaped me, and then Mads rolled her hips, and I swear to God, I saw fucking stars. I let her set the pace as she moved in slow circles at first, creating the sweetest torture my body had ever endured. It took all my control to not thrust deeper, to fully sink myself inside her.

She fit me so damn perfectly; every dip and curve matched mine. I ran my fingers over her plump ass as she rode me.

"More, Micah. I need more," she begged.

How could I say no? I increased the rhythm of my strokes, moving faster and harder. Her hands went above her head, flattening onto the surface of the headboard. Tangles of her hair fall forward over her shoulders, covering her breasts.

My hips lifted off the bed slightly as she matched my movements. Those dove-gray eyes held my gaze, and I was powerless to look away. "You know I'm the only one who can make you feel like this," I murmured, wrapping a hand around the back of her neck. "Tell me I'm the only one, Mads," I whispered as I dipped my head to take one of her nipples into my mouth.

Her head dropped back, a soft moan of desire slipping from her before she responded, "There will never be anyone but you, Micah." Her skin glistened, cheeks flushed. I didn't think there was a more beautiful sight than Mads coming completely undone.

The fingers pressing into my chest turned into nails raking down my body as I watched her chase her release. The sting of her nails only heightened my need for her. I welcomed it and the passion that flared within me. My name tore from her lips as she tumbled over the edge, her gray eyes so dark. Seconds later I followed, my body trembling under hers.

When the orgasm died down, my muscles went lax, and she curled into me, relaxing. Her chest rose and fell in tempo with mine, a comforting feeling. I closed my eyes. We lay tangled up in each other for minutes before Mads got up to use the bathroom. When she returned, she sank into the center of my bed, honey hair spreading over my sheets and lips swollen from our kisses. Tiredness came over her features, her eyes growing heavy to the point that she could no longer keep them open. This was good. She needed sleep.

I rolled to my side to get us both some water, but Mads's hand stopped me. "Stay. You said you would stay."

I gathered her in my arms, an affectionate smile nipping at my lips. "Is this better?"

She nuzzled into my side, the tips of her nails tracing the outline of my chest tattoo, something she did often when we were together. "Not even close."

A minute later, her fingers stopped moving and lay softly on my chest. Her breathing had evened, and I hoped that meant she'd fallen asleep. I was too afraid to move and risk waking her up. She'd suffered enough tonight. She deserved whatever rest she could find.

But I didn't sleep at all. I couldn't.

Sterling had gone too far, and I had to find a way to make sure he never touched her again. There weren't many options short of killing the bastard. And I didn't see how I could protect Mads without also hurting her.

For hours, I agonized over my options, what the best course of action might be. By the time the sun crested over the horizon,

I was filled with so much dread that it felt as if I were suffocating from it.

As much as I wanted this night to end for her, I never wanted the morning to come. I didn't feel good about what I would do, but I had to shift Sterling's focus off Mads and entirely on me. Then I could figure out what this asshole had against me.

I sat in the corner, cloaked in shadows, the first streak of sunlight peeking through the blinds, and stared at the girl in my bed. I never imagined someone would become so important to me that I would put them above myself. Or the Elite.

Fuck. That was a hell of a statement. Those three guys had been the only people who I could count on. They'd been my family, more than that of my blood. I would die, kill, and burn the world for them. I hadn't expected Mads to become that level of importance to me. Perhaps I should have seen her coming. She'd always been there, hanging around. The girl who had once been like an annoying little sister had grown up and become someone I couldn't ignore.

My heart mattered little to me in this situation, and yet tonight it was cracking. Each minute that went by, each second the sun grew brighter, those cracks deepened.

I just hoped that when this was over, Mads could forgive me.

Again.

CHAPTER SIXTEEN

MADS

I woke up the following morning alone in Micah's bed. Memories of the night came back in waves, a flow of highs and lows that had me feeling pretty fucking messed up. I couldn't seem to distinguish how I felt about what happened. On one hand, I was hurt, angry, ashamed, and sad that Sterling had violated my freedom. But on the other side, despite hating the drug, I had felt this connection with Micah. The way he'd been so gentle, how he'd held me afterward in his arms. I knew a huge part of what I'd experienced from his touch was heightened by the drug, but could it also be because I was in love with him?

Calling the sex magical seemed wrong considering the circumstances, but it did have a romantic quality to it.

I loved Micah.

Admitting such a big confession to myself was almost weight lifting. A part of me had loved Micah for as long as I could remember, but I'd suppressed it, homing in on the hurt and anger he'd made me feel. Somehow that had been easier than dealing with heartbreak.

Stretching, I rolled to my side, keeping the sheet around me. I had no idea what time it was, but the house was silent. A bottle of water had been left on the side table. I inched myself up into a reclined position, reaching for the water, when a movement from the edge of my eye had my heart sprinting in my chest. For a few split seconds, panic that someone had broken into Micah's house raced within me, making my organs pump harder. A someone like Sterling.

It was reasonable to think I would be jumpy and paranoid after what happened. I didn't want it to be a long-term reaction, me jumping at every shadow in the corner or constantly looking over my shoulder. It seemed wrong as the victim that I would have to continue to suffer.

I was a second away from scrambling out of bed when I heard my name.

"Mads," Micah whispered.

My blood pressure slowly returned to normal as I realized it was him sitting quietly in a chair nestled in the corner of his bedroom. The floor-length curtains covering the windows were slightly ajar, letting in slivers of light. Fully dressed, he sat forward, elbows pressed into his knees, wearing his serious expression.

I didn't like it.

It meant something was bothering him.

Micah was rarely somber.

I stared at him, suddenly finding myself tongue-tied. What

did you say after something like last night? *"Thanks for taking care of me?"* It sounded wrong on so many levels despite that actually being what he'd done.

"You're making me nervous. Just tell me what's wrong," I said, breaking the silence between us. "Did something else happen?"

Micah didn't move a muscle as he replied, "No. He wouldn't dare show up here, not with the four of us under one roof."

I dropped my head back against the wall, releasing the breath I'd been holding. "Then why do you look like you're about to tell me there's been a death in the family."

"I think we need a break," he blurted, the statement coming out so matter-of-fact, as if he'd given it considerable thought. Perhaps he had. I had no idea how long he'd been sitting in the chair. Hours?

I blinked, hardly believing this was a conversation we were having before coffee, let alone at all! "What do you mean, a break?" This was not something I expected after last night. How could someone show me such love, care only about my needs, and then cast me aside?

Because that was what this felt like, as if Micah didn't have a need for me any longer.

My mind knew that wasn't true, but hearing those words from his mouth caused my heart to doubt everything.

Was he angry?

I studied his face as I waited for him to explain, not surprised to pick up the tension in his shoulders.

He was doing his best to keep the fire within him from

surfacing, and I imagined he'd kept that rage buried all night. It had to be eating away at him, and I couldn't help but wonder if any part of that fury was because of me. Had I done something?

Hurt fractured in those light blue eyes like shattered ice. "It's not safe for you to be around me. Look what happened last night. That shit was my fault. Because of me, you ended up in danger. My past. My decisions lead to trouble. And I *refuse* to bring you into the danger."

I bolted upright in bed, the sheet around me slipping, but I didn't give an Elite ass about my nakedness. "Don't you dare take the blame. You didn't put a gun to Sterling's head and force him to drug me."

His shoulders dropped, right along with my heart as understanding dawned. Micah was self-sabotaging our relationship. "No, but I might as well have. Whatever beef Sterling has with me, he'll continue to use the most important thing to me because he knows that's where to cut me the deepest. *You*," he emphasized. "You're the most important thing in my life, and I can't risk you. Who knows how much further he's willing to go? Until I find out what it is he thinks I've done, you need to stay away from me."

Everything about this felt wrong. Why should Micah and I be the ones punished for someone else's fucked-up mental issues? I was convinced Sterling had more than a few screws loose. I'd seen it yesterday, and I believed that was only the tip of a giant iceberg regarding his mental stability.

I shook my head. "Like a few days? A week? How long of a break are you suggesting? And what do you mean by break? We don't see each other anymore? We don't talk?"

"I don't know," he replied, giving me absolutely nothing to hold on to.

I fisted the sheets, holding them to my chest. "You don't know," I repeated, punctuating each syllable with attitude. "That's rich, Micah. Why do you get to make this decision? You should have talked to me." I let my anger free. He wasn't the only one who was frustrated with Sterling.

He forked a hand into his sandy hair. Some days I missed the platinum locks he'd worn through high school. "What do you think I'm doing?" he bit out, finally releasing that locked-up anger.

I could see this escalating quickly. Micah and I were about to have a full-blown fight. "This isn't talking and coming up with a solution together. This is you making all the decisions because you think you know best."

"I get that you're pissed. Do you think I want to do this?"

"Does it matter? Because you are. How many times am I going to let you hurt me?" I shot back.

"I'm not doing this to hurt you, Mads. Just the fucking opposite."

"It doesn't matter. The outcome is the same." I snorted, shaking my head. "You're being just as big a fool as he is if you think he's going to buy into the crap that you don't care about me anymore. This *break*, as you call it, is pointless."

"Maybe. But I knew you wouldn't agree to leave school, and I couldn't ask you no matter how much I want you as far from him as possible." He took a deep breath. "Look, all I'm saying is that you can't be anywhere I am. It gives him opportunity."

From confused, to upset, to hurt, to pissed off. My emotions had just gotten off a roller coaster only to get right back on the worst ride of my life. The pain in my heart split into surging anger. "I'm not doing this," I said, tossing the sheet off me and jumping out of his bed. I didn't want to be here anymore, listening to the stupidest shit I'd ever heard.

"Mads." Micah sighed. "It's because I love you so fucking much that I have to let you go. Next time, I might not be there. I can live knowing you're alive and safe. But if anything happened to you... that I could never live with."

"This is stupid, do you know that? You love me, but you think we should break up. Fuck that, Micah." I began a scavenger hunt for my clothes, scouring the floor for something to wear. It didn't even have to be mine. "Screw your break," I snapped, whirling toward him. "How about I see you one better and just call this whole thing off? It's not like we ever really stood a chance."

He recoiled as if I'd slapped him. It was a low blow, but my tongue was irrational, acting out without thinking. I tended to get that way when I was furious and hurt. "Are you breaking up with me?" he asked quietly.

I grabbed a T-shirt and yanked it over my head. Micah's scent surrounded me, and I instantly wanted to rip it off. "If you insist on taking a break, yes. I don't want someone who won't stand by me."

His jaw hardened. "That's not what I'm doing. You know damn well this isn't simple or something I took lightly."

"You're fucking kidding, right?" I barked, jerking on my shorts. "This is a joke. You're being an asshole. And it's not cute or sexy this time. And it's not me who's doing this to us. It's you.

I'm just drawing the line. We're either a team or we're not. Simple."

He stood from the chair, coming toward me. "Mads."

I held up a finger in front of me before he could take one step closer to me, distance being key for me to keep my composure. I would not crumble under those damn light blue eyes or the fucking dimples. He would not use those on me. Not today. "No. I know what you're doing, and I refuse to let you do this to us."

He took a step toward me and another. "It might not seem like it right now, but I'd rather have you alive than see you tormented for being my girlfriend."

Snatching my bra and underwear from the floor, I clutched them at my sides. "If you do this, Micah, he wins. And I can promise that I'm not waiting around. Not anymore. If I walk out that door, I'm never walking back through. Do you understand? That's it. We're finished. Finite. Forever. You don't get to come in and out of my life when you fucking feel like it. I'm not a revolving door you can enter and leave when the mood strikes."

He said the worst thing he could. "You're being unreasonable."

I zipped up my shorts, angrily fumbling with the button. He knew I hated having my feelings invalidated. "I didn't think I could ever hate you as much as I did that night I found you in bed with another girl. Boy, was I wrong." Grabbing my bag, I stormed out, leaving him standing in the middle of the room.

He called after me, but I rushed down the stairs, not looking back. Fynn and Grayson were in the kitchen with Brock, drinking coffee as another pot brewed. Water percolating in the carafe joined the thumping of my bare feet as I padded across the room.

I hadn't even bothered to grab my shoes, and I wasn't about to run back upstairs and get them. The only thing I wanted was to get as far from Micah as I could. I didn't want to see or talk to the Elite.

"Mads?" Grayson called as I strutted past the table, not looking up at any of them. I didn't want to see their faces, see the sympathy or feel the awkwardness of them trying to work out what happened. It was bad enough that they knew Sterling had drugged me and what Micah and I had done most of the night.

Shame stained my cheeks as I shook my head, fighting back the well of tears that wanted to break free. I refused to let them. Not here. *You have nothing to be ashamed of*, I tried to remind myself, but the mantra hadn't stuck.

"Not now," I told Grayson and walked out the front door, feeling three sets of curious but worried eyes on me.

I hadn't thought Micah could be a bigger dick than when I found him in bed with another girl.

I was fucking wrong.

This whole shit of him thinking he was saving me somehow by pushing me away, it was such a pussy move, and so not like Micah. Yet it was such an Elite scheme. I had to wonder if it was Brock's idea, not that it mattered. All Micah had to do was say no, and he hadn't.

I didn't feel the shards of tiny pebbles cutting into my feet as I hiked back to the dorm, nor the strange looks I got from the few people moseying about this early in the morning on a Saturday. And because I didn't want to go straight back to my room and face my friends, I stopped and bought a coffee at one of the vendors on the sidewalk, the smell taunting me since I'd left Micah's.

Ugh!

Would my every thought circle back to him in all shapes and forms? It was like my brain couldn't go more than a few seconds without somehow thinking about *him*. He'd woven himself into all aspects of my life.

The guy making my flat white coffee eyed me once or twice but didn't seem fazed. "Fun night?" he asked, making small talk.

I was so not in the mood for chitchat. "Not exactly."

"Well, you've come to the right place for the perfect hangover cure."

Forcing a grin, I took my coffee. If only overindulging in liquor was my only problem.

I walked aimlessly around campus with no destination in mind. Just like my feet, my mind roamed, losing all sense of time and the world around me. I paid no attention to the campus slowly waking up, becoming busier, and it wasn't until a body sat down next to me and gave me a cheesy pickup line that I snapped out of the daze.

Blinking at the random guy beside me on the bench, I suddenly didn't feel comfortable being alone. Without saying a word, I got up and left, speed-walking back to my dorm. With each step, the anxiety that sprouted inside me thrived like a weed after a rainstorm. By the time I got to my building, I was positive someone was following me. My fingers shook as I took out my ID card, holding it over the sensor and waiting for the door to unlock. The second it clicked, I tugged the door open and bolted inside.

Exhaling, I pressed my back to the wall and dropped my head, staring at my bare feet.

What the fuck are you doing? Get a hold of yourself.

After pressing the elevator button, I chewed on my lip, watching the numbers highlight one at a time. *Why is this thing so slow?* My patience level shot, I decided to take the stairs, out of breath by the time I reached my room.

"Where have you been?" Kenna demanded the moment I stepped foot in our room. She had her hair in a messy bun on top of her head, arms tented on her hips, reminding me a little too much of my mother. "I was two minutes away from calling campus security and filing a missing Mads report."

The coffee I'd drunk earlier had worked itself out of my system, and the caffeine buzz crashed, leaving me fatigued. I dropped my bag. "I was walking."

"For hours?" she prompted disbelievingly.

Shrugging, I shuffled past her and sank down onto the edge of my bed. "I guess. I haven't really looked at the time." I didn't even know if my phone was in my bag.

Her eyes ran over me. "Where the fuck are your shoes?"

"I don't know. Micah's probably."

"He called me," she stated.

That got my attention. My head snapped up, and a snort breezed through my nostrils. "I do not want to talk about him."

She crossed her arms. "Fine. He doesn't exist in this room. Do you hear that, girls?" she hollered over her shoulder. "Micah Bradford no longer exists here."

I rolled my eyes.

Leave it to Kenna to be dramatic as fuck.

Josie came into the room and sat down beside me. "Are you okay?" she murmured.

Ainsley plopped down on my other side, sandwiching me in, the two of them essentially holding me up.

My chest ached, and I could feel myself withdrawing before I crumbled. "I just want to sleep."

Ainsley shifted, pulling back the blankets on my bed and tucking me in. "How about I order us some ramen from that place we like for lunch?"

"Sure," I mumbled, curling up into a ball, food the furthest thing from my mind. I knew the three of them were giving each other worried glances, but I was too tired to care.

CHAPTER SEVENTEEN

MICAH

Hurting Mads cut me deeper than I anticipated. If my will to keep her safe hadn't been so strong, I would have caved at the first quiver in her voice. The idea that she might be alone and crying somewhere tore at my chest like I was being clawed from the inside out.

I should have rushed after her instead of sitting in the dark, but I couldn't move. I wanted to run after her, stop her from leaving. I wanted to take her in my arms and tell her I was sorry. That she was right. That I was scared and being an ass.

But then I glanced at the rumpled bed and remembered what happened last night, how she'd been drugged right in front of me and I hadn't known. Not until it was too late. Sterling had come on my turf, fucked with my girl, laughing like a smug prick. The bastard was lucky he still had two legs to stand on, because when I was finished with him, he would be wheeled out of KU on a stretcher.

I didn't give a shit if it got me expelled. There were other schools. My dad's wrath would be fierce but nothing compared to mine. I needed to do more than hit something, and busting my ass in the gym wasn't going to give me the satisfaction I craved. Not just craved. Revenge was a pulsing demand. My muscles shook with it.

The front door slammed shut, and I stood, staring at the window, combating the urge to peek out as Mads stormed off.

Clenching my fists, I bashed my hand into the wall; it went straight through, battering the drywall. Still, it wasn't enough. Not nearly. I could picture Sterling's face and hit the wall a thousand times and it still wouldn't calm the beast roaring within me.

The twenty-ninth couldn't come soon enough. It was no longer just about some pictures. I had to find dirt on him, find a way to make him gone. And stay gone.

Knock. Knock. Knock.

"Not in the mood," I said gruffly, but the person behind the door wasn't discouraged. The hinges squeaked as they pushed open my bedroom door.

Brock leaned a shoulder on the doorway. "Micah, what the fuck did you do?"

He'd seen Mads leave and clearly noticed she'd been upset. Fynn and Grayson had probably also caught sight of her considering they were sleeping on our couches. Wonderful. Not only had I upset Mads but now my friends were pissed off at me too.

I shoved my hands into my pockets before I punched another wall. "What needed to be done," I said.

"I take it you did something stupid, then, like push her away. Again."

"She'll get over it," I replied, my tone sharpening. I didn't want to talk about this, not when it was so damn raw. Couldn't he see I was dealing with my own shit?

Brock rested a shoulder on the doorframe, cocking a brow at me. "Really? That's what you have to say? Don't be a fucking ass."

I heaved out a sigh. "Too late. And before you start, save the pep talk for someone who gives a shit." I turned my back on him and walked to the window, hoping he would leave me alone. I didn't want company.

He didn't leave. "Prickly. From someone who knows how you're feeling, make it right with Mads. Before it's too late."

I tilted my head to the side, regarding him with a narrowed eye. "What do you think I'm doing?"

"I think you're making a mistake if you think a girl like Mads will wait around a second time or even give you another chance."

He was right. Perhaps that was why my chest hurt so damn much.

If I lost her, truly lost her, then I had lost myself as well.

"Mads is good," I stated, returning my gaze to the window, although I didn't really look at anything particular. The world was nothing but shades of muted colors blurring together. "I'm not." It was that simple.

"I won't argue that she probably deserves better, but you're who she chose," he pointed out.

A snort breezed through my nose. "Makes me question her

taste in men. After all, she slept with Sterling, who's currently stalking, blackmailing, and drugging her." But even after the accusation left my lips, I didn't really believe Sterling had been anything to Mads but a rebound one-night stand. I'd had more than my share. She'd been pissed off at me and hurt... much like now.

A burst of panic exploded in my chest. "Shit," I muttered, scrubbing a hand over my face and staring at my reflection in the mirror. "What the fuck have I done?" Last night it seemed to all make sense.

Brock placed a hand on my shoulder and squeezed. I hadn't heard him move into the room. "What we all do. Fuck up from time to time. Own your mistake and fix it. That makes you more of a man. Besides, if you don't, Grayson's waiting downstairs to lay into you."

I turned and leaned my back against the window, shaking my head. "How the fuck did we both end up falling for the girls in his family?"

His lips curved in a wicked way that said he wasn't sorry at all for falling for his best friend's sister. "It drives him crazy."

My chest lifted and lowered as I took a deep breath. "We still on for tonight?" I asked.

Brock's eyes brightened with a speck of anticipation. "Fuck yes. Nothing's changed."

"Thanks, man. I couldn't do this without you, without them," I added, nodding toward the open door where the rest of my *true* family waited. The guys who'd always been there and never let me down.

He held my gaze and said, "You've always done the same for me."

* * *

I stared at my phone countless times throughout the day and into the night, debating whether to text or call Mads, but each time I came close, I chickened out. I couldn't do it. Not yet. Sterling had to be dealt with. I needed to break him. I needed just one night.

The problem was that night of opportunity wasn't until next weekend—rush week.

Brock and the others might not agree with my decision to keep Mads away, but it was better than her getting caught in the crossfire.

If anything, Brock should understand considering everything that happened last year with Josie and Carter. He'd wanted to throttle Josie for putting herself in danger, regardless that she handled herself like a damn Elite. Secretly, we'd all been a little proud, once the anger evaporated.

But that didn't mean I wanted Mads going off on some sort of vigilante mission. It would be better if she went home for the weekend and visited her parents, but the suggestion couldn't come from me. That would only have the opposite effect. Maybe I could get Josie to help, but that also had a chance to backfire. The girls in our lives were so damn willful. It was maddening.

Waiting was always the worst part when it came to taking

down a target. Time tortured me when I was rearing to go. But until all the pieces were in place, I was at a standstill.

Brock had Fynn and Grayson working on something. I received an email from our PI containing all he'd uncovered about Sterling and his family a few days ago. To keep my mind off Mads and the colossal fuckup I'd made of the one good thing in my life, I flipped through the information again on my phone as I sat in my car, making sure I hadn't missed anything.

It was all crap. Nothing of real importance, and that in itself was fishy. Everyone had something to hide, a secret they wanted to keep buried, and the fact that our PI uncovered nothing told me the Westons worked hard to keep their secrets just that—secret. But I was like a fucking dog with a bone. I wouldn't stop until I found what it was they had scrubbed squeaky clean from their lives.

For years, Brock, Grayson, Fynn, and I collected those little dirty secrets people desperately worked to keep from seeing the light of day. Some had the power to destroy lives, others to break up marriages, crush careers, or crumble futures. Politicians, teachers, friends, parents, school boards, police officers—no one was safe from the *kill book*. That was what we called it, but it really wasn't a tangible book. We weren't stupid. Fynn had a system that was too complex for my brain. The dude was a certifiable genius when it came to computers and techy shit. Our little brain. All I knew was it was secure, undetectable in how to access the information. That was enough for me.

I did learn one piece of information that was worth testing out. Sterling had a younger sister, and I was curious how close the two were. Would he care if something happened to her?

He wasn't the only one who could play games. If anything, he'd been playing in the minor leagues, and I was about to show him what happened when you messed with the big dogs.

Stifling a yawn, I let my car slowly roll to a stop at the light and rubbed my eyes. Exhaustion had been plaguing me for the last few hours. It didn't help that I hadn't slept in over a day, and although my body wanted to give in to the dark recesses of sleep, my mind had other plans. Not that it mattered, because the moment I closed my eyes, I saw Mads and Sterling. Unpleasant images that made my skin crawl, that boiled my blood, churned my stomach, and haunted me. The idea that one day the Elite or I might not be there to stop one of Sterling's twisted plots made my blood run cold. I'd be damned before I let him do anything to Mads.

He'd already done enough.

The light turned green, and I slammed my foot on the gas, lurching the Hummer forward with a rumble of the engine. A Hummer at college wasn't all that practical, but it was my favorite car and made a statement.

Get the fuck out of my way.

A few blocks down the road, I swung my car into a parking spot and hopped out to meet up with the guys. I hoped Fynn had better information for me than the PI did.

The neon sign in the window flickered as I walked by Mad Dog's Tap to the entrance. An annoying bell rang over the door as I pulled it open and stepped inside the seedy bar that reminded me an awful lot of Lazy Ray's. The scene was low-key for a Sunday night, exactly what we were looking for, to not draw attention, and the dim booth in the back was made for developing nefarious plans.

I nodded to the bartender, making my w a y down the row of empty booths. "Did you get it?" I asked, slipping into the worn leather seat across from Brock and Fynn. Grayson sat to my left.

Fynn eyed me, a twinkle of victory in his green eyes as he lifted a pierced brow. "Have I ever let you down?"

"I fucking love you, man," I said, our hands clasping over the table.

He slid a slim SD card over the sticky table. "Just download the file onto your phone and hit Play. Should do the trick."

Picking up the tiny device, I looked it over, a fragment of the guilt and pressure in my chest easing. It finally felt like I was doing something other than using my fists. "Brilliant. I can't wait to see his face."

Grayson pushed a full pint glass toward me. "We got you a drink and ordered some food."

I tucked the card into my pocket and shifted to unfold myself from the booth. "I'm not—"

"Sit," Brock clipped, his voice low and deep.
"Fuck," I cursed under my breath, relaxing back into the lumpy leather that had seen better days. Probably had once smelled better too. "What is this? Some kind of intervention?"

"Do you need it to be?" Grayson challenged, his eyes firm but serious. It was his default.

I didn't like the way they were looking at me. It made my guard go up, and I resorted to my usual defensive method: sarcasm. "Great. I love the whole deflect-with-a-question tactic."

"This isn't a tactic." Grayson sighed. "We're worried about you."

Brock leaned an elbow on the table, angling his head to the side toward me. "You need to be on your A-game. There's no room for mistakes."

He didn't need to tell me the importance of not fucking up. "This isn't my first takedown. I know what I need to do."

Fynn shifted forward and kept his voice down as he said, "That's not what we're saying. Just don't do anything that will jeopardize your future. If you get kicked out of school, it'll make it twice as hard to keep not just Mads safe but the other girls as well."

"We need you here," Brock added, his aqua eyes darker than usual.

I stared at the light gold liquid in my cup, my knee bouncing under the table. "I hear what you're saying, but if it comes down to Mads or KU, you know which one I'm choosing. There's no point in arguing or convincing me otherwise, because I would do the same for any of you."

Brock nodded. "And we would do the same for you," he agreed.

I glanced at Grayson and Fynn. "I need to ask a favor before this begins," I said, taking this moment to lay it all out. "If something happens and I get banned from school, will one of you think about transferring? I can't leave Brock here alone to deal with the fallout. I know it's a lot to ask, but there's no one I can trust."

"You don't even have to ask," Grayson replied with no hesitation. He and Fynn would uproot their own lives and education for my peace of mind. It wasn't often you found friends like mine.

"No matter what happens, we take care of our own," Fynn added.

"All right, then," Brock stated, grabbing his beer. "Let's show this fucker what we're made of."

"I'll drink to that." I raised mine in return and slammed it back a moment later, downing the entire glass before banging the empty pint onto the table.

The other three followed in succession.

I had no intention of staying out and drinking tonight with the guys, but they had a way of pulling me out of the dark hole. It was easier to stay angry and yo-yo between feeling my heart physically ache and wanting to hate the world, but for a few hours, my friends could make me forget all the shit and noise in my head.

The beer helped too.

I needed this.

Needed them.

And they knew it.

I didn't have to ask. Hell, I hadn't even known how much I missed this, the camaraderie we shared.

Grabbing another slice of pizza, I took a bite. It wasn't the best, not like Lazy Ray's, but the hunger gnawing at my stomach didn't care.

"The amount of time you guys spend here, you might as well transfer to KU," I joked to Grayson and Fynn. Partially joked, because in truth, I would have loved it more if they were here with Brock and me.

Fynn devoured a slice of pizza in two bites. "It's weird being separated, isn't it? I didn't think it would be a big deal, but not being in the same school makes me feel like I've lost a part of myself."

"I know what you mean," Brock muttered, brows drawing together.

We didn't often sit around sharing our feelings so that in itself made this a slightly uncomfortable discussion. The four of us knew each other well enough that words weren't necessary.

But sometimes they were.

Grayson reclined in the booth, his legs stretching out underneath the table, kicking me in the process. I kicked him back, nudging his legs out of my space. His lips twitched. "We haven't really had a chance to settle into our lives at college."

"No shit. Sterling has made that difficult," I grumbled, shoving the last bit of crust into my mouth.

After a few more rounds of beers, the bartender called for the last round. We were the only ones left. I drained the last of my glass and shuffled out of the booth. The alcohol hit as I stood up, or maybe it was the lack of sleep. Either way, my head spun for a heartbeat or two, and I swayed on my feet, my hand steadying on the back of a barstool.

Fynn appeared at my side. "Give me the key. I'll drive us back to the dorm." He held out his hand.

I dropped the fob into his open palm. "I fucked up, man."

He didn't need me to elaborate on which fuckup I referred to. "Nah, Mads loves you. She'll forgive you for being a dumbass."

Steadier now that my head had stopped spinning, I sauntered to the exit, Fynn beside me and Brock and Grayson behind. "I'm not so sure. Not this time." Before, we'd been young, and a part of me had loved chasing her and riling her up. The sarcastic banter between us had become our thing. But this time, I didn't think being snarky and cute would win her over.

Fynn held the door. "If you're that worried, then what are you waiting for? Call her. Text her. Send her some damn flowers."

"Mads hates flowers," I moped.

"The point is to make things better and apologize," Fynn clarified. "She'd be better off staying with you than at the dorms. They all would be."

I snorted. "Would you want to live with four girls?"

Fynn grinned, unlocking the Hummer's doors. "Did you just hear yourself? Micah Bradford snubbed his nose at the chance of living in the same house with four girls. I swear to God, a year ago, you would have jumped at the chance."

I opened the passenger door and hauled my ass into the seat. He was right. A year ago, all I'd given a shit about was how many girls I could bang just so I could forget about the one I couldn't. Now I finally had the girl I wanted, and I resorted right back to my old habits. "Maybe I need to get laid."

Starting the engine, Fynn glanced over at me. "If you do that, not only will I kick your ass, but Grayson will want in too."

"Fuck," I breathed. "Never date anyone related to your friends. It just complicates the shit out of everything."

"That's the problem with never trusting anyone. Our circle is too damn small."

I dropped my head to the back of the seat. "Can you

imagine if you started dating Kenna? Grayson would literally lose his shit."

Fynn shifted in the driver's seat, his eyes on the road. "No chance of that happening."

Was that regret in his tone? I'd been joking. I always joked. I studied him for a moment, and Fynn looked uncomfortable, like I'd hit a sore spot. He bit the inside of his cheek, hollowing out the sharp lines of his jaw. "Holy shit. Please don't tell me you have a thing for Kenna."

"Fine. I don't have a thing for Kenna," he quickly said. "Not that it's any of your business, but we're talking about your love life, not mine."

"What love life?" I groaned. "As far as I know, you're not seeing anyone. Not even casually. No hookups, and you haven't looked twice at a girl here. Is there something you're not sharing?"

The Hummer cruised down the road, Fynn handling the truck like he drove it every day. "Despite popular belief, I don't share everything with you."

His cynical tone rolled right off me like a bead of water on a waxy leaf. "Bullshit."

"How about we stick to your drama?"

"So you're admitting there is something."

"For fuck's sake, Micah, how many ways do I have to—" Fynn slammed his foot on the brake, the Hummer jolting to a jerking stop that had my chest restrained by the seat belt. "What the—"

I braced against the dash as the tires squealed to halt, peering out the front windshield. "Mads?" I murmured, blinking, unable to believe what I was seeing. How much had I drunk? It couldn't possibly be Mads running around this time of night, could it? She wouldn't. Not with what happened with Sterling.

But she wasn't alone.

Kenna popped into view of the beaming headlights. She grabbed Mads's arm and began pulling her off the road.

I stuck my head out the window. "What the fuck? Are you trying to get her killed?"

Kenna's head whirled at the sound of my voice blaring through the night. She squinted against the headlights until she saw me, her lips splitting into a grin. "What's up, fuckers?"

This girl. I sometimes wondered if Carter had permanently broken Kenna. She'd been through something traumatic, and we all carried around a chunk of guilt at not being able to stop what happened. Kenna had been like a sister to us—still was, just a different version of the sister we had grown up with.

"You're insane," I barked.

She winked. "Learned from the best."

"Get in the truck," Fynn ordered, his mouth a thin, straight line. He was as amused as I was. Less so. Fynn rarely got angry, but when he did, watch the fuck out. Hell, he scared me the way his features darkened.

But not Kenna. Girl was a fool. She grinned at him. "Sorry, they can't be seen together. Micah's orders. Isn't that right?" She lifted her brows mockingly at me. Underneath all the attitude, she wanted to kick my ass, and I couldn't blame her.

The headlights of the Hummer beamed over Mads like she was on stage. I could only stare at her, my fingers gripping the door handle, wanting to jump out of the car. She threw her hands in the air and stuck up two middle fingers with a spiteful, forced grin on her lips. "I'm not you're problem anymore."

"I'm going to kill her," I growled.

Fynn watched them skip away, shaking his head. The Hummer idled while he wrestled with deciding to haul their asses into the car or leave. He wrung his fingers against the steering wheel.

It was clear they'd been drinking, and I couldn't fault Mads for drowning her feelings in booze. I had done the same. "I'll text Grayson," I told Fynn, digging my phone out of my back pocket. He would make sure Thing One and Thing Two got home safely before they found trouble.

We drove back to the rowhouse in silence. Seeing Mads shook me. I wanted this over. I wanted Sterling out of our lives, by whatever means necessary.

CHAPTER EIGHTEEN

MADS

R unning into Micah the other night hadn't been planned, but it did turn out to be therapeutic for about five whole minutes, and then the pain set back in. That up-and-down, seesawing of emotions followed me all week.

But my feelings weren't the only thing that trailed me.

As I robotically went through the motions of going to class each day, I got the suspicion someone was watching or following me. Often it felt like both. At first, I assumed it was Sterling sleuthing around campus looking for another opportunity to stick me with a needle, which only skyrocketed my paranoia and, in turn, made me want to run to the one person I was avoiding.

Regardless of those creepy vibes, I never saw Sterling. He was either doing an excellent job of spying or was staying away from me. The latter seemed too good to be true, yet he didn't show up to our marketing class.

I did, however, spot an unmarked black car hanging around campus that was always parked near the buildings where I had classes or outside my dorm.

Micah put a security detail on me. Apparently he hadn't liked my little episode of rebellion the other night.

As much as I didn't like the idea of a stranger keeping tabs on me, it did finally give me a semblance of peace. Whenever the car was in sight, I was able to walk around feeling a bit safer. It was a bittersweet sense of security, seeing as it was Micah who hired the detail, but it was also because of him that my heart ached constantly.

"You've noticed him too?" Josie asked, nodding toward the black car.

I sucked on the end of my cigarette, drawing in a deep puff. "Yeah."

Her brows drew together. We'd just finished our English class together and were meeting up with Kenna and Ainsley for a study session at Break Zone, a café on campus. "And you're not angry?"

My normal vice of smoking wasn't giving me the calmness I wanted. "I should be. I'm pissed off at a lot of shit, but the assigned detail is at the bottom of the list."

"Is it weird that I feel better knowing he's watching you?"

I made sure to blow the smoke away from Josie. "No, of course not. It means you care."

"So does Micah," she added quietly.

I shook my head. "Nope, still don't want to talk about him." My mouth went into a pressed straight line.

It was windier than usual outside, and Josie wrestled her hair up into a knotted bun on top of her head. "Message received, but if you change your mind…"

"I won't," I assured her as we approached Break Zone. Kenna was leaning against the side of the building, talking to two guys. Just like in high school, she was more often than not surrounded by the opposite sex.

A smile started on my lips, but as I happened to glance to the side, my gaze was interrupted by a laugh that was carried by the breeze, and the beginnings of that smile died. I faltered, my feet coming to an abrupt halt.

Sterling finally emerged from his frat house, and unlike me, having my world flipped upside down, he looked… happy. Fucking happy! Where I'd been miserable. In a span of seconds, my shock and alarm moved straight into reckless fury.

I should stay away. I should keep going and walk into the café with my friends and forget I ever saw the devil. I shouldn't make a scene.

But why the fuck not?

At this point, a scene was expected from me, and I couldn't stand by while he laughed with his frat losers. "You have got to be kidding me," I grumbled, tossing my cigarette to the ground.

Josie's eyes found the source of my agitation, her body stiffening. From the side of my eyes, I noticed her reaching for her phone, but I was on a rant.

"How the hell can he show his face after what he did?" I demanded, talking out loud. "I'm starting to think the douche has no conscience." My feet were moving. Unfiltered rage poured through me, and all I could see was a red figure of Sterling. Everyone else became muted background.

"Fuck," Josie muttered, but it didn't stop me. Couldn't. "Kenna!" I heard her shout.

With purposeful strides, I crossed the courtyard, Josie and Kenna hot on my heels.

"Mads, think about this," Kenna called from behind me as she scrambled to catch up.

"Do you really want to confront him so publicly?" Josie asked, Kenna's counterpart, finishing each other's thoughts and shit. And the fucked-up part was that neither of them was aware that they'd started doing that.

I ignored them both.

Sterling had his back to me, still laughing with a group of guys. Each chuckle hit me like a slap in the face, memories of being backhanded, the tiny prick on the nape of my neck, the smoke filling my nostrils, and its putrid smell. The tiny cut on my lip had mostly healed, and the bruise on my cheek had faded, the discoloration nearly gone, but you know what hadn't faded? The internal scars. The memories. The aftermath of his actions lived with me every day. *He* had done that to me.

He had drugged me. It didn't matter that I had the most incredible sex of my life, not when he'd taken away my choice. Or that he'd probably planned for it to have been him, not Micah, bringing me to heavenly peaks of ecstasy.

He was responsible for my *break* with Micah. My heart still ached. My soul splintered. I felt incomplete. Despite my anger, I missed Micah, even when I didn't want to.

He had made what was supposed to be the best time of my life hell. My life was crumbling and falling down around me, and Sterling was to blame.

Each dilemma was like an electric shock that recharged the rising pain and storm of rage. By the time I was behind Sterling, my arms and legs shook. No voice in my head warned me this was a bad idea. Only the deafening throb of anger echoed in my mind.

I tapped his shoulder and waited for him to spin around. A flash of surprise encompassed his amber eyes, but it didn't last long. A smug smile curled on his lips right as I snuck my fist into Sterling's gut with all my might, enhanced by a clusterfuck of emotions seething within me. A satisfied grunt of both startlement and pain expelled from his mouth as he doubled over.

I wasn't done yet.

Bringing my knee up quickly before he could grab me, I sank it into his junk, fucking hard. The response was better than the punch. He sucked in a breath, holding it as pain rocked his precious manhood.

I'd just assaulted Sterling. And it had felt fucking good.

"Bring that to the school board, asshole." My jaw clenched, teeth pressing together. "Never again lay a fucking hand on me." I didn't give a shit about the mumbles that set off around us.

"Is this the chick? Damn, man, she really laid into you," one of his idiot friends joked, grinning widely at him.

Sterling straightened up fully. "Shut the fuck up, Mav." He turned to me then, lips splitting into a smile I recognized as unfriendly and scary, but I lifted my chin. "I might have deserved that, but remember, Splash, no deed goes unpunished."

Josie and Kenna flanked me now, subtly telling me they had my back. "Let's fucking hope not," I spat. "Because I think your luck is about to run out. Brace yourself."

On the outside, Sterling kept his composure except for a tiny twitch of his left eye. "Is it true that Micah cut you loose? His damn loss if you ask me."

He was good at getting under my skin, I'd give him that. "No one fucking asked you. And I'm not a caged tiger being released into the wild. My relationship is none of your business. Find another bitch to torment." With that said, I whirled and walked off with my head high, feeling damn good about myself. Powerful. In control. And less like a victim.

I didn't know how much I needed that.

"Holy shit, Mads," Kenna gushed, all but skipping on her toes beside me. "That was goddamn epic. I wish I would have thought to take a video."

Josie rolled her eyes, tucking stray pink pieces of hair behind her ears. "The last thing we need is evidence floating around for him to hurt Mads with, but I'm with Kenna. Girl..." She bumped her shoulder lightly to mine, grinning. "You have guns. That hit was spectacular. It made me want to try and sock him one too."

Kenna laughed, falling into Josie and somehow still managing to walk. "Micah is going to be pissed he missed that."

Not likely. If anything, he would be more pissed at *me* for coming within a hundred miles of Sterling. Despite KU being a large school, it would be impossible to avoid the prick for the entire time he had left at college.

Kenna beamed. "I'm so damn proud of you."

"Look at us, fighting back." Josie did an air kick like she was a ninja in training, making Kenna and me shake our heads, snickering. "The Elite who? We can take care of shit ourselves."

I rubbed my hand as we continued to walk, chasing away the sting radiating in my fingers as well as the shaking that just started. "God, I need a fucking cigarette."

* * *

The high of releasing days of pent-up anger didn't last long. Once the rush faded, I was left raw and more depressed than before.

I'd spent the remainder of the week feeling sorry for myself, indulging in horror films with my roommates, ordering every shitty food within a ten-mile radius of campus, and dragging my sorry ass to classes. Some days I left the dorm in my lounge clothes without showering.

I didn't agree with Micah's approach to keeping me safe and dealing with Sterling on his own, but damn if it didn't just smell like crap the Elite did. They were always like "you're family," "you're one of us, "we protect what's ours," and crap like that. What that really meant was, when shit got real, they only relied on the four of them.

Fuck that.

They weren't the only ones who cared or who wanted to see Sterling fall to his knees.

The fact that Micah wanted to take a *break* was utter bull-shit, and I saw right through it. I'd meant everything I said. Micah Bradford had hurt me for the last time. If he wasn't willing to fight alongside me, then what was the point? I was looking for a partner in crime. Well, not just in crime but in life. The good. The bad. The ugly. The beautiful. The tears. All the ups and downs that came with being a human living on Earth.

By Saturday night, Kenna, Ainsley, and Josie declared a mandatory girls' night, whether I was in the mood or not. I didn't admit it, but it was just what I wanted. When we were together, my mind had fewer chances to think about Micah and Sterling. I thought of Micah more often than the stalker. He seemed to crawl into every crevice of my mind at every available opportunity.

It had been a week since we'd last seen each other, talked to one another. Even when we weren't dating and I hated him, we'd still seen each other. Micah had always found a reason to tease me. Then I'd insult him, and he would laugh.

I missed his laugh.

The tears still hadn't come. I refused to cry, because a part of me denied that Micah and I were over, refused to admit the ultimatum I'd given was real. Sometimes deluding yourself was the only way to get through the day. Nothing about college had gone at all as I'd envisioned.

I missed the dream. What was supposed to be a happy time for Micah and me embarking on this college romance together had turned into a living nightmare I couldn't wake up from. Night and day, Sterling was there, wreaking havoc on my world.

"We're not taking no for an answer, so you might as well

give in now." Kenna whipped the covers off my bed. She had the bossy older sister vibe down.

"Do you ever take no for an answer?" I countered, not moving from my horizontal position on the bed. I enjoyed my view of the ceiling as I hugged the stuffed white teddy bear.

"No," she answered, grabbing my wrist and tugging me upright.

Josie rolled her eyes from where she sat on the other side of my bed. "We can do whatever you want. Watch another horror flick, eat buckets of ice cream, bash boys all night."

The second option was appealing, but I didn't want to talk about Micah or my feelings. I wanted to forget the jerk ever existed.

Ainsley stood at the foot of the bed. "You can't leave me alone with the Edwards sisters," she pleaded, pouting her black painted lips.

I saw an opportunity, and I took it. I hadn't spent the entire weekend moping, despite how it might have seen. "There's something I want to do, but you guys won't like it."

Suspicion immediately darkened Josie's eyes as her brows drew together. "This is going to piss off the guys, isn't it?"

I gave a light shrug, picking at a loose stitch on my bed. "It's my way of bashing them."

"Fuck yes. I'm in," Kenna said, jumping onto my bed. The mattress bounced under her sudden excitement.

"Me too," Ainsley piped up. Of course, in something like this, the two of them would be on the same side. Any other time, they'd be bickering just to bicker.

Josie glanced from me to her sister to Ainsley. "I've never been one to sit along the sidelines."

Micah might want me to sit around and do nothing, but after hitting Sterling the other day, I knew I had to do something. Of course, I roped in my best friends to help me out. It felt like I'd taken back my power, and I wanted to keep that momentum going. For days, I'd been chewing on the same question. What had happened that made Sterling hate Micah so much? My gut told me it was important I find out.

Who knew what Sterling had planned next, but I wasn't about to twiddle my thumbs and wait for him to do something. At some point, he would stop using me to hurt Micah and would just go straight for the cause of his hatred.

My friends came prepared. Josie pulled out a case of booze she had stashed under her bed—not the least surprising thing to find under there. Ainsley grabbed her insane collection of black candles, lighting and placing them around the room, making it look like we were holding a seance or a witches' coven meeting. And Kenna brought the snacks. With all essentials covered, girls' night was about to commence. It got me out of bed. It was a start.

The guys had their crew, and we had ours. They just didn't know about ours.

Kenna hauled a platter and two bowls into the center of our room. "We need a name."

"The moment we give this a name," Ainsley began, sticking a finger in the air and circling it between us, "is when the guys find out."

"She has a point," Josie agreed, tossing pillows onto the floor for us to sit on.

The goal here was to uncover where his vendetta against Micah stemmed from, and to destroy anything Sterling might have in his possession to use in hurting or manipulating Micah.

Was this dangerous?

Probably.

Was it stupid?

Definitely.

Was I still going to go through with it?

Hell yes.

Candlelight flickered around the room as the four of us sat in a circle on the floor between Kenna's and my bed. Josie passed out cans of Twisted Tea as Kenna opened a bag of tortilla chips and poured them onto the patter around two bowls of dip.

"Where the hell did you get guacamole and salsa?" I asked. Only Kenna would bring chips and dip as a snack. The rest of us were thinking popcorn, candy, the shit you get out of vending machines.

Not Kenna.

"I placed a carry-out order at the Mexican place just off campus. The one where everyone goes to get tacos," she explained.

"Julio's?" Ainsley supplied.

Kenna nodded, sending her dark ponytail swinging. "Yeah."

We were straying way off topic, but that was pretty damn typical when the four of us got together. Our mouths flapped, one thing led to another, and before you knew it, what was supposed to be a serious powwow turned into a discussion about tacos.

It felt so normal that I didn't even mind.

Popping the top on my warm tea, I took a swig before steering the conversation back on course. "First, let me say that none of you have to do this. If you're just here for snacks, drinks, and to provide input, I'm completely cool with that. I promise we'll still be friends."

"Fuck that," Kenna disputed, taking a chip and dipping it in the gauc. "This is ride-or-die. You're either in or you're out."

"So eloquently put," Josie mumbled, stretching out one of her legs to the side.

Setting the can between my legs, I tossed my hair up into a bun for some serious dipping. I was suddenly starved and secretly wished Kenna had gotten tacos too. I hadn't had a decent meal in days.

Kenna tapped a nail against the side of her drink. "I think we're all here for the same reason. No one hurts one of ours. It isn't just one of us Sterling is fucking with. It's all of us. And we've put this off long enough."

True, seeing as last Friday I'd been drugged, an incident I both wanted to forget and remember for the rest of my life. It was a mindfuck. I wish there was a way to separate the two from my brain. My mind needed to compartmentalize. Get rid of the bad and hold on to the good. Except that even the amazing sex was tainted by the morning after.

Too bad my brain didn't listen to my wants and needs. I swear to God, it had a mind of its own. My brain had a brain.

"Isn't tonight the Chi Sigma secret rush event?" Ainsley asked, shoving a chip smothered in salsa into her mouth.

From across the circle, Kenna shot me a chilling grin. "Not so secret considering everyone knows about it."

Ainsley reached for another chip. "The house will be empty."

"Probably," Josie agreed, the corner of her lips curving.

My friends were crazy. I loved their train of thought, but at the same time, I couldn't let them risk getting caught. It was one thing to jeopardize my future at KU but another thing for all of us to go down.

"I don't like the gleam in your eyes. We're not doing something stupid, just searching." I knew Josie, and she would use the opportunity to teach Sterling a lesson.

It was as if I hadn't even spoken. "Fuck yes we are," she replied, gleefully sounding like the cheerleader she'd been in high school, chanting the academy motto.

"We don't know that no one will be home," I argued, wondering why I was the only one being the voice of reason. Then I thought, *What the fuck am I doing?* This was precisely what I wanted. Reason could go fuck itself. At least for the night.

Kenna was right. We needed to try.

No one was backing down, not even the newest addition to our group, Ainsley. "It doesn't hurt to check it out," she offered.

I thought my cousins were scary when they schemed, but add Ainsley into the mix and they were frighteningly brilliant.

"Tonight is our best chance," Kenna pressed on. "With

fraternity doing rush shit, it's an opportunity we can't let slip by."

Ainsley held up her can in salute to Kenna. "I agree."

Kenna wasn't done yet, and Ainsley's agreement only energized her. "He fucking deserves so much more than us snooping about. I want to make him spend every day of his life looking over his shoulder. What he did to Mads, it's unforgivable."

The incident with Sterling shooting me up hit a little too close to home for Kenna. She had been given a date rape drug by someone she thought had been a friend. Unlike what happened to me, no one had been there to save her from her attack. She'd spent two years recovering from her wounds. It had been the internal scars that did the most damage. A few still remained. Some scars cut deep, and no matter how much they lightened over the years, an imprint lingered.

She'd come so far from that dark hole, crawling and clawing her way out. I was so proud of her.

But was this really the best idea? How much of her thirst for vengeance was she projecting? Did it matter? Carter, Sterling, and every other douchebag out there all needed to be held accountable for their actions. And if the system failed, sometimes you had to take matters into your own hands—Elite law.

It looked like this was happening tonight. A little sooner than I had anticipated, but Kenna was right. This was the perfect opening.

"What's the plan?"

"Are you sure we can't pull a Carter? Drug him, strip him, and torture the truth out of him?" Kenna asked, dead serious.

The funny thing was she had actually done just that with Josie last year.

Ainsley waved a chip in the air. "Same trick, different dog."

I wasn't going to lie. I kind of liked thinking of Sterling as a dog.

"How about we come up with new material?" I suggested. "Our goal is to get rid of anything he could use against Micah, like the pictures, and see if we can discover why Sterling wants to hurt him to begin with. It could be important."

Josie nodded. "Agreed. We need to get to the bottom of his grudge. It's the only way we put an end to it."

"So, a little B&E," Kenna mused. "Seems a bit tame, but we can always add a dash of spice."

I rolled my eyes, digging into the guacamole.

And so the four of us brainstormed, going over ideas and suggestions, strategizing the best way to get inside Chi Sigma unnoticed. There might not be anyone in the house, but they had neighbors, and Greek Row tended to be swarming with people at all hours. It wouldn't stop me from uncovering what it was that Sterling had against Micah. Something must have happened in the past that triggered such a deep-rooted desire to hurt him.

I knew virtually nothing about Sterling Weston, other than his parents had money and he was the president of a fraternity. Finding information on his background could be imperative, and there was only so much we could do online. And we did.

Out of the four of us, Ainsley was the most tech-savvy. I didn't know if that was saying much, seeing as the only device I really used was my cell phone and my laptop to take notes or watch YouTube. We needed a bit more in-depth skill. Fynn would be perfect, but I assumed the Elite were already using him to dig up their own dirt. I doubted they would be up for sharing. Not to mention it would lead to questions I didn't want to answer.

It would be better and more efficient if we all worked together on this, but Micah had made his position clear, and I wasn't ready to see the jerk. Not yet. Not any time soon. I was giving him his break, and that included seeing my face.

We had a few hours to kill before the guys headed out for their rush initiation or whatever stupid shit they had planned for their rushees. To pass the time, Ainsley pulled out her laptop and got to work scouring the Internet for any information on Sterling Weston.

KU had rules against fraternity and sororities using violence, sexual manners, and bully tactics during rush week, but something told me Chi Sigma was above college rules, or at the very least, they were overlooked by the university heads.

"So far, our boy is clean," Ainsley muttered, her eyes pouring over website after website. "Not squeaky clean. He had a few run-ins with the police, but nothing Daddy's wallet or Mommy's purse didn't fix."

"Typical," Josie said flatly.

His parents came from old money. Weston Real Estate branched not just across the States but overseas as well. Forrest Weston, Sterling's father, married Colleen Bass at the Plaza Hotel in Paris. We browsed through their marriage announcement, the photos online of the event, as well as the birth announcements of their children.

Sterling had a sister. Sadie. Funny how he had never mentioned her. She was a few years younger than he was.

I started to drift off, my eyes growing tired from reading lines of text on the laptop screen. The Twisted Teas weren't helping either.

I rolled over on the bed, the light from Ainsley's computer shining on the ceiling. She and Josie sat on the floor, their backs propped against my bed. "Time to switch to coffee," I mumbled, doing my best to suppress a yawn. "We need a pick-me-up to keep us on our toes tonight."

"I'll brew a pot," Josie offered, jumping to her feet. "I need to stretch my legs."

Kenna checked the time on her phone. "We should probably start to get ready soon. It'll give us time to canvass the house."

Ainsley closed her laptop, the room going dark, and rolled her neck. We hadn't found anything vital in our search, just facts about his family. Of course it would have been too easy to find the answers with a Google search.

"This is going to be fucking fun," Kenna said as she bounded off the bed with too much enthusiasm.

I rubbed a hand to my temple, trying to massage the tiredness out of me. "Christ, Kenna. Only you would think breaking into someone's house is fun."

Kenna ducked under the bed, searching for something. "I'll grab a few bottles of spray paint."

Bolting upright in bed, I replied, "What the fuck for? We're not tagging his house." Everyone in the dorm went still, all eyes on Kenna, waiting expectantly.

She shimmied out a bag. "Uh yes, we are. We need to leave our signature behind. And I never go anywhere without at least one can."

Who even was my cousin? "That sounds like a bad idea."

"And everyone knows that bad ideas are actually the best ideas," she retorted, undeterred.

Ainsley blinked at her from the floor. "What world do you live in?"

My cousin tossed her bag on the bed and unzipped it to check the contents. "The same fucked-up world as the rest of you. I just play in it more than you do."

"That's because the rest of us don't want to end up in jail," I said, frowning.

"Or dying," Ainsley added.

Kenna made a shushing sound like none of that was a big deal. "Josie and I are pros."

Josie snorted, popping back into the room after starting the little coffeepot she had on her desk. "One sting does not make us experts. The real experts are—"

"Don't say it," I interrupted. "Don't you dare say it. We are not talking about *them*."

Josie's lips twitched.

I gave Kenna a pointed look. "Sterling told me you tagged his house. How many times, Kenna?"

"Just the once," she admitted. "But I planned on going back again. Tonight is the perfect opportunity to leave the prick a little follow-up message."

"If Grayson finds out you're tagging again—" Josie started before Kenna cut her off.

"He won't," she snapped. "Because no one here is going to tell him. They have their secrets, and we have ours."

"She has a point," Ainsley agreed. Again with the out-of-ordinary alliance with Kenna, who she usually argued with for the sake of arguing. *What the fuck is going on with those two?* Them getting along actually unnerved me. It was scary, like trouble leading trouble. Nothing good would come out of a blooming friendship between them. The campus, let alone the world, wasn't prepared for an Ainsley-Kenna girlmance. That was totally a thing, right? Like bromance? If it wasn't, Ainsley and Kenna just coined the term. Or more like they were on their way.

Something about espionage brought even the strangest of people together.

Josie and I shared a look as if she were having the same thought. I could see the *WTF* in her eyes.

I gave her a slight shrug.

Before I could talk myself out of leaving and realize this entire plan was shit, I got up and rummaged through my closet for the appropriate attire.

What does one wear for a night of sleuthing?

It was nearly midnight, and a part of me wanted to text Micah. Were he and Brock on their way to the designated location? What would go down? Was Sterling planning something for Micah? A way to hurt him? Was Micah walking into a trap? If he was, he wasn't strolling in blind. Micah wasn't stupid enough to think Sterling wasn't setting him up, but still, worry set in whether I wanted it to or not. Regardless of my anger at Micah, I didn't want anything to happen to him.

I was willing to break into Sterling's house and risk going into the enemy's den. Micah wasn't the only one who could protect someone. I wanted to not care, to forget years of caring about him. My heart didn't regard logic.

"I knew there was a reason I brought these pants," Ainsley said, pulling me out of my head. She checked her ass out in the mirror, admiring a pair of seriously stellar black leather pants. Not exactly the most practical attire for breaking and entering, but we weren't your average criminals, so it weirdly made sense.

"God, this brings back memories." Kenna grinned as she slipped on a hoodie, and I noticed a slight paint mark on the cuff of the sleeve. I was pretty sure she was fucking enjoying this.

We were never on time... except for tonight. Somehow, we managed to get dressed in record time.

The four of us stepped out of the dorm in head-to-toe black getups, and I couldn't tell if we looked like strippers getting ready for a shift at the club or a gang of suspicious weirdos that campus security was about to bust for lurking on campus. I kind of felt badass, and for the first time since the Carter debacle, I understood how Josie and Kenna felt the night they fought back, standing up to the person who took away their right to say no.

It was my turn.

CHAPTER NINETEEN

MADS

Sneaking around in the dark toward Greek Row with three other girls was easier said than done. Someone always had something to say. Usually utter nonsense. Someone constantly had to remind the others to shut the fuck up. And that led to the giggles. At this rate, it was guaranteed we'd get busted.

And yet I didn't give two shits. Just as long as we came up with something worthwhile.

The grass was soft under my boots as we moved from yard to yard. "Remind me never to enlist your guys' help the next time I decide to break into someone's house," I griped.

"Who forgot the flashlight?" Ainsley hissed after stumbling over a rock that bordered a flowerbed. She glanced over her shoulder, glaring at the ground as if the concrete had jumped out at her.

"We don't have one," Kenna reminded. "Besides, it would defeat the purpose. We're supposed to be undetectable."

Midnight wasn't late for a college, particularly on a Saturday night. Someone was always awake at all hours, having a little too much fun, puking in the bushes, or stumbling home in the streets.

"Could you guys chill?" I said in a loud whisper. "We're almost there."

Josie jumped as a sudden beam of lights shot down the road. "Oh shit, a car!"

"Hide!" Ainsley shrieked, and like a bunch of scared cats, we dashed away from the edge of the yard, scrambling for cover.

Josie and I ducked behind a tree and waited as the car rolled past. Music blared from the stereo.

Kenna and Ainsley shoved off the ground from where they'd been squatting behind a row of bushes and brushed pine needles off their clothes and hands.

"Do you think they saw us?" Ainsley asked, pulling a twig out of her hair.

"Even if they did, they probably think we're drunk," Kenna reasoned, slipping the strap of her bag back over her shoulder.

We were only three houses away from Chi Sigma. So damn close.

"All right, let's go before I lose my spunk. Maybe we should stick to the shadows, stay away from the road," I suggested.

Veering deeper into the yard, we crossed the lawns connecting one house to the next.

"We should have brought a bottle of bourbon," Josie muttered.

When things got hard or made Josie nervous, she relied on Jim Beam to help her through. Not the best therapy choice but it was a hell of a lot cheaper than a therapist.

"How would that help exactly?" I asked.

"It would make me a hell of a lot less jumpy," she justified.

My cousin had a lot to be high-strung about. Her life had been anything but peaches and cream. Now might not be the right time to talk about personal family problems, but I realized I'd been so self-absorbed these last weeks that I hadn't given much thought to the mess Josie had left behind at home.

"Have you heard from Angie?" I inquired.

Despite Angie being a shitty mother who was also a drunk, I knew the situation was hard on Josie because a part of her still loved the woman who'd raised her.

Josie shook her head, her fingers fumbling with the ring on her thumb. "No, not for a while now."

Chewing on the side of my cheek, I broached another subject that was attached to a string of painful memories for all of us, but more so Kenna and Josie. "And what about Carter?"

She snorted. "The asshole still sends me letters, begging me to come see him."

I shook my head, glancing at Kenna's back and wondering if he was writing those same letters to her. Some evil, even when locked away, was never truly vanquished. It was hard enough that both my cousins had to live with the memories, but to get little reminders, like a letter or an email, when the memories were slowly fading took them right back, erasing any progress they'd made.

That shit pissed me off. Enough that I contemplated visiting the jail to tell Carter to leave my family alone.

"Even in jail, he still has balls. Was it too much to hope someone would have cut them off by now?" I half joked, hoping to lighten the mood.

Josie let out a stuttered laugh, like she was a little surprised she could find any humor in the situation at all.

Kenna, on the other hand, was all business tonight. She whirled around, pressing a finger to her lip, and let out a long "*Ssshhhh*."

I returned a hand gesture of my own, mumbling to Josie, "I guess we should behave, get serious, or some shit before Kenna goes postal."

We gathered under the canopy of a willow tree at the house next to Chi Sigma. It was another fraternity residence, one probably not as douchey as Sterling's.

"Oh, look, they left the porch light on for us. How considerate," Kenna sneered, glaring at the two-story home.

"We're sticking to the plan. Got it?" I said, looking directly at Kenna and Ainsley. If anyone was going to deviate, it would be one of them. Probably both.

"We got it, Sarge," Kenna answered snarkily. "Ainsley and I will stay stationed at the front and back exits as lookouts."

"Keep your phones on," Josie instructed, sticking her earbuds in. The rest of us did the same, connecting our phones on a four-way call. "Only talk when necessary."

"And don't spend the entire time tagging," I directed at Kenna with a frown.

"Worry about yourself," she replied as we started to break off and move into positions.

Josie and I slunk off toward the back door with Ainsley while Kenna took the front. I glanced over once before we went behind the house to see her crouching on the side of the porch, shadows concealing her.

Ainsley tucked herself next to a well-manicured bush a hair taller than she was. If there was one thing I could say about KU, it was that landscapers did a bang-up job keeping up the grounds.

Josie in front, I grabbed the back of her shirt as we came upon the rear entrance in the backyard. No lights other than the moon shone from this side of the house. The yard was small, not offering a lot of space for entertaining, but there was a long wooden table, a grill, and the grass was littered with cheap plastic chairs.

Lifting her hand to the doorknob, Josie checked the lock, pressing down on the latch. *Click.* Her eyes went wide with mine, and we both let out a collective sigh.

She pushed at the door slowly, careful to keep any noise to a minimum, and popped her head inside the dark room to see if any unexpected stragglers were lingering who might put a wrench in our plan.

With a quick wave, she signaled for me to follow, and I took that as the coast was clear. Inside, I closed the door softly behind me, leaving Ainsley outside.

"We're in," I whispered.

"No movement from the front of the house," Kenna's voice murmured in my ears.

Moving through the kitchen, I felt like a rookie FBI agent about to raid the place. But I also felt like throwing up. I wavered between the two.

Keep your shit together.

If Josie had qualms about breaking into the frat house, she didn't show it. Girl remained the picture of calm as we shared a glance, knowing our moment was up—it was time to shine. This was where we parted ways. The goal was to get in and out as fast as possible to lower the risk of someone discovering us.

With a quick nod, I headed for the hallway, going for the stairs. I had a general layout of the house from the last time I'd been inside. Josie would cover the main floor while I took the second, which consisted of mostly bedrooms and a few bathrooms.

Finding Sterling's room shouldn't be difficult, I hoped. He was bound to have something personal to give him away.

The stairs creaked as I ascended, but other than the little groans and moans of an old house, no other sign of life seemed present. I went through the methodical task of checking room after room, poking around and sifting through papers and mail. My conclusion after the first five or six rooms—college boys were gross.

There was messy, and then there was nuclear bomb messy. As a person who wasn't known to be super organized or clean, the fact that I was grossed out spoke volumes. My shoes were sticking to the carpet. Never a good sign, and I was damn sure going to shower when I got home.

I came to a door at the end of the L-shaped hallway, surprised to find that the doorknob wouldn't turn.

Why is this door locked? Suspicious? Fuck yes.

Or maybe someone really valued their privacy, yet I got a sinking feeling that wasn't the case.

I tried the handle again, but it wouldn't budge. Bending down, I inspected the lock. Unlike the other doors, this one had a tiny keyhole, not the turning mechanism the rest of the rooms had.

Now my suspicious nature went on high alert.

I knew one thing for certain. I had to get into this door.

Keeping my voice low, I started to speak. "Josie, I think I—"

"Mads?"

Jumping to my feet, I banged my elbow on the doorknob. Pain shot down my arm, and a series of f-bombs went off in my head. Narrowing my eyes at the last person I expected to see inside Sterling's frat house, I met his scowl with one of my own.

"Micah," I whisper-hissed. "What the fuck are you doing here?" Then I whacked him on the shoulder. "You scared the shit out of me. You're lucky I didn't pepper-spray the shit out of your eyeballs." I hit him again just because.

Micah glanced over me. "Just where exactly are you stashing pepper spray?"

That was the first thing he had to say to me in a week? Where was the pepper spray?

"Mads?" Josie whispered in my ear. "Did I hear you right? You said Micah?"

"We got a problem," I replied, keeping my eyes on the culprit. I didn't want to admit it, but seeing him, having him just feet in front of me, opened a flood of emotions. I missed the asshole.

"What kind of problem?" Kenna asked.

"The kind of problem where you suck at being a lookout. How could you let him in?" No mercy tainted the accusation.

Dead air greeted me through the phone, and I snorted, neither Kenna nor Ainsley owning up.

Glaring at Micah, I demanded, "Who else is here with you?"

"It doesn't matter. We're leaving." He grabbed my wrists to drag me down the hall, but I dug my heels in.

"No. Not until I get what I came for," I insisted, gritting my teeth in determination.

He turned back to face me, frown lines creasing the corner of his lips. "And what is that, Maddy? What did you think you'd gain from sneaking into his house? Did you not hear a word I said? You were supposed to stay away from this, away from Sterling, and yet I find you here, in the middle of the spider's web."

He called me Maddy. He was pissed and let me know by using the name I hated. I exhaled, somehow feeling slightly better regardless of my situation. "Stop yelling at me. I never said I would stay away. Your word isn't God. You don't get to decide what I do or don't do."

"Guys, as much as the two of you have to talk about," Josie interrupted, trying to be reasonable, "now might not be the right time."

Micah noticed the change in my expression, and his gaze went to my ears, seeing the earbuds. "What are they saying?" He didn't wait for me to respond, just plucked one of them out of my ear and stuck it in his. "Josie Jo, when Brock finds out—"

"Don't be a dick," Kenna intercepted.

Micah raked a hand through his disheveled hair. "Oh, fabulous. You brought the entire squad."

"Crew," Ainsley corrected.

Micah laughed, shaking his head. "The four of you are not a crew, and I suggest you make a quick exit before you end up with a disciplinary mark on your record."

It still begged the question, what was he doing here? Following me? Maybe. But there wasn't time to waste by asking. "I'm not leaving until I see what's behind this door."

"What door?" three voices echoed.

Micah pinned me with a hard stare. I shifted my gaze from him to the door in question. "Why do you have to be so damn difficult?" His hand moved to the knob as he brushed near me, the scent of his cologne fucking with my senses. The handle jiggled but didn't give way. "It's locked," he stated, brows furrowed.

"No shit, Sherlock. That's why I want in."

"I should have locked you up," he mumbled as he leaned down to inspect the keyhole. He dug something out of his pocket and began to unravel a paperclip.

"You just happen to have paperclips in your pocket?"

His lips quirked. "At least one of us came prepared."

"Uh-huh. Just what are you doing here, Micah?"

He still had my wireless earbud nestled in his ear and ignored my question, speaking to my cousin instead. "Josie, if you don't get out of this house, it won't just be your ass but mine too."

"You don't think I can handle Brock?" she replied.

"Normally I would be up for details on just how you handle

him, but not now. Besides, Grayson is somewhere downstairs, so unless you want to run into him, I suggest you sneak your little ass out."

"Goddammit," she hissed. "Why didn't you bring Fynn?"

Micah stuck the first paperclip into the lock, wiggling it around. "Because he lost at rock, paper, scissors."

Leaning against the wall, I eyed him, perplexed. "I genuinely don't know how any of you obtained the level of respect you're given."

"And you never will," he retorted like it was this great secret.

"Sorry, Mads," Josie said a second before...

Click. The lock gave, and Micah stood up, grinning like he'd just won the Nobel Prize for lockpicking. He turned the knob before pulling out the paper clips. "Usually I'd say ladies first, but I don't know what we're going to find behind this door."

A steady hum filtered from inside that made me think of fan blades whizzing through the air. Rolling my eyes, I kicked open the door. It was like ripping off a Band-Aid. You just had to go for it.

"You just couldn't..." Micah's voice trailed off as his gaze sharpened, taking in the spare room that had been converted into...

I blinked.

Just what the fuck am I seeing?

Dozens of small TVs lined the entire back wall in a grid formation. The setup looked professional. Not a cord out of place or cables tangled. Two desks were placed together in front of the wall, computers controlling the feed to each TV. I would say it was a command center of sorts if it weren't for the images on each of the screens. They looked like dorm rooms.

Hypnotized, I walked into the room, needing to get a closer look. There were too many pictures to view, causing chaos in my brain. It was as if my eyes didn't know where to focus, so I picked a screen.

And I didn't like what I saw.

Beds. Some with girls sleeping. Some empty. Some studying or watching TV.

My entire body went cold, and I lost all feeling. A weird detachment came over me. It was as if I was having an out-of-body experience. This couldn't be real.

What kind of shady shit were they doing?

Why were they watching all these rooms?

To get off? A frat group jerkoff party seemed a bit desperate when most of the guys in the fraternity could bang those girls on camera based on their rich reputation alone. *So what gives?*

Dark thoughts raced through my head.

This was not what I thought I'd be uncovering tonight.

Micah scrubbed a hand over his face. "Fucking hell." The exact expression descending upon his features reflected the same one that had appeared on mine. He moved deeper into the room, eyes fixed upon a screen and the muscles in his neck bulging at the hard set of his jaw.

Something was wrong.

CHAPTER TWENTY

MICAH

"Micah?"

I heard Mads say my name, but I couldn't tear my eyes away from the screen. This had to be a fucking joke—a sick prank. I didn't want to believe these cameras were real, especially one in particular.

It was the creamy white teddy bear sitting on a rumpled bed that caught my attention. That stuffed animal looked awfully like the one I had won Mads at the summer fair in Elmwood, but that would mean Sterling hadn't just been using my girl-friend, he'd been spying on her as well.

"If you don't—" She gasped, her gaze finally picking out what I'd been staring at so hard. "Holy shit, that isn't... Oh my God. It is. That's my room. That's my bed."

Unbridled fury tore through me. It took all my fucking self-control to keep from putting my fist through the TV broadcasting Mads's room like it was a primetime special. "I need to hit something."

"I'm going to be sick," she whispered, taking a step back. She trembled beside me, and I swept an arm around her hip, anchoring her to my side. A rough and choppy exhale left her lips.

"What is it?"

"What did you find?"

"You're killing us."

Three voices rapidly fired through the earbuds like little chipmunks. I ignored them all, trying to get a handle on the monster that raged within me. If I didn't get out of this room, I would blow a fuse. I turned to leave, telling myself to get Mads out of here. She'd seen enough.

Hell, I'd seen enough.

"I guess we know how he got photos of me in my dorm room," she whispered, her voice a tad shaky.

Sick prick. The idea of him watching my girlfriend while she slept, got dressed, and everything else in between made me feral. "We should go."

But Mads's feet remained planted, her gaze flicking from one TV to the next. "This must have taken forever to set up. They would have had to get access to every one of these rooms."

We really shouldn't have been discussing this, not in here. "Maybe that's the key. These are all the dorm rooms of girls they hooked up with."

"You think this is some kind of conquest trophy room?" she asked.

I rubbed my thumb over her hip bone to not just comfort

her but me as well. I needed to touch her. "Who knows, but if so, this takes collecting panties to a whole new fucking level."

Her skin went cold under my fingers. She shivered. "God, I don't even want to imagine."

"I don't think you need to imagine. It's all right here."

"So not helping, Micah." She groaned, leaning closer to me. "Do you think they keep the footage?"

She seemed so small in my arms. It was hard to not pick her up and run out of the house. "You don't want to know the answer."

She flipped her head back, glancing up at me. "Fynn could hack into these computers and check."

"Probably," I agreed. I planned on asking him to get me that footage and anything else on these computers, but Mads didn't need to see it. What good would it do?

I made the dumb mistake of glancing one last time at the white teddy bear on Mads's bed, and I knew I couldn't leave this room without sending Sterling a message. Stepping in front of Mads, shielding her with my body, I cocked my fist back and slammed it into the screen projecting her room. It shattered on impact. The sound blasted through the house.

"What the fuck was that?" Kenna shrieked in my ear. I'd forgotten Kenna, Ainsley, and Josie were still connected through their phones.

Mads scowled at me as she replied, "Micah being a dumb-ass." Her focus shifted to my hand, and her lips formed an O. "You're bleeding." She reached for me.

I hadn't felt the pain or the skin over my knuckles splitting open. My hand was so large in hers as she inspected the cut. "It doesn't matter. I will kill him."

"We got company," Kenna whispered through the earpiece. "You guys need to get out of there. Now." Then the earbuds went dead, the call between the girls disconnecting.

Mads grabbed my arm, tugging me toward the door. "Micah," she pleaded.

I reached into my back pocket and took out my phone, punching Grayson's name on the screen. A single ring sounded before he picked up on the other end. "Where are you?" he answered, short and to the point.

"Leaving. We've got trouble on the way. Get the girls out. I've got Mads," I informed him, glancing down at her. She chewed on her lower lip, unease swimming in her expression at the blood trickling down my fingers. "We don't have time for you to play nurse. Let's go." I didn't mean to snap at her, but no matter how much control I possessed, some emotions were harder to shove aside than others.

She looked at me with big gray eyes. They swirled like a storm, full of confusion, fear, and specks of anger. It wasn't surprising that her anger had been lit. She had a fire inside her that sometimes scared me. Mads's fighting spirit could get her in trouble.

Taking her hand with my nonbloody one, I rushed her out of the room, leaving the door open and unlocked purposely. I wanted Sterling to know someone had broken in, and it wouldn't take him long to realize it was me. He must have already concluded why I wasn't with Brock tonight and figured I was up to something.

I dragged her down the hallway, blood dripping onto the carpet. It was fucking inconvenient leaving behind DNA, but really, other than breaking a TV, we hadn't done anything wrong, and I highly doubted anyone in the fraternity would report the smashed screen considering what the room contained. So the little traces of blood I left behind weren't going to be a problem, not without the fraternity bringing heat onto themselves.

Mads's breathing came out rapidly behind me as she struggled to keep up with my long strides. We got to the bottom of the stairs, and I heard voices. Coming to a dead stop, I listened, pinpointing where in the house the voices were.

Mads bumped into my back. "Micah, your—"

My hand flew over her mouth as I indicated with a narrowed gaze for her to be quiet. She huffed, lips turning down beneath my palm, but remained silent.

They were in the kitchen, and if they stepped out at the right time, whoever had entered the house would spot Mads and me slipping out the front door.

Changing course, I guided her into the room adjacent to the stairs, spotting a window. It would have to do. I weaved around the deep brown leather furniture and wedged the window fully open. A gust of mild wind blew inside, sending the burgundy curtains dancing behind me. Mads shoved them out of her face, and I quickly helped her swing a leg out the window and climb out.

The voices were growing closer, and I knew we only had seconds to make our escape.

Her feet thumped to the ground. Following next, I jumped

out, landing in a bush. I grabbed Mads and shoved her against the house on the other side of the stone chimney. Her heart hammered against my chest, and despite the situation we were in, I had to tell myself not to get swept up in the feeling of her pressed to my body. I loved so many aspects of her, but the way she was soft where I was hard, the places where I swelled and she dipped, she drove me crazy.

She pressed her cheek against mine, holding her breath. I secured my arms around her as the flutter of voices floated from the window on the other side of the stacked stones.

"Someone was here," a deep, troubled voice said.

"Should we alert Sterling?" another asked, this one less sure than the other.

"He'll want to know," the first responded, his tone quieter. "Let's check the rest of the house. They might still be inside."

Josie and Grayson better have gotten their asses out.

Without a moment to lose, I waited just to make sure they had left the window, then whispered in Mads's ear, "Run."

She glanced at me for a split second, then took off into the night, darting under the trees as she headed for the street. I raced right behind her, risking one quick peek over my shoulder at the window. No one was there.

Ignoring the leaves and branches that smacked my arms, I made sure to stay close behind Mads. She slowed down only when we got to the corner of Greek Row and turned onto Scenic Drive, the road that would take us to my house. "Do you think they saw us?" she panted, bending over slightly to catch her breath.

I shook my head. "It doesn't matter. Sterling will know."

Panic shone in her eyes, and I would have given anything to extinguish it. "Micah, what am I supposed to do? I can't go home."

She meant her dorm. I had already been thinking down that road, and I'd planned to say and do whatever it took to convince her not to stay in her room. I didn't give a shit if she was still pissed off at me. I'd kidnap her and handcuff her to my bed if I had to. "You're not," I started.

She swiped the back of her forehead with the sleeve of her hoodie. "I can't live at your place."

Break over, I started walking down the lit pathway, keeping my strides slow. "You can, and you will. This isn't up for debate. The other girls will have to stay as well. At least until we can sweep your dorm and have Fynn check it out."

"I thought you wanted me to stay away from you," she retorted dryly, tossing my own words back in my face, but I deserved it.

My lips narrowed. "That was before."

"This changes nothing," she clarified.

"It changes everything." No matter what I did, I couldn't erase the sight of Mads's bed displayed in some sleazy back room. My fists curled at my side as we continued to walk. I had to draw on all my control to stop from bolting across campus and beating Sterling to a bloody pulp. Once I started, I didn't think I'd be able to stop. I *would* kill him.

Her frustrated huff was audible, and a beat of silence passed before she said, "This is a fight we're going to have to have later. For the night, I concede."

She must have been seriously shaken and exhausted to back

down so easily. Mads did not shy away from a fight, and Sterling was to blame. An added layer of anger festered in the pit of my gut.

When we trotted up the steps to my front stoop, lights were glowing from inside. I prayed that meant Grayson and the girls had made it home.

Chaos greeted us as Mads and I stepped inside, but that wasn't shocking. Any time the triplets were in the same room, mayhem tended to erupt. Kenna, Josie, and Grayson paced around the furniture, talking over each other so it was impossible to hear what anyone was saying. Ainsley sat in a chair enjoying the show. I nearly asked if she wanted me to get her some popcorn.

The trio turned their heads in perfect unison, finally noticing Mads and me in the doorway.

"Fuck, man," Grayson cursed, shoving a hand through his chestnut hair. "It's about time."

Kenna folded her arms over her chest. "What the hell took so long?"

"We were worried," Josie added with a sigh, her tense shoulders loosening.

"I can see that," I replied, devoid of any sympathy.

Ainsley sat up from her position on the couch. "Did you get caught?"

A snort breezed through my nose. "Did you forget who I am?"

"Mads?" Josie eyed her cousin thoughtfully, edging past Grayson. "Are you okay?"

Mads blinked and rubbed a hand up and down her arms. "I

need a cigarette."

I didn't stop her as she moved through the lounging area to the sliding doors that led to a small porch off the side of the house. She didn't want to stay and listen to me recount what we'd discovered, and she needed something familiar and calming. Despite wanting to be that for her, I knew she would shove me away. Mads wasn't ready to forgive me.

Grayson waited until Mads slipped outside with Josie behind her before he peppered me with questions. Ainsley and Kenna stayed. "What did you find?" he asked, taking a seat on the edge of the couch. Kenna sat on the other end.

My eyes flickered to the open curtains, seeing the burning spark from the end of Mads's cigarette. I plunked down into the chair opposite Ainsley's. "Are Brock and Fynn back yet?" I wasn't keen on having to relay our findings more than once. My barely contained anger couldn't handle it. I didn't think I'd be able to stop myself from confronting Sterling.

Kenna shook her head. "Josie tried Brock's phone, but he didn't answer."

Grayson and I shared a look, and I knew he was thinking the same thing I was. *Should we get them or wait?* Brock not answering Josie's call wasn't a good sign.

There was no question that Brock and Fynn could take care of themselves, especially against a group of frat boys, but that didn't mean it sat right with me leaving them. We always had each other's backs, and if something went down... If Sterling already learned I'd been in his house, found his secret room, would he try something with Brock and Fynn?

Shiiit.

This was one of those times I appreciated Brock making the decisions, except he wasn't here.

* * *

We didn't have to wait long for Brock and Fynn to show their faces. Josie rushed across the room and threw herself around Brock, who caught her in his arms without missing a beat. She promptly smacked him on the chest, scolding him for making her worry.

Seven of us were gathered around in the kitchen, all exhausted and ready to go to bed. Mads had come in from her smoke five minutes before I started to recount the events of tonight and went upstairs to my room, declaring she was tired. I wanted to follow her and tuck her in, hold in her my arms, but I said nothing, my eyes just trailing her as she climbed the stairs. It wasn't until I heard the click of my door closing that I told my friends about the hidden cameras and TVs playing the live feed.

"You're lying," Kenna snapped, denial in her eyes after gasping several times while I gave them details on the room.

"I wish I was," I responded to her outrage. I wasn't sure there was any other way to feel about being secretly filmed than utter shock and fury. Once it sank in, all those other unpleasant emotions would make themselves present.

This should have been a place of safety and security, a time of happy memories, not a school of horror. It was fucking bull-shit that any of the girls had to feel violated.

"And you're sure it was our room?" Ainsley asked with a grain of hope.

"Does it matter?" Kenna barked. "Our room, the one down the hall, or one in another building. They have access to all those rooms." She tossed her hands animatedly in the air with each statement.

Josie sat perched on Brock's lap. "Do you think he knew Mads would be in that room before we moved in?"

"I wouldn't put it past him." Grayson's response was low and thrumming with anger.

Dark energy radiated off Brock. "It's not just Sterling but the entire fraternity."

"We're burning it to the ground," Fynn said coldly. His green eyes didn't often go glacial like they were now.

A smirk played at the corners of Kenna's lips. "I like the way you think, Dupree."

I shifted my narrowed gaze from Kenna to Fynn. "Before we wreck the place, do you think you can find out what's on those computers?" I wasn't opposed to destroying the frat house, just as long as we made sure the members went down with it.

"I'll need to work fast before they try to erase any evidence," Fynn replied. I had no idea how he did the shit he did, breaking into other people's computers, phones, and tablets. The few times he tried to explain it to me as I watched over his shoulder, my brain literally shut down after a minute. It was beyond the scope of my understanding.

Fynn had always been the smart one.

"We'll also need to comb every inch of their dorm," Brock added, and we immediately delegated tasks.

"In the meantime, the girls stay with us," I said.

"Do you think any of this is connected to you or Mads?"

Ainsley asked, her knee bouncing under the table. As the newcomer who hadn't completely earned our trust, she was handling the situation better than most, but I could tell she was doing her best to put on a brave face.

I shook my head. "It feels different, separate."

"I agree," Brock added. "The cameras are probably a fraternity thing, something that's been around for years. Sterling's vendetta with Micah is personal, probably unrelated to the fraternity. They give him a cover, not to mention additional influence and resources."

Grayson leaned back in his chair, crossing his arms over his chest. "Did anything happen at the meeting tonight?"

Brook shook his head. "Nah, just some stupid hazing shit that I refused to participate in. He was definitely looking for you." His eyes were on me.

"Ah, how I hate to disappoint," I said flatly.

"I got the sense that he *was* disappointed," Brock reflected. "You not being there raised more than a few eyebrows and threw a wrench into his night. The bastard knew we were up to something. It's safe to say that I doubt either of us will be Chi Sigma fraternity brothers after this."

Kenna shuddered. "House of creeps."

Guilt wound its way inside me. "I hate that I'm dragging all of you into this mess. I had no idea..."

"None of us did," Brock declared with strong conviction.

Grayson's jaw remained rigid. "And this is no longer your problem. It involves all of us."

Fynn got out his laptop and set up for an all-nighter. Well, technically it was early in the morning, but regardless, none of us were going to get much sleep. If any.

We had a spare room that Kenna and Ainsley took. Neither was thrilled at having to share a bed, but it was either that or the floor. Grayson and Fynn—if he crashed—would take the couches again.

I glanced at the stairs for the umpteenth time. Was she sleeping? I'd procrastinated long enough.

Fynn noticed and lifted his head from the laptop at the sound of my sigh. "Stop pining and just take your ass upstairs. You're distracting me."

I tossed a coaster off the table at his head.

Fynn jerked to the side, his reflexes still sharp regardless that he had to be tired.

The coaster hit the wall behind him, causing Grayson to scowl. "Are you trying to wake up the house? Or just keep me from getting any sleep?" He adjusted the pillow under his head from where he was stretched out on a couch.

"The latter, obviously, because I live to annoy you," I bit back with no real ice behind the words.

Grayson settled his shoulders into the cushions. "What the fuck does my cousin see in you?"

This wasn't the first time he'd posed the question. It had been a running joke that only he didn't find much humor in.

"Do you want me to make a list?"

Eyes closing, he said coolly, "I want you to leave me alone."

There was a form of comfort in falling into old habits of riding each other's asses. "When are you going to get a girl?"

"Never," he stated, hands folded over his chest. "I have too many in my life as it is." With two sisters and Mads, it was true. Grayson was surrounded by females but none he could bang.

"What about Ainsley?" I suggested.

He scrunched his nose. "What about her?"

"You could hit that." She was cute in a dark anime way. I didn't watch the stuff, but I knew the style, and Ainsley had this adorable, street, badass chick vibe. I didn't know how she meshed it all together, but it worked for her. Maybe not Grayson's usual type, but maybe going out of his box would pull him out of this funk. She would be a fun distraction, at the very least.

"I don't need to have sex with every girl within a mile radius of me."

I gave him a quick grin. "Fuck, why not?"

"Go to bed, Micah," he groaned. "If you're lucky, my cousin won't kick your ass out of your own room. I'm not giving up the couch, by the way."

I longed to go curl up in my bed with Mads. But did I deserve to share a bed with her after how I treated her? Fuck no. "You guys suck," I grumbled, shoving out of the chair.

Climbing the stairs, I lightened my steps as I approached my door, careful not to wake her up. I turned the knob slowly, giving the door a gentle push. For once it didn't squeak. I stepped inside, my gaze immediately drawn to the bed and the form outlined in the sheets. The thin material hugged the shape of her curving profile. Like always, she slept curled on her side, back facing the door.

I shut the door behind me and sank against it. Her faint breathing drifted through the room, and to me, it was like a siren luring a sailor on a foggy night. She made me feel powerless, my body not in my control.

The desire came swift, as it always did with her. Just her breathing turned me on. My cock swelled in my pants, straining against the zipper on my jeans.

She didn't move or make a sound as I walked across the floor and removed my jeans and shirt. I had no intention of touching her. *Just sleep.* She needed it, and so did I.

My dick, on the other hand, was firm and pulsing in my boxers. I swear to God, it swayed in her direction as I slipped under the blanket and climbed in beside her. I told myself to stay on my side of the bed, but the moment I settled in and dropped my head on the pillow, Mads snuggled up to me, her body contouring to mine.

Fuck me.

This had to be karma torturing me for what I'd done by insisting we put space between us when that was the last thing I wanted. It was as if the universe was toying with me just as I had played with Mads's heart, despite believing it was for the greater good.

I lay still, afraid to move and disturb her because this was exactly what I wanted, what I craved, to be in bed alongside her.

Mads sighed contently in my arms, her breath warm and soft against my face. My heart thumped in my chest, followed by a squeezing flip that made me ache to do more than hold her. Too tired to deny the pleasure of her body against mine, I buried my nose in her hair and inhaled. I'd deal with the fallout when we both woke up. Every muscle in me went lax as her scent filled me. She gave me a contentment I had no right possessing, and I couldn't help but wonder if I would ever be a man deserving of her love.

* * *

The first thing I noticed before I even opened my eyes... Mads was gone. The weight of her head nuzzled on my shoulder, the warmth of her hand on my chest, and the scent of her skin were all absent. Vanished like an empty dream, leaving a gaping hole in my chest. The kind that made you gasp for air.

I'd never had my heart broken. Never cared enough about a girl to come close to letting her destroy me. I didn't want to depend on anyone else other than Brock, Fynn, and Grayson. They were exceptions, and I had kept that rule my whole life until Mads.

Now she was a part of me—vital. She was as important as my heart. I didn't know that I could live without her.

Groaning, I rolled over, getting a whiff of her shampoo that still clung to the pillow. I rubbed at my eyes, half contemplating going back to bed. Judging by the position of the sun, it was midday.

I made use of the bathroom and pulled on a pair of sweats. The kitchen smelled like coffee. A fresh pot was brewing, and I suspected it wasn't the first or even the second one. Used mugs lined the counter. Not waiting for the machine to finish percolating, I grabbed what I hoped was a clean cup and poured it to the top. Taking it straight with no cream or sugar, I sat down at the table beside Fynn. He looked like he had drunk a pot or two himself. "Anything?" I asked.

He massaged his forehead, eyes bloodshot and droopy despite all the caffeine he'd inhaled. "Someone over there knows their shit. Or did. They have tight-ass security." A frustrated sigh blew through his nostrils. "It's going to take me longer than any of us want." And he would beat himself up over it.

"Don't stress. Why don't you get some sleep? We have a big night ahead of us. We'll worry about the cameras after. Grayson and I will take care of the ones in the girls' dorm today."

Speaking of girls, where are they?

Fynn read the expression on my face as my eyes searched the family room, finding it empty. The house was awfully quiet, Grayson and Brock nowhere about either. "They went to stock up on food. And before you ask, Mads went too."

"Oh."

"Did you apologize yet?"

Sipping my coffee, I shook my head. "I'm working on it."

"Grayson and I both told you what would happen if you broke her heart."

"How could I forget?" I dryly replied, but it had momentarily left my mind. I recalled one or both threatening to tie me naked to the top of Fynn's Jeep, drive me through a carwash, and then run my ass over. Such violence.

But I would do the same if Brock hurt Josie. I understood their protectiveness, and yet, despite not agreeing with my methods, protecting Mads had been my only intent.

"Why don't we focus on tonight so we can kiss and make up?" I advised over the brim of my mug.

Fynn snorted. "You're delusional if you think it'll be that easy with her."

I flashed him a grin, falling back on my false sense of confidence. "I prefer optimistic."

He snapped his laptop closed, blinking heavily. "You should probably get your head checked out, then."

"Do you need me to do anything?"

"Everything for tonight is set," Fynn assured me. "You nervous?"

I met his gaze unflinchingly. "No, impatient."

He yawned. "Then I would use this time to write one fucking stellar apology, because you are going to have to grovel like you've never groveled before. I wouldn't take you back." His eyes were half closed by the time he finished, voice trailing off.

"Good thing we're not dating," I murmured, taking the coffee from Fynn and sending him to bed in the spare room.

While I waited for the others to return, I took a shower and screwed around in my room until the front door opened, the house suddenly filling with chatter. I bounded down the stairs into the kitchen, my gaze landing on Mads. She spared me nothing more than a fleeting look.

I deserved that.

The silent treatment and avoiding eye contact continued through the day. Grayson, Mads, and Ainsley made dinner. Nothing special, just a giant pot of spaghetti and french bread with garlic spread on it, as well as a salad. The girls had to have greens. I could have done without the veggies, but that wasn't saying it wasn't good. I didn't know what Ainsley did to give it such flavor, but for once I ate the lettuce without complaining.

It had been too long since the eight of us sat around and had dinner. We needed a night without tension, a moment to forget what we'd uncovered and what the guys and I were going to do tonight.

I wanted more dinners like this, more nights without the looming darkness over our heads like a storm cloud about to burst. This was how college should be. Friendship with the people who were important at the forefront of our thoughts.

But as the night grew closer, so did the ticking clock.

Grayson and I had pulled four cameras from the girls' dorm. My first inclination had been to smash them to dust, but he stopped me, and when he explained why, I grinned, loving his devious mind.

Josie and Brock took care of the dishes while Grayson and Fynn ran errands, pulling together the last-minute details while also keeping the girls in the dark. It wasn't easy, seeing as we were all temporarily living under the same roof, and in a few hours, it wouldn't be secret at all.

Mads cornered me in the bathroom. Her hand shot out, bracing it on the door just as I was about to close myself inside. "What are you doing?" she demanded, suspicious eyes on me.

"Taking a leak," I replied, stating the obvious.

She frowned, her brows creasing together. "Nope. Don't play that stoic game with me. I want the truth. You guys are planning something, and I want to know what."

I leaned a shoulder on the door. "Why?"

"Do you really have to ask?"

I regarded her for a moment. The hard set of her jaw and

firm press of her lips. I knew this Mads. "Telling you won't change anything. I won't let you be a part of this."

"Won't," she echoed through clenched teeth, her eyes darkening.

Poor choice of words. Angering Mads would lead to the exact opposite of what I was trying to do. "Now you're suddenly talking to me." She hadn't spoken two words to me all day.

"Haven't you learned yet? I will find out." She crossed her arms over her chest. "We can do this the easy way or the hard way."

She was serious. I could see it flashing in her gray eyes. Determination. Fierceness. Stubbornness. And still, it changed nothing. Not for me.

"No," I stated.

Her hands flew in the air. "Dammit, Micah. Enough."

I took a step forward. "Why do you have to make everything difficult?"

She put a finger into my chest. "Says the asshole who can't be straight with me for once in his life."

I wrapped my fingers around her wrist, intending to remove her finger poking into my ribs, but once I touched her, I couldn't seem to make my hand move. "I don't want to fight."

The center of her eyes eclipsed with shadows. "Too late."

"Mads, I have to go." We both knew I wasn't talking about taking a piss.

I didn't like the expression that flashed over her features. "Leave, then. No one's stopping you."

She didn't actually *want* me to leave, but I did so anyway.

When the time came, Brock, Fynn, Grayson, and I walked

out the door, leaving the girls at the house without a word. I didn't ask Brock if he said anything to Josie, and he never asked me about Mads. All that mattered was what we had to do, what waited for us, what we set into motion.

One more night.

That was what I told myself. One more night to finish this thing with Sterling.

It ended tonight.

The fraternity was a problem for another day.

CHAPTER TWENTY-ONE

MADS

Tiptoeing along the side of the house, I plastered myself against the bricks. Two seconds after the guys left, I snuck out the back door, leaving Josie, Kenna, and Ainsley in the family room watching a movie. The guys were up to something, and I was going to find out what. Josie knew, too, but she wasn't saying anything. My guess was that Brock hadn't given her the details of their plans, most likely so she didn't spill the particulars to Kenna, Ainsley, and me.

As if that would stop me.

I dared a quick peek around the corner. The four of them stood by Brock's SUV, huddled around something small like a phone. It was indeed a phone, the screen lighting up their faces in the dark. Fynn switched the device to speaker as he punched in a number.

What the fuck are they doing?

"What the fuck are they doing?" a voice echoed my thoughts.

Realizing who it belonged to, I spun, whipping a finger to my lips, silently telling Kenna to keep quiet. She and her big mouth were about to blow my cover.

She complied, but only after giving me the stink eye. It was a glare I'd been on the receiving end of frequently and had little impact on me.

Brrrring. Brrrring. Brrrring.

The ringing pulled my attention back to the guys just as the person on the other end picked up. "Hello?"

It was difficult to distinguish who answered the call from one common word and the distance from which I hid, but I had an inkling who it was.

Brock gave Micah a single nod. I had no idea what he was instructing Micah to do, but when another voice cut through the quiet of the night, I became even more confused. It was female, and she trembled one name into the phone. "Sterling."

Huh?

Did they have someone with them? Had they merged two calls? Where was this girl?

Kenna and I shared a look, her brows raised in question as she crowded against my side. I gave her a silent shrug, those same questions in my expression.

I squinted and counted the heads huddled together to make sure I hadn't somehow missed an addition. Four. There were definitely only four, but then I spotted something in Micah's hand. It looked like his phone. Not so weird. But I continued to watch him closely.

"Sadie?" Sterling's reply came through the speaker. A combination of surprise and befuddlement was evident in his tone.

Who the hell is Sadie?

Micah hit a button on his phone, lifting it toward his lips. "Sterling, help me," a female voice cried.

A recording. They were playing a recording of this girl Sadie. No, that wasn't quite right. They were using her voice to alter Micah's. Who was this girl to Sterling?

"Sadie? How...? Are you hurt?" He sounded concerned, but something else laced his words. An emotion I couldn't quite place. It appeared I wasn't the only one trying to play catch-up and figure out what the fuck was going on.

Kenna's fingers pressed into my shoulder as she leaned forward to hear better.

"Where are you?" Sterling asked, a hardening edge to his question.

Micah hit a button and held his phone up to his mouth. "I-I don't know. It's dark. A warehouse maybe."

I didn't have to wonder how they got a recording voice of Sadie and used it to make a program that would mutate everything Micah said to come from this girl.

Fynn.

Micah should have been nominated for an Oscar after the performance he was giving. The way his voice shook, even I believed the girl on the other end was frightened, alone, and desperate for help.

"Is there a window? Look outside, see if you can find something to tell me where you are," Sterling urged.

Micah turned off the app that masked his voice and said, "I've got a better idea. I'll text you the address."

A beat of silence passed. "Who is this?" Sterling demanded, the situation sinking in.

"You'll find out soon enough if you want to see your sister again," Micah said, and then Fynn disconnected the call.

They were threatening Sterling by using his sister. Or pretending to use her. Then what?

I had to find out.

I dug my fingers into the side of the house, watching the guys pile into Brock's Range Rover. I turned as the engine jumped to life, rushing by Kenna into the house.

"Mads," she hissed after me. I didn't have time to stop and explain what I was doing. If I did, I would lose them. "Fucking hell," she growled, her thumping feet following me.

Inside the front entrance of the rowhouse, I grabbed the first set of keys my fingers touched from the bowl sitting on the table. I twisted back around, bumping into Kenna. "Don't try to stop me."

She shadowed my movements. "I'm not. I'm going with you."

The movie played in the other room, Josie and Kenna reclining on the couch. I didn't waste time arguing, just bolted outside, hitting the Unlock button on the key fob to identify which car the key belonged to. It was Grayson's—one of my cousin's many vehicles. I was sure he wouldn't mind if I borrowed it. This was an emergency, after all. An emergency to me, that was.

If Kenna planned to go with me, she better hurry her ass up, because I wasn't waiting for anyone. I'd take off without her. I had to. It was the only way to ensure I caught up with the guys. The engine in the Jeep rumbled to life, and I rammed the car into Drive just as Kenna opened the door, hopping in. She dropped a bag onto the floor of the car, settling in as I hit the gas, the Jeep lurching forward from where it had been parked on the street.

Gripping the steering wheel, I searched the road for another set of headlights. "Help me find them."

"They couldn't have gone far. Go to the school's main exit," she directed, pointing slightly to the right. "Hopefully they got stopped at the light."

Luck was on our side. I rolled the Jeep up to the stoplight, seeing the rear end of the black Rover. Three cars separated us, but I still proceeded cautiously as the light turned green. I didn't have a cousin who raced cars and not pick up a thing or two. Two cousins, actually. Sawyer, the triplets' older brother, died while street racing. It was a very triggering topic in the Edwards's household, one we all avoided in front of my aunt and uncle.

Moving through town wasn't hard, not with the other cars, the bright streetlights, and the city glowing on either side of the road, but when the Rover steered into a more rural part of Elmwood, I had to put more distance between us. If the guys knew they were being followed, they gave no signal.

"Kill the lights," Kenna instructed. We were about to make a turn onto a somber street without a single lamppost. Nothing but darkness stretched out for miles.

I flipped the headlights off before I turned after them.

This took backwoods to a new meaning. The starless sky, the eerie darkness, and the canopy of trees all sent uneasy tingles through me. It seemed just a little too perfect for a murder scene.

"Remind me never to come to this part of town alone," Kenna muttered, rubbing her hands up and down her arms.

"Did you bring your Taser?" I asked, glancing at her before looking back at the road.

"Of course." I couldn't see her face, but she definitely rolled her eyes.

I should have guessed. She'd brought her fun bag of toys. God only knew what else was in there.

The occasional glow of the Rover's taillights acted as my guide. We eventually pulled onto a gravel road. Another five minutes and the SUV came to a stop. I steered into the woods surrounding the road, tucking the Jeep behind a tree.

Kenna and I waited until the guys exited the Range Rover; then we quietly opened our doors, lifting the handles and pushing them shut with a soft click. We walked around to the front of the Jeep, and I shoved the key into my back pocket, thankful I'd put on jeans today. If I would be traipsing around in the woods, then at least I didn't have to worry about ticks.

Ducking and twisting, I peeked through the branches to get a glimpse of the building. It was indeed a warehouse, a run-down one at that, complete with broken windows, missing planks of wood, peeling paint, and overgrown weeds. The place was the perfect hideaway for the homeless and junkies. Secluded and forgotten. Unless someone actually owned this shit hole, no one would bother checking on it.

What the hell had this place once been? And how did the Elite know about it?

I leaned a hand against a branch, needing something to hold on to, but the tree wasn't having it. A hunk of bark broke off, tumbling to the ground. I froze, Kenna shooting me a you're-going-to-get-us-caught glower. I didn't blame her; if the roles had been reversed, I would have given her an identical glare.

Grayson's head lifted, turning to the trees where we were hidden. "Did you hear that?" he asked the others.

A long stretch of silence proceeded, and I held my breath.

"Don't be paranoid," Micah said, clasping Grayson on the back. "It's probably a fox or a raccoon."

Kenna and I stayed in the trees, watching the guys move into the warehouse. "What do you think they plan on doing to him in there?" she whispered.

I batted a leaf away from my mouth, ignoring the mosquito buzzing in my ear. "Only one way to find out."

She raised a brow. "Do we really want to know?"

She had a point. It might be healthier for my mental state to not know what would happen inside the shambled warehouse. Yet my feet were moving. Crouched, I trotted across the road to Brock's SUV. Kenna was at my side, peering through the window. She adjusted the bag, securing it higher on her shoulder.

Clang. Click, click, click.

Something had dropped out of Kenna's bag, the small noise sounding like a gun going off in an empty field. I jumped, whirling toward her. The spray can rolled to my feet, hitting the toe of my shoe.

"Why did you bring spray paint?" I whisper-hissed, my heart still thundering in my chest. I fucking hated jump scares. It made my blood pressure soar.

"It was in my bag. You didn't give me a lot of time to sort through my shit," she defended, her eyes as big and startled as mine. We both needed to calm down.

Exhaling, I shot Kenna a glower and bent to pick up the spray can. My fingers brushed the tip of the metal bottle when I was suddenly jerked back. A hand wrapped around my waist, another clamping over my mouth. Hot air rushed over the nape of my neck as the voice of my living nightmare murmured near my ear.

"Hello, Splash. What an unexpected surprise. You just became my insurance policy."

Everything in me became hyperaware. A bolt of fear lanced through me, and my joints all locked up. I went rigid, unable to move, to scream. The few moments of frozen fear would haunt me later. My first reaction should have been to thrust my elbow or my head back, anything to dislodge the grip he had on me. That hesitation cost me.

Kenna let out a muffled shriek as her gaze landed on Sterling. She recovered quicker than I did, shock transforming into anger. "Let her go," she snarled as she reached into her bag and pulled out pepper spray.

He disregarded Kenna like she was a pesky fly buzzing around his head. Sterling reinforced his hold against me, caging me tighter to the point that I squeaked. "I don't have plans to hurt you unless you give me a reason to. All I want is a trade. You for my sister." He might have ignored my cousin, but that didn't mean he wasn't aware of her. The bastard kept his face cleverly hidden behind mine so Kenna couldn't spray him without also hitting me.

"I'm going to remove my hand from your mouth," he said. "If either of you screams, though, I'll be forced to hurt you." The hand cautiously lifted from my lips, and I contemplated biting him, but something sharp poked into my side.

I was afraid I knew what it was. Deathly afraid.

A knife.

I captured Kenna's gaze and gave just the smallest shake of my head, advising her not to do anything. Not yet. She wasn't thrilled, but perhaps she saw my face pale, or the shaking horror that trembled in my eyes.

It was difficult to keep still. My breathing became heavier due to the threat poking me in my side, and I feared if I didn't calm down, I would accidentally cut myself.

That would be just my luck.

Distract. Distract. Distract. It was the only thing I could think of. Buy time until the Elite were alerted. Or worse, I let Sterling take me and put my trust in that Micah would make sure I left here unharmed.

"Sadie is your sister?" I asked, doing my best to keep my shaky voice steady and failing.

"Don't fucking say her name," he seethed, sounding deranged.

Whoa, touchy much? I didn't see why he was so damn defensive about a name, but I packed that info away for later. I had a button to push, and when the time came, I would use it.

He took a breath, the tip of the blade shifting with the

movement. When he regained his composure, he ordered, "Move. You first," he instructed Kenna.

She flipped him off as she passed by, heading toward the sketchy warehouse. I took the fact that he wasn't worried about what she had in her bag as a godsend.

With his knee, Sterling nudged me forward. My legs obeyed, sloppily trying to trudge over the uneven ground.

I closed my eyes briefly, the severity of the situation sinking in. *Holy shit. I just put a supersized wrench in the guys' tactical plan.* Talk about a fucking plot twist, but I should have seen this coming, and I had no one to blame but myself... and Sterling. He was partially to blame seeing as I wouldn't be here if he hadn't used me.

It was fine. All I had to do was find a way to turn this around in my favor—in the Elite's favor.

Would Micah be fuming?

Yes.

But after what he put me through, fuck it. He could deal with it. All the secrets and lies... yeah, those were on him. Prick. I had about a dozen other colorful adjectives for Micah, but underneath my fear and anger lingered hurt. And love.

I couldn't stop myself from loving him. No amount of anger or heartache could white out the way I felt about him.

I tried for years.

It was time I accepted that Micah had my heart. Whether or not he ever stopped breaking mine, he was my one true love.

Kenna entered the warehouse through the same door we saw the boys disappear into. For a split second, I could see her considering her options. She bit the corner of her lip, holding the door, but ultimately she didn't want to leave me alone, even though she could have slammed the door in Sterling's face and taken off, yelling for the guys.

I couldn't decide if I was relieved or disappointed in her decision.

It didn't matter much. Once Sterling and I were inside and the door clattered shut behind us, there was no turning back. Already a nervous mess, I jumped at the echoing sound, the knife nicking me. "Ouch." I twitched forward, trying to keep my body away from the pointy object. It pierced my shirt, just scratching my skin, but probably enough to cause a little blood.

Of course I was wearing white.

"Sadie!" Sterling called, flustered, his voice vibrating throughout the abandoned warehouse. "Where are you?"

So much for coming in inconspicuously. He'd just fully announced his arrival. Did he want to draw out the Elite? I assumed so. Wandering around this massive place would take too much time, especially with a hostage and another one he had no real control over. Kenna glanced over her shoulder, shooting Sterling a nasty glare as she deliberately kept her pace at a crawl, still clinging to the pepper spray.

He caught on quick. "Keep moving, cunt," he snapped, ordering Kenna about and giving her incentive by letting her see the flash of his knife.

"Now you show your true colors. How hard it must have been for you to pretend you aren't a psychopath," I spat, letting that bead of anger burst through my fear. I could hear Micah's voice in my head, telling me that now was not the time to practice female empowerment with a blade pressed to my side, but shit if I didn't want to stand up for myself.

What if I spun really fast and brought my forearm down over his, knocking the knife out of his hand? Then I could kick him the balls. It could work, right?

He let out a bitter laugh. "When your boyfriend does shit like this, it's acceptable, but it makes me deranged? Hypocritical much?"

"So not the same thing," Kenna muttered sarcastically, loud enough for Sterling to hear.

I stared at the back of her head. "They're not going to hurt your sister," I assured him, hoping to calm down the crazy in his expression. It didn't work.

It was awkward walking with his arm looped around my waist, keeping me too close to him, but he didn't let up an inch. "You should know better than anyone. All they do is hurt people."

I wanted to argue, but I had nothing. In a way, he was right. The Elite did hurt people.

But they also fiercely protected those they loved. Sure, most of the time that was each other, but it also extended to a small circle of friends.

We came to the end of the first open room with its high ceilings and exposed rafters. Sterling prompted us down the corridor, keeping Kenna a few feet in front of us, directly in his eyesight. At the third door on the left, her demeanor changed, and I knew we had come to where the Elite were.

She halted, unsure what to do next, but Sterling was there in the next heartbeat. He turned me to the side and kicked my cousin forward into the room. From the doorway, I gasped, watching her tumble forward on her hands and knees to the ground. An oomph of surprise expelled from her upon impact, dark strands of hair curtaining her face.

"Should have known you wouldn't come alone—" Micah's voice abruptly broke off, and without looking at his face, I spotted the tension zapping through him. That was the precise moment his gaze landed on me. He wore streetwear of tattered black jeans and a dark T-shirt that hung long and loose.

A hush fell over the room.

With Sterling still holding me captive, I lifted my eyes, half afraid to meet Micah's gaze. Cold fury like I'd never seen radiated in the depths of his icy blue irises. A flicker of panic came and went like a flash of lightning on a stormy night.

It was about to open and pour wrath like Sterling had never seen. Four against one wasn't great odds, even with me as a hostage. I tried to apologize with my eyes alone, but Micah's focus shifted to Sterling.

The Elite assessed the change of events, four sets of eyes darting from Kenna to Sterling to me, in different orders, but once Micah's landed on me again, they never left. His whole body tightened, the vein running down his neck pulsing.

Grayson stood scowling on the other side of Micah, a beanie pulled over his dark hair. "Goddammit. Seriously! Couldn't the two of you stay put for once?" he seethed, more than annoyance lining the hard planes of his body.

Kenna shoved to her feet, dusting off her hands. Her knees were scuffed. Neither of us had dressed for a brawl. "This isn't our fault," she barked, irritated that her brother was scolding her instead of the guy with the knife.

Fynn flinched, watching Kenna compose herself after the fall. I could tell by his expression that he wanted to go to her. He touched the brim of his ball cap, twisting it around backward on his head.

Grayson's jaw flexed. "Next time we have shit to take care of, we're tying them up."

"What a good idea," Sterling sneered, propelling me forward and pushing the blade deeper into my shirt. A single chair sat only a few feet in front of me beside where Kenna had hit the ground. "Why don't you have a seat, Splash? It's going to be a long night for you."

What did he mean by that? Surely he didn't plan on keeping me here all night.

Nothing in me wanted to sit in that chair already equipped with ropes on the arms and legs. Fun. The chair had been prepped for Sterling, I assumed. I immediately stopped my mind from wondering just what the Elite planned to do to him while tied up.

The room was devoid of any other furniture but had an ample supply of dust, dirt, and critters scuttling in the corners. A faint trace of piss lingered in the chalky air. Moonlight spilled from the windows on the east side of the room, providing little light, and since there was no working electricity, the Elite had a portal fog lamp in the other corner of the room.

Kenna turned around and faced me, giving the Elite her back. The fire in her brown eyes made them look almost amber.

Her fingers were clenched at her sides, the pepper spray still in one hand.

"Kenna," Grayson rumbled, upset that his sister was in the crossfire, about to do something stupid.

She wanted to hurt Sterling; I could see it in her eyes. "He has a knife," she finally said after staring him down.

"Mads, it's going to be okay," Micah assured me. Hearing him say my name gave me a burst of strength, not the reassurance itself.

Sterling let out a manic chuckle at Micah's attempt to calm me, shoving me into the rickety wooden chair. "Be a doll and tie her up," he ordered Kenna, sliding the blade up to my throat as he waited for her to secure the ties on my arms.

Micah cursed under his breath, the muscles in his neck pulsing.

"Sorry," Kenna muttered, her brown eyes brimming with remorse and ire. It wasn't me she wanted to tie to this chair. Her fingers fumbled with the knots, shaking.

When she finished the last knot, Sterling was quick to growl, "Now back the fuck up."

She did so slowly until she was in front of Fynn, who promptly secured Kenna at his side. I exhaled, assured she was safe with the Elite.

"How did you find out about Sadie?" Sterling snarled, leaning down on the back of the chair in a show of dominance. He believed he had the upper hand, and maybe he did. I had no real idea what the Elite planned. This entire place could be rigged with explosives for all I knew.

But I found Sterling's question strange. Then again, this

entire situation was fucking unusual. He hadn't asked where
Sadie was but how they'd learned about his sister, as if she was
this dark family secret.

Why wasn't he pissed off that the Elite had tricked him?
Obviously Sadie wasn't at the warehouse.

Something was wrong here, more than just me having a
knife jabbed into my throat.

"Why don't you put down the weapon so we can talk?"
Brock suggested, keeping his hands in front of him where Sterling could see them and his tone smooth, cool.

"How about you fuck off? You think I came here to save my
sister?" Sterling snorted. "I told you not to underestimate me."

Fynn's brows drew together like he was figuring out a
puzzle, his arm still protectively in front of Kenna, not trusting
her. "If you knew we didn't have your sister, why come at all?"
he asked.

Sterling's voice increased in anger. "Because your friend
took something from me, and I want him to pay." The knife
against my throat trembled, making me very fucking uncomfortable. He lifted the weapon from my throat and pressed it to the
side of my cheek. His face moved alongside mine. "Do you think
he would love you if I mutilated your pretty face?"

"You touch her and you won't walk out of here alive,"
Micah growled, his glacial eyes steady on Sterling. Contempt
oozed from his pores. He wanted to get his hands on the
psycho.

"See, all he cares about is how pretty you look on his arm,"
Sterling taunted, talking crazy nonsense again, but at least he
was talking and not attacking anyone.

"You lied," I rasped, my voice tart as my eyes narrowed sidelong at him.

He flashed his teeth, and I wanted to knock them out. "Hardly the first lie I've told. You should be used to being deceived, seeing as that's all your boyfriend has ever done."

Micah's jaw worked, fighting back the fury sparking in his eyes. "What the fuck do you know about my relationship? Who are you to judge?"

Sterling dipped his face closer to mine, our cheeks brushing so I could feel the prickly stubble. "I know she isn't the first girl you've lied to or used."

I jerked away, careful not to make the move too immense. "And?" I prompted, showing Sterling that his words didn't affect me. Nothing he said was news to me, so if he wanted to shock me, he was failing miserably. It was going to take a lot more to shake my perception of Micah.

Crouching down beside me, he let the blade rest between my breasts, too close to my heart, his other hand gripping my chin. "He got a girl pregnant. Did you know that?"

Okay, I had not expected him to say that. He managed to surprise me after all.

Micah's expression contorted. His fists clamped together at his sides. "What fucking absurdity are you spewing? You really are a pathological liar. You even believe your own lies."

"This is your lie, not mine." Sterling tilted his head to the side. "Or don't you remember? There have been so many girls, I guess it would be hard to recall everyone who claimed you knocked her up."

This was a long overdue conversation, and no one wanted to

stop the reasoning behind Sterling's madness from being unveiled. Brock, Fynn, and Grayson were quiet but alert. Not a part of their bodies wasn't poised for action. When the opportunity came, they would take Sterling down.

Micah stepped forward, making sure the prick's gaze remained focused on him. "I might have slept around, but I always used protection. My dick never went unwrapped."

"Condoms break," Sterling snarled, releasing my chin.

Micah was losing his patience. "I'm telling you, I'm careful. Not to mention, no girl has ever claimed to be pregnant with my kid."

"Why had I expected you to remember? They mean nothing to you. You can't even remember their names," he said disgustedly.

"Sadie, right?" Micah bit out.

"She was my sister!" Sterling hurled. "And you killed her!"

A bomb could have fallen through the corroded ceiling and no one would have moved a muscle. My breathing became more prominent, my chin throbbing from the indents of his fingers.

"Well, that took a dark turn quick," Micah mumbled, inappropriately as usual. He didn't believe for one second that he was responsible for Sadie's death.

Kenna gripped Fynn's arm, glancing over the mountain that blocked her path. "Sadie's dead?"

"That's why you're doing this. You blame Micah for her death." Brock scoffed.

From the darkening of Sterling's eyes, he'd hit a bull's-eye.

"It's your fault," he directed at Micah, speaking to him as if he were the only person in the room. The rest of us mattered little. Well, maybe me, because I was his ticket to hurt the guy I loved. "If you hadn't slept with her, she wouldn't have died."

Micah's gaze flicked to me at the hysteria rising in Sterling's voice. I did my best to express that I was okay. "I'm a little confused. Just how did my dick kill her?" he asked.

"This isn't a fucking joke." As if to hammer home his point, he lifted the hand holding the knife and lashed out, faster than I could have prepared myself. I didn't know he cut me until after the fact when my cheek stung, and that stinging turned into sharp, throbbing pain.

"No!" Micah roared and lunged. Brock and Grayson grabbed him, holding him back, but not without difficulty.

I instinctively wanted to touch my face, but the ropes stopped me. A drop of blood splattered onto my shirt, and I swayed into Sterling. "You fucking cut me."

"Just the first of many, Splash, if your boyfriend doesn't take me seriously," he said, laying the knife dripping with my blood against the side of my neck. If I so much as twisted my head slightly, I would risk injury.

Micah's whole body went from panicked rage to desperate surrender. "Don't hurt her. She has nothing to do with any of this."

Sterling cocked a brow. "Doesn't she?"

Kenna sniffled, tears welling in her eyes as I looked at her. It wasn't reassuring.

"It's me you want to hurt." Micah held up his hands and took another step forward. "Everyone can leave. Let them take the girls out of here, and then it's just you and me. If you want to beat the shit out of me, I won't stop you. I won't fight back. You have my word."

"Micah, no," I pleaded, tears blurring my vision. "I'm not letting you do this."

"Do we have a deal?" Micah asked, lifting a brow.

Sterling's response came without hesitation. "I don't think so. You took something from me. It's only fair that I take what you love most."

It became clear to me then. He was going to kill me and make Micah watch. Sterling had to know that if he tried it again, he would have four very pissed-off guys on top of him. He wouldn't just be sentencing me to death but himself as well.

"How did she die?" Fynn asked, shifting the conversation from me. His tone was mellow and even, like he was talking a jumper off the ledge of a building. He kind of was.

Sterling replaced the knife, glazed in my blood, near my throat. "Do you remember the night we met, Splash?"

It took me a few moments to realize he'd posed the question to me. The pain throbbing in my cheek, the blood rushing to my face and trickling down my chin, made it impossible to concentrate on anything he was saying. I tried to shove aside the spike of my fear. "Y-Yes," I stammered.

Sterling laid out the details for those who didn't know. "You found him in bed with another girl. Isn't that right?"

I stiffened my lower lip. "I don't know why that matters."

"Oh, it does, Splash, because that girl he was fucking, that was Sadie."

I didn't want to believe him. I shook my head, but he didn't stop. "She dragged me to the party that night, saying she had to go. All her friends would be there, and she couldn't miss it, despite my parents already telling her no. At that time, I lived to piss off the old man. I have regretted taking Sadie to that party every day since. If I'd known she would end up in his bed, I never would have agreed."

"You were on the porch," I said, finding myself sucked into the past despite not wanting to go there.

"It wasn't my scene, but I wanted Sadie to have a good time, do all the things girls her age experience. I thought I was being a good brother. Then you came rushing out, eyes glossy with tears. I had seen you arrive not long before, and I couldn't help but wonder what happened in such a short time to cause you such sadness. It didn't take long for a reason to appear. I believed fate sent you to me that night."

"I don't believe in fate," I rasped. Karma, perhaps, but fate... no. We had the choice, the power to change our future. "The only thing that night gave me was regret."

He brushed a chunk of hair off my face, strands damp with blood, and I shuddered.

Micah's terrifying expression bored into Sterling's, promising unimaginable pain.

Sterling's hostile glare turned to Micah. "She saw you two months later, just after learning about the baby. Your football team played against Crown Royal, and she waited until after the game to approach you. She told you she was pregnant, but you barely spared her a glance. You said it couldn't possibly be yours because you would never have fucked a girl like her. And if that wasn't humiliating enough, you added salt to an open wound, telling her to try and tie down one of the other guys she'd opened her legs for."

Fynn had Kenna tucked against him. Her eyes were red. "Did she have the baby?" he asked.

Sterling swallowed hard. "No. I took her to the appointment. She cried the entire drive. Up until the moment they put her under she doubted her decision, but without your support or my parents', I understood why she went through with the abortion."

I had a sickening feeling about how this story ended, and I didn't want to hear it. Nor did I want to admit the pain in Sterling's voice. I wanted him to remain a monster, not a brother who was hurt over losing his sister.

My eyes went to Grayson, and I wondered what he would do if Kenna or Josie found themselves in a similar situation. Although, I didn't have to think too hard about it. Truth was, Grayson would be in Sterling's position, seeking his retribution without hesitation.

"She refused to tell me your name, and I didn't find out until after her death. She never woke up. Whether it was a complication or something else, my parents made sure the truth about Sadie's death remained locked away, from the press, from her medical records, and even from me. But it didn't matter. The truth never stays buried. Once I uncovered your name in a journal she kept online, I knew I had to make you hurt the way you hurt her."

There was no proof that Micah had been the father of Sadie's baby, but if she hadn't been with anyone else, Micah could have been a father.

I didn't know how that made me feel.

Not good.

Sterling's fingers gripped my hair, yanking my head back and forcing me to look up at him. "When I saw you were with him even after what he'd done to you, I realized you were as bad as the rest of them. You deserved to be humiliated just as Sadie was."

Coiled tight, Micah spoke in low tones. "I could try and convince you all night that I had no idea, but you won't believe me. If you won't let Mads leave, then let everyone else go. Mads and I will stay."

"No fucking way are we leaving you with him," Brock snapped, his face tightening.

They shared a look. It was only for a split second, but I caught something between the boys. A flash. It caused my already pumping adrenaline to soar. There was a sense of urgency in them all.

Micah took another step forward, and Sterling reacted. The tip of the blade pierced the thin skin on the side of my neck. "I wouldn't do that again if I were you."

I whimpered, closing my eyes briefly, thinking death was surely close. I clutched the chair's arms to the point that I had no feeling left in my hands.

"Don't hurt her." Micah's voice came out gruff.

"Better," Sterling sneered, a corrupt smile curving on his lips, "but not nearly enough pain."

I braced myself, sensing the next slash was coming and there was little I could do to stop it.

"Relax," the asshole whispered in my ear. He reached into

his pocket, pulling out a cigarette and sticking it between my lips. "We both could use this."

I spat out the slim stick despite desperately wanting to inhale its familiar taste.

The Zippo flicked, a flame burning near the other side of my cheek, the one not still dripping blood. He tsked in disapproval. "What a waste."

Before Sterling could pull out another cigarette, Micah moved, bolting across the warehouse.

"Fuck," the other Elite chorused, all having the same reaction to Micah rushing at Sterling. They were a step or two behind, Fynn grabbing a hold of Kenna to keep her out of the mess that was about to unfold.

Seeing Micah rushing forward, Sterling dropped the lighter and, a second later, plunged the blade into my side.

I sucked in a sharp inhale of shock, and my eyes widened.

The fucker stabbed me. Actually, stabbed me.

My disbelief stunned me before the scorching pain registered. The full brunt of it broadcasted through my body when he ripped the knife out of muscle, fat, and flesh.

His movements were jerky and sloppy, making it clear that stabbing people wasn't something he did for a living. But fuck if it didn't hurt like hell. So much worse than anything I'd seen on TV.

"Mads!" Micah bellowed, stark panic on his face as he surged toward me, toward Sterling.

Hot wetness soaked the side of my shirt. Instinct told me to cover the wound with my hand and put pressure on it. Only problem... I didn't have a free hand to do so. They were both tied to the stupid fucking chair.

This was how I died. In an abandoned warehouse, bleeding out on a dusty, dirty floor in front of my friends and the guy I loved. Murdered. I had to say, this was not how I thought the end would come. Not for me.

I heard the crunch of bone connecting with flesh. "You're dead, motherfucker," Micah seethed. A splatter of blood landed on my thigh, but I had no idea if it was mine or Sterling's.

The blade he'd used to threaten and intimidate me all night clattered to the floor. Micah dropped low, slamming his shoulder into Sterling's gut and taking them both down.

Heat crawled up my leg, singeing the skin. I felt as if I was on fire. Was it a reaction to being stabbed? The heat deepened, and I couldn't decide whether the wound at my side or the burning was worse.

It was then that I saw something near my feet had erupted into flames. Kenna's discarded bag. She'd left it there when Sterling kicked her to the ground.

Spray paint. That's flammable, right?

Oh shit.

I lifted my eyes, wanting to scream to my friends to run, wanting to warn Micah he was in danger, but that was when the explosion rocked the warehouse.

It had been close. Too fucking close.

All hell broke loose.

The blast knocked me over, chair and all, tossing me backward. I hit the ground hard, my whole body jerking from the impact. The back of my head smacked the hard surface, my wrists jostled against the rope, fibers of thread rubbing into my skin.

The world went eerily silent for a moment before the ringing started. I whipped my head to the side, away from the swelling flames that blistered the right half of my body, but I couldn't escape, not tied to a chair. Fear and frenzy clawed violently within me like a headless beast.

Despite the pain and terror coursing through my veins, thoughts of Micah overtook the agony I suffered. Where was he? Had the explosion knocked him around as it had me? Was he hurt? What if Sterling managed to find the knife?

Rotted and decayed beams started to fall from the ceiling, loosened and detached by the explosion. They crashed to the ground, immediately eaten by the raging fire. In less than a minute, it had grown out of control.

I tried to wiggle and scoot myself around to see if I could spot him—see if I could find anyone—but the pain was too much. I was growing weaker. I was losing too much blood too fast, and moving only made it worse. I laid my head down, tears streaming over my cheeks as I watched flames crawl over the floor, engulfing everything in their path. It came straight for me, the wooden chair underneath me kindling for the hungry fire consuming everything in its path.

I was so fucked.

Smoke blanketed the room in a dense fog, and I lost sight of everyone. They could all be dead or unable to move like me. I coughed, the plumes filling my lungs. Heat scorched my legs, advising me that the fire had grown closer. Burning to death was one of my biggest fears. I'd rather die any other way. Hell, I'd rather Sterling stab me to death. Maybe I should just beg the asshole to finish me off before the fire ate me alive, but I didn't know where he was. He could have run for all I knew, leaving me to perish in this building.

The coughing wouldn't stop. I had no way to prevent my lungs from inhaling the smoke-coated air. My eyes grew heavy, and although my outer flesh was fiery, inside I shivered, an iciness flowing into every crevice of my body.

I didn't want to die alone. I didn't want to die at all, but if this was my time, I longed to be with someone I loved. Someone who loved me. Someone to tell me not to be afraid. Someone to hold my hand until the final second.

"Mads," a voice called. They called again and again, repeating my name yet sounding so very far away.

Micah, my mind cried in answer. I couldn't tell if it was the impending unconsciousness, my damaged hearing, or the burning building that made him sound as if he was calling me from another dimension.

I opened my mouth to tell him to leave, to get out of here, but smoke filled the space and I coughed instead. A shadowy figure stumbled through the heavy smoke, jumping over a wall of flames that boxed me in.

"Mads." My name wrenched from his lips as he crouched down beside me, his fingers immediately going to the knots tied at my wrists. "Just hold on. Don't you dare give up on me. I'm going to get you out of here. Do you hear me?"

Micah wouldn't leave. The stubborn ass would fight to get me out until his last breath, and that scared the shit out of me. We both couldn't die in here. I refused to let that happen.

"Get out of here," I rasped, coughing afterward. The few words cost me.

"Never without you," he said, freeing one hand and shifting quickly to the other.

I didn't have it in me to argue. All I could do was lie bleeding on the floor, staring at his face under heavy eyes. Dirt and soot smeared his cheeks and forehead in gloomy streaks. His shirt was torn, and he had blood on him, but it was hard to say if it was his, mine, or possibly even Sterling's.

I had so many things I wanted to say, the top being how much I loved him. And that I didn't regret a single moment in our crazy up-and-down relationship. He had been worth it. Every tear. Every heartache. Every lonely night. I only wish I'd had the chance to tell him.

He slid his arms underneath me, tears glistening in his bright eyes. The flames curled and licked along the floor, seconds away from swallowing the legs of the chair.

"I got you, Mads," he murmured, scooping me up in his arms, and it no longer mattered if I lived or died. I wasn't alone.

CHAPTER TWENTY-TWO

MADS

The incessant beeping of a machine woke me. Before I opened my eyes, the sterile scent of a hospital filled my nostrils, and I wanted to go right back into that bliss of oblivion.

Reality meant I had to deal with what happened.

And I wanted it all to be a dream.

Sterling.

The warehouse.

The fire.

I could hear screams. Mine. Kenna's. Micah roaring my name.

Were they alive? Had they all gotten out?

Hysteria seized my chest as each memory flooded into my mind. The explosion still rang in my ears, my hearing muffled from the blast. So much fucking smoke. Swallowing only confirmed that my lungs were raw and scratchy from the amount I'd inhaled. Pressure ached on my side where I'd been stabbed.

Holy shit. I was stabbed.

I forced my eyes open, needing to know how this night ended. No matter how terrible the news might be, I had to find out if my friends were alive. Micah had carried me out of the building, but after that... nothing. My memory hit a brick wall. I had no idea what happened to Kenna, Micah, or the Elite.

Or Sterling, for that matter, but right now, I didn't give a shit about him. The bastard had nearly killed me.

A low groan pulled from my lips as I tried to move, shifting my head a bit higher on the pillow, but that was a bad idea. Instant pain flared at my wound. Taking a breath, I waited for the throbbing to subside and looked around the room, seeing a figure slumped over in a chair. Their elbows were braced on their knees, head hung down.

Seeing him, a rush of overwhelming emotion pricked at my eyes. I blinked to clear the haze of sleep, the medication coursing through my body, and the moisture gathering at the corners. Just like the memories that I wanted to be a dream, I was afraid this moment was also a figment of my imagination. I longed for him to be alive, to be unhurt and in front of me. If any moment of the last few hours was going to be real, let it be this. The universe couldn't be so cruel as to make me see him and it not be real.

"Micah," I whispered. It was all I could manage, and even then, my throat protested.

His head snapped up, eyes devouring my face. I could see how pale his skin was, how tired his eyes were.

"You're awake," he said, scrubbing a hand down his mouth and chin as he exhaled. "Christ, Mads. Don't ever scare me like that again. I—" His voice broke off, he, too, struggling to speak.

I reached out to him, needing to feel that he was flesh and warmth. All the fighting and anger from the last week didn't matter. "I'm okay," I assured him.

Moving off the chair, he laced his fingers with mine and gently sat on the edge of my hospital bed. It wasn't close enough for me, but I understood his carefulness. I must have looked a fucking mess. There was a reason they didn't have mirrors in hospital rooms, and thank God. If I saw my reflection right now, I'd probably scare myself.

Despite having cleaned his face, his clothes had seen better days, and he smelled like a bonfire. Remorse twisted at his mouth. "I can't decide if I want to scold you or beg for your forgiveness."

I squeezed his hand, repressing the urge to pull him onto the bed. "Is everyone okay? Did they all get out?"

He nodded. "Just a few scratches and smoke inhalation. They're all fine. You don't need to worry."

My whole body sank deeper into the thin mattress, relief releasing the tension. "And Sterling?"

A long pause swelled between us before he replied, "He didn't make it out." Not an ounce of contrition. "Kenna called 911 as Fynn pulled her out of the warehouse. By the time the firemen arrived, the entire building was engulfed, and they couldn't get inside. I imagine once they extinguish the flames, the cops will comb through the debris, and with any luck, they'll find his remains."

Dead? Sterling was dead? It probably made me a shitty person for feeling... relieved. The air in my chest moved in easier knowing Sterling wasn't out there to hurt anyone I loved. An audible exhale released from my lips.

Micah's head dropped onto my arm. "I'm sorry," he murmured. "I'm so sorry. If I—"

I couldn't stand to see him like this. Broken. I was the one in the hospital bed, but he seemed to be suffering more. Or maybe it was because I was on some good drugs. I slid my fingers into his hair. "Micah. Micah, look at me." I wanted to see his eyes when I said this. He didn't just need to hear me. He needed to see the truth of the words on my face. I almost called his name again, but he finally lifted his head. "I don't blame you."

He reached to touch me with his free hand but then remembered half my cheek was bandaged. His hand dropped to the bed. "But I do blame myself." I could see it in his eyes, the guilt, the shame, the pain. It all swam in his gaze, dulling the usual brightness that shone in them.

"Stop." I swallowed, trying to ease the dryness that scratched my throat. Micah grabbed a glass of water from the tray and handed it to me. I gave him a small smile of thanks as he lifted it to my lips, and I drank a few slow sips.

"Better?" he asked, putting the cup back onto the moving tray.

I nodded, reclining into the pillow. "I can't let you take on this guilt. The choices and decisions of someone else are not your responsibility. You can speculate all day and night about whether what Sterling said was true, but it won't change a thing.

And the only person who made me follow you last night was me. I owe you my life, Micah. If you hadn't..."

"I would have died in that building alongside you rather than leave you alone," he said softly.

"I know."

He released a breath, his stormy eyes holding mine. "I can't live without you, Mads. There is no life worth living if you're not beside me."

Tugging on his arm, I urged him into bed next to me. I bit my lip against the movement he created lying on his side, not wanting him to see the discomfort even the tiniest jostle caused. I needed him close. He placed a hand over my heart, careful of any bruises I might have suffered on my body and staying away from the wrapped wound on the other side. I buried my face into him, breathing in and not caring about those hints of smoke mixing with his scent. "Stay a little longer," I muttered.

"I'm not going anywhere. Not as long as you're here." Gentle fingers ran through my tangled hair. "I don't deserve you."

He didn't. But my heart only wanted this jerk, flaws and all.

"I promised myself that when you woke up, I would do whatever it takes to make it right between us." He shifted his head so we lay face-to-face on the shared pillow. "The moment you walked out of my room that morning, I regretted what I'd done. It's never been easy for me to trust someone with my heart, but I love you, Mads. You mean more to me than I ever thought possible. So much more."

My eyes misted. I was going to be one of those sappy girls who cried.

"I never want to go back to being that guy whose life was empty and meaningless," he continued. "You make me want to prove everyone wrong about me. I can be more than a rich asshole who doesn't take anything seriously. I take us seriously. And that's what matters to me."

The tears couldn't be stopped, but they were happy tears, mostly, falling tenderly down my cheeks. "I've waited years to hear you say those words, would have given anything to hear them last week."

Panic trembled in his eyes. "Mads, I swear—"

"It's not that," I quickly interrupted before he thought for another second that I wasn't accepting him. But I couldn't stop the shadow of self-doubt. "I love you, Micah. I've loved you since I was five years old."

He caught one of my tears with the pad of his thumb. "What's wrong?"

"Look at me," I whimpered.

"I am looking at you," he said, confusion bunching his brows.

Was it vain to be so concerned about my outward appearance? Yes. But I had just woken up. I had no idea how bad the side of my face was, but I could assume that a reminder of last night would be etched into my cheek—the line of Sterling's blade running down my face. I was more worried about that wound than the one on my side.

"Who knows what I'll look like when they take this bandage off?" The admission felt like sandpaper on my tongue that had nothing to do with the smoke damage.

He propped his hand on the side of his temple, glancing

down at me. "You think I give a shit about a possible little scar?" He ran a finger over my trembling bottom lip. "We all have scars, Mads. Not all of them are visible, but they're there all the same. Sometimes it's those invisible wounds that cut deeper than any outward scar. I have more than most, and not once have you seen me only for the wrong I've done or the damage I've created. You see all of me. Accept all of me. Love all of me. Why would you think I wouldn't do the same?"

The injury was so raw. I should be thankful I survived instead of wallowing in vanity, but I also thought I needed to mourn the old Mads to be able to embrace the girl I would be. "I think I might need some time to process everything."

Dipping his head, he lightly dragged his lips over mine. "You will always be my Mads no matter what, and if you want space, I can give you that, for as long as you need."

I shook my head. "Space is the last thing I want. At least from you."

His lips hovered over mine. "I can do less space. Is this better?" Glint sparkled in the eyes that held mine with a heated promise.

"Almost," I whispered, catching the front of his shirt and pulling him to me.

He kissed me, and it mattered little that I was in a hospital bed and suffering. The need for him began to rise inside me.

Someone cleared their throat, and Micah regrettably pulled away, glancing toward the door. The doctor gave us a warm, friendly smile, moving into the room. "I see the patient is awake. How do you feel?" he asked. "Are you in any pain?"

Color stained my cheeks as I readjusted myself on the bed,

fixing the sheet draped over me. "Nothing that isn't tolerable. It only really hurts if I move."

"Good, that means the medication is doing the trick. We're going to monitor you for a few days, but you're going to need to take it easy for a few weeks. You were lucky. No organs were damaged. The wound itself was less than an inch deep. Would you like us to contact your parents?" the doctor asked while reading one of the machines beeping beside the bed.

I shook my head. "No, I don't want to worry them."

Micah continued to lie on the bed beside me. "It wouldn't be a bad idea to go home while you recover and heal," he said. "You know your mom would love to dote."

"I'm fine, really." The last thing I wanted to explain was how I got hurt or ended up stabbed in an abandoned warehouse. Too many questions I didn't want to answer.

The doctor gave me the rundown of my care. I was also being treated for smoke inhalation, and they'd stitched my cheek. He informed me that it would most likely leave a scar, but after the healing process, I could consider cosmetic surgery or other methods to lighten and diminish the mark.

When he finished checking my vitals, the doctor ordered me to rest and went to check on his other patients.

A knock came a few minutes later, and Grayson's face peered around the door. "What the fuck, asshole? You couldn't let us know she was awake?"

Micah's expression was unapologetic. "The doctor just left."

Grayson was shoved inside the small room, Fynn filling up the space behind him. Then I heard Kenna's voice. "Bunch of Neanderthals," she mumbled under her breath as she waltzed through the door after them. Her brown eyes grazed over the guys and found mine. "Fucking hell, Mads. If you hadn't just escaped death tonight, I would kill you for scaring me like that." She pushed herself to the side of my bed, weaving around the guys standing awkwardly.

When I saw Kenna, the tears threatened to come back. She was safe. Her hair might have been messier than usual, her clothes sooty, but she was unharmed. "I'm happy to see you too."

"Can I hug you?" she asked, her voice hitching.

Nodding, I swallowed. "I'll be upset if you don't."

Arms flung around my neck. "I've never been so scared," she whispered, clinging for another moment before pulling away and wiping at her eyes.

I brushed at my cheeks, mopping up the tears that had escaped. "You're okay?"

"I've been through worse. The world is better off without him, remember that," she said.

Fynn maneuvered around Kenna to lean down and kiss my cheek. "I always knew you were a tough chick."

I grinned and then promptly winced. "Don't make me smile or laugh."

"Watch where you're putting those lips," Micah grumbled, scowling at his friend.

Fynn only chuckled, caring little about Micah's half-hearted threats.

The real threat was over.

Maybe I could finally start enjoying college.

Grayson moved forward next, giving me a quick hug. "Josie

and Ainsley are freaking out. Brock went back to the townhouse to make sure the two of them stay put," he shared, knowing I would want to know. Everyone was accounted for. He rubbed a hand over the back of his neck. "The cops are going to want a statement."

I fumbled with the IV cord stuck into my arm. "Is there anything I should know beforehand?" I glanced at everyone in the room. We had to have our stories straight. I didn't want this to fall on the Elite.

"Just stick to the truth," Grayson advised. "Tell them only what you want to tell them. No more, no less."

Kenna scrunched her face up at her brother. "Did you take that from one of Brock's playbooks?"

Fynn intercepted before the sibling war broke out in my hospital room. "Maybe it's time this brat goes home." He ruffled Kenna's hair, further irritating her, but before she could open her mouth and protest, his eyes returned to me. "You don't have to worry, Mads. We've made some calls, and none of this will blow back on us."

Once again, the connections these four guys had staggered me. "I'll be home soon. They're releasing me in a few hours, assuming I don't flatline," I said in a sad attempt at humor.

"That's not fucking funny," the queen of drama chided.

Micah chuckled beside me, and Grayson rolled his eyes. "You have a twisted sense of humor," my cousin mumbled, shaking his head.

They started to head out of the room.

"Kenna," I called.

She halted at the door and half turned toward me, brow lifting. Grayson and Fynn looked back as well, but my eyes were on Kenna's.

My expression turned grim, the events of the night hitting me like a truck. "I'm sorry. I never should have let you come with me," I told her, voice pained.

She lowered the questioning brow, her features softening. "As if I would have ever let you go alone. You're my best friend, Mads. I'd follow you into Hell every time. No questions asked."

Micah wiped at the corner of his eye and sniffled. "Stop. You're going to make me cry."

Kenna grinned. "We're going to be all right."

I smiled back. "We always are."

Grayson shoved his hands into his pockets. "Yeah, because of us. Imagine what would happen if we weren't around."

"There would be no trouble, that's what," Kenna bit back.

Fynn, Grayson, and Micah all snorted in unison. Fynn hooked an arm around Kenna's shoulders, holding the door open with his large foot. "Come on, brat. Let's go before you blow up the hospital."

Kenna rolled her eyes. "Me?" she shrieked as Fynn steered her into the hallway. "You're in the Elite of Destruction."

"Cute," Fynn retorted, ruffling her hair again, something Kenna despised.

Grayson lingered another minute in the doorway. "I'm sure this doesn't have to be said, but don't tell your mom."

I shot him a disparaging look. "What do you take me for, an amateur?"

He came back with one of his usual smartass remarks. "Does that deem a response?"

Amusement danced in Micah's eyes, but he was smart enough not to laugh.

I wanted to toss something at my cousin, but I wasn't going to give up my pillow, and the only other thing within reach was the bed remote, which was attached to the fucking bed. "Get out of here before I have my doctor cast the broken leg I'm about to give you."

Grayson looked more relaxed now. "I'm glad you're still in there."

Both a chilling and warm stream washed through me, colliding like the ocean meeting the sea. I was still me, but also, I wasn't. "Where would I have gone?"

"Don't fuck this up," he told Micah.

EPILOGUE

MADS

I held the mascara wand between my fingers, carefully coating my lashes as I arched over the bathroom sink, wary of the wound that was mostly healed. It only gave me problems if I bumped it, something I was cautious of not doing.

My recovery hadn't been easy, but I'd been surrounded by people who cared about me. I didn't have to lift a finger for shit. Hell, the first two weeks I rarely left my bed. Micah remained at my side day and night, waiting on me. After that, I insisted he resume going to class. I stayed at his house during my recovery. My roommates helped make sure I didn't fall behind on my classes, bringing me my assignments and speaking with my professors. The school allowed me to complete my work online.

Keeping my injuries from my parents had been difficult. Too many times I wanted to hear my mom's voice, have her nurse me back to health as she had with all those bouts of colds and touches of flu I'd had growing up. I would have given up a night of sleep for a bowl of my dad's creamy tomato soup. The homesickness hit hard during the early days of being stuck in a bed. But slowly, it passed, and my friends were a big part of easing the loneliness. Not that I was ever really alone, but there was such a thing as feeling empty even when surrounded by people.

In the weeks that passed, not a stitch of news was released about Sterling. No body had been recovered. No remains had been discovered in the ashes. He was just gone. And whether the police found that suspicious or not, his disappearance remained an open case. I'd been questioned more than once by the detectives, as had the Elite. The fire itself had been ruled an accident, and as much as I wanted to believe Sterling perished in that warehouse, I couldn't fully believe he was dead until proof was discovered. Until then, I needed to move on with my life, regardless of how hard it was.

Tonight was the homecoming football game, and the first time I'd be going out in public without my bandages. Nervous didn't begin to describe the butterflies fluttering inside me. It was enough to make me sick, climb back into bed, and tell my friends I couldn't go.

My wounds had healed. The stab wound on my side still gave me problems but was so much more manageable than when I'd first come home, but the mark on my cheek wasn't something I could hide under clothes.

Makeup was my best friend. I added a light layer of concealer to tone down the redness. It would take time to get used to seeing the scar on my face. What bothered me wasn't the imperfection but the reminder it created. I hoped over time it would dull, not just the jagged line but the imprint it had stamped in my memory. I didn't want to relive that night. It was bad enough seeing it again in my dreams. The rope burns on my wrists had faded as well and were easily covered up with bracelets. Another week and that reminder would vanish.

But I couldn't avoid the world.

Life went on.

I stared at myself in the mirror and took a breath. It was time to lift my chin and get out there or college would pass me by. "You don't give a shit what anyone else thinks of you. Never did, and you're surely not going to start now," I told my reflection.

"You done giving yourself a pep talk?" Josie leaned in the doorway, a smile on her lips and strands of pink hair falling over her shoulders. "It was a pretty good one, though." She stepped into the bathroom and glanced at me through the mirror. "No one else's opinion matters. When I first came to Elmwood Academy, it was one of the things I admired most about you. That and your ability to tell the Elite to fuck off."

I chuckled, releasing the smile that wanted to curl on my lips. "They were such dicks in high school."

"They're still mostly dicks."

No argument there.

"I can't believe we're in college still going to watch the same boys play football." Neither Josie nor I was big on sports, but once she got a glimpse of Brock in his uniform, her interest in the game developed, though it was only him she cared about. The girl still didn't know shit about offense or defense. Dragging Josie to her first academy game was an experience I'd never forget.

She toyed with her necklace, a charm that said PERFECT with a crooked T. It had been a gift from Brock. "We might be watching some of them a lot longer than college," she replied wistfully.

I wrinkled my nose. "Fynn for sure. I know Micah loves the game when his father isn't shoving it down his throat, but I think college ball will be the end for him. What about Brock?" I asked, shoving my makeup back into its travel bag.

Shrugging, she straightened off the doorway. "He hasn't made up his mind, but a part of him wants to go to the pros like Fynn. Maybe not quite as much, but I wouldn't rule it out."

Fluffing my hair one last time, I grabbed my phone and shoved it into my bag. "I think it's time I moved back into the dorm."

"Are you sure you're ready? No one would fault you for not wanting to move back in. It's kind of cozy here, you all snuggled up with Micah every night." She gave me that look like she knew a lot more than snuggling was going on and then turned to the side so I could leave the bathroom.

"Do you wish you'd moved into the house with Brock instead?" I asked, walking to the bedroom door.

She shook her head as we entered the hallway. "No. Don't

get me wrong. I miss the jerk. A lot. But I need this time alone and with my crew." Her lips twitched over the newly coined name we'd given ourselves. "I don't want my life to just become about Brock or the Elite."

The cameras in our dorm had been dealt with, but the fraternity had not. The time would come, sooner than I was probably ready for. Despite Brock's ordering, pleading, barking, and pouting, Josie moved back into the dorm with Kenna and Ainsley the week I came home from the hospital. "When did you become so wise?"

She gently linked arms as we descended the stairs and rolled her eyes. "Obviously the day I met you."

I didn't believe that for a second. Josie James was not someone who made decisions lightly. She had a tough life, and I admired her fighting spirit—her survival instincts.

Together we walked through campus with the dozens and dozens of other students all making their way to the field. It was a busy day at the university, the grounds decorated with school pride on every corner. A buzz of excited energy vibrated through the air.

We shuffled our way into the stands along with the hundreds of other students, parents, and college staff to watch the Kingsley Knights tear down the opposing team. The stadium looked like a sea of silver and purple, the university's colors.

Ainsley and Kenna had saved our seats. They were bickering over who had the best pizza in Elmwood when Josie and I arrived. Somehow seeing the two of them back to giving each other attitude seemed right, as if the world finally returned to normal.

"Did we miss anything?" I asked, plunking down onto the bleachers. My ass would be screaming at me by the end of the game. Someone needed to consider padding these damn things.

"Only Kenna throwing herself at some guys," Ainsley retorted in a judging way.

Kenna was quick to throw a barb of her own. "Until you scared them off with your witchy eyes."

This was going to be a fun night. I could tell.

When the Knights came barreling through the tunnel a few minutes later, the crowd surged to their feet in an uproar, banners and signs waving proudly. There really wasn't an experience like an entire school coming together to support their team, especially in a town that worshipped football and its players. They were treated like celebrities, and if they came from money, their status rose to godlike.

My eyes immediately detected Micah on the field, and as if he were the opposite side of my magnet, those light blue eyes found mine. Dimples graced either side of his cheeks. He lifted the helmet dangling from his fingers into the air. I shook my head, grinning like the hopelessly-in-love fool I was.

Over the next three hours, the four of us watched the Knights battle against the Hurricanes on the field. It wasn't like high school in the sense that our team didn't slaughter the visitors. The Knights had to fight tooth and nail to stay head-to-head with their opponent, something neither Brock nor Micah was accustomed to. At one point they looked worried.

We were well into the fourth quarter when Ainsley glanced at her phone, a frown marring her lips. It wasn't the first time I caught her scowling at something on the screen; she'd been glancing at it off and on throughout the game.

"Is everything okay?" I asked during a moment of quiet. Well, relatively quiet considering the constant chatter from the stands.

She looked up, shoving her phone into her back pocket, and smiled, but it didn't reach her eyes. "Yeah, just a wrong number."

I couldn't say why, but I didn't believe her. It was clear she wasn't ready to talk about what was bothering her. No pressure from me.

With only a few minutes left in the game, the Knights trailed the opposing team by three points. We had to score on this next drive or kiss our homecoming game victory goodbye. No one wanted that dark cloud over their head tonight. It would definitely put a damper on the after-parties.

Our offense got into formation, Brock behind the center. His strong voice called out the countdown right before the ball snapped into his waiting, sturdy hands. He shuffled backward and then to the side, avoiding not one but two tackles as the right tackle and left outside linebacker rushed to get their hands on our quarterback.

Then Brock dropped his hand back, finding his opening, and tossed the ball. It spiraled down the field straight into the hands of my boyfriend. Micah's fingers secured the catch, and the race against the clock began. He never stopped running, and as he tucked the ball into his chest, his legs pumped toward the end zone.

The entire stadium fell silent, watching Micah haul ass. I glanced at the clock, holding my breath.

Ten seconds.

Two of the defensive players for the other team were on his heels, chasing after him.

Five seconds.

Micah ran, his feet flying over the ground, dirt kicking up behind him.

Two seconds.

The end zone was in sight. Just a few more feet. My heart thumped in my chest. This was nearly as stressful as getting stabbed. Nearly. A different kind of adrenaline rush.

Micah crossed into the end zone, and I exhaled.

The Knights won.

Cheers erupted throughout the stadium, hands clapping and feet stomping in thunderous rhythm. Kenna, Josie, Ainsley, and I jumped, the four of us screaming from the stands.

Within seconds, Micah was surrounded by his teammates as they dashed off the sidelines and scrambled down the field. Micah tossed the ball onto the ground right before he was engulfed by the other players. He was born to be at the center of everything he did with a damn crooked smile on his lips.

Tonight would be one long-ass victory party.

As much as I wanted to hurdle over the bleachers and run onto the field to congratulate him, I hung back with my friends, giving Brock and Micah their moment of glory.

But I didn't have to wait long. Micah jogged over to my section of the stands. He already had his helmet off, and once his eyes connected with mine, he pointed at me. "Get down here!" he yelled, shaking out his hair and grinning. The crowd around me only encouraged him, growing louder.

Josie nudged my shoulder, and the next thing I knew, I was moving down the row. People parted, letting me pass by; all the while, I was suppressing the urge to hide under the bleachers, my cheeks warming with embarrassment. "You're crazy," I told when him I reached the bottom.

He grabbed my hand and pulled me into his chest. The crowd went nuts. "Crazy about you."

Shaking my head, I replied, "When did your lines get so cheesy?"

His laugh, like the man himself, was enamoring. He tilted his head in a side jerk, indicating he wanted us to leave. The celebration had already begun on and off the field. As we walked the long length toward the players' locker room, coaches, teammates, students, teachers, and parents all congratulated Micah, slapping him on the back, shouting his jersey number, shaking his hand, or calling his name. It was mayhem but in the best possible way. He kept me at his side the entire time, fingers curled against mine.

Unlike a lot of the players, his parents weren't in the stands. They were overseas and hadn't come to the game, but for Micah, it was far less stressful not having them here.

When we cleared the stadium, the crowd could still be heard but at a much more manageable volume. My ears would probably ring for a week, and I told myself not to compare it to the explosion. Today was not the day for bad memories. This was a day for happiness, pride, and fucking parties, as Micah would say.

I could tell he wanted to sweep me up into his arms, but his fear of hurting me kept my feet planted on the ground. "You can hug me, at least," I offered, gazing up into his face. Arms came around my shoulders and neck, careful to keep his hold far from my injured side, and I instantly relaxed, loosely wrapping my hands around his waist. "You need a shower," I protested weakly, loving his intoxicating scent even when it was almost masked by sweat and earth.

The ends of his hair were damp. He was exhausted from the grueling game, yet excitement danced in his eyes. "Maybe you can help me out of these clothes. I could sneak you into the locker room," he said with a playful hook of his lips.

The dimples did me in. If he kept smiling at me like this, I'd be a puddle at his feet, following him anywhere, even into the guys' locker room. I wanted to taste his lips. "Stop trying to tempt me."

He kissed my neck. "So, is that a yes?"

I squealed with laughter as he bit the column of my throat. Not hard, but just even pressure to send my blood singing. "Definitely not. You are not dragging me into the locker room."

"Five minutes. Hell, two minutes. That's all we need." The stadium behind us started to clear out, but we were oblivious to everyone else but us.

I wrinkled my nose. "How romantic." I drew him in, no longer resisting the desire to kiss him. He tasted of salt, but I didn't care. God, I loved this prick.

"You kill me, Mads," he groaned, his breath teasing my lips.

"Good," I said, dropping a quick peck on his mouth. "Because we're going to celebrate your win, and what I have in mind for the rest of the night is going to take a hell of a lot longer than two minutes. That's how much time you have to shower and get your ass back to the house." I slapped his backside.

His eyes darkened. "I love you."

Blinking, I basked in the sudden warmth that flooded through my system. "Say it again," I demanded.

Gentle fingers brushed at the sides of my face. "I love you, Madeleine Clarke."

A thrill went through me. "Four minutes," I declared, taking a step out of his arms, my eyes twinkling.

Brows drew together, confusion descending over his expression before he caught on. His hand went to the back of my neck. "Screw the shower here. We can take one together at home."

From the heat in his eyes, he was seconds away from kissing me again, and I wanted him to very much. I grinned, curling my fingers into the front of his jersey. "I like that idea better."

"You were always meant to be mine," he murmured, claiming my lips just as he had claimed my heart.

THANK YOU FOR READING!
I hope you enjoyed Mads and Micah's story. There is more to come...
Book Five: Unchained
Ainsley and Grayson

READ MORE BY J. L. WEIL

ELITE OF ELMWOOD ACADEMY
(New Adult Dark High School Romance)

Turmoil

Disorder

Revenge

Rival

DIVISA HUNTRESS
(New Adult Paranormal Romance)

Crown of Darkness

Inferno of Darkness

Eternity of Darkness

DRAGON DESCENDANTS SERIES
(Upper Teen Reverse Harem Fantasy)

Stealing Tranquility

Absorbing Poison

Taming Fire

Thawing Frost

THE DIVISA SERIES

(Full series completed – Teen Paranormal Romance)

Losing Emma: A Divisa novella

Saving Angel

Hunting Angel

Breaking Emma: A Divisa novella

Chasing Angel

Loving Angel

Redeeming Angel

LUMINESCENCE TRILOGY

(Full series completed – Teen Paranormal Romance)

Luminescence

Amethyst Tears

Moondust

Darkmist – A Luminescence novella

RAVEN SERIES

(Full series completed – Teen Paranormal Romance)

White Raven

Black Crow

Soul Symmetry

BEAUTY NEVER DIES CHRONICLES

(Teen Dystopian Romance)

Slumber

Entangled

Forsaken

NINE TAILS SERIES

(Teen Paranormal Romance)

First Shift

Storm Shift

Flame Shift

Time Shift

Void Shift

Spirit Shift

Tide Shift

Wind Shift

Celestial Shift

HAVENWOOD FALLS HIGH

(Teen Paranormal Romance)

Falling Deep

Ascending Darkness

SINGLE NOVELS

Starbound

(Teen Paranormal Romance)

Casting Dreams

(New Adult Paranormal Romance)

Ancient Tides

(New Adult Paranormal Romance)

For an updated list of my books, please visit my website: www.jlweil.com

Join my VIP email list and I'll personally send you an email reminder as soon as my next book is out! Click here to sign up: www.jlweil.com

ABOUT THE AUTHOR

J.L. Weil is a USA TODAY Bestselling author of teen & new adult paranormal romance, fantasy, and urban fantasy books about spunky, smart mouth girls who always wind up in dire situations. For every sassy girl, there is an equally mouthwatering, overprotective guy.

You can visit her online at: www.jlweil.com or come hang out with her at JL Weil's Dark Divas on FB.

Stalk Me Online
www.jlweil.com
jenniferlweil@gmail.com

Printed in Great Britain
by Amazon

15256143R00242